AMBROSE

A Modern Rendition

by

M. W. Wolf

Cover Design by eCover Makers

Photographs by Dreamstime

Saints on Bicycles,
Publisher

Images by Dreamstime. The appendix lists image copyrights.

Cover design by eCover Makers

Ambrose: A Modern Rendition
Saints on Bicycles, Publisher
Tudor Towers
936 Nebraska Ave. W
Saint Paul, Minnesota 55117-3329
Logo design by www.logoyes.com
First Edition, paperback

ISBN-13: 978-0-9892737-0-1
ISBN-10: 0-9892737-0-9

Saints on Bicycles
A Publishing Division of Mark W. Wolf, LLC

AMBROSE

A Modern Rendition

AUTHOR'S NOTE

In the fourth century of our Lord, in the waning moments of the Roman Empire, lived a charming fellow named Aurelius Ambrosius. After his father's death, his mother moved the family from Trier (Germany's oldest city), to Rome. There, Aurelius, along with his sister Marcellina and brother Satyrus, received a top-notch education. A popular figure, Ambrose began his career as a lawyer and then became a governor living in Milan, Italy.

To his horror, however, parishioners elected him bishop (the former archbishop having recently died) when he went to the cathedral to silence a disagreement over Christian doctrine. Ambrose hid out but ultimately yielded to his clerical fate after Emperor Valentinian I signed a proclamation declaring him legal. Despite his reluctance to serve, Ambrose took to his new occupation, becoming a pastoral doctor, then saint, of the Roman Catholic Tradition. People the world over celebrate his feast day on December seventh.

AUTHOR'S NOTE

This novel chronicles the saint's life, but not as he lived it. It's historical fiction, a fiction of how his life may have unfolded had he lived in the modern, perhaps futuristic, United States. The United States, due to large-scale policy changes, is different than most of us recognize. It resembles Ambrose's Roman era in several important respects.

First, Congress outlawed guns, so only knives, daggers, machetes, and swords are available to terminate life. In addition, President Constantine I, who served in office thirty years prior, changed our beloved democracy into an autocracy without shedding a drop of blood. Now, thanks to President Valentinian I's weak heart, America includes an east and west president: one residing in Washington, D.C., the other in Denver, Colorado. The United States resembles Rome in lesser ways, too. At sporting events, contestants battle ferocious lions for points, and inmates fight gladiators to win back their freedom.

This novel highlights three important challenges the saint faced in his life. First, he lived a comfortable, secular existence until his mid-thirties. In other words, he was rising to the top, fulfilling the Italian Dream. However, his life abruptly changed when someone called out his name in church: "Ambrose, bishop!" Now, Ambrose grew up Catholic, mind you, but he wasn't religious, nor did he regularly attend church—he hadn't even received all the sacraments! However, he brought himself up to speed by studying the writings of famous clergy. Saint Ambrose became a competent diocesan cleric by the end of the week.

Second, in his day a contentious debate had arisen over the meaning of the Trinity. The First Council of Nicaea declared Jesus begotten not made; an equal member of the Godhead. Arian Christians, on the other hand, believed God the Father created Him; thus, Jesus held an inferior position in the Trinity. The debate between denominations led to fighting in the streets. Ambrose, a man of gifted speech, calmed their fears while siding with the Council.

Lastly, Ambrose matched wits against nobles and other government officials. Emperors, empresses, and local politicians gained supremacy and endeavored to usurp the church's power. Their egos had grown large protecting the empire against Visigoth, Huns, and other invading marauders. However, Ambrose let them know in his calm and civil manner that the Lord of Hosts was in charge; the saint had a marvelous time rebuking political figures. For Saint Ambrose, aristocrats and senators were earthly beings under the church's dominion—mere mortals beneath the cathedral's great dome—not sovereigns reigning over it.

I hope you enjoy reading about Ambrose as much as I have enjoyed bringing him back to life. His skeletal remains, adorned in white vestments, are found in the crypt of Sant' Ambrogio Basilica, Milan. Many fine websites exist if you wish to read more about him.

Please note that the theology discussed herein, bent toward Catholicism, will not exactly reflect the views of any institutionalized faith or religion. Also, character resemblances to living persons are strictly coincidental. Finally, you will encounter much literary violence, much of it senseless. Of course, its inclusion is intentional. I meant to depict the cold-blooded times in which the saint lived, and the equally unbending modern times in which he is depicted. I am sorry if the violence troubles you—if not, then I'm even sorrier.

M. W. Wolf

ACKNOWLEDGMENTS

I owe much gratitude to many people. My first thank-you goes to my wife, Roberta, who is a lot like Mary, herein. Mary never gave up on the good people of Dionysius, and Roberta has never given up on me.

My next round of thanks goes to my beta editors. To Susan, my daughter, who kept the text convincing and provided her expertise in Spanish. To my sister, Claudia, who scored an "A" on everything she had ever written in school—you made the book infinitely better by suggesting I use a prologue. To Rachel Young, a colleague of mine at Impact Physical Medicine and Aquatic Center in Saint Paul, who thinks ever so clearly and has a pleasing disposition. You put a smile on my face when you said that you liked the book and would recommend it to others. Lastly, to Rachel's brother-in-law, Lucian Young, who gave it a quick look-see and provided words of inspiration.

A hearty thank-you goes out to my professional editor, Ashley Brooks, of www.brookseditorial.com. Ashley has a keen eye for detail and taught me grammatical rules I never knew existed. Thank you, Ashley, for a job well done! I hope that I can count on your services for my next project.

A big thank you to Derek Chiodo, of www.ecovermakers.com, for his superb artistic expression in designing my cover and improving its interior layout. Your one-page creative manifesto captured the essence of this book—what took me over four hundred pages in writing.

To the folks at www.dreamstime.com, who provided the wonderful stock photographs herein—your fabulous selection is overwhelming! Please visit the appendix at the back of the book for a listing of all the amazing photographers who snapped the pictures.

I also cannot forget a lifetime of learning: To the sisters and lay teachers at St. Jerome's Parish in Maplewood, Minnesota, for giving me a fine Catholic education. To the physical therapists I know, and the patients I've treated, you taught me a lot about people. To the professors at William Mitchell College of Law, you gave me the confidence to write. Finally, to my son David, whose courage serving in our armed forces a few years back helped to push me out of my comfort zone. To all of you, a hearty thanks.

CONTENTS

AMBROSE

A Modern Rendition

Prologue

The watery call from a yellow-breasted Western Meadowlark disturbed creaking from unpainted floorboards as Mr. and Mrs. Aurelianis rocked back and forth, sitting in old mahogany chairs. "I'd love to stay the whole day and have coffee with you on the porch," he began.

Laura smiled. "Yes, that would be nice." Then she slowly turned her head and looked out at the lazy river. "It's such a lovely day."

"The conference won't take long, a few days at most," said Mr. Aurelianis. "We need to learn more about this Constantine fellow. Leonard's quite religious, you know, and his rise to power seems legitimate; he might just be our next president."

"Well, he can't be any worse than the one we have now . . . shoo . . . shoo," she said, waving off several bees.

" 'Ommy, 'ommy," whined two-year-old Satyrus, standing by her side, reaching for her hands.

"Hmm, looks like he wants that button you're holding," interjected Mr. Aurelianis. "Shoo . . . shoo . . . gosh these bees are something else," he continued, motioning with his arms.

"Here you go, honey, but don't put it in your mouth," said Mrs. Aurelianis to her toddler. "I hope you don't mind, hun," she continued, redirecting her gaze at her husband, "but I had two thousand of these campaign buttons made up. I plan to start giving them away at my women's auxiliary club this afternoon."

Mr. Aurelianis sighed and then spoke in a loathing manner, "I had hoped you would say it was too early to start campaigning, but I suppose there's no time off in a campaign fight." He gazed out at the Beaverhead River moving peacefully in a southerly direction, then directed his eyes toward the opposite end of the porch. "Look at her," he continued, pointing at his four-year-old daughter seated on the deck reading a book.

Mrs. Aurelianis rolled her eyes. "I swear she'll be reading college textbooks by the time she enters kindergarten next year!"

"You're probably right, dear," he chuckled. "Our Marci is a smart one . . . shoo. So, where's our little guy?"

"I put him back in his crib; he started to fuss. You know, he always seems to protest whenever you leave, it's like he can sense you're going away."

"Well, I'll go up and give him a kiss good-bye. I need to get my bags anyway; the taxi will be here soon. Shoo!"

"Hun, when you're up there, would you shut his window? I don't want any bees getting into Aurelius's room." Mrs. Aurelianis looked down at her toddler after watching her husband leave. "No we don't, do we, mister . . . no bees in Aurelius's room."

"Bee," mimicked Satyrus, staring intently at his button.

After a half-minute passed, Mrs. Aurelianis heard her husband shout down from an upper floor window, "Laura, come up here, quickly!"

Part One

Autumn,
34 Years Later

I

EUCHARISTIC CELEBRATION

The Cathedral of Dionysius stood high on a hill looking down on Milan. A sacred edifice, its architecture exhibited prominent cornices and baronial columns, each with decorated capitals. Its balconies, embellished with balustrades, swags, and medallions, and its saintly sculptures, all fashioned in rich white marble, were of central European tradition.

Frater Natalia Theodosia had authorized its massive, Beaux-Arts design as a reminder to all that God was in charge. The Frater relocated to North America in 1922 from the Order of Augustinian Recollects at the Monastery of Marcella, Spain. He commissioned Pirelli T. Lazarus of St. Louis to construct it. The Most Reverend Aldfrith Gelasius, Archbishop, consecrated the building in near-blizzard conditions in November of

1930. The cathedral lists among the premier worship sites in the United Provinces.

Sister Angela, blind since birth, now in her late twenties, anxiously waited in the cathedral's main aisle; she paced back and forth, lightly tapping her cane. After hearing the massive doors to the church open wide, she implored, "Hurry, Reverend Mother, more parishioners are arriving."

"Calm down," replied Sister Anne, giving her subordinate a contemptuous look. Sister Anne Larson, also known as Mother Superior, or Reverend Mother, had a pleasing face and figure for a woman fifty-nine years of age. A loyalist of the Benedictine tradition, she had taken her vows thirty years earlier before the Congregation for Institutes of Consecrated Life and Societies of Apostolic Life. Like the Dominican Sisters of Corpus Christi, who pray in support of the priests of the Archdiocese of New York, Sister Anne commanded a small group of nuns doing similar work in Milan.

Sister Anne walked under an arched doorway leading out from the baptismal. She strolled briskly down the corridor toward the vestibule directly beneath the cathedral's great dome. The structure measured 335 feet above its base. Its height surpassed the Basilica of the National Shrine of the Immaculate Conception by seven feet. A thirty-foot steeple stood atop the dome, making the Cathedral of Dionysius the tallest church in North America.

The church's great hall basked in the morning sun; bright light radiated through a prodigious pane of Saint Jerome. The window consisted of thousands of red, blue, yellow, and green glass pieces arranged in his likeness. The pieces, held together by strips of blackened lead in an angulate frame, loomed high on the cathedral's eastern wall. Thirty-two stained-glass windows, sixteen on each side—each twenty-seven feet by eleven feet wide—stood like soldiers on its northern and southern walls.

The nun, cleansed in the sunlight's glory, greeted an elderly man ambulating toward the front of the church. He wore battered sneakers, dirty tan trousers, a ball cap, and a dusty, brown leather jacket. A large red ribbon lay fastened to the jacket's lapel. "Good morning, Mr. Schmidt," she said.

"Don't bother me," he replied in a hushed and gravelly voice. After speaking, Clarence Schmidt lurched forward and grabbed hold of a mahogany pew to prevent himself from falling. Clarence, ninety-two years old and hard of hearing, suffered from a mild case of Parkinson's. After serving as master sergeant in the Army during the Second World War, he worked for fifty-two years at Goose Head brewery, where he served as headmaster for the nationally acclaimed distillery. Though married for most of his life, he now lived alone and walked slowly using his great-grandfather's walking stick. President Theodore Roosevelt had autographed the cane, "best wishes John," back in 1902. Mr. Schmidt carried a church-key bottle opener in his left pants pocket, and a six-inch, UP Army-issued stiletto folding knife in his right. They reminded him of better days.

Sister Anne paused shortly to give Clarence directions. She wore the conventional wardrobe of a monastic Catholic nun, which included a black habit and well-fitted white coif. "I think you want to go up another five . . . let's see now . . . five more pews, Mr. Schmidt," she said. Clarence had never missed a Sunday Mass in all the years she had known him. In addition, he always sat in the third pew from the front since his devoted wife Clarice died of a massive stroke fourteen years ago.

"I know where I'm goin'," he snapped, as he continued toward the front of the church. "Why don't you find someone else that needs help?" Mr. Schmidt counted his way to the third pew and plopped himself down on an old wooden bench, where years of friction had extracted nearly all the varnish and stain. Clarence secured his cap and cane to a bronze-metal hook and shrugged off the annoying conversation. He fixed his gaze upon the altar and pined away in thought. After several moments of reflection, he closed his eyes and prayed softly, "Oh Lord, where is Clarice, where is my beloved Clarice?"

Sister smiled, watching him settle into his seat. Her black Oxford shoes clicked against the myrtle-green marble floor as she resumed walking toward the vestibule. Like horseshoes clomping on slate, the sound of her gait echoed throughout the church as she hastened her steps past forty rows of near-empty pews.

Sister Anne was the oldest of three children of a well-to-do family from the Lake Forest region of northern Chicago. As a child, she had lived in an all-white neighborhood closely surrounded by hot-tempered minorities. Her father, an orthopedic surgeon, specialized in knee-joint replacement surgery. Although he seemed happy, he'd been a workaholic; Anne felt she never really knew him because he spent so little time with the family. Now, after retiring, he lived by himself at Mother of Peace Senior Center in Abingdon, Illinois. Anne's mother, a stay-at-home alcoholic, died of liver cancer when Anne turned twelve. Anne matured quickly, having spent a good portion of her teenage years looking after her two younger brothers. Sadly, despite her hard work, the boys followed their mother's example and became alcoholics themselves.

Brisk wind greeted Sister after she pushed open the doors at the back of the church. The October sky was perfection in blue, not a cloud in sight. The air, fresh and crisp, twirled the autumn leaves in a lighthearted dance. Sister Anne, awe-struck by the yellow, brown, red, and amber complexions radiating from birch, elm, hackberry, and maple, watched a group of boys playing touch football at the far end of Orchard Park. One of the boys appeared exuberant after catching a pass and scoring a touchdown.

The Mendoza family ascended the cathedral's concrete steps just as its massive doors swung wide. The family unit consisted of Francisco and Lareyna, and their six children: Antonio, Miguel, Mario, Rafael, Elsa, and little Yesenia. "Whoa," cried Sister Anne, moving out of the way. Mario and Rafael, eight and six years old, zoomed past her in an effort to be first inside the church.

"¡Más despacio!" shouted Francisco. He pointed a finger at the two boys as he yelled out, but they had already gone inside, gawking at the twenty-foot metamorphosed statute of St. Mark.

"Sorry, Madre Superiora . . . buenos días," said Francisco, lowering his arm and turning his attention toward Sister.

Sister Anne quickly scanned the family's appearance. "Bueno," she replied. "Is everyone well, Francisco?"

"Si, Madre Superiora."

"Lareyna, you look so beautiful today." Sister's compliments were indeed a treasure, for she administered discipline more readily than pleasure. The nun stared at the woman, and then stated her assertion more clearly. "What a lovely dress."

"Gracias, Madre Superiora," replied Lareyna. "Mi madre made my dress." Lareyna wore a majorelle blue ruched crew-neck sweater dress that hung several inches below her knees. A sash of the same material served as a belt. "Mi madre gave it to me on my birthday last week," she continued proudly. Lareyna had added a silver necklace with a crucifix attached at the end to complete the ensemble.

After wishing her happy birthday, Sister Anne commented, "And look, you've lost all your baby weight, too!" Sister praised Lareyna an unprecedented third extolment for a distinctly selfish reason. She peered down at the bundle in her arms, "May I please hold Yesenia?" Yesenia, the newest member of their household—born six weeks premature—had required a period of incubation at Our Lady of Hope Hospital on Milan's east side. Her anxious parents had waited several weeks before bringing her home.

"Si, Madre Superiora; I'd be honored."

Sister Anne positioned her arms to receive the child. "Oh, how precious . . . how old is she now?"

"She'll be sixteen weeks next Wednesday."

Sister stared at the fidgeting baby. "My goodness, aren't you just the most precious thing," she said again. "Oh, and look at those little fingers, and gosh, those big brown eyes . . . oh, you're adorable." Sister glanced up at Yesenia's mother. "You must be so happy, Lareyna," she said, sounding a bit jealous.

Lareyna had a sad look on her face. "Madre Superiora, Pancho lost his job at the plant. We don't know if he's going to get called back."

Sister's eyebrows shot up as she looked at Lareyna's husband. "When did that happen, Francisco?"

"Hundreds of us got a pink slip yesterday. We don't know if they're going to close it or retool it; we just have to wait." Magra, a car and truck manufacturing plant, was Milan's largest employer. Situated close to the Awanata River in the city's southwestern corner, it covered 850 acres and required a small train to get from one end to the other. Thirty-five hundred middle-class citizens consisting of whites, Latinos, blacks, Asians, and several Native American tribes drew a paycheck from there. For many, their fathers and grandfathers labored there before them.

"My heavens, did you know that would happen?"

"We knew they stopped making the Commando. A rumor was circulating that they were constructing a factory in India; they want to start building the Delont."

Sister looked at him inquisitively. "Is that a car?"

"Sí, it's their newest truck series; it's bigger than a Commando, but smaller than their T series."

"Well, I hope you're called back, and soon, Francisco," Sister said, smiling firmly at Lareyna. "You'll be in my prayers tonight." Then she looked down at Yesenia, who smacked her lips and made delectable cooing sounds, "Especially you, my precious." Sister gave Yesenia back to Lareyna, and the rest of the Mendoza family proceeded into the church in search of their two missing boys.

Hundreds of parishioners flowed into the church's parking lot for the mid-morning Mass. Sister observed vehicles of every make and model. The Henderson family pulled up in their Cadillac; the Thomas' in their old, green Chevy station wagon; the O'Leary's in their black Magra Commando; and Mr. and Mrs. Sebastopoulos, who resided a few blocks away, walked carefully onto the lot, sideswiping cars.

As Sister gazed out at the multitudes, she heard percussion from three enormous bells perched high atop the cathedral's bell tower. Each bell stood five feet tall and weighed over two thousand pounds owing to its cast iron resonator, its flared rim, and a clapper hanging down from inside its center. Archbishop Gelasius had blessed each bell separately before mounting them in the steeple. To ring them, an altar server—usually an eighth grader from St. George's Catholic School—pulled on a rope inside the cathedral's sacristy. The bells rang five minutes before every Sunday Mass. Their sound pierced the air for miles in all directions.

"Reverend Mother, Reverend Mother," called Sister Martin, a young woman with boyish features and exceptional athletic talent. She wore a white habit over her white sneakers; she had not yet taken her final vows. The apprentice sprinted to the back of the church in a desperate search for the archbishop. "It's time for Mass to start, Reverend Mother, but I can't find His Excellency."

Sister Anne shook her head in disgust, thinking, *that old fool is going to be the death of me yet.* "Look in the basement, Sister. I saw Mrs. Williams walk down there a few minutes ago; you'll probably find him with her."

The Archbishop of Dionysius, the Most Reverend Claudius Auxentius, was seventy-three years old. He had faithfully served the diocese for twenty-one years. Bishop Titus G. Bassinis, now a prominent cardinal in Rome, ordained Auxentius in 1966. The Archbishop conversed with Naeem Williams, a forty-two-year-old parishioner who had never finished high school. They chatted in a confessional in the cathedral's damp, murky basement.

"I wants to kill 'em, Father . . . ain't that wrong? I know I ain't perfect, but dose people is makin' things lots worser for my son . . . lots worser, you understand."

Auxentius, speaking through a darkened screen, asked the frightened woman, "What branch of the military did you say he worked in?"

"Da army."

"I see . . . and where's he stationed?"

"He's at . . . oh, for pity's sake. I can't think of it, Father . . . he's at Fort Drum, in New York." She thumped herself on the head after remembering the name. "He's wit da 10th Division."

"Oh yes, yes, the 10th Mountain Division . . . I know it well."

"Oh no, Father, my son don't work in da mountains."

"I'm well aware of that, Naeem. See, the word *mountain* is used for historical significance. Your son's unit is trained to fight in very harsh weather."

"I knows dat, Father, but it ain't da weather dat worries me. It's dose Goths! We gives 'em a place to live, but dey only wants to cause trouble."

"What sort of trouble?"

Mrs. Williams's eyes opened wide; she replied in an anxious voice: "Dey wants to kill us, Father . . . and da President too. Dey 'specially wants to kill soldiers in our military; dey's crazy people, Father!"

"Did Travus tell you this?"

"Tavius, Father," she corrected. "No, my son's too proud to tell me dese things. But I listen to da news."

"Mrs. Williams, let me assure you, your son is well trained. The 10th Mountain Division is one of the finest units in all the military. And those East Africans, Thrivingi, or Goths as you like to call them, are mostly teenagers—kids kicked out of their homeland from civil strife. They have little or no military training whatsoever. Your son will know how to defend himself against them. He's going to be fine . . . just fine, Naeem."

"Oh, thank you, thank you, Father. I couldn't bear to lose him, you know." Tears glistened in her eyes in the dim lighting of the cathedral's basement. "He's my boy, Father . . . he's my only boy!"

"Mrs. Williams, I can assure you Travus will be fine," he repeated.

"Tavius, Father."

"But, as an extra measure, Naeem, I'll say devotion for him later today. Is there anything else on your mind?" After hearing a faint "no," the Archbishop felt compelled to dismiss her. However, he couldn't let her leave without levying some form of contrition. "Naeem, if memory serves me, you talked about killing Visigoths. For your professed hatred, you'll need to pray three Hail Marys and five Our Fathers."

"Oh gosh, I did say dat, didn't I, Father."

The archbishop smiled after hearing her answer, and then considered taking their conversation in a completely new direction. "Naeem, are you aware that our heavenly Father created Jesus to exemplify a sinless life and open Heaven's gate to mankind?" He magically hoped for a scholarly retort from the simple parishioner.

Mrs. Williams merely replied, "I knows dat, Father." She lifted the handle and exited the cubicle. "I'll say all dose prayers, Father, and I hope you keeps your end of da bargain, too." She closed the door behind her and walked back up the steps to prepare for Sunday Mass.

Auxentius sat back in his chair and closed his eyes. He felt satisfied knowing he had helped her emotionally unburden. But he also felt disheartened knowing she couldn't cognitively grasp the meaning of his question—that God the Father *created* Jesus, the Christ. He had tried different ways over the years to introduce Arian Christianity to his parishioners, but few seemed ready, or sophisticated enough, to grasp its meaning.

Arian belief derived from Arius, a Christian scholar from Alexandria, Egypt, who lived AD 250–336. Arius suggested that Jesus didn't always exist, that He'd been created, and thus, He was inferior to the Father. His idea purportedly sprang from Jesus's words: "The Father is greater than I." However, the First Council of Nicaea shot down his belief; they considered it heresy. A half-century later, the First Council of Constantinople also dismissed it.

However, Auxentius couldn't let it go. He hadn't always believed it—he'd never have become a priest if he had. At age twenty-seven, he'd graduated with a doctorate in Christian ministries from Liberty University. He began his career in the Jesuit Order where he dutifully served God's glory carrying out the Formula of the Institute of the Society of Jesus, which undeniably declared Him an equal member of the Trinity.

As a Jesuit, Auxentius served the poor throughout Central America for nearly twenty-three years. During that time, he developed a liberation theology—that Jesus's teachings freed the impoverished from unjust economic, political, and social conditions. Auxentius used his religion to incriminate the Salvadoran government of unrighteousness. Church hierarchy viewed his thinking as controversial; the Salvadoran government forbade it. Thus, on a warm September night in 1989, Auxentius narrowly escaped death. The army brutally murdered six of his fellow priests and an innocent housekeeper and her favorite grandson on the campus of the university—killed on suspicion of subversion.

Following that travesty, Auxentius had moved to Dionysius. He became bishop after serving three years as a diocesan priest. He dutifully served his parishioners, as well as patients in area hospitals and inmates incarcerated in Stillwater prison.

In Milan, Auxentius came across Father Wulfila Palladius, a Roman Catholic priest and an Arian extremist. Father Palladius loved debating Christian theology as much as he cared for the homeless on the city's east side where he served as a traveling priest: a street-priest. They made quite a pair: Auxentius, a slow-moving, robust man with thick spectacles, contrasted sharply with the thin, keen-eyed and highly spirited Palladius. They spent many hours playing chess together, discussing Christian doctrine in the cozy, richly paneled study of the cathedral's vicarage. The archbishop, still sitting in the basement confessional, recalled a moment years ago when he began taking Arianism seriously.

"Claudius, they criticize us for polytheism," said Father Palladius. "My pawn takes your castle."

"Yes, I know dear friend, that's the bane of Arianism . . . my knight takes your rook." After moving the chess piece, Auxentius reached for his wine. "Wulf, you can't have one God creating another without it."

"Claudius, the Vatican avoids the problem by insisting God has three natures." After Palladius spoke, he uncrossed his legs and leaned forward in the ruby-colored chair. "My queen takes your knight!"

"Yes they do, don't they, Wulf. Why, just the other day I overheard Sister Anne teaching the Trinity to a class of second graders. She used the analogy of water, you know. Ice, liquid, vapor: one substance with three distinct properties." The archbishop took a second sip of the pristine liquid. "Gosh, Sister Henrietta chose a fabulous wine. This is incredible stuff! I must ask her where she got it."

"Yes, yes, Claudius, lots of people use that simplistic analogy." Father Palladius leaned farther forward and spoke with passion, "but don't you see, if each member of the God-Head has a distinct nature, then by reason, each can't have the other's essence. Are you going to make a move?"

"My rook takes your rook," said the archbishop, setting his glass of wine down on the table. He began focusing more closely on his colleague's words. "So what's that supposed to mean, exactly?"

"It means Jesus can't be Supreme. Claudius, water changes its properties by adding or subtracting energy. But nothing can be added or subtracted from God; by definition, God is perfect. Since Jesus is restricted to His nature, that restriction precludes Him from omnipotence. And if He can't do as He pleases, He can only be one of God's creations. Check!"

"Let me get this straight, Wulf, you're saying . . . what . . . check? . . . Oh darn it all," declared the archbishop, staring intently at the board.

Palladius leaned even farther forward, literally face to face with the archbishop. "What I'm saying, dear Claudius, is that Arian polytheism trumps Vatican psuedodeism! Do you concede the game?"

Auxentius examined the board for a solution to his problem. "What are you talking about? Omnipotence isn't foreclosed because members of the Godhead are restricted to a given nature. That sounds like Jesus can't be First Cause unless He puts a round peg through a square hole . . . or, well, vice versa." A smile came over his face. "I found an answer to your check," he said, reaching for his wine.

"For argument's sake, even if Jesus can assume the Father's nature—without adding or subtracting anything to his own, that is—He still needs authority to do it. Claudius, I believe Jesus holds an inferior position in the Trinity because He lacks power to command the Father.

I do not believe for one second Jesus could have compelled the Father's incarnation. And since Jesus believed the Father was greater than He, why should we believe any different?" The priest relaxed in his chair. "Go ahead and make that move, it won't get you very far."

"My knight takes yours," the archbishop proclaimed; he had a measure of satisfaction in his voice. Auxentius sat back and refocused on his colleague's words. "Are you saying Jesus isn't an equal member of the Trinity because He lacks authority to will the Father?" The archbishop briefly recalled his friend's response when a woman, shouting in the hallway, disrupted his daydream.

"Your Excellency, are you down here?" Sister Martin's yell pierced the dark foyers of the cathedral's basement. Two bulbs had burned out in the short time since Mrs. Williams's departure.

The archbishop, irked by the sudden interruption, left the confessional in search of the bellowing woman. He groped for a light switch while replying with his own bit of yelling. "Who's down here, and why are there no lights?"

Sister Martin approached him slowly. "Thank you, Lord," she said softly. Then she raised her voice to a normal decibel. "Your Excellency, I was sent here to get you. Oh, I'm so glad that I found you, are you all right?"

"Sister Martin, is that you?"

The apprentice trembled with fright. She didn't enjoy conversing privately with him—even when he was in a good mood. She feared him because he had become a national celebrity, a noble. Auxentius not only became Dionysius's archbishop; he had replaced the Most Reverend John L. Secundianus to become the nation's third superintendent archbishop. People outside Dionysius affectionately called him "exarch." As superintendent, he reviewed federal policy enacted by the president. His office also decreed local law for the province in collaboration with the governor. Sister Martin hid her nervousness. "Your Excellency, Mass is about to start."

The archbishop squinted at his Victorinox Swiss Army watch. One of the Jesuit priests brutally murdered by the Salvadoran Army had given him the timepiece on his forty-first birthday. "Oh, yes . . . it's 10:30," he said, calming down. "Well Sister, they can't start without me, now can they."

Sister answered him with a respectful but nervous chuckle, "No, Your Grace, you're right about that." A momentary pause in their conversation ensued before she asked him a question. "Your Excellency, if I may inquire, I was wondering why you no longer use the upstairs confess—"

The archbishop interrupted her, asking a question of his own. "Tell me, Sister Martin, what's the weather like outside?" He looked at her in a serene and fatherly manner, but with bleak and distant eyes.

"Haven't you been outside, Your Grace?"

"No, Sister . . . I came through the tunnel, and well . . . I've been rather preoccupied."

"It's a beautiful day . . . sky is clear; sun is shining. The leaves are gorgeous, Your Grace—they're peaking. The air is a bit chilly now, but the temperature is expected to reach sixty-five degrees."

"Thank you for that report, Sister. I'll be on my way; I wouldn't want to keep the congregation waiting. Oh, Sister, did you want to ask me something?"

"No, Your Grace, it can wait." Sister Martin sensed oddness about him, but she couldn't explain it or put her finger on it. She blamed herself for standing too close to him in the dark.

"Well then, may God's joy be with you always."

"As with you, Your Grace." She gave a respectful nod before turning and walking away. The archbishop watched her disappear into the shadows. Then he walked through dimly lit corridors, relishing his vision of the outdoors. He passed the smaller of two statutes of Saint Peter, traveled up a seldom-used staircase, and steered himself along a narrow hallway tessellated with dingy, yellow carpeting.

"There you are, Your Excellency," said Father Liguria, standing in the sacristy. *Liguria* had been Father Simplician's middle name, in honor of his maternal uncle. He changed it to his surname after people called him a naïf once too often. Father, a forty-something-year-old priest, managed the secular affairs of the archdiocese. He also served as churchwarden to Auxentius before the mid-morning Mass. "I sent Sister Martin off to find you; Mass is about to start."

Liguria kissed the archbishop's Episcopal ring while motioning with a finger at two altar servers to bring forth his liturgical garments. The archbishop's wardrobe consisted of several memorable articles: First, a green chasuble, its beauty derived as much from its draping contour as the intricate crosses and elegant weaves hand-stitched into the fabric. Next, a white pallium, containing three black crosses made from luxurious handcrafted wool. A conical mitre, made of fine linen, which also included a sacred diadem of pure gold secured by a violet-colored ribbon. Finally, the crosier, a seven-foot staff curved at the top and made of champlevé enamel over gilt copper in the likeness of a lion.

Auxentius ducked his head through the chasuble opening, striking the corner of his spectacles; they lay crooked on his nose. After his head emerged, he fixed his lenses, inquiring, "Tarquitius, how did the bells sound today?"

Liguria's expression turned puzzled. "Didn't you hear them, Your Excellency? They sounded only a few moments ago!"

Auxentius shook his head, causing his glasses to slip down his nose. "No, Tarquitius, I've been . . . rather preoccupied."

Liguria fought for the right words. "Well, Your Grace, they rang ten times per usual. They had a deep quality . . . very opulent . . . an almost copious richness. I'm sure they lifted the spirit of anyone who heard them."

"I'm fond of the second strike," blurted the archbishop. "No one hears the first one—people are too busy doing this and that, you know, it catches them off guard. But if they think they've heard something, then they prepare themselves for the second one; they quietly anticipate its chime. And when they hear it, Tarquitius—especially if it's got that deep resonance to it—it makes people stop in their tracks. It's as if someone is telling them to forget all their troubles because there's more to life than making credit. The opulent sound vibrates the heart more than the ears, Tarquitius. As Donne said, 'it tolls for thee.' That's why Jesus followed John. John was the first strike. He prepared the way; he got people's attention. However, it was Jesus who made them think."

Father stared steadfastly into the archbishop's eyes. "Are you all right, Your Excellency?"

Auxentius emerged from his thoughts. "Yes, yes, I'm perfectly fine, Tarquitius," he replied. "But I need you and the servers to leave me alone for a few minutes; I must have some time to pray."

"Certainly, Your Excellency." Father Liguria looked over at several of the older servers. "Follow me, fellas, and bring those two youngsters along with you. Let's give the archbishop his privacy."

Auxentius looked around the vacant sacristy as the last server disappeared from sight. Cabinets and drawers, made from imported cherry, had stood the test of time exceedingly well. The archbishop stroked his hand over the grain, smooth as an elephant's tusk. However, he soon came to a spot near the handle of the chasuble closet where the finish felt marred. He recalled the precise moment when two altar boys engaged in a sword fight. One of them had struck the finish with the handle of his processional candle.

As Auxentius continued looking, he noticed a small white ceiling fan—a necessary tool in the summer since the building had no air conditioning. An unpretentious sink, used to discard liturgical wine, stood on the far side of the room. A small stained-glass window, in the middle of the northern wall, tucked behind a three-foot set of drawers, depicted the Archangel Michael. Although Auxentius and visiting priests easily reached the window's latch, it provided good fun watching young servers climb atop the cabinet to open it.

The archbishop, holding the crosier in his left hand, knelt down on a kneeler directly beneath a golden figure of Christ. He made the sign of the cross and began praying the words of Thomas Aquinas:

> Lord, in your great generosity, heal my sickness, wash away my defilement, enlighten my blindness, enrich my poverty, and clothe my nakedness. May I receive the bread of angels, the King of kings and Lord of lords, with humble reverence, with the purity and faith, the repentance and love, and the determined purpose that—

He ended the prayer early after hearing the clatter of people returning. He rose to his feet and silently prayed the words *munire me digneris*, asking the Lord for strength and protection against evil. Father Liguria poked his head into the sacristy. "Your Excellency, are you ready to begin?"

The archbishop nodded his approval. "Yes, Tarquitius, you may signal the organist." Six altar boys, two deacons, Father Liguria—along with four other priests who had just arrived through the tunnel—and the archbishop, all lined up in procession. They walked out of the sacristy and onto the altar to the tune of the opening hymn:

♫ Holy God, we praise Thy Name,
Lord of all, we bow before Thee!
All on earth Thy scepter claim,
All in Heaven above adore Thee.
Infinite Thy vast domain,
Everlasting is Thy reign . . .

The walls reverberated as fifteen hundred parishioners, standing tall on their feet, and another thirty-two choristers, sang all seven verses of the popular hymn. Father Ignaz Franz, a Catholic priest, gets credit for scribing the words—though a slightly different version had appeared four years prior to the year that he wrote it.

Colorful red, orange, and purple banners, draped from four large, black marble pillars, energized the cathedral's altar. Tapered beeswax candles too numerous to tally radiated brightly on gold-plated stands in front of the stage. Forest-green vases containing pure-white and blood-red carnations dotted the railing that divided the altar from the people. An immense oil painting depicting the Last Supper, with its rich browns, blacks, and ruddy reds, hung on the back wall of the altar. Painted by Monsignor Santino Bartelli of Italy and commissioned by Archbishop Gelasius in 1936, the new painting replaced the original; a small fire had destroyed it two years earlier.

Bright sunlight pierced stained-glass windows, illuminating a thirty-foot crucifix suspended high above the tabernacle. Sweet smoke from sacred incense hovered over parishioners like a heavy blanket. Except for the archbishop, every priest, deacon, and altar server wore a fire engine-red surplice over a black cassock; each took his place on the altar ready to perform a liturgical function.

The aging archbishop, nearly out of breath after climbing the steps, stood facing the effusive crowd with his arms extended. After regaining his air, he boomed, "The Lord be with you."†

"And with your spirit,"† came a thunderous retort from the congregation.

"Lift up your hearts."†

"We lift them up to the Lord."†

The archbishop was as comfortable in front of fifteen hundred people as he was in front of a single parishioner in a dimly lit basement. He knew people. He had a sense for them, not only for the afflictions they suffered as individuals, but for how to excite and impassion them as a crowd. He had learned compassion for people in the small villages of El Salvador where he led advances against their belligerent government. Regrettably, those conflicts had gotten most of his colleagues killed and he expelled from the country. Auxentius slowly stepped down from the altar and walked over to the lectern to read the Gospel.

As he approached the pulpit, a loud noise arose as everyone stood up in unison. "The Lord be with you,"† he said to them again, speaking confidently into the microphone.

"And with your spirit."†

"A reading from the Gospel of Mark."

"Glory to you, O Lord."† Most everyone traced their fingers in the form of a cross over their forehead, lips, and heart, in a deep-rooted Catholic gesture. The archbishop began reading:

> And one of the scribes came and heard them arguing, and recognizing that He had answered them well, asked Him, "What commandment is the foremost of all?" Jesus answered, "the foremost is, 'Hear, O Israel! The Lord our God is one Lord; and you shall love the Lord your God with all your heart, and with all your soul, and with all your mind, and with all your strength.'"[1]

After the passage concluded, Father raised the book in the air for everyone to see. "This is the Word of the Lord,"† he proclaimed.

"Praise be to God."† The congregation sat down on the old mahogany pews to listen to his sermon.

"Brethren, we're told that our Lord is one Lord, and that the greatest commandment is to love Him. Though we speak of Jesus as the Son of God, the Father actually created Him, and He has remained subservient to God ever after. The Gospel today clearly falsifies any unity within the Trinity, and possibly denies any Trinity at all. Nonetheless, Jesus is united with the Father; a bond that is beyond all comprehension. A bond more closely connected than any mother to her infant." He spotted Mrs. Mendoza holding Yesenia in her arms sitting in the pew behind Clarence.

"Many people have said," he continued, "that the Father created Jesus for one specific purpose—to take away man's sin. Hogwash! Look around you; how many of you stopped sinning because Jesus came into the world? Jesus, a divine servant of God, had not the authority to remove or forgive sin. In the *Pater Noster*, why does Jesus tell us to pray to the Father for forgiveness? It's because He couldn't do it himself, that's why. The Father only commissioned Jesus to exemplify a sinless life, and by His death, to open the gates of Heaven."

Sister Anne sat with her arms folded listening to the archbishop pontificate. She had heard enough of his Arian antics; she considered him a heretic. Sister felt appalled that he had won over nearly half the congregation, the other half being too busy or ignorant to understand anything about the concept. Sister had written letters to the Vatican asking for their help reforming or replacing him, but they never responded.

The archbishop continued his rhetoric. "And how are we supposed to love Him? What does it mean to love Him with all our heart, soul, mind, and strength? 'With all our heart' means we're supposed to love Him unconditionally; we're supposed to love Him whether He bestows grace or sends swarms of locusts down upon us. 'With all our soul' means we're supposed to strive for Him, put our energy toward Him, and not just sit back and wait for Him to call us on our phone."

A small chuckle arose from the congregation.

"Third, 'with all our mind' means we're supposed to understand Him, learn about Him, observe his ways, and make discoveries about Him. God hasn't finished revealing Himself to us. Finally, 'with all our strength' means we are to go out into the world and make things happen. We're supposed to care for the homeless, not just bemoan them. We're supposed to build homes, schools, hospitals, and churches. We're supposed to make cars, Francisco, even if the company won't build them. We're supposed to protect ourselves, Naeem, even if that means our sons and daughters go off to war . . ."

"He's talked for twenty-five minutes," blurted Sister Catherine De Luca, who, at ninety-seven years old, long exceeded the age of talking quietly. "Did you piss him off again, Sister Anne?"

"Hush," responded Sister, using her suppressed voice. She asked herself why he talked about Francisco, or revealed the confessions of a frightened parishioner. Sister looked down the pew and spotted the apprentice. "Sister Martin, did the archbishop tell you he'd spoken to Francisco?"

"No, Reverend Mother. He said that he never went outside . . . that he'd been . . . rather preoccupied."

The archbishop's sermon continued. "People, the time is at hand to fight for what you believe in. There are those in this very room who will work against us; they'll shake our fervent faith to the very core . . ."

"You pissed him off again didn't you Sister Anne," blurted the elderly nun, "that's why he's still talking."

Sister Anne, now hot under the collar, extended her stare past Sisters Henrietta, Angela, and Martin, and onward to Catherine. "No I did not, and please don't use that dreadful word again," she insisted. As the archbishop's sermon ended, Sister kept pondering how he knew about Francisco. She watched him leave the pulpit and walk back up the altar steps to prepare for the Eucharistic celebration.

The congregation watched intently as Ben and Louise Corrigan brought gifts to the altar. The gifts included a gold plate containing a three-inch diameter circle of unleavened bread, and cruets, consisting of two gold-plated cups, one containing a small amount of water, the other, unpretentious white wine. The couple headed a fine Irish family of five grown children. Ben managed a food warehouse in Milan, while Louise worked in the library at St. George's. They believed strongly in Arianism and had served as church volunteers for years. Ben and Louise walked slowly up the aisle with the gifts while the choir sang another melody.

An altar server jingled a small bell while the archbishop prayed over the bread and wine, lifting them up high as he spoke. His prayers transformed the nutrients into the body and blood of Jesus, a feat no mortal man could do, not even an experienced priest. The feat was possible only because Christ had sanctioned it. Arians still believed in transubstantiation despite downgrading Jesus's divinical stature. After Auxentius completed the prayers, he and his subordinates made their way to the railing to distribute sustenance to a spiritually hungry congregation.

"The body of Christ,"† said the archbishop, before placing a host on Clarence's tongue. The elderly man received the bread in his mouth before sipping on wine and shuffling back to his pew. Clarence smiled at four-year-old Elsa Mendoza seated behind him. He remembered his daughter, Addie, being about that age, the last time he had seen her alive. He wondered what she would look like today.

It all began on a Sunday morning in July years ago when he had taken her for chocolate ice cream in Milan's town square. As they walked along a cobblestone sidewalk, Clarence looked away for just a moment at a streetcar headed in their direction. In that moment, a young man ran up to them from the side and snatched Addie into his arms. However, he slipped darting across the tracks. Addie dropped from his grasp and tumbled headlong into the path of the oncoming car; she died instantly. The malefactor brushed himself off and ran off forever, leaving behind a pack of Clannic cigarettes.

Clarence never had any more children, and his relationship with Clarice remained tenuous thereafter. The thing he remembered most about the ordeal, however, was the terrified look on Addie's face after she turned her head around. She had peered over the abductor's shoulder and looked at him with frightened eyes. "Help me," she had yelled. "Please help me, Daddy!" Clarence would forgo twenty lifetimes—even Heaven itself—if he could have done something to save his daughter.

Sister Anne walked in the communion line for only a few minutes, but kept staring at the archbishop for what seemed like an hour. She gazed deeply into his eyes as he distributed hosts. *Something is going on; his eyes seem so blank. Something about him isn't quite right.* Sister arrived at the railing. "The body of Christ,"† said the archbishop. He patiently waited for her reply before giving her a host.

"Amen,"† she responded. Sister received the bread in her cupped hands before placing it in her mouth. She always passed on the wine, remembering the drunken state of her mother and two alcoholic brothers. As she walked back to her pew, she convinced herself that things were fine. "I must be out of my mind," she muttered.

Archbishop Auxentius ascended the altar after communion ended, breathing hard; he felt short of breath again. He placed the conical mitre on his head before sitting in the cathedra, then grasped the crosier in his left hand and waited several minutes for parishioners to return to their seats. "*Munire me digneris*," he whispered, just before standing up to recite the final prayers. Then he said aloud, "The Lord be with you."†

"And with your spirit."† The walls reverberated again as those gathered round rose to their feet in unison.

"Let us pray: Oh great and merciful Father, Thou didst create and commission Jesus your servant to live a sinless life and lead us into Heaven. The Mass is ended, go in peace to love and serve the Lord."†

"Thanks be to God."†

The choir began singing its final hymn of the morning, "Crown Him With Many Crowns," a nineteenth-century English anthem. Mathew Bridges and Godfrey Thring wrote the text while George Elvey scored the music:

> ♫ Crown Him with many crowns,
> the Lamb upon his throne.
> Hark! How the Heavenly anthem drowns
> all music but its own.
> Awake, my soul, and sing of Him who
> died for thee,
> And hail Him as thy matchless King
> through all eternity . . .

Liguria felt relieved that Mass had ended flawlessly. He had felt nervous ever since the archbishop's comments about the bells. Now, he looked for signs from Auxentius to get back into procession and return to the sacristy.

The archbishop listened to the hymn's first verse before silently asking one last favor from God. *Oh Lord, protect Travus Williams from all earthly and Satanic harm. Let him share with You the gift of eternal life when his time on earth is through.* He kissed the altar, and then genuflected on unsteady legs. As he straightened up, he spotted Sister Anne and the other Benedictine sisters; he humbly nodded in their direction. Then, without hesitation, he pulled out a six-inch, stainless steel, serrated knife from under the altar cloth and plunged it deep into the left side of his neck. It severed the jugular—and more than nicked the carotid. Blood spattered across his chasuble, gushed across the altar, and dripped onto the marble floor, where he collapsed in a heap. His mitre, crosier, and spectacles tumbled down the steps to the feet of Father Liguria.

The choir stopped singing at precisely 11:26 a.m. amidst a stunned and confused faithful. Archbishop Claudius Auxentius, most beloved archbishop of Dionysius, third exarch to the nation, lay dead in a pool of blood.

II

POLITICIAN'S APPOINTMENT

Aurelius Ambrosius, or Ambrose to most of his friends and colleagues, stood six foot one inches tall and weighed 165 pounds. With short-cropped, sepia-brown hair, Egyptian-blue eyes, and olive-colored skin, he was a fine-looking thirty-four-year-old attorney. He toted a chestnut-brown leather briefcase and wore a pinstripe suit, hand-made, imported directly from Friuli-Venezia Giulia, Italy. He walked down a ramp onto a curved cobblestone sidewalk lined by rows of three-foot tall *Sorbaria sorbifolia* plants. Ambrose headed for the Salamis County Courthouse.

Salamis County, one of thirty-five counties in Dionysius, sat in the southeast region of the province. Densely populated, over three million people occupied 7,500 square miles. Milan served as the county's principal city, closely followed in size by Titus to the north, Domitilla to the east, Agnomen to the west, and Messalla to the south. Two million European Americans, mostly German, English, and Irish, along with a sizeable number of Norwegians and a growing number of African, Hmong, and Latino, called Milan—the capital and business district of Dionysius—their home.

The Awanata River, a tortuous stretch of water receiving tributaries from the Balba and Camillus, divided the city into northern and southern districts. The business district, with its enormous skyscrapers, lay to the north, while the best shops, restaurants, and theaters lay to its south.

The courthouse, a thirty-story building, stood tall in Milan's northern district. The edifice, constructed of sand-lime brick—a lean mixture of slaked lime and fine sand baked in a unique German tradition—shone as a golden backdrop to a brick-laden waterfront overlooking the Awanata River.

"Is your client guilty?" one reporter asked.

"Thompson's case is awfully believable!" interjected another.

"Can you tell us more about what's happening, Mr. Ambrosius?" Inquisitive reporters repeatedly asked questions as flash after flash exploded from cell phone cameras. "I hope Llinos burns in hell," shouted a female bystander walking in the opposite direction.

Ambrose turned to face them while showing off his resplendent smile. "Do you really want to know how my case is going?"

The reporters all nodded.

"Then let's set the record straight. Criminal cases aren't decided by whose facts are more credible—that's how civil cases are won. In criminal court, the prosecutor—in this case my distinguished colleague, Mr. Leonard Thompson—has the sole burden of proving my client's guilt beyond a reasonable doubt." Ambrose looked around and smiled at his inquisitive audience. "My client is, and shall remain henceforth, ladies and gentlemen, not guilty, without ever having said a word in defense."

A tough-looking, redheaded reporter who displayed a scar rising vertically above his right upper lip, mocked him. "You get paid well for doing nothing, Counselor!"

Ambrose ignored the imbricate man and carried on, "Ladies and gentlemen, the phrase, 'beyond a reasonable doubt' . . ."

"You'll need to dig deep to win this one . . . A u r e l i u s," interrupted the repugnant reporter. He intentionally dragged-out the lawyer's first name before whipping up saliva in his mouth and spitting on the ground.

Ambrose turned to look at him. "Friend, you seem to know me. May I inquire who you are?"

The man reached into his pocket for a pack of cigarettes without looking up. "Mock," he replied. "M-O-C-K," he said again, spelling it out.

Ambrose moved his eyes up and down, memorizing the aggressive man's features.

"Mr. Mock," he asked, "I'd like to pick your brain on this case. Would you be kind enough to meet me after court today?"

"I'm sure I'm too busy," he replied, striking a match and lighting up a Clannic cigarette—a cheap roll of tobacco sold exclusively in the Ukraine. Ambrose watched the ruffian inhale deeply on the leaves, making his scar stand out more distinctly.

"I'll make it worthwhile."

Mock dragged out the lawyer's first name again, then said, "Supposin' you can be my date tonight."

Ambrose pretentiously nodded before turning himself back to the others. The reporters waited patiently for a succulent comment to write in their columns. "Where did I leave off . . . oh yes, 'beyond a reasonable doubt' is open to interpretation. It generally means . . ."

The gathering immediately objected, "Ambrosius, give us a break, just tell us about your case."

"Very well, my client is being maliciously prosecuted." The defense lawyer spoke in a direct and serious tone, watching his detestable friend amble across 9th street. Ambrose regained his composure and pointed his index finger in the direction of several reporters. "Picture yourselves—you sir, or you madam—being viciously prosecuted for a heinous crime you didn't commit. You're upstairs at the time of the murder, and you have no alibi. The assailant, whose identity is unknown, knocks you out, stabs your wife, and frames you for the murder. Now, how do you think my case is going?"

Without waiting for an answer, Ambrose pushed himself through a set of revolving doors leading into the courthouse. After walking by security, he passed a black marble statue of Chief Justice Marcus and took an elevator to the twenty-second floor. From there, he turned right and walked twenty feet down a wood-paneled hallway where he entered courtroom B.

"ALL RISE. The case of Harold P. Llinos versus the people of Dionysius is now in session. The Honorable Harvey Devoe, of the district court, presiding," bellowed the clerk.

"Be seated," commanded the judge, shuffling a few papers. "Are all members of the jury present and accounted for?"

"Yes, Your Honor," the clerk replied.

"Bring in the accused." The judge always spoke in an exasperating tone. A black man, he grew up on Milan's west side. At fifteen years of age, his family won a multi-million-credit lottery and used part of it to send him to college. Now, at age sixty-two, he'd sat on that courtroom bench for thirty years and had seen it all. The judge planned to retire soon and delighted in the thought of never officiating another DUI, rape, murder, personal injury, divorce, or child abuse case again. He dreamed of the day when his toughest decision would be whether to use a five or six iron to reach the green.

Henry Llinos, escorted by Deputy Sheriff Johnny Scarsdale, appeared at the side entrance of the courtroom. Llinos, dressed in an orange jumpsuit, had steel shackles fastened around his wrists and ankles. Ambrose asked the judge several times if his client could enter the courtroom before seating the jury—and be permitted to wear a suit and tie without restraints—but always to no avail. Judge Devoe was old school; he enjoyed watching the accused writhe in front of the jury.

Llinos, born on Anglesey Island, the largest island off the coastline of Wales, immigrated to the United Provinces with his older sister when he turned eighteen. He had come here more to escape dysfunctional family relationships than to seek fame or fortune. Although he possessed a scrawny, bird-like physique, he had become a national celebrity; some said a bigger-than-life international celebrity. Now fifty-something, he'd become a premier radio host on KGPK-AM. *Utterers Magazine* featured him on its "Heavy Hundred" list and named him a top ten most important personality in the radio industry.

Henry, a Republican through and through, relished taking pot shots at Democrats as often as possible. Unfortunately, the province didn't charge him with verbally assaulting liberals; rather, with first-degree murder for stabbing his wife with a nine-inch, black-handled machete.

In times past, victims like Mrs. Llinos would have died instantly—a shot to the head from a loaded pistol. She wouldn't have suffered slowly like she did after being butchered by a knife; in her case, she lingered for hours. Fifteen years ago, Archbishop Auxentius and Governor Probos made it a capital offense for anyone to use, store, house, carry, or conceal a gun—or firearm of any type, including air and paint guns—within the province. The statute kept pace with the rest of the country. Thus, knives, daggers, machetes, and swords became the contemporary means of killing.

Scarsdale seated the radio host moments before Judge Devoe proclaimed, "You may call your next witness, Prosecutor."

"Thank you, Your Honor." Thompson stood up and turned around to face the gallery. "I call Mrs. Piedmont back to the stand." Betty Piedmont had worked as the Llinos' housekeeper for the past fifteen years. The job did not pay well, but she and her daughter Nancy received free room and board. The Llinoses had also promised to pay Nancy's college tuition if she ever made it that far in school. Mrs. Piedmont, a homely, robust woman, testified on the stand because she cooked in the house at the time of the murder, and because she knew about the tempestuous relationship Henry had with his wife, Carminea, better than anyone else did.

Judge Devoe looked at her sternly; he had little patience for oblivious people, especially uneducated women. "Mrs. Piedmont, I must advise you that you're still under oath."

Thompson began his examination. "Mrs. Piedmont, we've already established that someone stabbed Mrs. Llinos in her home, on the balcony, just outside her bedroom between 6:45 and 7:00 p.m. on the evening of May eighteenth. Would you please tell the court where you were at that time?"

"At home," she said quietly.

"You'll need to speak up."

The housekeeper regained her composure and replied in a stronger voice—remembering also to look at the jury as she spoke. "I cooked and cleaned at the Llinos' home, but . . . I live there, too . . . me and my daughter."

Thompson looked up from a stack of papers neatly arranged on the walnut-colored desk in front of him. "Mrs. Piedmont, where exactly in the house were you at that time?"

"In the kitchen, preparing dinner," she said, using her hands to gesture slicing a vegetable.

The prosecutor leaned back in his chair, confident the simple housekeeper would remember her lines. "Was anyone besides yourself and Mrs. Llinos in the house at that time?"

"Yes, Mr. Llinos."

"How about your daughter?"

Betty's eyes grew wide. "No, thank God, she went away to a friend's house."

Thompson brought himself back upright in the chair, giving the housekeeper a reassuring nod. "Mrs. Piedmont, what area of the house did Mr. Llinos occupy at that time?"

"He had just talked to me in the kitchen and marched his way up the stairs to Minea's . . . I mean, Mrs. Llinos's bedroom."

The prosecutor glanced at Ambrose before turning himself toward the jury. "What did you and Mr. Llinos talk about before he . . . went up the stairs?"

The housekeeper cleared her throat and repositioned herself in the box before answering. "He looked upset . . . I mean, visibly shaken. He stressed over her choice in the upcoming election."

"Mrs. Piedmont—now this is very important—can you remember his exact words to you before he ascended the steps?"

She nodded her head. "He said, 'I can't believe that bitch is voting for Martin, I'm going to kill her.' " Mrs. Piedmont felt relieved knowing she remembered the most damaging part of her testimony.

Llinos, who listened intently, leaned toward Ambrose and whispered, "Can't you object to any of this?"

The lawyer smiled and softly patted his client on the shoulder. "Relax, Henry, we'll get our chance."

Thompson continued, "Now, Mrs. Piedmont, it's your testimony that Mr. Llinos went upstairs immediately after saying those words. Do you know where he went when he reached the top floor?"

"He went to her bedroom."

"How do you know he went to her bedroom?"

"Well, I didn't actually see him go there, if that's what you mean. But I heard Minea, I mean, Mrs. Llinos, a few moments after he'd gone up . . . I heard her shouting and screaming." Tears began welling in the housekeeper's eyes.

Henry squirmed in his seat, "Ambrose, aren't you going to object to any of this?

Ambrose turned toward his apprehensive client. "Calm down, Henry," he whispered.

"Mrs. Piedmont," continued Thompson, "now I ask you, did the shouting and screaming you hear come from upstairs?" Soon after he asked the question, he peeked at the jury's reaction.

"Yes, of course."

"What'd you do after you heard shouting and screaming?" Thompson wanted to say those words as often as possible; a hundred times more if he could in order to paint the jury a better portrait of the malicious happenings.

The housekeeper looked up at the courtroom ceiling. "I yelled upstairs; I asked if they had a problem."

"And?"

"No one answered."

"What'd you do then?"

"Well, I waited a little while, and then I called 911." The housekeeper pretended to dial with her finger.

"Did you go upstairs?"

Mrs. Piedmont bowed her head. "No, sir, I didn't move until the police arrived. I felt too scared." The rest of her testimony consumed nearly the entire morning. Thompson elicited detailed information about Llinos's extremist personality and the stormy relationship he had with his wife. To Henry's consternation, Ambrose remained quiet. He had failed to utter a single objection throughout Thompson's entire examination.

The prosecutor smiled at the homely housekeeper at half past eleven. "Thank you, Mrs. Piedmont." He rose to his feet and addressed Judge Devoe, "That's all the questions I have for this witness, Your Honor."

The judge glanced up at the clock, then down at Ambrose. "Defense counsel, you may cross."

Ambrose rose to his feet. "Thank you, Judge. Mrs. Piedmont, between the time you heard my client walking up the stairs and the time you heard a woman scream, did you make any noise of your own?"

"Like what?" The housekeeper felt renewed anxiety now that someone else asked the questions.

"Well, for example, did you open a squeaky oven door, or slide a heavy pot across the stove, or maybe drop a metal utensil on the tile?" Ambrose gestured with his hands as he commented on each example.

"Now that you mention it, I do recall dropping a metal spoon on the floor about that time; spaghetti made my hands slippery. It made quite a mess. What does that have to do with anything?"

Ambrose stood up and addressed the judge. "I've no more questions for this witness, Your Honor." Ambrose sensed a small chill run up Henry's spine the moment he closed out his questioning. He knew his client was articulate; a man accustomed to words. He knew ending his cross so abruptly without damaging her testimony was, in his client's eyes, equivalent to committing a crime.

Henry desperately tried keeping his wrath to a whisper. "What . . . are you crazy? You're not going to destroy this wretched woman?"

"Trust me, Henry, she's not your enemy," Ambrose replied, in his calm and reassuring manner.

Llinos stood up, unable to contain his fury. "Not my enemy, didn't you hear the terrible things she just said about me?"

"Henry, sit . . . and keep your voice down," whispered Ambrose, waiving his hand in a downward direction.

"Please control your client, counselor," ordered the judge, glancing up at the clock.

Llinos sat back in his chair, his arms crossed in front of him. With rage in his eyes, he tried hard not to condemn his attorney. *He's supposed to be one of the best*, he thought. *Christ, he's going to get me the quick-sword!* Salamis County had legalized the death penalty, and it was carried out swiftly after one failed appeal. A sword or dagger ended the wrongdoer's life since the county had banned firearms and injections. The remains were quickly burned inside a crematorium; hence, "quick-sword" became the popular title.

"Prosecutor, do you wish to redirect?" asked Judge Devoe. Thompson didn't bother looking up. "No, Your Honor."

"Okay, since the noon hour is upon us, I think we'll break for lunch. Does counsel have any objections?"

"No, Judge," they replied.

"We'll reconvene at 2:00 p.m. Deputy, please escort the accused from the courtroom." After saying those words, Devoe looked squarely at the jury. "Ladies and gentleman, I'll once again remind you not to talk about this case among yourselves or anyone else. You're excused until 2:00 p.m. this afternoon."

"ALL RISE," bellowed the clerk; Judge Devoe stood up and left the courtroom.

Ambrose gathered papers, watching his agitated client disappear from the room. He was convinced that an assailant snuck into the Llinos' home before Henry had ascended the stairs. He believed the assailant knocked out Henry at the exact moment Mrs. Piedmont dropped her utensil. Thompson argued that Henry never lost consciousness, and that he self-inflicted the blow to his head. Ambrose believed that, after subduing Henry, the assailant entered Mrs. Llinos's bedroom and found her smoking a cigarette on the balcony. She screamed at his approach; he stabbed her repeatedly with the black-handled machete. After wiping off his prints and putting the knife into Henry's hand, he had climbed down the fire escape attached to the balcony.

Ambrose had two problems with his theory. First, Henry seemed the only person wanting Mrs. Llinos dead. Carminea, by all accounts, didn't have another enemy in the world. Although she voted Republican in most elections—just to appease her husband—she voted against the party on occasion if she truly believed the opposing candidate represented the better choice. In this case, Thompson built an elaborate theory that Llinos wanted to kill his wife because she planned to vote for John Martin Stanton, a staunch liberal opposing the incumbent, Aegyptus Tiberius, for Mayor of Milan. Henry insisted his passion for politics extended only to national affairs, but he held such high regard for all social science that no one believed his words.

Ambrose also lacked evidence that a third-party assailant had ever entered the Llinos' home. Nothing turned up missing, and no one found footprints or extraneous fibers. Other than Mrs. Llinos's blood, no extrinsic spatters showed up anywhere in the house or on the fire escape.

Another thumbprint on the machete turned up, but it belonged to novice detective, Bill Heinz. Llinos insisted that he'd never owned a knife—certainly not one of the caliber that killed his wife—but Thompson had presented evidence that he purchased one online from the Gladius Mercantile Exchange two years ago.

Ambrose exited the courtroom and made his way down the elevator to the second floor. He walked through a convoluted hallway and crossed a skyway leading to the Manchester Hotel for a quick lunch at Dickies. Entering the restaurant, he came upon Chijioke Gowon, a security guard at the courthouse who emigrated from Nigeria ten years ago. Gowon, also known as "Tiny," a six-foot-six, 345 pound man, had played one season as an offensive lineman for the San Antonio Valeros before rupturing the anterior cruciate ligament in his left knee. He never fully recovered after two failed surgeries, forcing him to leave the game he loved.

"Hey, Brozie," said Gowon, in a deep and raspy voice. Only Tiny called him by that name, and Ambrose, perceiving the sheer size of the man, never felt inclined to correct him.

"Hey, Tiny," Ambrose replied, "Would you like to make an extra hundred?"

"Sixteen?"

"No, twenty-two."

"I'll be there." Gowon lumbered out of the restaurant with two other guards. Before going far, he turned back toward Ambrose. "Say Brozie, you've never met my friend Michael Mariano."

Ambrose took a few moments to shake hands and make polite conversation before walking into the establishment. The restaurant had become a favorite bar and grill for anyone working at the courthouse.

He spotted Andrew Lierchetsky drinking coffee and sitting alone in a red, vinyl booth at the far end of the eatery. Ambrose sat down opposite his investigator. "Please tell me you have good news?"

Lierchetsky, a lanky man with a receding hairline, became the lawyer's favorite detective after Ambrose joined Agrippa, Leontius, and Drusus. They had worked closely together on a number of criminal cases. Their collaborative efforts had earned Ambrose partnership in only four years at the firm. "I'm sorry, Ambrose," he replied. "Everything he said in his deposition checks out. Nothing comes up on this guy; he's clean."

"No way, Drew, Mary remembers this guy getting booked a year or so ago, and she's never wrong." Ambrose referred to Mary Peterson, a thirty-two-year-old brunette who worked full-time as a clerk for the Salamis County Sheriff's office. She attained a baccalaureate in English literature and worked at a public law library for several years before working for the sheriff. Now she pursued a master's in criminal justice, attending part-time at Cassius College, a private institution on the outskirts of Fausta County. Her brother Winston had studied in the class ahead of Ambrose at Phoebus School of Law, located in the heart of Agnomen. He graduated at the top of his class and worked as an intellectual property attorney for a software company in southern California.

Lierchetsky looked the defense attorney square in the eyes. "Does she even know you exist?"

Ambrose and Mary had never dated, and he, being on the defense, more often worked on the opposite side of the case. But one day he noticed her muguet-oil fragrance, which then brought his attention to her pleasing figure, her pretty, dark-chocolate hair, and her emerald-green eyes. "Who are you talking about?"

"Mother Teresa! Who do you think I mean?"

"Gosh, I don't know, Drew . . . probably." Ambrose was shy when it came to women, and he felt uncomfortable talking about Mary in Lierchetsky's presence. Although he had started liking her, he hadn't conveyed his feelings to anyone, at least not directly. Unbeknownst to him, however, his flirtatious behavior had become so obvious that everyone figured he would ask her out in time. "Look, Drew, there's got to be dirt on this guy," said Ambrose, trying to redirect the conversation.

Ambrose meant Darwin Cooper, a recent informant for Prosecutor Thompson. Cooper would testify tomorrow that he had been walking his eight-year-old yellow lab in an alley next to the Llinos' house when he witnessed Henry stab his wife on the balcony. Ambrose looked squarely at Drew, feeling exasperated, sounding desperate. "Does he have an alias, several names, or multiple personalities? Is he behind on taxes, did he beat up his wife, or sell his kids into slavery?"

"No, Ambrose," Lierchetsky fired back. "Nothing in the computer comes up on the guy. If he's anything but a model citizen, I haven't found it."

"Keep trying, Drew, we've got to have something on him before tomorrow or Henry will be stabbing me next." The two men ate their lunch in silence. Ambrose picked at his plate of shrimp scampi while Lierchetsky gulped down a burger and fries. Then they each paid for their meal and went their own separate ways. Ambrose removed his phone from his front trouser pocket and called his secretary on his way back to the courtroom. He spoke to her while crossing the brightly lit skyway overlooking Julius and Robert streets. "Hey, Hermi, it's Ambrose. Any messages?"

"Yeah, the governor just called; he wants to talk to you."

The lawyer stopped walking and gazed out the window at the Awanata River. "Yeah right, I suppose he wants to sell me a swamp in Messalla!"

"I'm not kidding; he wants you to give him a call."

The attorney remained quiet for a moment and then asked, "Why would the governor want to talk to me? He has a hundred qualified lawyers at his disposal. Besides, it's premature to grant a stay of execution."

"I don't know . . . but privately, he's a client of this firm. Mr. Yang says you need to call him as soon as possible—that means today!"

Ambrose stared at the sparkles reflecting off the river. "All right, Hermie, I'll go along with this; I'll give Probus a call after court today. Anybody else . . . the emperor, perhaps; do I need to call him, too?"

Herminius sensed sarcasm. "No Ambrose, please just call the governor."

"All right, thanks Hermi—don't know what I'd do without you." Ambrose shut off his phone and put it back in his pocket before hurrying through the convoluted hallway. He stepped inside mirrored elevator number five just before it closed; it quickly brought him up to the twenty-second floor. Ambrose sat down at the defense table at precisely 2:00 p.m., just as the clerk entered the courtroom and instructed everyone to rise. Always punctual, Judge Devoe tendered a fifteen-minute lecture to any attorney even half a minute late. After everyone was situated, the deputy paraded Llinos back into the courtroom; the lunch break had done nothing to quell his anger.

"If you don't defend me better this afternoon, Ambrosius, I'll fire your ass and do this myself," he snapped, plopping himself down at the defense table. "You know Thompson hates me . . . you're letting him wallow in the moment."

It wasn't that Thompson hated Llinos—he fervently despised him. Two years ago, Thompson had fought for his political life during a contentious election. Many Democrats took a beating that year owing to excessive spending and an inability to balance the budget. During the campaign, Llinos lashed out at Thompson for being soft on crime, especially between Arian and Nicene Catholics and between newly arriving Goths and everyone else. "The situation with Goths is getting worse," Llinos had told his listeners, "and Thompson won't do anything to stop it. Our fair city is going to pot because he won't control the situation. Maybe Thompson secretly wants Muslims to take over our land. Maybe he enjoys praying to Allah on his knees while being panty-whipped by his leather-clad, dominatrix wife, Darlene." Although Thompson survived the election, he never forgot the personal attacks Llinos made against him and his family. To say that he hated Llinos was an understatement.

"Settle down, Henry," said Ambrose. "If you start making frivolous objections, the jury's going to think you're guilty. Now sit back and relax. I promise we'll get our chance tomorrow." Ambrose hated making promises to clients, especially ones he couldn't keep. Nevertheless, Llinos needed to be controlled; he gave Ambrose no choice.

The afternoon droned on as long and as badly as it had in the morning. Thompson brought two more witnesses forward, both of whom testified for over an hour that Llinos's political rhetoric soared out of control and that he'd been emotionally abusive to his wife. Just as before, Ambrose made no objections during the prosecutor's examination. And on cross, he asked few, if any questions. After testimony ended—just before Scarsdale escorted Llinos from the courtroom—Henry turned around and spoke to his lawyer in a serene and melancholy manner. "I sure hope you know what you're doing, Ambrose. For Christ's sake, don't let me die by the quick-sword."

Ambrose sat quietly in the empty courtroom; his aching head pounded. *There has to be an answer*, he thought. *Llinos may be a strange piece of work, but that doesn't make him a murderer. What am I missing? Why can't I get my head around this?* Before delving deeper into thought, Ambrose heard clapping from the back of the room. "Mock," he whispered to himself. The lawyer turned around to face his pugnacious friend, "Mr. Mock; I'm so glad to see you," he said aloud in a light and airy voice.

"Like I said, A u r e l i u s, you make a good living doing nothin'." Mock dragged out his first name again; it became an annoying habit. Moments after exchanging greetings, the door to the courtroom swung wide and in stepped an enormous figure. Mock gazed intently at Tiny while addressing his words to Ambrose. "What the hell . . . is this some kind of setup?"

"I told you I'd make it worthwhile," replied Ambrose. "Now, I've got some questions for you, unless, of course, you'd prefer to tangle with my gridiron friend?"

"You're bluffing."

"Mock, if that's your real name, I spent the whole day listening to damaging testimony against my client." Ambrose rubbed his eyes. "I'm really not in a good mood. If you prefer to have your balls pulled out through your throat, then so be it." He motioned to Tiny to step forward.

Mock's eyes grew wide, feeling the shade of the giant's shadow—though the titan remained a good twenty-five feet away. "All right, Counselor, what do you want?" He asked his question with a slight quiver; the scar on his lip inadvertently moved up and down.

Ambrose crossed his arms in front of his chest. "Let's start with your name."

"Keller . . . William Keller."

"How do you know me, Keller?"

"I don't . . . well, not really." He briefly glanced at Tiny. "See, back in '83 my father ran against yours for mayor. Like you, I was just a kid."

Ambrose stared hard at the repugnant man. "You mean to tell me your father was Octavius?" Without waiting for a reply, the lawyer continued talking. "I remember my dad telling me that he'd won that election by the slimmest of margins . . . and that afterwards, your dad killed himself and your family."

"Yeah, 'cept he forgot about me." Keller's scarred lip quivered again as he took his eyes off Tiny and directed them at Ambrose. "I was visiting my grandma when he did his cowardly deed. I stayed with her for a couple of years after that, but then she died. I've lived with my uncle ever since."

"Who's your uncle?"

Keller reached into his pocket searching for a cigarette. He took another glance at Tiny, "Darwin Cooper."

Ambrose stood up and began rattling off questions: "Your uncle is Darwin Cooper? The same Darwin Cooper who will testify against my client tomorrow? Are you telling me he's testifying to get even with my father?"

"He hates your guts—your whole family's guts. My uncle had big plans for when my dad became mayor, but your father ruined all that."

"Keller, has your uncle committed any crimes recently?"

"Sure, lots of 'em," Keller began, relaxing now that he began talking about someone else. "After Dad died, Coop became a drunk, a drifter. I think we lived in, oh . . . twenty-five places over the past twenty years. My uncle can't hold down a job; I know he's done plenty of stealin'."

"Has he ever killed anyone?"

"No, not that I know of."

"I've no further questions." Ambrose motioned to Tiny to step away from the door. "You can leave now, Keller."

The offensive man took a few abbreviated steps, moving closer to the exit, and then hastened his gait after Tiny lumbered his large body out of the way. Keller burst into a sprint, pulled on the handle, and ran out of the courtroom. He ran all the way down the wood-paneled corridor to the stairwell; he didn't have patience to wait for the elevator.

Tiny looked at Ambrose and asked in a deep and raspy voice. "Do you think he told the truth, Brozie?"

"Doubtful. See, Octavius did kill himself and his wife after losing the election—but he had no siblings or children. Tiny, give me a call after you lift his prints off the handle; I'll be at home. Oh, and don't forget to bill the firm . . . and be sure to take a hundred credits for yourself."

"You got it. Do you need an escort out of the building?"

"No, he's gone. He won't be bothering anybody for a while."

Ambrose gathered his Baroni topcoat and leather briefcase. He boarded car sixty-three at Julius and 9th, just around the corner from the courthouse. The air felt cool, though not as crisp as it felt earlier that morning. The sun was sinking fast; bright reds and yellows of daytime autumn gave way to twilight shades of grey. Ambrose sat in a seat toward the front and loosened his necktie. He stared out a window at a woman with a chocolate labradoodle pup; behind her stood two unruly teenagers. They waited to board the streetcar just as soon as a blue-haired woman using a walker got out of their way. The streetcar made two more stops, one at Julius and 12th and one at 12th and St. Peter, before hitching with ten other cars on Basillius Avenue. Once hitched, a diesel pulled the cars out of Milan's business district and into its northern suburbs.

Train 15-B traveled north and west, close to the banks of Lake Aeliana. The lake, once a beautiful freshwater reservoir, spanned one thousand surface acres and reached a depth of one hundred feet at its center. Originally used for Milan's drinking water, the county permitted no houses or cabins along its shoreline. However, after discovering deep drilling technology, the lake opened up to recreational and industrial uses. It suffered from sulfur dioxide pollution emitted from power plants and heavy metals discharged from motor vehicles. It still offered anglers a great opportunity to catch walleye, muskie, and perch. It just wasn't a good idea to eat more than one fish in a lifetime.

Ambrose rode the train past four stations to Candria—its farthest hub. The station, located on the outskirts of Titus, positioned itself twenty-five minutes north and west of Milan. The county drew plans to extend the tracks into downtown, but it hadn't received final approval yet. After Candria, the train returned to Milan's business district where it separated into individual streetcars that circulated the city. Cars reconnected and traveled out every hour. In all, sixteen trains moved about, each with ten streetcars; north and south trains exited the city just as east and west trains returned.

Darkness had descended when Ambrose stepped onto Candria's platform. He walked over to his two-year-old midnight-black Mercedes Benz SL552 roadster parked under a burned-out street lamp. The lawyer fired up the engine and sped down Wellington Lane going east past a row of Juniper hedges. From there, he turned left onto Hortensi Place and drove two miles to Lavinia Townhomes. No sooner did he step through the door to his home than he received a call on his phone.

"Mr. Ambrosius, this is Marcia Hathaway at the 5th precinct in Milan. I'm giving you a call at the request of Mr. Gowon, security down at the courthouse. We analyzed the fingerprints on the door."

"Wow, that was fast," he said, speaking with energy in his voice, fumbling for the light switch.

"The prints belong to Mr. William Cameroon Heinz."

"Hmm, I'm guessing he's not a red-headed guy with a scar on his lip."

"No, Bill's a detective in our department; black, middle forties . . . he wears wire-rim glasses . . . you've probably seen him around."

"Yes, I know who he is. Thank you, Ms. Hathaway, you've been very helpful." Ambrose stood in the dark; he still hadn't found the light switch. "Would you print a copy of your report? I'll have my investigator pick it up in the morning. Oh, and if you'd be so kind, please send a copy to the sheriff."

"I've already done that—that's standard procedure."

"Great . . . well . . . once again, thank you very much for the information." Ambrose clicked off his phone and put it back in his pocket. Then he put more effort into finding the light switch.

After illuminating the room, he threw his topcoat over the back of a black leather sofa. The garment blanketed Lava, his twelve-year-old, orange-colored tabby. "This case is beginning to make sense." Ambrose noticed a tail sticking out beneath his jacket, but before uncovering the feline, he received another call on his phone. "Ambrose," he said, after fumbling to retrieve the device from his pocket.

"How are you doing, Bee?" Ambrose's parents had given him that nickname one day in August when Ambrose was a baby. His dad, now deceased, used to tell the story that a swarm of bees had settled on Ambrose's lips while he laid in his crib. They left behind a golden drop of honey. His parents considered it a promising sign of his future fluidity in speech. Anyway, the nickname stuck, but only members of his immediate family used it.

"Sy, it's good to hear from you; how you doing?" Ambrose used that name to refer to his older brother, Satyrus. Ambrose waited for his brother's news, kicking off two-tone wing-tip shoes and stepping onto a thick, handcrafted Persian rug in the middle of the living room.

"I'm doing great, Bee, but listen, the convention is still going. I can't break away and make it over to your place tonight. We're finishing with the mayoral speeches, but the governor still has to speak."

"Oh, shoot, Sy . . . that reminds me I'm supposed to call Probus."

"Probus . . . what does the governor want with you?" Satyrus didn't wait for his brother's answer, "Frankly, Bee, I can't get near the guy. Do you realize I've served as mayor of one of his cities for four years, but I've never once spoken to him directly?"

Ambrose moved the phone to his other ear. "He supposedly called my firm and asked to speak to me directly. But to be honest, I think people at my firm are having a little fun with me—you know, breaking up the tension of a difficult case. But according to my secretary, Hermie, Mr. Yang wants me to call him."

"Yang . . . he's one of your firm's senior partners, isn't he?"

Ambrose stared down at his half-covered cat. "Yeah, he's one of four head-honchos around there."

"I've heard his name bantered around once or twice. Is he looking for a political office?"

"Gosh, I don't know, Sy. I'm not big enough to be in his circle. Anyway, looks like you're mixing with the heavy-hitters now." Ambrose uncovered Lava and scratched under her collar. "The only one missing is Auxentius."

"Can you believe that, Bee? The archbishop slits his throat at the end of Sunday Mass! Where did he get the knife?"

Ambrose flicked a finger at the sleepy cat's nose, trying to wake her up. "Well, from what I've read, he hid it under the altar cloth. But I've never heard a good reason why. All I know, Sy, is that he's been the raging talk around here for a week. At least his suicide took attention away from my sorry case."

"Listen, Bee, I need to go. We're still on for tomorrow night, aren't we?"

"We'd better be; I'm not letting you return to Trier without seeing me." Ambrose picked up his sleepy cat and placed her on his lap. "Have you talked to Mom or Marci yet? I think they want to take you to some fancy Greek restaurant."

"No, but they're on my list. All right, Bee, got to go; I'll see you tomorrow night."

Ambrose tossed his phone on the couch and lifted Lava's face to his own. "You sleep all day without a care in the world," he said softly. Lava opened her eyes to the sound of his voice, "and we *sapiens* are supposed to be the smart ones!" Ambrose playfully nudged the feline's nose when he heard another lively jingle from his phone. *I'm going to toss that thing in the Awanata River.* He retrieved the device from the cushion of the couch and put it next to his ear. "Hello."

"Mr. Ambrosius, this is Mary Peterson from the Salimas County Sheriff's office. Marcia Hathaway sent us fingerprints and asked me to contact you when we finished our analysis. I must admit, Mr. Ambrosius, the results are confusing."

Ambrose put the cat down on the couch and began pacing the carpet. "Let me guess," he started, "almost every precinct shows those prints belong to a black guy with glasses—a Mr. William C. Heinz. But I'm hoping that a handful of counties say they belong to a tough-looking, red-headed guy with a scar on his lip."

Ms. Peterson sounded disheartened. "Why, yes, that's correct . . . I guess you already knew what I had to say. Only a few counties still use old software. They are the ones showing the prints belong to the man with the scar. His name is Michael William Farthington." Then she added, sounding confused, "but that still doesn't explain why two people share the same prints."

Ambrose closed his eyes and sighed, "I've got a hunch, but it's going to take a lot of work to prove it. Mary . . . I mean, Ms. Peterson, does it say if Farthington conspired with anyone?"

"It shows armed robberies and a host of misdemeanors. But I don't find any other names listed alongside his. Is there anything else I can do for you?"

Ambrose's heart started beating faster. "Well . . . um, there is actually," he stammered, "if you'll permit me to ask a personal question. I mean . . . well, I hope you don't think I'm being presumptuous, Mary . . . but, um, would you consider seeing a movie with me sometime?" Ambrose pulled the phone away from his ear shaking his head in disgust over the manner in which he asked her out.

"Oh, that's sweet, Mr. Ambrosius, but I'm too busy working here in the evenings, and I'm in school during the day. I thought you knew about my criminal justice degree at Cassius College. I'm really sorry; I just don't have time to see a movie."

Ambrose's heart sank. "That's okay, Mary. I don't know what came over me; I should have known better."

"Oh no, Mr. Ambrosius, I didn't mean it that way. Maybe we can have lunch together on campus sometime . . . if you're in the area, that is."

"Really? Oh, that would be wonderful, Mary; I'd like that very much." The electrified lawyer pulled the phone from his ear again. He pumped his fists up and down and danced on the Persian rug like a crazy man. Then he closed out the conversation with confidence, "Mary, I'll give you a call later in the week—I'll arrange to be in the area."

"Sounds great."

"Bye, Mary—I mean, Ms. Peterson—and thanks for the information on Farthington." Ambrose hung up the phone and placed it gingerly on the beechwood table next to his black leather sofa. "Come here, sweetie," he said, lifting his sleepy cat. "I'm going out with Mary, I'm going out with Mary," he repeated in a light-hearted voice, dancing on the rug holding his cat to his chest.

"Meow."

"Oh, that's right . . . thanks for reminding me, girl, I need to make one more call." The frightened cat leaped to the floor and scampered off to another room. Ambrose picked up his phone and dialed his investigator. "Hey, Drew" he said, sitting down on the couch. "If you're not busy, I've got another job for you."

"Thank god; it's been boring as hell watching Cooper's house. Nothing has happened here the entire day. But you know, Ambrose; I was thinking, this house was in foreclosure when I first investigated the murder."

The lawyer shoved his coat to one side of the couch to lie down. "Well, that fits my theory, Drew, but you can check that out later. Right now, I need to know if you've got good forensic skills."

"Lost a file on your laptop?"

"Funny guy!" For the next twenty minutes, Ambrose explained all that he had learned. He discussed the conversation that he had with Michael Farthington at the courthouse and the recent conversations with Marcia Hathaway and Ms. Peterson—although he left out the part about asking Mary on a date. Ambrose turned onto his side and asked, "So, partner, do you know what I need?"

"Yeah, I get it . . . but that's one tall order."

"I know; don't know what I'd do without you. Do you think you can get me the results before Thompson finishes with Cooper?"

"Goodnight, Ambrose."

"Night, Drew." At half past six in the evening, he finished talking to Lierchetsky. The lawyer shut his eyes for what he thought would be a short nap on the couch. At quarter past midnight, he awoke with a jump. "Oh geez, I forgot to call the governor!"

"ALL RISE. The case of Harold P. Llinos versus the people of Dionysius is now in session. The Honorable Harvey Devoe of the district court, presiding." The clerk's bellow came at exactly 9:00 a.m.

Everyone in the courtroom watched Scarsdale parade Llinos in front of the jury. Henry sported shackles and Salimas County orange just as he had done the previous days. "Call your next witness, Prosecutor," said Judge Devoe.

Thompson looked at Ambrose and smiled. He believed today would be his finest hour; the day he'd drive a thirty-inch gladius deep into his enemy's bird-like pancreas. "Your Honor, I call Mr. Darwin Cooper to the stand."

Cooper, a sixty-something-year-old man, bald, weathered, with a stubbly grey beard ripe for scratching, stood up. He wore a light-blue, button-down shirt with a pack of cigarettes in his left front pocket. He also wore brown slacks in desperate need of washing. Cooper had a bad left leg, noticeably smaller than his right. Using a single-point cane—held in the wrong hand—he hobbled out of the gallery overflowing with reporters. Each hoped to write a succulent story about the fall of the great Henry Llinos. Cooper limped past a wrought-iron railing and entered the courtroom's altar where he plopped himself down in the box. After the clerk swore him in, the prosecutor went to work.

Thompson proceeded with boyish exuberance, "Now, Mr. Cooper, would you please tell the court where you were on the night of May eighteenth, sometime between 6:45 and 7:00 in the evening?"

Cooper responded slowly, but with a measure of confidence in his speech. "I walked my dog, Boots, down the alley between Cloelius and Zavier. I live on Zavier, not far from the Llinos' house."

"From where you walked, Mr. Cooper, could you see the balcony of the defendant's house?" The prosecutor looked down at his notes. "I'm referring to the house located at 1835 Cloelius."

"Yep, I saw it," the weathered man responded. He projected his voice and looked straight at the jury.

Henry had a foul look on his face. He leaned toward Ambrose and whispered, "I've never seen this guy before in my life. I'll be a monkey's ass if he lives in my neighborhood, or anywhere close to my house!"

Ambrose gave his client an affirmative nod, but said not a word. A few moments later, after eyeing the witness intently, Ambrose leaned in toward Llinos and whispered, "Henry, can you make out the brand of smokes in his pocket?"

"Why do you want to know about that?"

Thompson continued questioning his witness; he felt the passion building—his inquisition rising to a summit. "Mr. Cooper, did you see anyone on that balcony?"

"Yep . . . a man and a woman."

"Could you identify the woman?"

"It was her all right. I know what Mrs. Llinos looks like. I seen her plenty of times when I walked Boots. She stood on the balcony enjoyin' a smoke."

"And you saw a man?"

"Yep," came an assertive reply.

Thompson responded with equal assurance, "Is that man in this courtroom today?"

"Yes sir."

The prosecutor leaned forward in his chair. "Mr. Cooper, would you please identify the man you saw—"

"Your Honor," interrupted Ambrose, "may we please approach the bench?" The lawyer stood up after receiving a stack of papers from Lierchetsky, who had just entered the courtroom.

"You'd better have a good reason, counselor," bellowed Judge Devoe, "Now come up here, both of you." The attorneys glanced scornfully at one another walking toward the bench while Devoe flipped a switch creating white noise over the jury. The judge looked squarely at Ambrose and asked, "Now, Son, what's this all about?"

"I've got proof of evidence tampering, Your Honor."

Devoe's eyes widened; he desperately wanted to yell and scream, throw a six iron at someone. However, he managed to maintain control—still, the sheer size of his eyes, and the engorged veins in his neck betrayed the volcano inside him. He barked out an order: "BOTH OF YOU, IN MY CHAMBERS, NOW!" The attorneys, like two innocent bear cubs walking behind an angry grizzly, followed him out of the courtroom. They walked along a narrow passageway past several offices until arriving at their destination at the end of the corridor. Devoe slammed the door shut after both attorneys entered. His raging demonstration sent a Jack Nicholas square-grooved, ultra-forged five iron falling to the floor. The judge curled his aging body around his desk and sat hard in the chair. "Now, Mr. Ambrosius, what's this nonsense all about?" He spoke with nasty temperament; the veins in his neck still surged.

Ambrose spoke calmly, "Your Honor, the thumbprint on the black-handled machete that allegedly belonged to Detective Heinz . . ."

"What? That fact's not alleged," interrupted the judge, "Thompson established it. Now get to the point before I have you disbarred!"

The lawyer set documents down on Judge Devoe's desk. "These documents show that fact isn't conclusive, Your Honor. Some counties match that print to Heinz; others to Michael Farthington."

"Who the hell's Farthington?"

"Michael William Farthington—he's our murderer, Judge. He's being detained by Tiny as we speak."

Devoe glanced at Thompson, then back at Ambrose; his veins hadn't softened. "How'd this mix-up happen?"

Ambrose didn't hesitate. "It wasn't by accident, Your Honor. My investigator performed an analysis on the 5th precinct's servers last night. The keystrokes transposing Heinz's identity onto Farthington's print occurred on my esteemed colleague's computer. Unfortunately for Leonard, his permutations only took hold on precincts with updated software."

Thompson stepped back; a mean scowl swept over his face; pointing at Ambrose, he shouted, "Liar, you're trying to frame me, you piece of shit, but it isn't going to work. I'll have your sweet hide for this when it's all over. Go to hell, Ambrose!"

"That's enough, Leonard," hollered Devoe, rising to his feet. The judge picked up the papers and performed a cursory examination, then looked at Ambrose. "What about that Cooper fellow out there who claims he saw Llinos kill his wife?"

"He's conspiring with Farthington. They may be related as uncle and nephew, but I'm not positive of that, yet. Moreover, the county foreclosed on the home Cooper claims to have owned at the time of the murder. I've also discovered both men smoke Clannic cigarettes."

"Who cares what they smoke?" interjected Thompson.

Ambrose continued speaking, "It matters a lot. See, Your Honor, Detective Heinz investigated an unsolved child-abduction case—a case that resulted in murder. It happened many, many years ago; so old Heinz thought all potential suspects were dead. But he did his job, Your Honor, bringing Cooper in for questioning after learning he smoked Clannic cigarettes—the only evidence left behind by the abductor.

"Heinz began building his case around Cooper and brought his information to Thompson. That's when Leonard cut Cooper a deal. In exchange for dropping the abduction case, Cooper agreed to testify against Llinos—after using Farthington to murder Mrs. Llinos, that is. Sadly, Farthington left his thumbprint on the machete, so Thompson covered it with Heinz's identity. Who would have questioned it, Your Honor? Heinz is inexperienced; he could have easily touched the evidence in his exuberance." Ambrose looked at his colleague, "And after it ended, Leonard would get sweet revenge over the man he despises. Unfortunately, a fly flew into the ointment—the cover-up didn't extend to all counties."

"Go to hell, Ambrosius!"

"That's enough," said Devoe, buzzing for Scarsdale and several other deputies to come to his office. "I guess your client walks, Counselor. Leonard, I'm placing you in contempt until we get this mess sorted out. Son, I hope you've got a good explanation."

Ambrose walked back to the courtroom—after Judge Devoe gleefully showed him his Tommy Aaron 52-degree gap wedge. Only a scrawny, bird-like figure of a man wearing orange remained in the courtroom.

Llinos danced in a circle, raising both arms and a leg to highlight his freedom. "Look," he said, "no shackles around my wrists or my ankles."

"That's wonderful, Henry," Ambrose said, slowly approaching his client. "They never looked that good on you anyway."

I won't say I'm going to miss you—you miserable punk." Tears welled in Llinos's eyes as they came closer together. Then Henry broke down and cried, hugging his attorney profusely. "God damn it, Ambrose, I don't know what you did or how you did it, but thank you; thank you from the bottom of my heart."

"You're welcome, Henry. Now go make this world a better place. Go out and make Minea proud of you."

Llinos released his hug and wiped his eyes with a sleeve. "I'll do that, she'll be proud of me; you'll see."

Ambrose watched Henry walk toward the side door of the courtroom. Scarsdale arrived, holding a bag with a few personal items inside it. After waving good-bye, the lawyer strolled over to the table to gather his things. Then, just as before, he heard clapping in the back of the room. *That can't be Mock . . . I mean Keller . . . I mean Farthington . . . he's in custody.* Ambrose abruptly turned around. "Who's there?"

"I didn't mean to startle you, Aurelius—may I call you Aurelius?"

Details of the mysterious figure emerged as Ambrose walked past the railing. "Governor, what a surprise," he called out. Ambrose bowed his head and lowered his eyes out of respect for the office.

A governor and archbishop ruled each American province; the latter holding a slight advantage over the former. Any issue became law without further discourse if the two heads agreed on the matter. If they disagreed, however, the secretary of state e-mailed a referendum to every cell phone registered in the province. Anyone so registered, and at least eighteen years of age, had forty-eight hours to respond. If the plebiscite favored the archbishop's proposal, then it became law without further discussion. If it favored the governor's proposal, the bill went down to the Senate. Dionysius had thirty-five senators, one from each county; passage required three-fifths majority. Dionysius' judiciary consisted of twenty-six district courts and two appellate courts. The Supreme Court had authority to overturn statutes, but only those enacted by the Senate.

The governor emerged from a corner. "Well, I figured if you weren't coming to me, then I needed to go to you," he said. Governor Anicius Probus clothed himself in a royal-purple toga, which had complex folds and ultra-thin gold-stitched lace. Designed exclusively for him by the Etruscans, it came hand-made from the finest fabrics in the world. The dye used to color the garment came from marine mollusks caught near Lebanon, off the shores of the Mediterranean.

"I'm sorry about that, Governor, I—"

"Aurelius, I'm not here for an apology," he interrupted, "I've little time before my guards burst through that door to ascertain my whereabouts. So let us speak briefly; what do you know about politics?"

"Well sir, I guess what I've read—"

"I'm not interested in what you've read, Aurelius," he interrupted again, "Do you know how it works?"

"Well, my brother is Mayor of Trier, and my father used to be Mayor of Gaul, so I've some idea—"

"Aurelius, I'm dying," Probos said bluntly. The governor sat down on a seat and looked Ambrose straight in the eyes. "Do you know you're the only one besides my wife and doctors privy to that information? They tell me it's some kind of intestinal cancer . . . pretty fast growing, too. I guess I ate one too many walleye out of Lake Aeliana. Anyway, Aurelius, I'm not expected to make it to my next election."

In most provinces, politicians cycled between elections and appointments every four years for as long as they wished to serve. Governor Probus proposed the legislation sixteen years ago to cut down on the expense—and the nastiness—of campaigning. He had had the support of the people, but not Archbishop Auxentius. The bill went down to the Senate, where they approved it by a twenty-one to fourteen margin. Seven months later, the Supreme Court upheld the law against a barbarous challenge.

The statute meant that any politician could appoint himself for four more years after his elected term expired. Leaders could also replace themselves with someone else—someone at least eighteen years of age, a citizen of the province, and free of any felony convictions. Local appointees required written confirmation from the Federal Agency on Reappointment (FAR), located in Washington, D.C. and Denver, Colorado. The gubernatorial office also required written validation from President Valentinian I, the present-day emperor.

"It saddens me to hear that," replied Ambrose, speaking in a somber tone. "If I may say, Governor, you've served our province well."

Probus formed a small smile. "You're very kind, Aurelius. But I feel disappointed in my performance. I should have achieved more than I did. It seems I often commanded the will of the people, but I lingered too often on the wrong side of the archbishop and Senate. Now I'm faced with appointing another before my ultimate departure."

The lawyer looked at him with steadfast eyes. "If you've come for advice, Governor, I've no one to recommend."

"Not even your brother, Satyrus?"

Ambrose leaned against the seats. "Sy's in your employ, Governor. He's dutifully served as mayor of Trier for the past four years. Am I to believe that you have not already considered him? After all, he's got a lot of political savvy; he's the most resourceful person I know."

"Yes, Aurelius, I've considered your brother. In fact, I've spent a great deal of time thinking about him lately. I wanted to speak with him at the conference last night, but I just never found the time. And you're quite right, Aurelius; Satyrus is a resourceful man . . . he knows how to get things done. He's like your father in that respect." A twinkle appeared in the governor's eyes as he looked off in the distance. "I knew your father well. He worked in Gaul about the same time I began managing Alexandria. To put it succinctly, I had profound respect for Mr. Ambrosius Aurelianus."

Ambrose remained quiet.

The governor resumed looking at the lawyer. "In some ways, Aurelius, you're the exact opposite of your father. Oh, I don't mean that negatively, Son . . . I wouldn't be here if I did. What I'm trying to say is that this office doesn't require someone who knows how to get things done. It needs someone who can move people, someone who can speak eloquently and motivate others to do things . . . things they may not want to do."

"Ms. Lalia is like that; she'd make a fine replacement."

"Yes, well, I've considered my lieutenant," replied Probus, shaking his head side-to-side. "She's different than she used to be, Aurelius. I can't put my finger on it, but she's grown troubling to me. I think her head has grown too large ever since they named the channel in her honor. Anyway, I've already made my decision about her."

Ambrose stood upright, speaking with a heavy heart. "We're certainly all going to miss you, Governor. I'm confident you'll find someone special to replace you."

Probus rose from his chair after hearing a noise in the hallway. "I think my guards finally found me," he said. He walked up to Ambrose placing a hand on his shoulder. "I've watched you closely these past several years, Aurelius. You are that special someone who can speak eloquently and motivate others to do things. Son, I wish to appoint you the next governor of Dionysius."

"Me?"

III

SIBLING ACQUAINTANCES

Sunshine radiated brightly through prodigious rectangular windows on the western side of the classroom. Marcellina Ambrosius sat quietly in the second of twenty-five rows of bistre-colored benches, listening intently to Professor Nero. Each bench rose eighteen inches higher than the one preceding it, if one began at the front and walked to the back of the room, owing to the upward slant in the floor.

Marcellina had Persian-blue eyes and was sufficiently pretty to forgo makeup. She had auburn-colored hair with only a hint of red, and, except for her bangs, she kept it in miniature curls. She wore a carmine-colored, long-sleeve woolen sweater over a white t-shirt. Her high-cut boots, tan in color, fit snugly under her close-fitting jeans. Marcellina sat between two other students and rested her arms on a shelf secured to the bench in front of her. The shelf, extending all the way down the row, displayed meaningless graffiti dating back nearly 105 years.

"All right," said Nero, gazing out at his pupils, "let's conclude today's lecture with a brief discussion of ancient Jewish communes."

Professor J. Celcius Nero, PhD, graduated summa cum laude from Lynchtown College decades ago. He devoted his life to ancient history and became an authority on comparative religion. He taught classes to graduate students at Dionysius University, formerly known as Dionysius Polytechnic Institute. The school, located in the City of Agnomen, on the western edge of Salamis County, changed its name in 1833 after offering degree programs and scholarships to students.

Nero, now in his mid-seventies, wore a plaid sport coat and olive-drab trousers to class every morning. A crotchety man, he sometimes showed a sense of humor. He showed it by making tired jokes when he felt comfortable in his surroundings. His students regaled him a curmudgeon because he made them stand whenever he called upon them to answer a question. They also hated him because he permitted no computers, pens, notebooks, or texts in his classroom. Every student discussed the assigned reading using only his or her memory for a tool. Nero paced back and forth, his eyes fixed upon the black tile floor in front of him. "Mr. Vergil," he began, "sitting in the last row won't get you excused from participating. Please tell us the principal characteristics of a commune."

"Um . . . egalitarianism . . ."

"Stand up and start over, Mr. Vergil."

The young man rose to his feet and continued, "Egalitarianism, anti-enceinte, and . . . and anti-bureaucratic." After he finished, he boasted a beaming grin on his face making his freckles stand out.

"Thank you, Mr. Vergil. Please remember to stand whenever you contribute to class. Now, Ms. Ambrosius," he continued, turning himself toward his next victim, "what do these words mean?"

Marcellina quickly stood up. "Egalitarianism means the members reject social hierarchy. They believe no one in the commune should have greater or lesser status than anyone else. Anti-enceinte means they don't care to live in a large and impersonal society. They would much rather live closely among a smaller group of people who share a common vision."

"A place where everybody knows your name," interrupted the professor, scanning his audience to see if his remark elicited any smiles.

Marcellina wasn't amused. "Yes, something like that," she replied. "And anti-bureaucratic means they reject an outside government running their lives. In essence, they want to be self-sustaining, be their own authority."

"Indeed, Ms. Ambrosius." Nero made his remark before interjecting a peripheral comment, "Speaking of government, Marcellina, please send along my congratulations to Aurelius. I do hope they confirm your brother; I think he would make a splendid governor. Of course, his appointment won't earn you a better grade." The professor explored the room for more chuckles.

"Nor will my conveyance render you more funding," countered Marcellina, speaking laconically to the elderly instructor. Marcellina was the eldest child in the Ambrosius family. At thirty-seven years, she came into the world fifteen months before Satyrus, and had circled the sun three and a half more times than Aurelius. Their parents had wanted them close together since they lived on an isolated plantation off the Beaverhead River in the northwestern territory of Gaul. The river's name stemmed from a rock in its middle, not from the many creatures along its banks. Historians said Sacajawea first noticed the rock during the Lewis and Clark expedition.

Marcellina had acquired her mother's wit and intellect. She was surefooted in the classroom, and smarter than a whip—smarter than her brothers put together. Unfortunately, her zest for people made her a bit naïve in the real world. She cared for people so much that she had developed the bad habit of taking them at their word. Marcellina was the kind of person, who, if someone told her that she failed an exam, she would start crying before she looked at her score.

Nero formed a tenuous smile and laughed heartily at Marcellina's comment. "Touché, Ms. Ambrosius," he said, after regaining his composure. "Ms. Ambrosius, do we find evidence of communal living among the Jews around the time of the first century?"

Marcellina stood tall, answering his question, "Yes, Professor. Archeology has uncovered countless evidence of people living simple lives in small clusters around Jewish towns and cities."

"Thank you, Ms. Ambrosius, you may be seated." The professor scoured the room for another person. "Ms. Teresa Jackson, where are you?" After diligently searching, he spotted a black woman weakly raising her hand. "Ahh, there you are, Ms. Jackson; do we have evidence that Jesus supported communal living?"

"Well—"

"Stand up, Ms. Jackson," interrupted Nero, shaking his head side to side. "Why does this class have such a hard time remembering that simple rule?"

Teresa rose to her feet and answered him nervously. "Well, Professor, Jesus ate with prostitutes and tax collectors, so I'm guessing He rejected that whole status thing going on at that time. He mostly, like, hung with his apostles. So, I'm pretty sure Jesus preferred living in small clusters."

"Did He, Ms. Jackson? I thought Jesus enjoyed preaching to the multitudes."

The student stood fidgeting, cracking her fingers as she thought up an answer. "Well, Professor . . . I mean . . . preaching became his job . . . I mean his second job. I think He intended to be with people who shared his vision."

"Was He anti-bureaucratic?"

"I don't think so," she replied, hoping beyond hope he would start picking on somebody else. "I think Jesus felt indifferent toward government. Many different groups existed at that time: Pharisees, Sadducees, Essenes, Sicarii, Zealots—they all hated government, at least Roman government . . . except maybe the Sadducees. But Jesus is like, 'give 'em whatever they want, whatever belongs to them.' He could look past the Romans because He knew His Father was in control."

The professor glanced up at the clock. "Did Jesus rebel against the nuclear family, Ms. Jackson?" He didn't let her answer before clarifying his question. "I mean, if Jesus has a heavenly Father, can we seriously believe He disapproved of man's family structure on earth? If life in Heaven is designed with family in mind, could He sincerely rebel against conventional domestic life here? Do you believe He lived one way on earth and another way in Heaven?"

"Me still?" The woman mindlessly traced her index finger along a line of graffiti in an effort to ward off anxiety.

"You're doing fine, Ms. Jackson." Nero spoke with cynicism in his voice while staring at the skittish woman. The professor carried on, "Can you picture Jesus rebelling against his mother and father in favor of communal living? 'Sorry, Mom,' He'd say, 'but I need a place I can grow my hair, or shave it bald if I want. Dad, I'm going where I can drink lots of red wine, and where I can paint a peace sign on my donkey.' " Nero looked around for smiles. He disliked speaking in a blasphemous manner, but sometimes he needed students to open up.

"I don't think He was subversive," Jackson replied. There is a passage in the Bible . . . one of the Gospels, I think, where Jesus asks, 'who is my mother, or my brother?' Family, in his mind, consisted of people who believed in the same things He did—more so than blood relatives who didn't. However, that doesn't mean He rebelled against the family. I think He would have separated himself to live among like-minded people, but if He felt happy at home—felt a sense of convergence—He would never have left them."

"Food for thought, Ms. Jackson; you may be seated." Nero watched her sit on the bench and smile at her neighbor before he scanned the room for other targets. "Does anyone else have a comment?"

"Professor, I agree with Terri that Jesus probably had a communal mind-set, but I don't think He actually lived in one," said Marcellina, remembering to rise before speaking. "Members of a commune believe society is big, impersonal, and unchangeable. They isolate themselves from the mainstream in order to create their own utopia. Jesus didn't have that luxury; He needed to educate society, not seclude himself from it."

"Good point, Ms. Ambrosius. Of course that's true if first-century communes existed for the same reasons they do today. We don't really know that for sure, now do we?" Nero reformed the tenuous smile that he'd had earlier. "Well, that'll be all for today, class. Read chapters six and seven out of Brossan and chapter nine from Aquila. We need to bring ourselves up to Mohamed."

Marcellina gathered her things, reflecting silently on Nero's last comment. She walked slowly up the sloped floor toward the back of the classroom. *Did I inject too much present-day thinking into my remark? The professor is right*, she continued, *knowing about something in existence today doesn't mean it existed that way thousands of years ago.* It became painfully obvious Nero's questions had no simple answers. The difference between him and his students was that he had contemplated more queries, not necessarily that he had arrived at any more answers.

Hordes of bustling students heading for their classrooms greeted Marcellina as she passed through the doors leading into the hallway. She walked awkwardly along the side of the yellow corridor with her shoulders turned inward, trying to avoid striking oil on canvas paintings of famous academicians, including one of Professor Nero. Upon reaching the outer doors to the building, Marcellina donned a light-blue jacket and walked out into the cool autumn temperature.

A brisk October wind blew past her as she watched yellow and brown oak leaves twirling in the distance. Marcellina descended the steps leading away from the building and came upon her roommate, Jacqueline Meadows. Jacqueline sat at the bottom of the steps talking on her phone. "Okay, look . . . yes; I know that already . . . look . . . I've got to go, Toni. I'll meet you guys at the Gallus." She looked over her shoulder at Marcellina after disconnecting her cell. "Hey Marci, how did you like your class?"

Marcellina sat down beside Jacqueline. "All right, I guess. I mean . . . I like Nero; he makes us think. What's up?"

"Nothing; just got done watching a demonstration in front of the Lucretius," Jacqueline replied, dropping her phone in her backpack. "Anyway, I knew you'd be finishing up about now so I stopped by to see you."

The Lucretius stood as the multicultural building where most of the dramatic arts and musical performances took place on campus. Located on the west end of the mall, the building was named in honor of the university's first president, Edgar Lucretius. The mall comprised fifteen acres of manicured Kentucky bluegrass enclosed by a five-foot hedge of Alpine currant, thornless barberry, and belle poitevine bushes. Fifty-foot oak trees impregnated the lawn, providing much-needed shade in the summer.

Consisting of twelve enormous buildings of classical Greek design, the university's principal colleges surrounded the meticulous grass. On the north: biology, physics, chemistry, mathematics, and engineering; on the south: law, journalism, history, language, and the Publius, the university's main library. The student center arose opposite the Lucretius; capping the mall's eastern end. The buildings—made from a mixture of white marble and limestone, each with ornate columns in front—stood tall to welcome strangers. The mall contained the university's entirety before it expanded in the early 1900s.

"Wasn't much of a demonstration," quipped Jacqueline, "just a handful of Goths claiming maltreatment. I really don't understand their grievance, but this guy came around wearing bright orange high-top sneakers. He was cute, but he seemed awful mad about something. Anyway, I came by to ask if you wanted to join us at the Gallus tonight."

"I shouldn't, Jackie; I need to finish my thesis."

"Marci, you're not going to finish it tonight." Jacqueline stood up and shook off leaves that had blown onto her boot-cut jeans. "It's Friday night; you need to get out of the house. As I told you before, you're blending into the furniture."

Marcellina smiled and pulled her collar tighter around her neck. "I'll be at the library for the rest of the day—does that count?"

"Look, Marci, I know you're not comfortable with my friends, but I promise you'll have a good time; no one will bother you. We'll have a few drinks and do some dancing." Jacqueline swayed her hips from side to side in front of Marcellina. "Look," she continued, demonstrating a signal, "if one of them tries picking you up, all you have to do is cross your middle finger over your index, like this."

"What does that do?" Marcellina tried mimicking her roommate's gesture with her left hand.

"It tells them to back off . . . that you're not interested. But you have to use your right hand, sweetie, not your left!"

"What's the difference?"

Jacqueline sighed. "Look," she began, sounding flabbergasted, "you wipe your ass with your left. People don't appreciate getting messages from that hand." She shook her head side to side signaling her protest. "Don't you know anything?"

"Look, Jackie, I appreciate the offer, but—"

"Then I'll see you at ten." Jacqueline flung her backpack over her shoulder and began skipping down the sidewalk. "Bring no date . . . and don't be late," she shouted, turning partway around to wave goodbye.

Marcellina shook her head, watching her roommate disappear from sight, reflecting on what had gotten her to this point in her life. She had gone into the Peace Corp after graduating from the University of South Florida with a political science degree. Then, she volunteered for four years in the Republic of Uganda, happily serving as a group coordinator. Marcellina loved teaching life-skills workshops to young people, especially the Ugandan Presidential Initiative on AIDS.

In Kampala, Marcellina met Dembe Binaisa, half-brother of Kukango Lukongwa Binaisa, who served as their country's president two decades earlier. Dembe had represented Uganda at the United Nations in Nairobi, arguing for better living conditions, improved human rights, and more abundant assistance for his people. Marcellina became one of his secretaries and worked closely with him for nine years. She worked on a number of interesting projects, most notably the Zero Under Eighteen Campaign, which helped eradicate children's involvement in armed combat.

Marcellina adored her work and considered making it a career—until someone raped her. One evening around seven, she stayed late to finish a report; she walked into Dembe's office to file it. No sooner did she enter the room than the lights went black and the door closed forcefully behind her. Only the light from a failing outdoor lamp flickered inside the room. Marcellina whirled around, her psyche aflutter, straining to catch a glimpse of her would-be attacker.

Her assailant promptly tackled her to the ground, sending papers strewing into the air and across the floor. With eyes ablaze, Marcellina kicked, clawed, scratched, and bit at any body part not her own. She felt resolved to win the fight—but she was keenly aware that the beastly man had ripped open her blouse and bra and that he now pawed at her slacks.

After incurring horrific blows to the head, Marcellina's sense of reality turned surreal; she struggled to remain in the moment. With consciousness, strength, and purpose failing, Marcellina vaguely sensed her breasts being fondled. She also sensed a hand, or what seemed like many hands, forcibly stroking between her legs. With tears streaming down her face, determination yielded to numbness and submission. Marcellina stopped thrashing; she reluctantly closed her eyes and turned her head away.

At that moment, the flickering light from the outdoor lamp had given way to a bright light inside the room. Dembe had returned to his office to fetch a small piece of jewelry from the top drawer of his desk. He planned to fasten a pin on his lapel for a special engagement later that evening.

Dembe had tried convincing Marcellina to stay on. He told her Androa Gwondoya, his eighteen-year-old nephew, received severe punishment for his crime. Nonetheless, Marcellina remained unconvinced; Androa received no jail time for rape simply because he had not penetrated by the time the violation halted.

Marcellina returned home to pursue a doctorate in comparative religion. She chose Dionysius University, home of the Vespids, because Professor Nero had such an impeccable reputation. After her doctorate, Marcellina hoped to return to the UN and continue working with children. She would serve as a diplomat, she told herself, or at least someone higher than an ambassador's secretary; someone worthy of constabulary protection.

She had progressed to her final year at the university. For the past three years, Marcellina had lived alone in an apartment north of the mall on Palisade Avenue. She provided for herself working part-time as a teacher's aide at Fairbrook Middle School, but the work delayed her dissertation. With time running short, she cut her hours and searched for a roommate. She saw Jacqueline's advertisement posted on a wall at the student center. After Marcellina called her, they met for coffee at the Tea and Brew. Jacqueline's sense of integrity impressed Marcellina, and she accepted her as a cotenant. A week later, however, she begrudgingly learned of Jacqueline's sexual preference for women and her proclivity to party.

Marcellina stood up and walked eastward toward the Publius. *Great job, Marci,* she thought to herself, *you've gone from hobnobbing with aspiring ambassadors to imbibing with lustful lesbians. Jesus would be so proud!* She neared the southeast corner of the mall, turned right at the sidewalk, and walked up twenty steps to the library. Marcellina needed the strength of both arms to open a massive door leading into the foyer, and again to enter the building's principal quarters. The library's enormous hall shone dim, though six chandeliers hovered high above the desks; its main source of lighting came from incandescent lamps permanently affixed to each table.

The building provided welcome relief from the wind. Marcellina unzipped her jacket and walked along a creaky floor past twenty rows of rectangular, country-maple tables until arriving at a lonely spot in the back. Stacks of books, journals, periodicals, and newspapers dating back hundreds of years lined the walls from floor to ceiling. Despite being neatly indexed by subject matter, author, and keyword, students ignored these materials in favor of Internet sources accessible on laptops and cell phones. In a facility formerly known for its quiet, the clatter of hundreds of students pecking away on personal computers made it difficult for anyone to concentrate. *I must be nuts thinking I'll accomplish more here than at home,* she thought. She sat at a table and plugged her laptop into an outlet. *Remind myself to bring a few cushions to sit on next time,* she pondered. After settling in, she turned on her computer and began reading where she had left off.

Her dissertation, titled "Ecclesiastes: Differences Between the Catholic Nun, Eastern Orthodox Monastic, and the Anglican Community," approached 162 pages. It listed over two hundred references and began with a cursory examination of non-Christian nuns, beginning with the Buddhist.

"It is said that in India," she quietly read aloud to herself, "Shakyamuni Buddha appointed five male disciples, creating Bhikshu Sangha. Once he ordained men, he decreed Shakyan women, including his stepmother, Mahaprajapati. He reluctantly ordained them after they had agreed to follow the gurudharmas meticulously. Buddha initially resisted female ordination because he thought the lifestyle would be too hard on them, as most converts subsisted of wealthy women of the court. Still, others say he desired to shelter them from social disgrace because a male would no longer protect them. In any event, scholars agree Buddha gave comparable chances to women.

"Bhikshuni ordination moves through stages; it begins when a woman feels dissatisfied with life. She visits a monastery and does nothing more than wander the grounds and examine the library. If she discovers something of value, she returns to spend several weeks as a guest. The woman learns to liberate worldly possessions and denounce secular evils, such as swearing, drunkenness, and sex. Perceiving gratification, she stays on as a resident and becomes a novice, in which case, she wears all-white clothing, helps with chores, and stays on for a year, receiving Sangha guidance. After serving various branch monasteries for a few years, the novice receives bhikshuni, or full ordination."

Marcellina stopped reading and gazed across the room. *I wonder how dissatisfied with life a woman must get before joining a nunnery?* Without reaching a conclusion, she moved on to the central part of her thesis: differences between nuns and sisters in the Christian tradition. "Let's see," she began, still talking quietly to herself, "Catholic nuns profess solemn vows while sisters profess simple ones. Hmm, I need to delve more deeply into that. Catholic nuns and sisters undertake a postulate—a devotional period of testing and training for the ascetic life.

"Apprentices wear the garments of the order, usually a white veil instead of black, to distinguish them from the avowed. The terms *nun* and *sister* are interchangeable, but generally, *nun* refers to one living a contemplative, cloistered existence in prayer, while *sister* refers to one active in the community serving the poor, afflicted, and uneducated." Marcellina sat back in her chair. "I always knew nuns were useless."

Marcellina glanced at her silver-plated watch and discovered she had worked on her thesis for over five hours—time had leapt to 9:30 p.m. She remembered her invitation to meet Jackie's friends at the Gallus at ten. Marcellina closed her eyes and thought about whether she wanted to go. *Gosh, I'm so tired; I'll be nothing but a party-pooper.* She looked about the room, pondering her decision, noting that three-quarters of the students had left and that two more of them had stood up, getting ready to leave. A dreadful feeling came over her. "The library's not closing, is it?" The sound of her voice carried several tables away.

A handsome man in his mid-thirties responded. "No, ma'am, it doesn't close until eleven."

Marcellina smiled back. "Thank you," she said. Then she pushed her chair back from the table and stood up on two very stiff legs. *Whoa, I've been sitting here awhile—either that or I'm getting old.* She grabbed her green backpack and tottered off to the restroom. Fortunately, it was in the back near to where she sat.

As she made her way along, the thought of useless nuns returned—*Sister Mary Winthrop sure qualified.* Sister Mary taught fourth-grade Latin at Marcellina's school in Gaul, where she and her family first lived before moving to Milan. Whenever the class had gotten loud or unruly, Sister hauled out a ruler and started whacking students on the hand. Marcellina remembered having passed a note to her friend, Debbie. Sister saw it, insisting that she bring it forward and read it aloud before the class. Marcellina refused, whereby Sister ran after her with the stick. A chase ensued around the room that lasted several minutes, ending with Marcellina apologizing in front of Principal Danos. To Marcellina's gratification, however, the class never heard the note.

After exiting the bathroom, Marcellina laughed quietly, thinking about the incident. Then, she spotted another student closing her laptop and disconnecting its power cord. "What are you doing?" she shouted. She dropped her pack and started running toward the perpetrator. The student, a black man dressed in bright orange high-top sneakers, scooped up the processor and ran in the opposite direction. "Stop," she screamed. Marcellina slowed her pursuit when it became obvious she had no chance to catch him.

To her delight, however, the handsome man who had given her the time tackled the criminal from the side. He had witnessed the event and came bounding at the unscrupulous guy before he had gotten ten tables away. They hit hard, falling to the floor in a heap. The computer flew out of the offender's hands, crashing into a table leg before hitting the floor. The crook, unhurt from the assault, kicked the handsome man in the stomach. With an angry look, the thief rose to his feet and scampered away, leaving the laptop behind.

"Are you all right?" Marcellina asked her question while running up to the recumbent man.

"I will be . . . in a minute," he grunted, rubbing a painful spot.

"Should I call an ambulance?"

"No, no, please don't do that." After making a painful grimace, he took hold of a chair and climbed to his feet.

Marcellina wanted to help, to offer him support, as she hovered over him like a mother hen with her chick. "I can't tell you how grateful I am. I had over two years of notes in that computer."

The handsome man rubbed his stomach. "What's your name?"

"Marcellina—Marcellina Ambrosius. My friends call me Marci. And you?"

"Nadif, Aamir Nadif."

"Mr. Nadif, you deserve a reward for heroism. May I give you fifteen credits?" She looked around for her backpack and spotted it near the bathroom.

In Dionysius, like the rest of the country, people handled financial transactions using a creditizer. The most common model, the Lottorola C200, resembled a thick credit card. Small windows displayed credit remaining in up to three accounts. When purchasing a product, a buyer swiped the card across the merchandise. When purchasing a service, they stroked it across the service member's card. The same process happened whether procuring objects in brick and mortar or online. A green light appeared when depositing credit; red if it was removed. People read their financial statements over their phones; the pecuniary establishment fined them for requesting paper.

"No, that isn't necessary," replied Nadif. He stopped rubbing his stomach and started paying attention to her pleasing figure. "I'm content to have righted a wrong without gaining an advantage."

Marcellina reluctantly put her creditizer back into her backpack. "Then may I buy you lunch?"

"You're very kind, Ms. Ambrosius. Yes, I'd like that very much." Nadif brought his eyes up to her face and took note of her Persian-blue eyes.

After agreeing on a time and place, Marcellina gathered her things and waved good-bye to her hero. She exited the Publius, walking out into a dark and chilly night—fortunately, the wind had died considerably from its ferocity earlier that day. Marcellina misted the air with each exhalation and gazed upon millions of stars; some twinkled, but most shone steady through a black and cloudless sky. Marcellina made her way to the Gallus, situated ten minutes north of the Publius. *At least I have a good story to tell them*, she surmised.

The Gallus was as old as the university itself, having changed owners many times over. Barely inhabitable, the establishment defined the word *dive* in its truest sense. The outside of the burgundy-colored, two-story building consisted of crumbling, wet-cast concrete brick. It abutted the Agricola, a health-food store specializing in gluten-free consumables, and the Tea and Brew, where Marcellina first met her lesbian roommate. The Gallus served as a mecca for underclassmen but was beloved by graduate students as well.

Marcellina opened the door and entered the cabaret, immediately becoming deaf to any sounds other than obstreperous music from the Balba Stuarts, a popular rock band. She transferred credits to a dagger-carrying bouncer and walked into the crowded establishment. Grey smoke filled an otherwise dim enclosure—except floodlights sprinkling the stage with red, blue, and yellow colors.

Marcellina excused herself profusely as she moved through clusters of faceless people. After passing some spirited students, a discourteous man mimicking a Vespids goalie struck her from behind. He unintentionally lurched to the side, bumping hard into Marcellina, throwing her forward into a drunken man's chest. The inebriated man instantly wrapped his gangly arms around her.

"Hey J . . . Jen," he began, his breath reeking of scotch. "I just kn . . . knew you'd come back." Tears welled in his eyes as he bear-hugged the frightened woman.

"Please, sir, you're mistaking me for someone else." The sound from the band drowned out her voice as she struggled to escape his clutches.

The besotted man came to a realization. "Hey, y . . . you're not Jen," he said, trying to focus on the woman before him. "Did Jen send you here to 'pologize?" An intruder suddenly emerged from the darkness, forcibly yanking the man's head down by the earlobe. "Ow, ow, ow," he cried, letting go of Marcellina.

Jacqueline grabbed Marcellina's arm and wrenched her away from the drunk. "Come with me," she shouted, guiding her through the crowd. The women moved with the speed of lab rats winding their way through a maze. They arrived at a gathering near the dance floor where her friends had pushed two small tables together. A smorgasbord of imported beers, Captain Morgan rum, a glass of house chardonnay, Stolichnaya vodka, and one Bacardi mojito lay scattered about in varying degrees of consumption. "Everyone, this is my roommate, Marci," Jacqueline yelled, trying to make her voice heard over the music.

"Hi," shouted three women in unison.

Marcellina instantly realized that she was the oldest woman by over a decade. *Why did I worry? No one is going to make a pass at me; I must look like a grandmother to them!*

Jacqueline sat on the edge of a chair looking at Britannia. "Where's Accalia?" Accalia had recently become Jacqueline's girlfriend. She had been Beth's lover for the past several years. Beth tried repeatedly to convince Accalia to move to California where they could be legally married. However, Accalia felt reluctant to move so far away from family. By the time she agreed, they had reinstated the ban on same-sex marriage. Accalia's delay upset Beth so much that she broke off their relationship, disavowed their friendship, and moved into a separate apartment.

"Dancing with Beth," interrupted Antonia, pointing her finger toward the back of the dance floor.

"Come on, Marci, let's dance." Jacqueline stood up and grasped Marcellina's arm, forcibly dragging her onto the floor. "You're a good dancer," she continued, steering herself and her roommate toward Accalia and Beth. The four girls, now grouped together, partied wildly for the next hour and a half, occasionally joined by the three women at the table. Throughout the evening, Jacqueline kept a close eye on Accalia, looking for any subtle changes in their tentative relationship.

The foursome returned to the table after Jimmy Cummings, lead guitarist for the Bulba Stuarts, stated that the band would take a break. White luminosity supplanted dark surroundings, and the murmur of soft voices replaced deafening music. Before sitting down, Marcellina glanced toward the bar, searching for the lanky man who had held her captive, but he had left.

"Don't touch me, you guys are all sweaty," whined Britannia, moving her chair away from the oncoming women.

"Marci, we got you some wine, a chardonnay," said Cardea. Cardea, a manly, brutish-looking woman, whose name meant "door hinge," was aptly named after her father ripped off the screen door of the porch trying to get her laboring mother to the hospital. "I hope you like white wine."

"I'm not much for alcohol, but thank you," Marcellina replied, wiping her brow with a napkin. She grabbed her backpack and began searching for her creditizer. "How much do I owe you?"

"It's on the house if you take a sip," interrupted Britannia, nudging Antonia with her elbow.

Jacqueline bristled; she peeked around Accalia, who sat comfortably on her lap. "You guys didn't spike it with anything, did you?"

"No, we'd never do that," said Antonia, glancing at Cardea. " 'Course not," snorted Cardea.

"Don't believe 'em, Jackie," chimed Beth in her masculine voice, "I wouldn't trust these bitches as far as I could throw them."

"All right, what'd you put in it?"

"Maybe a little cat valium," Britannia replied.

"Ketamine . . . again?" Jacqueline looked over at her sweaty roommate. "Marci, don't you dare drink that wine; you'll be in la-la-land before you know it."

Marcellina pushed the chardonnay away. "Look, can I just have some water?"

"Take mine," said Britannia, staring into Jacqueline's vigilant eyes. She pushed her goblet toward Marcellina. "I swear; I haven't touched it."

Marci swallowed several gulps of the refreshing liquid and then pressed the glass to her forehead to chill her steaming body. "Hey, I've got a story for you," she began, trying to lighten the mood. "A man tried stealing my laptop in the library this evening . . . but he got tackled by another—"

"Oh, please . . . are guys still doing that?" Antonia interrupted.

"Boys are so stupid," Beth interjected, looking disgusted, "They'll do anything to get into a woman's pants."

"Yeah, that happened to my sister a few weeks ago," said Cardea, shaking her head, and then downing a big swig of beer.

Marcellina sat in her chair dumbfounded. "Are you telling me those guys staged that whole thing?" She reached for the goblet and took another sip of water, waiting for their reply.

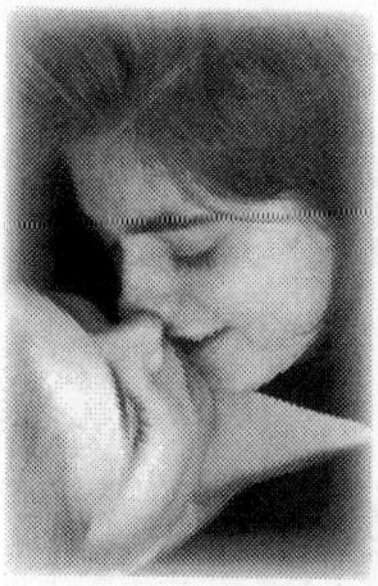

"Listen, honey," began Britannia, "you might be older than us, but you're naïve if you think guys are after your laptop. They want your vertical smile, sweetie. They pull that prank to meet women because they're too stupid to do it the right way." Marcellina sat speechless, hearing the band return to the stage. She glanced at Jacqueline hoping for a scintillating comment, but she was busy nuzzling Accalia.

"Alll rightyyy," blared Jimmy into the microphone, "we're back ladies and gentlemen, and we'll be starting this hour with a little *slowww* music. So, bring your sweetie up here and squeeze her to the sound of S & G." The band started softly playing the melody of Simon and Garfunkel's "Bridge Over Troubled Water."

Beth looked at Marcellina, "So what do you do, honey?" She asked her question moments before Jacqueline and Accalia stood up to dance.

"I'm completing a doctora—"

Beth ignored her answer; staring up at the two lovebirds walking away from the table. "Hey, who wants to dance?"

"Not me, you're too sweaty," Britannia replied. Marcellina stayed quiet; placing her hands on the table, crossing her right middle finger over her index.

"Toni, you'll dance with me?"

Antonia shook her head. "No way, my stomach isn't feeling good." She turned away and popped a pill, then chased it with some water.

"I'll dance with you," said Cardea, downing her last swig of beer.

"Next time, sweetie. Come on, Marci, let's see what you got." Beth yanked Marcellina out of her chair, "Maybe a little cuddling will relax those palsied fingers." Marcellina reluctantly walked onto the floor with her new captive. Firmly embraced in Beth's arms, they sidled over to Jacqueline and Accalia. The lights dimmed; a yellow spotlight beamed at a revolving globe high above the dance floor. Flecks of saffron flickered in a counter-clockwise direction. The band played on:

♫ ". . . And pain is all around . . ."

Marcellina clung tightly to Beth; swaying slowly in a caring embrace as the music took hold of their emotions. Marcellina felt her partner's heartbeat as the young woman reacted strongly to lyrics of pain and tough times. She felt her own pulse rise as a dreamy state took hold of her. Beth's soft, wet lips kissed Marcellina's ear and the side of her neck. Her hands, once fastened around the waist, now slid up to Marcellina's shoulders.

More hands started appearing. Marcellina felt hands groping her breasts, then stroking between her thighs. Hands pawed beneath her carmine-colored sweater and unzipped her faded jeans. Still more hands appeared; her body felt entombed. Marcellina's heart raced as she tried to pry herself away from her would-be attacker. "I can't breathe. I can't breathe," she cried, collapsing on the floor, struggling to remain in the moment. Only the light from a failing outdoor lamp flickered inside the room. "No, no, Androa," Marcellina cried out, feeling horrific blows to the side of her head. Tears streamed down her face as she reluctantly closed her eyes and looked away.

"Hey, you're awake," Jacqueline said softly. She sat on Marcellina's bed taking hold of her hands. "How are you feeling?"

Marcellina lifted her head off the pillow and looked around the room. "Where am I?"

"You're home. You gave us quite a scare last night; you were really tripping. I thought for sure we'd have to take you to the hospital. I guess you really don't like lesbians pawing at your body."

"No, that wasn't it," Marcellina replied, stroking her aching head. "Your friends are cool," she continued, returning her head to the pillow, "but that hand signal you taught me didn't work. Beth thought I had paralysis."

"Sorry about that; see, I had to find some way to get you to come."

Marcellina shot her roommate a malicious glance. "Speaking of Beth, you'd better watch out; she wants Accalia back."

"You noticed that, huh?" Jacqueline pumped her fist in the air several times. "Let her try; I'll knock her flat on her ass!"

They remained quiet for several moments, then Marcellina broke the silence. "Am I wearing pajamas?" She pulled the bed covers down revealing pink cotton butterfly jammies. "Did you change me?"

"You threw up on your other stuff. What should I have done? I didn't take advantage of you, Marci, not that there's a guy in the world who wouldn't have if they'd been in my shoes."

Marcellina smiled pulling the covers back up. "I trust you, Jackie."

Jacqueline smiled. "But you've got a nice ass!"

"Hey!"

The women conversed for several minutes before a question popped into Marcellina's mind. "Jackie, why did I throw up? I don't recall drinking any alcohol last night."

"The water was drugged, not the wine. God, Brit can be such a bitch sometimes."

"What'd she give me?"

"Ketamine; steals it from her brother's dental office. Brit must have given you a hefty dose 'cause I've never seen anyone trip the way you did. It's just supposed to relax you, Marci, not cause you to lose all control. Beth doesn't usually use enough to cause full-blown hallucinations. Can you recall what you thought about at the time?"

"The flickering lights, they reminded me of my rape three years ago."

"What? Oh my God, Marci, I didn't know . . . oh, honey, I'm so sorry," she said, taking hold of her roommate's hands.

Marcellina reflected on the night she spent in Dembe's office. "All I remember, Jackie, is a dark room—except for a flickering yellow light coming in through the window. That awful man had his hands all over me . . . I couldn't get away no matter how hard I tried. I just couldn't—"

"Don't relive it," Jacqueline interrupted, "it's bad enough experiencing it once without replaying it in your mind."

Tears rolled down Marcellina's cheeks. "I felt awful, Jackie. Do you know you're the only one I've ever told that story to?" Marcellina sat up in bed and the two women cried in each other's arms.

After ending their embrace, Jacqueline spoke up. "Here's a tissue," she said, sniffling, drying her own eyes with the sleeve of her sweater. "Now, you need to get up and get going."

Marcellina looked at her with red, puffy eyes; her head still ached. "Why, what do I need to do?"

"Aren't you supposed to meet your hero for lunch?"

"Oh my gosh, Jackie; I forgot all about Aamir."

IV

UPA PRESIDENTS

On a grey, drizzly day in April, President Flavius Valentinian I jogged past nine members of the O'Farland Garden Club. Owing to the weather, only half of their members showed up, freshly arrived from their meeting at the Bubalishious Bagel. They eagerly dug holes, raked leaves, and sprinkled granulated fertilizer, fastidiously planting row after row of crimson geraniums near the old clock tower.

Valentinian was chief executive officer of the United Provinces of America. He went by the interchangeable titles: president, emperor, Caesar, and Augustus. He boasted a mesomorph physique, was fifty-two years of age, and he had not run more than two 10k races in his life. Thus, to anyone remotely competent with endurance races, Valentinian was unsuited to run a marathon; he qualified for Boston because of his status, not his athleticism.

Caesar, never one to flaunt majestic habiliments, doffed his royal toga and sported a bargain-priced short-sleeve purple tunic. The garment hung well below his knees, concealing black neoprene wraps that suppressed his degenerative arthritis. The emperor ran rigidly, not smoothly and effortlessly like the lead runners; he ran as if each stride required a difficult policy-making decision.

"Go, Mr. President!" shouted one bystander. "You can do it, Caesar," shouted another.

Six hulking guards wearing bronze lorica squamata and a red-horsehair crest down the middle of each helmet encircled the muscular ruler. They also wore caligae—special sandals with metal hobnails on their bottoms. They had relinquished their shields at the start of the run and carried nothing but a sword and serrated dagger. Each guard was in excellent condition and could neutralize the most notorious malefactor using nothing but his bare hands.

The crowd, estimated at 750,000, lined the sides of the road. Spectators, standing in fifteen layers at the beginning and end of the race, stood considerably fewer in between. Many supporters got soaked by the rain, except those who had bought plastic ponchos from street vendors. Intelligent onlookers brought umbrellas from home to ward off precipitation, but police made them stand in the rear.

"You're coming up on a surly group to your right," said a military man into Acanthus's earphone. "One of them is leaning way out over the line. Do you have a visual?"

Acanthus, a strapping guard with blond hair flowing freely over his shoulders—a striking resemblance to Thor—jogged ahead and to the right of Augustus. "I spot them; should I break formation?"

"Negative, Canthi, keep your alignment."

No sooner did the man finish speaking when exhilaration overtook him. "I spot a knife, Canthi! Break formation . . . I repeat, break formation! I have confirmation on the weapon," he continued. "You're clear for kill, Acanthus. I repeat, you're clear for kill!"

Acanthus's eyes lit up as he bolted from his position. He quickly came upon the egregious spectator leaning well out over the tape. The guard raised his arm—about to deliver a deadly blow with his sword—when he noticed the man peeling aluminum foil from his dagger. Acanthus forcibly grabbed the candy bar from his hands and threw it to the ground. "Now get behind the line," he yelled, lowering his armament to his side, "and stay there!" Acanthus sheathed his gladius and jogged back into position. "False alarm," he said into his mouthpiece. "I'm returning to formation."

"Roger that, Canthi, checkpoint one signing off."

Caesar's goal to run the distance failed at mile three; thus, he and his entourage jog-walked the course for the next ten miles. Fortunately, the train at Framingham Center did not run away like it had in the past—the President wasn't fast enough to have eluded it. At the twelfth mile, Caesar began running a series of rolling hills. Gasping for breath, he gestured for water by gracefully lifting a finger toward his mouth. He wanted to look extra fresh before entering "screech tunnel" where Wellesley students and faculty chanted the whole daylong.

"Augustus requires hydration," said another man into Acanthus's earpiece.

"Acknowledged, checkpoint twelve." After speaking, the guard looked over his surroundings, observing nothing but hundreds of faces bobbing up and down in the rain. "Breaking formation in search of the nearest liquidity station," Acanthus said, darting to the side of the road.

Upon finding a suitable depot, Acanthus observed hundreds of open bottles of ordinary water all neatly lined up across a roadside table. No less than ten banausic volunteers lended their assistance. A gaunt man in his early thirties reached toward Acanthus with a clear plastic

Worthington
scream
Meskony?

container. "Here, give this to Caesar," he said with a smile, "I just plucked it from the fridge."

"Where's the imperial water?"

The man's smile soon left him. "I'm sorry, sir, there's none at this table. The closest is a quarter mile back."

Without hesitation, Acanthus grabbed the table and flipped it over, sending bottles spilling to the ground. "If Caesar can't drink here, nobody can," he roared. After snarling at the worker, Acanthus turned around and sprinted back down the road. Upon arriving at the imperial station, he asked a pretty woman, "Royal water, please?" Acanthus asked his question doubled over trying to catch his breath.

The woman, about eighteen years old, wore a white and red dress with cupids and hearts in honor of President *Valentine*, as she preferred to call him. The pretty ditz exhibited two notarized documents, one attesting to the water's purity, the other to her solemn virginity. Acanthus carefully studied the records, and then signaled for her to pour twenty ounces of water into a goblet.

Without delay, he raced up the road without spilling a drop and presented it to a thirsty Augustus. The brawny guard breathed heavily into his mouthpiece, "Hydration executed . . . I'm resuming formation."

"Acknowledged, Canthi; checkpoint twelve signing off." The men arduously jog-walked another eight miles, and like many before him, the president showed signs of debility climbing Heartbreak Hill at the twenty-first mile.

"Core temperature is holding, but his heart rate is erratic," said Dr. Ornuf Caecilius, Caesar's chief doctor. "His monitor isn't registering; Canthi, can you give us a visual?"

Brushing champagne-colored locks away from his face and jogging backwards up the hill, the guard turned around to look at Augustus. After studying the president, Acanthus mumbled, "Looks like a baby with gas!" Using his outer voice, however, he remarked, "He's giving me a thumb's up, doctor; a wire must've come loose off his chest."

"Roger that Aca—"

A frantic voice interrupted the physician. "Aegidius," a man began, speaking to one of Caesar's rear guards, "female racer approaches wearing number three-niner-niner, do you have a visual? She appears to have an orange bandana wrapped tightly around her head. Let her know that she's getting too close to the President."

"Copy that," Aegidius replied. The sentry instantly turned around and waved his arms at the approaching woman. With broad, sweeping gestures, he directed her to the side of the road. He spoke into his mouthpiece after noting her reaction. "Subject is running erratically; she is unresponsive and still approaching."

"Take evasive action."

Aegidius unsheathed his sword as the lethargic woman sprang into action. She veered right, darted left, and then bolted past the guard. The half-crazed woman rushed toward the President holding a six-inch serrated knife. Aegidius lunged at her legs in desperation. The cold steel of his gladius gouged her ankle—enough to slice a tendon. The infuriated woman tumbled headlong to the pavement and dropped the dagger, wrapping her trembling hands around her leg in an effort to stop the hemorrhage. Aegidius slowly regained his feet, perspiring profusely, using both arms to wipe sweat off of his Neanderthal brow. "Subject contained," he muttered, "recovering the knife and resuming formation." Aegidius shook his head and stared up into the rain.

"Roger that, Aegi, we'll send out a unit to retrieve her." After finishing his words, the man in the tower resumed speaking to Acanthus. "Canthi, Dr. Caecilius still needs a report on the President."

"We just crested the hill—and Mr. President's got a big ol' smile on his face. I'm turning around and resuming formation."

"Copy that, Canthi. Checkpoint twenty-one signing off . . . the president is down! I repeat; the president is down!" Acanthus turned and looked behind him. Valentinian stumbled forward, falling onto his side, appearing senseless but still conscious. Acanthus knelt down and grasped the emperor's arm, gently rolling him onto his backside.

Caesar's hand stroked the scales along Acanthus's squamata. "Canthi," he began, "I so wanted to break six hours." Augustus spoke with little strength in his voice. Then, a few moments later, after events deteriorated, the president mumbled, "Canthi, don't let me die." Caesar lost consciousness; his arm dropped limply to his side.

"Cassian, Corvinus, Manius—maintain crowd control," shouted Acanthus, scanning his surroundings with vigilant eyes. He returned his attention to the fallen monarch, placing his fingers lightly across his carotid. "Damn it, I'm not getting a pulse!"

"Administer AED," said Caecilius, speaking into Acanthus's earphone. "A heliport's on the way."

The sentry's eyes grew wide; he had a man's life in his hands. Acanthus forcibly ripped open the president's tunic from neck to navel. "Christ, would you look at that!" He peered down at a forest of statesman-grey hair intermeshed with two-inch electrodes. Black carbon pieces lay scattered on the president's chest in varying degrees of adhesion. Two were completely dislodged, six lay half-attached, and four—two on each side of his thorax—remained intact where Caesar's hair grew scarce.

Acanthus glanced at Aegidius and barked out instructions. "Scrape off that hair using that knife you found." Meanwhile, Acanthus removed a portable defibrillator from his pocket. The electronic device measured the size of a pack of cigarettes. He prepared new electrodes for application and stuck them on the president's shaven body. "AEDs are ready, doctor."

"Stand back and employ AED." The device took fifteen seconds to diagnose ventricular fibrillation, which occurs when the heart's lower left chamber beats erratically and is unable to move oxygenated blood through the body. The machine delivered a strong electric shock, causing the president's torso to rise off the pavement involuntarily.

"We're losing him," shouted Acanthus, watching the president's facial color turn blue after the instrument failed to restore normal rhythm. "Where's that blasted heliport?"

Acanthus and Aegidius took turns pushing on the president's chest. They performed cardiac compression and rescue breathing for what seemed like an hour before a Brookline City heliport appeared in the distance. "Manius, restrain the crowd," yelled Acanthus, "keep people back so that chopper has room to land." The guard took a moment to relax his weary arms. Looking toward Boston College, he muttered, "God, I wish to hell that band would stop playing."

The heliport landed without incident. Two paramedics quickly emerged and took charge of Caesar's condition. One took his vitals and applied an oxygen mask; the other established an intravenous line of epinephrine. With help from the guards, they hoisted Augustus onto a gurney and wrapped a special device around his chest. They wheeled the president to the chopper while the device delivered cardiac compression. Marine One lifted high in the sky after everyone sat, carrying five occupants, plus the pilot, to Massachusetts General. Acanthus studied the face of one of the paramedics. "Is he going to make it?" The guard spoke loudly, trying to be heard over the whirlybird's engine and rotors.

"Doctors control him now," shouted the medic. After attaching several more leads to the president's body, he inserted a central catheter. "You guys did a bang-up job keeping him alive until we got there. You beat the hell out of his chest; did you see how red it got?"

Acanthus sat back in his seat; he wanted a straightforward answer, a simple yes or no. He wasn't looking for conversation, or accolades, for that matter. Surmising a premature query, he glanced at Aegidius sitting on the opposite side of the aircraft. They studied each other's eyes and then turned their heads to look through portals at jets accompanying their journey. At two in the afternoon, cloudy skies and drizzle gave way to partly sunny conditions.

The heliport landed safely on the hospital's rooftop. Acanthus remained with the president while Aegidius met with officials discussing evacuation procedures and security sweeps of the entire medical complex. Time ticked slowly for Acanthus. He sat in a small room next to the emergency ward awaiting news from the doctors. Aegidius had just joined him when Dr. Caecilius walked into the room.

The doctor grinned; he had a broad smile on his face. "We're upgrading his condition from critical to serious," he said. "You boys saved his life; you should be awfully proud of yourselves." Caecilius looked away and walked toward a conference room packed with reporters. Before entering, however, he turned around and made one final comment. "By the way, fellas, the knife you used to scrape his hair had sulfuric acid on it. It caused a nasty chest burn; did you see how red it got? Well, I'm off to tell the rest of the world the good news."

The dumbfounded guards shook their heads. They both thought the same thing: *Why did that infuriating Hun have to coat the knife with a caustic substance?* They looked at one another as they removed their latex gloves and headed toward the exit, feeling generally satisfied with the day given its ugly circumstances.

The president, wearing a royal-purple gown pulled down to his navel, moved about in bed using his powerful legs. His left arm lay motionless, connected to an intravenous line; his right hand held onto a cell phone. "Look, Larry," he said, "I'm not letting Visigoths into the country. What . . . yes I know there is a civil war in Thrivingi . . . yeah; I realize Huns will probably annihilate them. Look, Larry, we're a Christian nation now. I can't risk bringing Islam into the country—damn it; that's my final answer!"

"Mr. President, you have another call on line six," said an aide standing by the bed. "Oh, and the German Chancellor is waiting on line three."

"Emperor, this fax just came in from Russia," said another.

At that moment, Dr. Caecilius entered the presidential suite. "What's going on? All of you, get out, and take your phones and faxes with you." He circled the room and herded them all into the corridor. After slamming the door shut, he implored, "Augustus . . . Caesar, you must slow down! Your weary heart needs time to rest. Please, Mr. President, I'm not sure you'll survive another attack."

Caesar shut off his phone and gazed up at his physician. "Perhaps I can accommodate you, doctor, but I'll need to speak to Tina."

"By all means, I saw limousines pulling up a few minutes ago. The First Lady should be here any moment." Caecilius had barely uttered the words when Valentinian II, or Ian, as his family called him, burst through the door and jumped into bed with his father. The doctor smiled at the boy before giving one final glance at a monitor. "Your rhythm is holding steady; I'll let myself out, Your Highness."

"Hey, hey, there's my boy," Caesar cheerfully remarked, squeezing his four-year-old son with one arm. "Hey, baby," he continued, watching Justina walk into the room. The president waited anxiously for the rest of his family. "Tina, where's Gratian and the girls—didn't they want to come?" Caesar asked his question while controlling Ian, who was busy spreading his cream-colored blankie over his father's chest.

"The girls are staying with Lolitta," she replied. Justina was utterly gorgeous for someone thirty-seven years old. She had a luscious shape, and her skin radiated a silky, golden hue that, as they say, dazzled the eyes of the beholder. She had originally been married to Adalberto Rodriguez, a former Mexican leader whose jet mysteriously crashed under ideal weather conditions. At the time of his demise—thirteen years ago now—Rodriguez had been flying in a private plane to get a closer look at immigration controls along the Mexico-Arizona border.

Justina first met President Valentinian when he attended her late husband's funeral. Valentinian had appeared with his wife, Marina Savera, and their son, Gratian. At the funeral, the widow's appearance had captivated Savera. Thereafter, she revisited Justina once a month just to make love. After exposing their lesbian affair, President Valentinian divorced Savera and took Justina for his bride. Together, they had had four children in short order: Galla, Grata, Justa, and Ian.

"Lolitta promised she'd show the girls a better way to apply makeup. And you know how teenagers are, Val; Gratian just wants to be with his friends. I'm sure he sends his love." Justina pushed aside a metal tray holding a cup of water, a box of tissues, and the television remote. She pushed his leg to one side and sat down on the edge of the bed, looking at him straight in the eyes. In her soft, maiden-like voice, she inquired, "So how you doing, Val?"

Caesar pushed himself up in bed. "I'm getting stronger; they'll be letting me go pretty soon." The president grabbed the remote and clicked off the television. "Listen, Tina, how would you like to move to Colorado?"

Justina's eyes lit up. "By Colorado, do you mean the mountains, the fresh air, the skiing, and all that peace and quiet kind of stuff?" She squeezed his hand, "Oh, Val, I could get used to that!"

The president smiled, but then a concerned look came over his face. "Great, baby, now if I can just get our nation used to the idea." Caesar pondered the nation's reaction to another big change in American policy. The United States, now the United Provinces, had changed markedly over the years. Most of it had occurred during the reign of Leonard Fitzgerald Constantine I thirty-some odd years ago.

At that time, America felt the grips of a painful recession. Then, without warning, large-scale climactic disasters struck China, India, and Indonesia. These lands were devastated, and, quite naturally, starved for credit. Conditions had forced them to expedite debt repayment from the United States. America could not meet its accelerated obligation and appealed to the UN and the international business community for help. Unfortunately, these organizations ignored her plight. With its rating lowered, the United States could not secure financing to stimulate its sluggish economy. The federal government, despite slashing a number of programs, defaulted on mandated payments to states. That action caused many states to make drastic cuts, and more than a few declared bankruptcy.

In an effort to salvage a nation in chaos, Senator Akiva Bercu, a prominent Virginia Republican, authored a bill permitting wealthy states the right to purchase ones that were failing. President Constantine signed the bill into law after it narrowly passed both Houses. Opponents challenged the statute, to which the Supreme Court, in a five-four decision, declared the new law constitutional.

The Supreme Court's affirmation proved what most precocious people already knew: the term *constitutional* bore no resemblance to the founding fathers' intentions. It meant nothing more than an archaic expression suggesting the statute in question held sufficient benefit to warrant passage. One could make a plausible argument that faith-based organizations, such as those with roots in Judaism, Christianity, or Islam, had done a much better job than the Supreme Court of adhering to their originators' principles. The argument is even more persuasive if one considers that religious traditions have maintained their values across thousands of years. The Supreme Court, on the other hand, had mangled the meaning of the Constitution in less than a few hundred.

The law gave rise to unfriendly mergers and acquisitions as affluent states purchased poor ones. Many holding companies, called provinces, soon formed. However, before the dust settled, only a dozen of them remained; each one, on average, holding four states. Thus, America no longer consisted of fifty states, but a league of twelve provinces, called the United Provinces, or UPA. That situation brought another crisis to the forefront.

States retained their names, boundaries, and representation at the local level. At the federal level, however, power resided in the provinces, each zealously represented by a board of directors in Washington. Bickering between Democrat and Republican congressional leaders paled next to the battle between legislators and the boards. The directors refused submission to Congress. "We don't take orders from subsidiaries," one director was quoted as saying.

President Constantine, a prominent businessperson himself before the people voted him into office, used their squabble to his advantage. In November of his second year in office, he began hosting a series of White House parties. His parties always served high-ranking military officers, FBI, CIA, and other defense-agency personnel, including local police. At every function, the president drilled his visitors with excessive talk about gridlock legislation and erratic funding for those putting themselves in harm's way. "Legislators are a hindrance to America's future," he would repeatedly say. "They need to go!" By the end of six months, President Constantine had nearly all of them singing his tune.

Then, on April 1 of the following year, at exactly nine in the morning, the president took his plan to the next level and had every legislator arrested. At first, people seemed stunned, and their reaction, bitter. However, everyone soon realized its potential as one of the finest April Fools' jokes ever envisioned. People subsequently cheered and danced in the streets. Bands played across the nation in honor of the prank. News analysts frothed at the mouth, conjuring joke after joke why the president should continue his tomfoolery. More importantly, no defense agency or foreign ally put a single combat plane into the air; America seemed jubilant with its current affairs.

The following day, of course, held crucial importance. Constantine, still holding the legislators imprisoned, sat at his desk perpetually on the phone. He used every ounce of reasoning he could muster, as well as insight gleaned from analysts the day before, to ward off police and other agency officials. In the end, those White House parties won the day, for no one released the prisoners, or came to arrest or impeach the president. "Let's see if he can get something done—God knows legislators can't," was the general reaction. "We've got boards, what do we need Congress for?" came another common response. Thus, President Fitzgerald Constantine I, partway through his third term in office, succeeded in changing America from a democracy to an autocracy without shedding a drop of blood—the nation had suffered only hangovers from the previous day's partying.

In his first act as monarch, Constantine released each legislator after abdicating power. Then he went to work on the final laws that distinguished his administration. He declared English America's official language, and Christianity its religion. Although he tolerated most faiths, none received federal funding or tax-exempt status except those declaring Jesus Christ as Lord and Savior. Constantine further declared he would enact no law contradicting the Bible as a Catholic bishop, elected from a province, understood that book to mean. Thus, the Most Reverend Antoine Alexander, Archbishop, became the country's first ever superintendent bishop, its first exarch. He hailed from the southeast province of Natalia and dutifully replaced the Supreme Court. Caesar promptly dismissed the body of nine justices formerly holding that position.

"Abra . . . cadabra," said Ian, pulling his blankie away from his father's stomach.

Valentinian suddenly awoke from his thoughts; a forbidding look appeared on his face as he watched Ian perform his magic. "Son, what are you doing?" he hollered, "I won't tolerate that!" He looked angrily at Justina. "Who's teaching him this stuff?"

"Probably the guards; they spend more time with him than you do."

"Well, that's about to change. Dr. Caecilius says I need to slow down. Look Tina, the way I figure, if we move to Colorado, I'd control the western half of the nation. My brother could stay in Washington and rule the east. That'd cut my work in half, baby. People would be okay with that, don't you think?"

Justina's eyes grew large. "You're going to split your presidency with Jules?"

Five months passed; President Valentinian stared out the window of the picturesque Chalet Aspenia. The Chalet, located at the base of Mount Aspen, served as his temporary office, his interim White House. Construction workers erected Caesar's permanent place of business several hundred yards away. He could see cranes, scaffolding, and other heavy equipment through fifty-foot Scotch pines dotted with pure-silvery snow. The emperor's eyes suddenly focused on a vintage 1948 Buick Roadmaster turning into the parking lot.

"Talk to me, Larry," said Caesar, speaking into his phone. "I heard about Probos—intestinal cancer, isn't it? . . . How long has he got? . . . No kidding . . . is he up for election? . . . Aurelius Ambrosius, where have I heard that name? . . . Oh, right, his old man served in Gaul . . . really, his brother governs in Trier. . . . What's that? . . . Ambrosius is a lawyer? Geez, is it asking too much to find a businessperson? . . . Yeah, now I remember; he defended that loudmouth Llinos—murder trial, I think? Say, that reminds me, have they found anyone to replace Exarch? . . . No, not yet . . . geez, Larry, you want me to approve this kid for governor, but he hasn't got a lick of business sense and no ecclesiastical guidance? . . . Fine, I'll take a look at his dossier when I get it from Appointments . . . hold on Larry." Caesar moved away from the window to view his secretary's message.

"Mr. Shapiro," she texted him on her cell.

"In," he texted back. The emperor returned to the window and gazed at the colorful sites. Looking down, he saw Acanthus and Aegidius having a lively conversation with the visitor in the Buick. "Send Canthi & Aegi," he texted again. The president resumed talking to his advisor. "What else you got, Larry . . . geez, what did my idiot brother do now?"

Caesar clicked off his phone after hearing a knock on the door. "Welcome, Mr. Shapiro," he said after Ms. Clarkston escorted the man into his office. Augustus directed his guest to a Victorian chair. "My secretary will take your coat. Can she get you any refreshments, Mr. Shapiro, a sparkling water perhaps?"

"No, I'm fine, thank you." Shapiro took his seat in the overstuffed chair and laid his briefcase beside him.

"Now, what can I do for you, Mr. Shapiro?"

"Mr. President, I'm with the special services division of the FBI. We, um . . . well, we continue investigating matters after the Bureau's made a definitive statement." The agent pulled a handkerchief from his pocket and wiped sweat from his brow.

"You follow up on crackpot theories."

Shapiro produced a small smile. "Yes, Mr. President, that's essentially correct."

"I can assure you, Mr. Shapiro, I'm legitimately head of the United Provinces. President Julianus, God rest his soul, had no heirs, not even a distant cousin. Upon his death, the boards appointed Jovianis his successor in accordance with the law. Then they rightfully appointed me to the throne after Jovianis's untimely fall. I assure you, Mr. Shapiro, Procopius—whatever hole he's crawled out of—is nothing more than a fraud." The president stood up from his chair. "Procopius is no cousin to Julianus; he has no right to the presidency. WHY, HE'S JUST ANOTHER LUNATIC TRYING TO GET HIS FIFTEEN MINUTES OF FAME!"

"Yes, well, I'm not here to discuss that, Mr. President."

"Oh!" Caesar returned to his seat and composed himself. "All right then, what are you here for?"

"I'm afraid it's of a graver nature. I've concrete evidence that your brother, President Valens, killed Jovianus."

The president laughed, "Jules . . . a murderer? You're a bigger lunatic than Procopius. Now listen here, Mr. Shapiro, President Jovianus died accidentally of gas asphyxiation from a faulty ventilation duct in the Manhattan Commons Hotel. No one has ever detected foul play."

"With all due respect, Mr. President, I've detected foul play," the agent replied, sporting a tiny grin. "I found a small hole in the ventilation shaft leading to our former president's stateroom. I've further evidence that someone inserted a gas hose through that hole. Now, in order to access the shaft, the assassin would have had to remove a plate secured with four bolts, and then replace them when he finished. Mr. President, three of the four nuts to those bolts were original to the building. But the fourth one was different. I eventually found the original; it had dropped to the floor and rolled under some heavy equipment. Its replacement, I discovered, came from Pete's Hardware store in Virginia. That store is not two blocks away from your family's plantation."

"Lots of people shop at Pete's, Mr. Shapiro."

"Of course, but that nut had your brother's fingerprint on it. Make no mistake, Mr. President, your brother fiddled with the ventilation shaft in the basement of that hotel."

"What possible motive would Jules have to kill Jovianus?"

"Mr. President, your brother blogged profusely against him." The agent lowered a hand and patted his briefcase. "Your brother became quite upset after Jovianus sold Hawaii and Alaska to pay down our debt. If you recall, Mr. President, that short-list of territories for auction also included Virginia. The board somehow narrowly saved her."

"Have you informed the bureau?"

"No, I haven't spoken to anyone yet. I wanted you to know before I took my information to the agency—before the . . . shit hits the fan, so to speak. That's why I drove here in my private automobile."

The president stood up and walked to the window. "I see; you're the one who drives that vintage Buick. It's a beautiful car, Mr. Shapiro; I'd love to take it for a ride sometime."

"I'd be honored." A half-minute lull in the conversation followed; Shapiro grew anxious. "Mr. President, you've not yet told me what my information is worth?"

Caesar turned around and looked at him directly. "My guards will escort you to the procurement office. I think you'll find the amount more than satisfactory, Mr. Shapiro. I do trust this conversation will never surface?"

"The case is officially closed, Mr. President."

Augustus walked back to his desk and spoke into the intercom, "Send in Canthi and Aegi." Then he looked at the agent still seated in the chair. "I do appreciate your coming here first with that information, Mr. Shapiro." A few moments later the president's office door swung open and in walked the guards. "Get in here and close the door," Caesar demanded using an unforgiving tone. "This man is making threats against my family."

"Do you want him arrested, Mr. President?"

"No, Canthi, I want him dead—now!"

Shapiro's eyes grew wide after hearing the message, growing even wider after the guards charged at him with their swords. "Aahh!" he cried, bolting from the chair. Aegidius reached him first. The blow from his gladius lacerated the agent's back near the shoulder. "Aahh!" he screamed again, managing to stay on his feet. Acanthus swung next, striking Shapiro's outer left knee, dropping him to the floor. Blood splattered everywhere as the guards took turns hacking away at the defenseless investigator. Seconds after the execution started, Aegidius delivered a final plunge into Shapiro's solar plexus. The agent glared up at the ceiling with fixed eyes, his chest no longer heaving.

"He's dead, Mr. President," said Acanthus. "Do you require anything else?"

The president had walked back to the window during the siege, preferring to gaze at the vintage automobile than watch the execution. Caesar spoke to his guards without turning around. "Both of you had a lengthy conversation with this man when he first arrived. Tell me, what did he say?"

Being the more articulate, Acanthus spoke first, "Nothing, Mr. President. We talked about his vehicle, and then we gave him directions to your office through the main entrance."

Augustus continued staring out the window. "Did he mention the good news? He had evidence absolving my brother of any wrongdoing in former President Jovianus's death."

Aegidius looked at Acanthus with an exuberant expression. "Why, yes, Mr. President, he did speak of that wonderful news." The loutish guard instantly realized he should have kept quiet.

Augustus smiled, tearing himself loose from the window, encircling the men before stopping in front of them. "Give me your sword, Aegi." The guard glanced quickly at Acanthus before reluctantly giving the handle of his sword to the president. Caesar grasped the gladius firmly in his right hand and raised the blade to within inches of the sentry's abdomen; the sword still dripped with Shapiro's blood.

Caesar stared at the steel as he spoke in a monotone voice, "Fellas, I was wrong not to attend your awards ceremony." He pulled out a kerchief from his pocket and began wiping the blade. "After all, you two did save my life." Augustus tossed the weapon back and forth in his hands. "Your sword, Aegi, it has excellent weight, but you have many dings in the metal."

"Lots of use, sir." Aegidius felt less apprehensive than he did a moment ago now that the sword pointed elsewhere.

"What about this jewel in the handle?"

"A pearl, Mr. President, to honor my father." The guard stood erect, raising his chin high. "He was the finest soldier I ever knew."

The president turned toward Acanthus. "May I have your sword, Canthi?"

"Certainly," he replied, placing its handle squarely into Valentinian's left hand.

The president raised the blade to within inches of Acanthus's abdomen. "You, too, have a gem in your sword."

Glistening tears appeared in the eyes of Thor's likeness. "A ruby, Mr. President, to honor my mother. I never knew my dad."

Caesar sighed deeply, then spoke after completing his inspection, "Well, fellas, I shall have your blades replaced by the finest steel in the entire world. I shall put your gems into a new handle and add five more of my own." The guards looked at each other with broad smiles—until Caesar pierced each man's belly with his respective gladius.

"Ummph," gasped the guards, losing their breath, clutching one another in a desperate attempt to remain upright. Their free arms tugged at the cold steel embedded within them. Blood gushed from their wounds like a raging river and pooled on the carpet below. It splattered in all directions after their knees buckled. As the shivering men knelt before Caesar, their vision faded to blackness, their hearing to silence. They valiantly clung to life amidst warm, scarlet fluid gurgling in their throats. As the last of their strength failed, their souls departed. Their lifeless hulks collapsed prone on the floor to the sound of clanging metal.

"Sorry fellas," whispered Augustus, "but I couldn't risk my private murder leaking out, even if that idiot Shapiro was going to wrongly incriminate Jules." He wiped his prints off their swords and carefully stepped over their bodies. He cracked open the door and hollered in the direction of his secretary, "Ms. Clarkston, come here."

She dutifully left her station and walked into his office. Her face grimaced after stepping inside. "Oh my gosh, Mr. President, are you all right?"

"Yes, yes, I'm fine. I need you to call Bob in security."

"Right away, Mr. Presi—"

"Wait, Ms. Clarkston," he interrupted, "Tell Bob I need the guards taken far away and disposed of without a trace. Tell him to use Marty's. I've used their landscaping company before; they'll know a suitable place to bury them. But, Ms. Clarkston—and I mean this sincerely—tell Bob he needs to be kind to them. After all, they were two of my best men." The emperor scanned the room to see what else he had forgotten. "Oh, and tell Bob he can do whatever he wants with the agent. And, Ms. Clarkston, call an interior decorator . . . and a jeweler . . . and have Jenkins gas up that vintage Buick. I may want to take it for a spin.

V

THRIVINGI GENERALS

WHIZZ—KABOOM, came the sound of an exploding warhead delivered by a short-range ballistic missile. The blast toppled the terra-cotta rooftop of the Eastern Thrivingi Railway Station. *WHIZZ—KABOOM*, thundered another, then another, each blast sounding louder than the last as warheads pelted the old Visigoths' city. "They're getting closer," shouted Lieutenant Dirie, nervously monitoring his GPS for the origin of the explosions.

"Allah will protect us, Aashif," shouted General Fritigern. "What's their position?" The general spoke calmly, yet felt desperate to relay the coordinates to his field officer, General Athanaric. The generals, often at odds with each other, weren't per se commanders of their country's military as much as warlords out for their own interests. But, at least for today, they cooperated in defense of their nation, protecting themselves against Huns stationed near the Gruethungi coastline.

Huns, a savage military group beginning centuries ago north of China, originated as a wily collection of prisoners, captives, homeless, and unfortunates. They were vagabonds and down-and-outs who had come together for the sole purpose of wreaking havoc on society. Under notorious leaders like Attila the Hun, they formed a vast empire that spread across Europe: an imperium exceeding the greatness of Rome.

Today, however, Huns no longer served as a political body but as a secret society. Their members numbered in the tens of millions, yet they possessed no territory of their own. They had absolutely no ambition for land, money, religion, power, or fame. Members, spread across Asia, Europe, and the Americas, enjoyed killing and mayhem for killing and mayhem's sake—at least, that is how the world perceived them. Insiders, however, believed themselves nature's little helpers. Each Hun felt a calling to eradicate the world of its weak, sick, and dying, believing assets and resources should not be wasted prolonging or enhancing the lives of nonproductive persons—except children, of course. For Huns, principle came before people. Outsiders considered them irrefutably cold and heartless, but Huns felt justified keeping humanity attentive and focused.

Huns usually attacked individuals and small private institutions, but on occasion would assault large groups of people, whole societies if they appeared disorganized enough. Members included doctors, teachers, politicians, engineers, clerics, and librarians—virtually all occupations. Their members included children as young as ten. Each person served for three weeks out of the year engaged in annihilation somewhere around the world. Adherents became recognizable only during military campaigns when each wore a brightly colored bandana around his or her head—worn so tightly it deformed the skull of anyone younger than twelve.

Huns preferred hand-to-hand combat to subdue victims—victims who often lay weak and defenseless. The dagger served as their weapon of choice, but recently it had become the dagger laced with sulfuric acid. They were excellent archers and bombers from afar when called upon to attack large numbers of people. But targeting people at a generous distance got innocent bystanders killed, which didn't serve their intention.

The Huns' most recent campaign nearly annihilated Ostrogoths living in Greuthungi, a sister state of Visigoths living in Thrivingi. Both clans lived off the Eastern Seaboard of Africa, situated east of Kenya near the Shibeli and Juba Rivers. First British, and then Italians, ruled their Commonwealth nation.

However, in the late twentieth century, General Mohamed Siad Bakke, following the assassination of Abdirashid Ali Sherpete, became the country's leader.

Bakke declared Goths an independent Islamic republic and eradicated foreigners from the land. He decimated paganism, including many Christian supporters. Under Bakke's rule, however, the republic soon divided. Shia Muslims, favoring Mohammed's succession by blood, became Ostrogoth. Sunnis, favoring Mohammed's succession by Abu Bakr, his close friend and adviser, became Visigoth. Thereafter, each nation created its own government and ruling classes. Since Ostrogoths embodied the smaller percentage, they lived along the harsh, rocky coastline of the Indian Ocean. The more abundant Visigoths moved inland and enjoyed the fruits of the Serengeti.

No one is sure why the Huns attacked the coast-dwelling Ostrogoths. Some scholars believe it started when foreigners regained entrance to the city. Travelers quickly converted to Islam, which, according to tradition, requires memorizing the Qur'an in its original Arabic. Foreigners insisted that the language add letters and punctuation to make it easier for them to read and pronounce the words. Ostrogoth leaders, to the mortification of its native inhabitants, consented.

Now, most Huns professed to be atheists, agnostics, Unitarians, Deists, or Naturalists. They could not have cared less if Islam distorted itself due to changes in its native language—weakness within the Ostrogoths' leadership caught their attention. Huns asked themselves: why would these leaders buckle to the querulous demands of outsiders, distorting a message that presumably came from God? In their minds, these leaders had to go. They would replace them with more precocious leaders in order to protect the world from any more small-mindedness.

But other scholars disagreed with that theory. Some believed the Huns attacked Ostrogoths because their leaders attacked one another, creating civil war that weakened their country. Still, others thought it had more to do with a change in Hun leadership than anything the Ostrogoths were doing. Young Huns asserted themselves, firmly believing in religious fusion, which meant taking the best from each religion and forming a new, grandiose faith. In their minds, they had reason to attack any prominent individual or group entrenched in one ecclesiastical tradition. Scholars believed young Huns took this position because they seemed more interested in preventing another war than saving financial resources.

Whatever the reason, extracting Ostrogoth leaders proved difficult. Huns had resorted to archery and bombing after hundreds of failed assassination attempts over a two-year period. Though their campaign ultimately succeeded, they killed over two thousand Ostrogoths and left a third of the coastal city in shambles. After inserting fusion-minded leaders, Huns directed their offensive at Visigoths living in Thrivingi.

"I've lost coordinates, General," cried Lieutenant Dirie. "The generator's out." *WHIZZ—KABOOM, WHIZZ—KABOOM* came the sound of more and more warheads. Each blast destroyed a section of wall of the Danubrian National Museum. The repository initially served as home to the Thrivingi National Parliament—an insignificant democratic organization trying to take hold in the country. However, a warlord general, Abdul Karim Fritigern, and his intelligence officer, had easily ousted them. *WHIZ—KABOOM* sounded another blast, sending parts of the museum wall crashing down on them.

"Everyone, retreat to the back of the museum," hollered Fritigern, throwing a useless phone on the table. Wearing his customary fatigues, he sidestepped rubble and escorted women through the fallen debris where they entered the room of Shah Ismail I. Fortunately, a farmhouse deep inside the country's interior currently housed the Shah's writings and other valuable manuscripts. The general and thirty-two members of his staff stood silently as they anxiously awaited the next round of shells. After ten minutes, the general stroked his beard and addressed his assemblage, "They've moved to a new target everyone; get back to your post and do what you can to get us back up and running."

Lieutenant Dirie walked back to his station and spotted something peculiar. "General, look," he said, pointing to a wall of the museum. The blasts had ripped open a three-by-two-foot section of an interior wall on the museum's main floor. It exposed a small room that antiquity had sealed off for centuries.

"Fetch me a flashlight, Aashif." After receiving the tool, Fritigern bent down and stepped into the opening. A small beam of light danced around the room revealing a thick layer of plaster particles floating about in the air. The first recognizable object, besides paper scattered across the floor, was a winding metal staircase. The steps wound tightly toward the ceiling. "Hmm, looks like it's closed off at the top," muttered Fritigern. The general redirected the light to the walls of the room and pulled a manuscript from one of the shelves. He pointed the beam at some unusual documents. "Sahaba, peace be upon Muhammad! This room contains the original writings of the companions . . . come here, Aashif."

Dirie entered the room just as the front doors to the museum's entrance burst open. Thirty-five Thrivingi guards, all dressed in green camouflage and equipped with AK-47 rifles, marched toward Fritigern's service men and women. General Athanaric followed the troops; he quickly made his anger known. "Fritigern's a traitor," he barked, grabbing hold of a table and flipping it over. Spittle clung to his black mustache as his act sent phones and computers crashing to the floor. "All of you," he continued, staring out at the terrified people, "all of you work for me now. Now, where's the general?" People timidly pointed toward the back of the museum causing Athanaric and ten of his men to make haste in that direction.

"So, the coup d'etat has begun," muttered Fritigern. He tucked the sacred documents under his shirt and handed the flashlight to Dirie. Then he dashed up the staircase. "Aashif, douse the light and follow me," he whispered. Upon reaching the top, Fritigern pressed his shoulder to the ceiling and pushed with all his might. "Aargh," he grunted. He felt the overhead tile start to budge, "Aargh," he grunted again, moving it another inch.

"Hurry, General," whispered Dirie, "I hear footsteps approaching."

One of Athanaric's guards pointed at the room. "General, I hear voices inside that small opening."

"Get in there and shoot at anything that moves."

The guard entered the space and noticed a flicker of light at the top of the stairway. Lieutenant Dirie hoisted his foot through the ceiling and replaced the tile behind him. "He's escaped to the second floor, General." The guard looked straight at Athanaric, who had poked his head into the room. "Shall I pursue him?"

"No, I know where he's going."

Fritigern and Dirie made their way past exit doors at the back of the museum. They kept low as they walked down crumbling steps leading to the front of the armory. "Aashif," began the general, panting furiously, "get my father and move him to a safe location. I'll head through here and see if I can find Saphrax or Alatheus." The two men had barely separated when sounds of *WHIZZ—KABOOM* resumed overhead.

"The Huns are attacking again," yelled the lieutenant.

The general glanced back, shaking his head. "It's not the Huns—now go!"

After Dirie got some distance away, he glanced back to see if anyone had followed him. As his head turned around, his eye caught sight of a flash. In an instant, a warhead blighted the armory off the face of the earth. Aashif's heart sank as he watched it burn; a demoralized look overcame his face. "My general . . . he's gone!"

Athanaric posted a five-hundred-credit reward to any civilian finding Fritigern's remains in the rubble. He wanted to recover the body—not to give it a proper burial, but to confirm the general's demise. However, with the Huns threatening to attack less than fifty miles away, he could ill afford to waste military resources on the effort. "I founds me another," yelled Abbas, clearing burnt debris, getting a closer look at the decedent. He held a rag to his nose to ward off the stench. "No, Captain; it ain't him."

"Then moves on, laddie," said Captain Riley. "It's startin' to shadow, and we still have lots of ground to cover." Captain Caragan Riley, a stout sixty-two-year-old, red-bearded native of Ireland—and a lifelong member of the Merchant Marines—had traveled up and down the Eastern Seaboard of Africa from Mecca to Mozambique. He had converted to Islam four years ago after Turkish sailors rescued him and his vessel, the *Aigneis*, a fifty-meter cargo ship, after it crashed on the reefs during a violent storm in the Red Sea.

"Captain, over here! I hears a voice."

The captain frowned, addressing his long-standing apprentice, "You've been snortin' again, haven't ye, mate? The blast is seven days old, laddie; no one is takin' a breath 'o air 'cept those of us standin'." But the captain had just enough faith in Abbas that he made his way closer for a personal inspection.

"Aahh," sounded a feeble voice beneath the pile.

"Subhanallah!" shouted Riley. "Quickly laddie, helps me move these boards."

The men worked feverishly to clear debris away from the potential survivor. "I see him . . . it's the general," cried Abbas.

Fritigern had wavered in and out of consciousness since the day of the blast. He had found himself in a small cubicle unable to move. He lay sandwiched between splintered beams that crisscrossed in their descent to the basement. The beams not only created his coffin but also saved his life, for they blocked the path of over two tons of scrap that lay over him. It may also be said that Allah saved the general's life, for two days' rain over the roofless armory dowsed the flames and provided valuable water that trickled into his mouth. The general had tried many times to wriggle from his cell; however, intense pain from a fractured humerus, tibia, and ribs—not to mention a punctured lung—was too much for him. He'd been buried alive and did his best to keep his wits about him.

"We're here, General . . . we're here to get you out," shouted Riley.

Abbas tapped his boss on the shoulder. "The credit is only good if we find the general's *remains*."

Captain Riley straightened up, stretching his back. "Well, laddie, I'm not figurin' to let a man die who'd come seven days 'o Satan's fury. Besides, he'll likely pay us more than five for savin' his pretty hide."

They worked well into the night to free the general. At approximately four o'clock the next morning, they had removed enough debris to pull him from the carnage. "Put him over here, laddie," said Riley, pointing to wooden planks he had laid across a wheelbarrow. "We'll cover him with these shirts."

"Did you pull these off—"

"Now, don't you be askin' no questions. Not a one of 'em gots any further need of no wears. Just get the general to the ship so's the doctor can gets a good look at 'em."

Abbas lowered the limp and bloodied general down a flight of stairs into the *Aigneis*'s belly. The ship, named in honor of Riley's mother, sat moored in the Indian Ocean ten miles south of the Gruethungi coastline.

"Slowly . . . slowly . . . aye," said Riley. "Now fetch Lynch while I wheel our lamped friend to sick bay."

Snap, sounded Fritigern's fractured humerus as Dr. Murray Lynch manipulated the upper arm into place. The captain wrinkled his nose during the course of the treatment, causing his bushy eyebrows to stand out. "Don't you have somethin' for the pain?" he asked. "The general cringes every time ye do that."

"I don't have anything; this ship isn't due to sail for another month. I gave him my last bottle of saline and a shot of penicillin. If he wakes up, I can give him an aspirin. It won't do much for pain, but it might help with clots. Now, Captain, hand me those planks so I can make a splint out them."

Captain Riley began walking out of sick bay after conveying the wood to the doctor. Before getting far, however, he turned 'round to address his crew. "Doc," he began, "lets me know if the general dies. I'll turn 'em over to Athanaric for a wee bit o' credit. Oh, and this goes for the both of ye," he continued, staring squarely at Abbas, "don't ye be tellin' the likes of no one who we gots aboard this ship."

One week passed before Fritigern stopped his incessant groaning. He'd become conscious enough to articulate his thoughts: "Where am I? Get me out of here! I demand to speak to the Gerudo in charge around—"

"Well now, that gerudo be me—Captain Caragan Riley at your service. I figures you must have had a quare temper; any man survive seven days o' ruins must have had a burr in his belly. Welcome aboards me *Aigneis*, General!"

"I demand you release me immediately!"

"Well now, me banjaxed friend," quipped the captain, "as much as I care to oblige, I've a wee problem with yer request. First, if we walked on the dry, there'd be no mistakin' ye could hang me by me throat for detain'n yer whereabouts. But, we's on the water, General, where mar' time rules apply—and them be my rules. But I must admit, I feels the gimp when I tries pulling rank on a man, so lets me offer you another reason. When you shows me proper use of the head, and me mate don't mop yer manky piss off the floor every hour, I'll consider yer demand. Is that fair 'nough, General?"

Fritigern looked around the room, then at the splints surrounding his extremities. He came to his senses and began speaking more calmly. "You . . . you saved my life, didn't you? How long have I been here?"

"Well, that's a wee more civil," said Captain Riley, pouring himself a cup of tea. "You've wimpered aboard me ship for seven days, General. I admits to savin' yer skin, but I can't takes all the credit. Me mate has the nose and ears of a canine, he does—I'd never have found ye if he hadn't been along." Riley set down his cup and looked squarely at the general. "I needs say I come lookin' fer ye only 'cause there be a price on yer head."

"Of course, I'll pay you four hundred for your trouble."

"It was five if ye'd taken yer final breath, General."

"All right then, six."

"We took a mighty risk bringin' ye here."

"Fine, eight."

"Doctors don't come cheap."

"Thousand."

"Me mate gave round the clock nursin'."

Fritigern raised his head off the pillow and stared up at Riley, who took another sip of tea. "Twelve hundred, Captain; that's final."

Riley wiped his mouth on his sleeve. "Ah, it's been a pleasure doin' business with ye, General. We'll have ye up and fightin' yer war in no time. Oh, by the way, ye kept callin' out a name the likes of Aashif. I sent me mate to fetch 'em. They be back in no time."

"Fifteen hundred."

"Ah, General, ye be a true gentleman; ye knows how to tip the house."

Captain Riley escorted Lieutenant Dirie through the dim and narrow passageways of the *Aigneis*. Upon entering sick bay and seeing his commander in bed, Aashif uttered, "Praise be to Allah! General, I can't believe you're alive!"

"Is my father safe?"

Lieutenant Dirie approached the bed, "Yes, General, he's with my cousin in Kismaayo." He lowered his face close to Fritigern's and whispered, "American ships are there . . . your father is safe from the Huns; they won't let anyone harm him."

Fritigern looked confused. "What are you saying, Aashif?"

"Remember, General, remember you thought it was all futile? Well, guess what? President Valens got your letter; he's accepting our people into the provinces."

The general looked away; his head pounded. He thought to himself, *Why would President Valens agree to Islamic immigration when his brother Valentinian was so adamantly against it?* Fritigern returned his gaze to Dirie and spoke with fire in his eyes, "Under what conditions, Aashif?"

"I don't know, General; Colonel Saphrax did the negotiating."

"Not Athanaric?"

Now Lieutenant Dirie looked confused. "No, General; Athanaric wants everyone to stay and fight the Huns—says we'll defeat them without anyone's help. That's why he tried killing you. He thinks you are a traitor for enlisting American support. Don't you remember?"

Fritigern tried, but nothing came to mind. Feeling uncertain about recent events terrified him. He'd never been this out-of-sorts before in his life. He looked up at his officer. "Have the Huns starting attacking us?"

"Not yet, they're calculating the strength of the American forces. But General, our people are divided: some want to stay with Athanaric and fight, while others wish to flee to the Provinces. Our civil strife is making us weak, General, and the Huns can sense it. I think it's only a matter of time before they attack."

Fritigern started remembering. "Aashif, get me Colonel Saphrax."

"Aye," interrupted Riley, "I couldn't help but hear yer last request—Captain's privilege if ye please. Now, if any fetchin' needs done, I insist ye use me mate. Abbas is a bloodhound who leaves no traces. I hopes ye understand, but I can't affords me ship lookin' like the armory should yer man be followed."

"Just say the word, Admiral, and we'll get underway," said Captain Troy.

Sixty-one-year-old Rear Admiral Frank T. Covington, UPN, gave Captain Troy a contemptuous look. "The word, Ed, is damn us all to hell—now shove off!" The admiral, in full dress whites, made his remark on the bridge of the *UPS George P. Sanford.* The ship, a 106,000 metric ton Nimitz-class aircraft carrier with all the planes removed, carried a skeleton crew of 1,500 service members and 4,500 Thrivingi refugees. The crew began its second voyage from Kismaayo to New York. "Adjust for the starboard list," barked Covington, "and I don't want to hear a peep from anyone until we've rounded the Cape."

"Admiral?"

"What is it Lieutenant Jackson?"

"General Fritigern's father is aboard; he's accompanied by Lieutenant Dirie and his four-year-old daughter.

"Well, let's all applaud," replied the admiral. He removed his glasses and rubbed his eyes; he felt a headache coming on. "Set them up in a private room, Lieutenant—at least until separation."

"Sir, shall I request their presence at dinner?"

The admiral continued rubbing his eyes. "Lieutenant, is this your first voyage?"

The ship sailed at thirty knots southwesterly in calm seas around the island of Madagascar and ports Elizabeth and Cape Town. After pointing north, the crew prepared for separation. "Come with me, sir," began a navy man. "Helicopters have landed above; they've brought medicine and valuable supplies." Sailors repeated this verbiage, assisting over one thousand sick and elderly Visigoth up to the flight deck.

"Separation's complete, Admiral," said Captain Troy.

"Admiral?"

"What is it, Lieutenant Jackson?"

"We've apprehended a Hun."

Admiral Covington stroked his head as he thought about what to do. "Bring him to me, Lieutenant."

"Sir?"

"What is it now?"

"Shall we separate General Fritigern's father?"

"Put him in sick bay." Covington felt another headache coming on as he slowly paced the bridge. After several minutes passed, he spoke to Captain Troy. "Take the com, Ed; I'll be in the infirmary."

The admiral walked swiftly, descending two flights of stairs, hurrying along narrow passageways until he arrived at his destination. He entered sick bay and came upon an elderly man wearing an all-white dishdasha made from 100 percent mercerized cotton. The garment had a small front-button opening at the neckline and came with a matching scarf. "I'm Admiral Covington," he began, "It's a pleasure having you aboard." The admiral shook the man's hand before sitting down next to him.

"Peace be upon Mohammed, and thank you for bringing us to your country. I am called Najid." The man bowed his head and gestured with open arms as he spoke.

"Where are you planning to live?"

"After I arrive in New York City, I shall travel by train to a province called Dionysius. Are you familiar with it?"

Before the admiral answered, he heard a disturbance outside the infirmary. "Excuse me a moment, Najid." The admiral stood up and left to investigate the ruckus. "What's going on?" he asked, watching two men struggling in the hallway.

Lieutenant Jackson looked up at the admiral, maintaining both arms around his prisoner. "The Hun, sir, as you requested. He's being a bit unruly."

Covington curled his lip, looking down at a twelve-year-old boy. "Shit, you've got to be kidding me."

The boy stopped struggling and began speaking, "I heard crew telling people to go above and get medicine. That's just wrong. That's exactly what they'll do in America: waste our healthcare, eat up resources the rest of us pay for—and for what? So they can sit and do nothing but piss in their pants watching television!"

The admiral continued staring at the youth. "Son, have you got a name to go along with that opinion?"

"Danny Mathews."

"Where you from, Mathews?"

"Milwaukee." The boy spat on the floor before resuming his crusade. "Look, these people need to die—before they waste any more resources." The boy grimaced while struggling to break loose against Lieutenant Jackson's arms.

"Relax," said the admiral, examining the boy's face. "Where'd you get these scars?"

"My parents cut me when I was a baby; said they didn't want me growing a beard when I got older."

Jackson pulled off Mathew's yellow bandana. "And look Admiral—look at his misshapen skull!"

"Enough," barked Covington, "Where are your folks, Mr. Mathews?"

"My dad died in Gruethungi, during the Ostrogoth campaign two months ago. My mom is still in jail, in Boston. She lost her court case. She's supposed to die by the quick-sword next month so I snuck aboard to hitch a ride back to the Provinces."

"What did your mom do?"

"She almost killed President Valentinian," he boasted. "She had Caesar's guard on his heels, but he got lucky." The youth shook his head, "That Neanderthal turned around at the last second and lunged at my mom with his sword. He gouged her ankle—enough to cut a tendon; otherwise she'd have had a clear shot at Augustus."

"When did that that happen?"

"Last spring . . . the Boston Marathon."

"If memory serves me, Mr. Mathews, your mom's murder attempt came before anyone knew Caesar had a bad heart. How did she know about that?"

"She didn't. It's 'cause he won't let Muslims into the country. In his case, it ain't about old people abusing healthcare; geez, Mom didn't try killing him over that." The Hun stared up at the admiral with anger in his eyes. "You don't get it, do you? If we don't start fusing religions, we're going to annihilate one another. It won't matter if old folks use up all our assets 'cause no one will be around to care."

Covington wasn't about to get into a theological discussion with a child imprisoned in his hallway. He glanced at Lieutenant Jackson before returning his gaze at the youth. "Son, have you got any brothers or sisters?"

"No, I'm on my own now."

The admiral smiled. "Well, I guess it's your lucky day, Mr. Mathews." He reached around to his backside and retrieved a six-inch switchblade from his belt. "Son, I've got an elderly Visigoth in this room," he said, pointing in the direction of the infirmary. "He's going to receive a very expensive medical exam when he gets to the Provinces. Now, you'll have exactly thirty seconds to do whatever it is you're going to do; do I make myself clear?"

"That's more than enough time," the boy replied. The admiral nodded toward Jackson to release the prisoner. Mathews secured his yellow bandana, grabbed the knife, and raced into the room.

Covington closed the door behind him and listened intently from the hallway. He winced at his Lieutenant several times after hearing screaming, thrashing, and chairs being thrown about in the room. After a half minute had passed, the admiral spoke to his officer. "Take out your pistol, Mr. Jackson, it's time."

Covington opened the door—both men cringed at the scene. The Hun, awash in red, knelt over the elderly man lapping blood with his tongue. The youth had slit the throat of Fritigern's father and stabbed him numerous times in the chest. Najid lay gruesomely dead, his eyes open, his head scarf removed, and his all-white dishdasha colored in crimson.

"Shoot it," ordered the admiral. The two men raised their pistols and shot the youth in the chest from a point-blank range. The jolt hurled Mathews against a wall several feet away, dead before his body ever hit the floor. "Wrap them up and ship them both to Fritigern, with our condolences, of course," said Admiral Covington. He looked at Jackson after finishing his orders. "Now do you understand why I couldn't dine with him, Lieutenant?"

Jackson stood glaring at the youth. "I don't understand any of this, Admiral, but I'll find people to clean up this mess. He began walking out of the infirmary when he suddenly turned back around. "Sir, should we stow the guns and break out the swords?"

"The day isn't over, Lieutenant. And before you clean up this mess, bring me Lieutenant Dirie." A few moments later, the Goth appeared outside of sick bay. "I'm sorry to have troubled you, Lieutenant," the admiral began, "but we recently found a renegade Hun aboard." Covington looked squarely into Aashif 's eyes. "I'm afraid we arrived too late to subdue him. I need you to identify the body of one of your people."

Dirie walked into the room and instantly recognized Fritigern's father. "NOOOO," he shrieked. He dropped to his knees and grabbed hold of the bloody corpse, caressing the elderly man, rocking him back and forth like a baby. He lovingly kissed him on the forehead, saying, "Najid, you were my responsibility." Aashif lowered his head and cried profusely.

Shortly afterwards, rapid-fire gunshots came from above. Dirie let go of the decedent, rose to his feet, and placed his bloody hands on the wall, steadying himself as he peered out a portal. His sorrow soon turned to horror, then rage, as he witnessed hundreds of elderly Visigoth falling off the flight deck and into the ocean. He turned around to face the admiral. With puffy eyes flowing with tears, and in a restrained but angry voice, he muttered, "You murderers!"

The admiral smiled at Dirie, "My instructions are clear, Lieutenant. I'm to return to the Provinces with able-bodied Visigoth capable of brandishing a sword in President Valen's army. I think you'll agree bed-wetting, cane-carrying arthritics hardly qualify."

Aashif looked straight at the admiral and spat on the floor. "We'll never fight in your army!"

"You'll do as you're told."

"We'd rather die."

"Be careful for whom you speak, Lieutenant."

Just then, the lilting voice of a sweet four-year-old girl came from the hallway. She carried a black doll with hazel-brown, marble eyes and a lovely pink dress. The girl spoke directly to one of the crew, "My daddy says Maali—she's my doll," said Azziza, "—she can have her own room once we get to America."

Lieutenant Dirie put his hands to his face and shouted, "NOOOO!" He lost his strength and sat down in a pool of blood still wet from Fritigern's father. He held his hands up to his face and wept.

Admiral Covington looked down at the lachrymose Goth. "Welcome to America, Aashif." Then he turned toward Lieutenant Jackson. "Now you may stow the guns and break out the swords."

Part Two

The Ensuing Winter & Spring

VI

VATICAN RESPONSE

Wispy flakes descended from Gainesboro clouds outside the Cathedral of Dionysius. Today began the second week of Advent—it was tradition to add ornaments to the nativity in preparation for the birth of Christ. Sisters Anne and Angela conversed as they decorated three nine-foot pines inside the church prior to Sunday Mass. "Reverend Mother, I believe this is a chicken," began Sister Angela, palpating the head of a ceramic figure. She pointed to a spot on the floor and asked, "Do you think it would it go well here?" Sister pointed with white cotton balls securely taped over her eyes.

Sister Angela, it may be recalled, lacked eyesight. She had recently undergone a medical operation aimed at restoring her vision. She had been one of fifty people selected for the experimental procedure after purchasing a walking stick and submitting its mail-in-rebate. Her surgery had proven extensive: first, doctors implanted optic nerves removed from the remains of a ten-year-old girl Then they robotically lasered hundreds of tiny blood vessels aimed at restoring minute circulation. Afterwards, they gave her stem-cell injections from pig fetuses to alter genetically dormant genes. Finally, she took massive doses of anti-rejection medication, which often made her nauseous.

"No, I think we have enough chickens," Sister Anne replied. She brought her nose close to a spruce and breathed deeply. "Mmm, I love the smell of pine. I think we should add more fake snow, don't you?"

Sister Angela groped along the far side of a tree. "This one could use more snow, but I think we're all out of that stuff. The janitor got carried away and sprayed too much on the tops when he first put them up."

"Pity . . . well, we'll have to do without." Sister Anne gazed out into the church's atrium and spotted Mr. Schmidt walking up the center aisle toward his customary pew. "Does Clarence look all right to you?"

"You're asking me? Well, if you want my opinion, Reverend Mother, he looks like his ornery, slow-moving self. I'll bet he's wearing a ball cap, and a dusty, brown leather jacket with a large red ribbon pinned to his lapel. Yep, Reverend Mother, he looks the same to me all right." Sister searched for cans of fake snow and never looked up from the overstuffed cardboard box as she spoke.

Sister Anne narrowed her eyes and looked scornfully at her subordinate. "Honestly, Sister," she replied in an exasperated tone. "I'm going to go check on him all the same." Mother Superior inspected the nativity before throwing Angela one last glance. "I'll be making my way to the vestibule. After you clean up here, you can join me at the back of the church."

Sister Angela looked up from the box. She loathed greeting parishioners before Sunday Mass. She would sooner spend time with the dead than make small talk with strangers. Actually, that was no exaggeration. She had frequently spent time as a child with her uncle, a mortician, alongside her cousins in his place of business. She remembered how disheartened he felt after installing a crematorium in the basement. "Mortuary science is becoming a lost art, Angela; people just want to be burned." Sister had another reason for not wanting to greet parishioners: she supposed her face looked hideous. "Can't I at least wait 'til I'm healed?"

Let me remind you, Sister," began Reverend Mother, puffing her chest and standing tall, "you're a Dominican—not a useless, cloistered nun. I won't allow you to spend all your time pining away in prayer, or doing meaningless chores until you're well. In case you are not aware, Sister, we Dominicans have a long tradition of helping people despite our facial imperfections. So, whether you like it or not, you're going to be at that door—just keep those cotton balls firmly taped to your lids!"

Mr. Schmidt ambulated directly under the cathedral's great dome heading toward the third pew using his autographed cane. Grey luminescence, radiating through Saint Jerome's window, bathed him in a milky, almost ghostly pastel. The elderly man looked toward the altar. "I see movement in those trees up ahead, Sarge."

"How many, Private?" asked Sergeant Dickinson.

"Two, Sarge, maybe more. They're dressed in black camouflage."

"All right, Private, I'll alert the others. We'll need to fan out from here . . . everybody stays low."

Clarence heard bombs and gunfire off in the distance. He crawled arduously on his belly through damp, myrtle-green grass as his chest labored for breath. The air smelled heavy, as if someone had stoked it with incense. The 10th Mountain Division slowly advanced into enemy territory. "Sarge," whispered Clarence, "I hear one of 'em coming this way. Should I take 'em out?"

"Damn straight, Private, let them know who they're dealing with."

Clarence brought his Fee-Tuckfield SMFT Army-issued gun around from his backside and quietly released the safety. His heart raced: he had never killed a man before. He waited patiently until the dark figure appeared prominently in the cross hairs of his rifle. When that moment arrived, he charged to his feet and lifted his cane to take aim. The abrupt act sent him reeling backward into a pew. "Whoa, I've got you, Mr. Schmidt!" Sister Anne took hold of the elderly man's belt before he had fallen completely.

"I don't need your help," he snapped, "why don't you find someone that does?" Clarence looked around at his new surroundings and restarted his walk up the aisle. He ambled slowly under the milky-white light of the cathedral's great dome. After plopping himself down on the bench, he closed his eyes and prayed, "Oh Lord, where is Clarice . . . where is my beloved Clarice?"

Sister Anne smiled watching him settle into his seat. Her black Oxford shoes clicked against the myrtle-green marble floor as she resumed walking toward the vestibule. Like the click from her displaced temporomandibular, which kept snapping in her jaw, the sound of her shoes echoed through the church as she hastened her gait past forty rows of near-empty pews. Upon nearing the last bench, Sister spotted a woman flagging for her attention. "Sister, Sister," shouted Mrs. Williams, waving her arms in a fluster.

Sister Anne directed her walk toward the excited parishioner and took hold of Naeem's hands. "It's so good to see you. Tell me, how's Tavius?"

"Dat's what I wanted to tell you, Sister. Tavius is comin' home to visit me over da next weekend. He's in da army, you know."

"That's wonderful news, Naeem."

"Oh, but I'm so scared for him, Sister. More and more Goths keep comin'—de's crazy people."

"He'll be fine, Naeem. I'm sure he's well trained; he'll know how to defend himself." Sister hugged the woman before continuing her walk. She had not gotten very far when she turned around. "Naeem, tell Tavius I want to see him at Mass next Sunday."

Cold air greeted Sister after she pushed open the doors at the back of the church. The December sky was perfection in blue, not a cloud in sight. The air felt dense and heavy; a spirited vapor arose with each respiration. Sister, awe-struck by the twinkles reflecting off nestled snowflakes, watched a group of energetic boys playing hockey at the far end of Orchard Park. One of the boys appeared exuberant after skating the length of the ice and scoring a goal.

The Mendoza family, consisting of Lareyna and her six children: Antonio, Miguel, Mario, Rafael, Elsa, and little Yesenia—the latter held in her mother's arms—ascended the cathedral's concrete steps as its massive doors swung open. "Whoa," cried Sister Anne. Mario and Rafael, eight and six years old, zoomed past her in an effort to be first inside the church. "¿Donde está Francisco?" Sister Anne inquired. She had asked her question while sidestepping the two racing youngsters.

Tears trickled down Lareyna's cheeks. "Oh, Madre Superiora, Pancho is so depressed. He is still out of work and can't find a job. He's drinking heavily now; we're fighting all the time. He thinks God is useless. That's why he's not here."

At that moment, Sisters Martin and Angela arrived at the scene. Sister Martin ran up from behind, wearing all-white vestments and white tennis shoes. "Sister," began Sister Anne, "take the children into the sacristy and show them how to ring the bells. Oh, but please, just show them how it works, let the servers do the ringing." Sister Martin took Elsa by the hand while Antonio and Miguel followed closely behind. They entered the church in search of the two missing boys.

Sister Angela stood motionless with a disconcerted look on her face. "I suppose you want me to stay here and greet people?"

"What a splendid idea."

"What do I do when the governor arrives?"

"Show him in, Sister. Oh, but do it with a smile on your face." Sister Anne lifted up the corners of her mouth using her thumb and index finger—fully cognizant Sister Angela could not see her intentions. Sister Anne turned to the forlorn mother and wiped a tear from her cheek.

"Don't cry, Lareyna, you and Yesenia come with me. We'll find a room in the church and have ourselves a chat before Mass."

Inside the sacristy, Father Wulfila Palladius donned a violet chasuble as he jawed easily with churchwarden Liguria and several altar servers. Tom, one of the older boys, asked, "Father, did you know the archbishop well?"

"Indeed I did, Thomas; I knew him very well. I met Archbishop Auxentius when he first came to Milan many years ago. He and I worked closely together serving the homeless on the city's east side." Father Palladius shook his head. "He was a man on a mission in those days, Thomas."

"In what way, Father?"

"Well, he began as a missionary priest in Central America. By golly, Thomas, Claudius rebelled against unrighteous governments. He nearly got himself killed in El Salvador pressuring them to do more for the people. Well, one day the regime fought back and killed quite a few of his comrades; I guess their government had had enough of his guff. Anyway, Thomas," continued Palladius, "soon after that, he transferred here. Within, oh, three or four years, he became Dionysius's Archbishop. Soon after that he took over for the Most Reverend John Secundianus and became America's third exarch. He and I had many long talks playing chess in the rectory. Don't tell anyone, Thomas, but the archbishop played poorly."

Tom straightened wrinkles in the back of Father's chasuble as he asked his next question. "Do you believe in Arianism, too, Father?"

The priest let out a bellow. "Too? Why, Thomas, I convinced His Holiness the doctrine was sound."

"Tom," interrupted Father Liguria, "you should go ring the bells now." He pointed down a lackluster hallway leading out of the sacristy. A two-inch diameter rope dangled from the ceiling midway along its stretch; knotted at one end, the rope rose all the way to the steeple and was attached to the bells. "We'll be starting Mass soon."

After the boy had left, Father Palladius approached Liguria. "But I've never been able to convince you of Jesus's creation, now have I, Tarquitius?" Palladius spoke in a quiet voice. He didn't want to publicize their religious differences—not in front of the youth still present in the sacristy.

"No Wulf, you haven't. It's my belief the Nicaea Council got it right."

Palladius resumed speaking in a muted voice. "Tarquitius, please tell me how you managed to get along so well with the archbishop? After all, you and he had such profound theological differences."

Before Father answered, a cluster of Latino children came running into the sacristy, closely followed by Sister Martin. "What's the meaning of this, Sister?" Liguria asked his question while sidestepping the onrushing youngsters.

"Forgive me, Reverend, I'm taking them to watch the bells being rung—orders from Sister Anne. See, Reverend, their father isn't doing well. He's very depressed, and not attending church any longer." Sister Martin pointed in the direction of the congregation. "Mother Superior needs time alone to console their mother."

"Very well, Sister, carry on . . . but, please, slow down." He watched the ensemble march down the hallway before returning his attention to Father Palladius. Before answering the cleric's question, Father Liguria interjected one of his own. "Speaking of Sister Anne, Wulf, do you recall our earlier conversation?"

"Sadly, I do, and I've informed the deacons as well." Palladius looked at him with fervent eyes. "Now, you still haven't answered my question, Tarquitius. How did you manage so well with the archbishop? After all, it couldn't have been easy putting up with him if you didn't believe in what he was saying."

Father Liguria reflected a moment. He almost responded when Max—Tom's younger brother, the youngest altar server present—interrupted him again. "Did he really walk on water, Father?" Max directed his question at Father Palladius while pointing to a picture on the sacristy wall.

Palladius smiled. "I guess I'll have to wait a little longer for your answer, Tarquitius." They both heard deep, tonal chiming from the cathedral's bells as Palladius turned his attention away from the churchwarden.

Father formulated a response to the youth. "Well Max," he began, "the archbishop did some miraculous things, but even he couldn't walk on water. See, I was present the day someone snapped that picture of him. Perhaps Father Liguria will permit me some time to tell a story before Mass."

"Be quick," he replied, looking out a sacristy door at the congregation, "the governor has arrived, and he's almost in position."

"Okay, Max, that day began two days earlier, when torrential rain swept over Milan. I kid you not; the rain pelted our fair city for forty-eight hours straight; seemingly no let-up in sight. A lot of homes and businesses got flooded. Anyway, Max, when it finally stopped, Archbishop Auxentius—we called him Father Claudius back then—insisted we deliver supplies to the needy. So off we went to the banks of the Awanata River. We headed under the highway overpasses where most of the homeless live in cardboard boxes.

"Max, we spent an hour handing out blankets, food, and clothing, when suddenly I heard the loudest crack I've ever heard in my life. We both looked at one another; neither one of us knew where it had come from. I thought to myself that a car had crashed on the bridge above us, or maybe the bridge itself was coming down. Well, as we pondered, we began hearing a rushing sound, which only got louder the longer we listened. See, Max, as fate would have it, a section of the dam gave way that very moment, and a river of water rushed toward us. Claudius and I got swept away by the current before either one of us could react; only God's grace saved us from being pulled down to our deaths by a raging undertow. Many of the homeless weren't so lucky," he continued softly, "many of them perished."

"Well, Max, as we moved helplessly downriver, I met up with a channel buoy. My feet struck its metal hard, but it slowed me enough to grab a line. I pulled myself out of the water and stood panting on top of the float. That's when I looked around for the archbishop, and lo and behold, Max, there he was. Father Claudius stood on water, just like that picture shows."

"Just like Jesus!"

"Not exactly, Max," continued Father. "See, what you don't see in that picture is a tug boat that had sunk in that very spot about five years before any of this happened. The pilothouse roof sits about two feet above the water, and all the skippers know to stay clear of its position. However, after the dam broke, Max, the river rose and submerged the roof an inch below the surface. Well, that's what Claudius stood on when someone on the bank snapped that picture."

"The governor is ready, Father," interrupted Liguria. "And for what it's worth, Wulf, I hope you reach fifty-one percent. I may not believe in Arianism, but I think you'd make a fine bishop."

Father Palladius became the second priest to bid for the office of bishop of Dionysius. The position had remained vacant ever since the tragic death of Auxentius. Father Liguria, as acting churchwarden, made a list of potential candidates. He selected individuals from within and outside the province. He had no obligation to disclose the list and kept it a well-guarded secret. Prospects, selected at random, said Sunday Mass at the cathedral for four consecutive weeks.

The province broadcast each service on over fifty television and radio stations. Adult residents of any religious denomination, and even those not affiliated, voted with their cell phone or laptop on whether to keep the celebrant on as their leader. The Dominican Sisters of Milan—mostly Sister Henrietta, since she had the best head for numbers—were responsible for tallying the results. If the priest incurred fifty-one percent of the people's votes during any one of his presiding weeks, then he became their bishop. Those still on the list lost their chance for the office as the inductee held the position for life.

"Thank you, Tarquitius," replied Palladius, "that means a lot to me. Father smiled before his next comment: "I've got one more opportunity;

let's all pray I score a touchdown." Then he nodded at the churchwarden. "You may signal the organist." As the organ began playing "O Come All Ye Faithful," six altar servers, four deacons, and Father's Liguria and Palladius lined up in procession and walked onto the altar.

♫ O Come All Ye Faithful
Joyful and triumphant,
O come ye, O come ye
To Bethlehem . . .

The cathedral walls reverberated as fifteen hundred standing parishioners plus thirty-two choristers pounded out all three verses of the popular hymn. John Wade, an Englishman, originally crafted the lyrics in Latin and named it *Adeste Fideles*. Frederick Oakely translated it into English; he converted to Catholicism from the Reformed Church of England and became Canon of Westminster. John Reading, another Englishman, scored the music.

Colorful red, green, and silver banners draped from four marble pillars energized the cathedral's altar. Tapered beeswax candles too numerous to tally radiated brightly on gold-plated stands in front of the stage. Dark-green vases containing vibrant poinsettias dotted the railing that separated the altar from the people. Three scotch-pines, each nine-feet high and coated in fake snow, stood behind the manger—along with chickens and an assortment of other barnyard animals. The immense oil painting depicting the Last Supper, with its rich browns, blacks, and ruddy reds, served as the altar's backdrop, beckoning everyone to a pre-holiday banquet.

"The Lord be with you,"† boomed Palladius. Father stood facing the crowd from the top of the altar, arms extending out from his sides, mimicking Jesus welcoming the multitudes. Father gazed earnestly at the people, watching thick smoke from sacred incense descend over them like a spiritual blanket.

"And with your spirit."†

"Lift up your hearts,"† he boomed again.

"We lift them up to the Lord."†

"My dear people, we have special guests with us today. Please join with the choir in singing "Hark! The Herald Angels Sing" as we welcome Governor Anicius Probus and Governor-Appoint Aurelius Ambrosius." The cathedral walls reverberated as everyone began singing another tune:

♫ Hark the herald angels sing
Glory to the newborn King!
Peace on earth and mercy mild
God and sinners reconciled . . .

Charles Wesley originally wrote the hymn as a slow and solemn score. However, Felix Mendelssohn's lively cantata met up with the words over one hundred years later. The governor, dressed in an Etruscan-made, royal-purple toga, mouthed the words as he walked painstakingly up the aisle. Six guards surrounded him, while Ambrose, following ten paces behind wearing his Italian-made, blue-pinstripe suit, walked alone.

Ambrose turned into the second pew with two of Probus's guards. As he made his turn, he noticed children running into a small room on the south side of the church. Inside the room, he saw a concerned nun rocking a fussing baby while conversing with an anguished Latino; the tormented Hispanic appeared to be crying profusely. Ambrose pondered the pitiful setting—two troubled women sitting alone, attempting to silence a whining child with a bunch more kids on the way and no father in sight. *Now, that's a more realistic manger scene than the one they have set up*, he surmised.

Father Palladius resumed Mass after his guests found their pews. Liguria read two epistle readings before the thin, keen-eyed, and highly spirited Palladius stepped down from the altar. The Arian priest walked over to the lectern in preparation for the Gospel passage. "A reading from the Gospel of Luke," he said.

"Glory to you, O Lord."† Most everyone traced their fingers in the form of a cross over their forehead, lips, and heart as they muttered the words. After applying incense over the holy book, Palladius started reading:

> Now the time came for Elizabeth to give birth, and she brought forth a son. And her neighbors and her relatives heard that the Lord had displayed his great mercy toward her; and they were rejoicing with her. And it came about that on the eigth day they came to circumcise the child, and they were going to call him Zacharias, after his father. And his mother answered and said, "No indeed, but he shall be called John." And they said to her, "There is no one among your relatives who is called by that name." And they made signs to his father as to what he wanted him called. And he asked for a tablet and wrote as follows, "His name is John." And they were all astonished. And at once his mouth was opened and his tongue loosed, and he began to speak in praise of God.[2]

Father raised the Bible up for everyone to see. "This is the word of the Lord."† He set it down and began preaching. His sermon, meant to teach parishioners a little something about God, also served as his best opportunity to win the prize of his life—bishop of Dionysius. As he began speaking, Ambrose received a series of calls on his phone, calls that began with Mary Peterson.

"Hey, Mary, what's up?"

"Ambrose, why are you whispering? I can barely hear you."

Ambrose smiled at the perturbed guard sitting next to him. "I'm in church."

"Oh my gosh, I'll hang up and text you."

"No, Mary, what is it?" Ambrose preferred hearing her soothing voice to reading black characters off a colorless screen.

"I called to say I can't meet you for lunch," she whispered, "I switched hours with Kiara down at the sheriff 's office. But I can see you tonight."

"Mary, *you* don't need to whisper," he interrupted. "How about if I pick you up at seven."

"That'd be great; see you then, Ambrose."

Soon after Mary's call ended, he received another call on his phone. He shot the perturbed guard another smile. "Hey, Sy, when are you getting in?"

"That's what I'm calling about, Bee . . . but I can barely hear you; we must have a bad connection. Look Bee, I'm snowed in. We got ten inches of the stuff over the last few hours, and it is still coming down. Everything is grounded until tomorrow. But don't worry; I'll be at your inaugural on Tuesday."

"Where're you staying?"

"Senator Leontius's home, but I'll be sure to see Mom before I head back to Trier. Bee, our connection is getting worse; I should go . . . see you on Tuesday."

Ambrose considered his brother's words as he put his phone back in his pocket. Satyrus, being the first-born male, held a special bond with their mother. Ambrose wasn't jealous; to the contrary, he went out of his way to make sure Sy visited her when he came to Milan. Although he knew his mother to be more intellectual than emotional, he knew she still longed for a sensitive relationship with her boys.

Ambrose slouched in the pew, focusing on Father Palladius's sermon. "The Immaculate Conception isn't Jesus's conception," he bellowed. "It's got nothing to do with the Holy Spirit out-bidding Joseph for the job. Rather, it's about Mary being conceived in the absence of original sin."

Ambrose struggled to remain in the moment; his eyelids began drooping and his head started bobbing. *Church is amazingly boring. It never changes; maybe that's why older people find it so appealing.* Ambrose soon nodded off when the guard next to him kicked him in the shin. He quickly sat up and glanced at his watch; rubbing his eyes he peered at the room where he had first noticed the troubled women, but they had left. To his relief, he received another call on his phone. Ambrose retrieved his cell from his pocket and forced another smile at the guard. "Hey, Hermie, I don't work there anymore, remember?"

"I know, Ambrose. And I'll bet you're pretty darn glad you took my advice and called the governor—do you have a cold?"

"No, I'm in church; I need to keep my voice down."

"Ambrose . . . in church? Wow, I can't picture that—that's a hoot. Remember to bring holy water home to your cat."

"Funny girl . . . now, are you calling for a purpose?"

"Ooh, Mr. High and Mighty is getting snooty," she replied jokingly. "Well, don't worry, Your Majesty, I called for a reason. I wouldn't dream of wasting your governorship's time!" A brief pause in their conversation ensued before she continued. "Anyway, Ambrose, you forgot a box after you cleaned out your office. Can you swing by and pick it up this afternoon?"

"Is the firm open?"

"Come on, Ambrose, you know associates work 'round the clock at this joint. Don't you remember trying to make partner?"

The lawyer crinkled his brow at the image. "All right, I'll stop by later—anything else?" He heard a faint "no" amidst party-favors blaring in the background. Ambrose ended the conversation, "Thanks, Hermie, I liked hearing your voice." He shut off his phone and put it back in his pocket when he heard the bellow of an older woman sitting several rows behind him.

"You pissed him off again, didn't you Sister Anne. That's why he's still talking."

"No, I did not, Sister," she shouted in a suppressed voice. Sister Anne gently nudged Angela with her elbow. "Sister, would you please pass along to our dear demented Sister that she's to stop using that dreadful word!"

Father Palladius heard the disturbance and began wrapping up his sermon. He didn't want to chance losing votes because some found him long-winded. "In conclusion," he said, "Advent is about preparation; about readying ourselves for hope, miracles, and joy. We need this time to gear up for the coming of Christ, who is, was, and ever shall be, our best hope for eternal salvation. My friends, Advent isn't about decorating trees or buying presents. Those are secular pretenses aimed at lightening our wallets. Our preparation must go deeper; each of us must strive to cleanse our impious souls. Finally, let me end by saying don't ever stop believing in miracles. I realize that some people say it's impossible to fool Mother Nature—but they forget about Father Time. Ask yourselves, what if—what if the Three Wise Men looked up and saw airplanes flying overhead? They'd quickly pronounce their vision, 'a miracle' and just as quickly be labeled fools. Yet, brethren, that is a vision we all take for granted. So don't forget, whether it's turning water into wine, loosening a dumb tongue, or the Immaculate Conception, these things may be miracles to us, but they'll be ho-hum to future generations who've figured out the science."

Father Palladius left the pulpit and walked up the altar steps to prepare for the Eucharistic celebration, winking at Father Liguria. Ben and Louise Corrigan brought up the gifts while the assembly sang another hymn. After praying over the bread and wine, Palladius, along with the other ascetics, walked to the railing to distribute the body and blood of Christ to a spiritually hungry congregation.

Walking in the Communion line, Sister Anne gazed deeply into Liguria's eyes for what seemed like an hour. *Something strange is going on; his eyes seem destructive.* Sister finally arrived at the railing. "The body of Christ,"† he said.

"Amen,"† she responded, expecting a host in her hands. However, Liguria never gave her one. He'd gone through the motions—pretended to comply—but he never supplied her with spiritual nutrition. "I'm a Catholic in good grace," she told him quietly, looking up at the irascible priest. He beckoned with his eyes for her to move on. *What have I done wrong?* Tears began welling in her eyes.

The exchange didn't escape Ambrose. He recognized the distraught nun walking back to her seat. She had consoled the Latino less than an hour ago. *Sure is a lot of lamenting going on*, he thought to himself. Ambrose turned and watched the agitated woman walk all the way back to her pew. Sadly, none of the other Sisters in the row seemed to notice her shaken situation.

After Communion, Father Palladius said the final prayers. "Let us pray,"† he began. "O great and merciful Father, Thou didst create and commission Jesus our Savior to exemplify a sinless existence and bring us into everlasting life. The Mass is ended, everyone; go in peace to love and serve the Lord."

"Thanks be to God,"† the people all thundered. The choristers began singing the final hymn of the morning, "O Holy Night." Placide Cappeau, a Frenchman and wine merchant, wrote the poem. Adolphe Adam, known for composing operas and ballets, composed the music.

> ♫ O Holy Night! The stars are brightly shining,
> It is the night of the dear Savior's birth.
> Long lay the world in sin and error pining . . .

"He's at forty-nine," blurted Sister Henrietta, to no one in particular. She spoke rather loudly after gazing intently at the tabulations on her phone. "Father Palladius needs two more points," she continued. After Mass ended, she gawked at Governor Probus and appointee Ambrosius as they slowly walked along the cathedral's main aisle toward massive doors guarding the exit. Sister noticed Ambrose looking up at the ceiling. He'd spotted several television cameras strategically hidden in the beams. He had also spotted a gaggle of reporters waiting to interview Probos at the end of the line.

"Governor, how's your health?"

"Do you think Father Palladius will get enough votes?"

"Ladies and gentleman, please," replied Probus, "I'll make one brief statement. After all, people behind me are waiting to leave."

Several minutes passed before the line started moving. Ambrose came upon Sister Anne crying and kneeling alone in the pew. She prayed with her hands clasped together, resting on the backrest of the bench in front of her.

"Mr. Ambrosius," shouted Father Liguria, who had weaved his way through the crowd after stashing his chasuble inside the sacristy. Wearing a black, button-down cotton shirt and ebony, polyester, cuffed slacks, he swooped down upon the governor-appoint. "Would you come with me please?"

Ambrose pointed toward Sister. "May she come with us?" The Benedictine nun overheard his request and looked curiously at the two men standing in the aisle.

Father sent a menacing glance in her direction. "I'll deal with her later."

"Well, if she doesn't come, I don't come," countered Ambrose. He sensed he had struck a nerve with Father and played hardball to arrive at the answers. Liguria, puzzled by the connection between the two of them, reluctantly agreed to his proposition. They said introductions and made their way through a non-conspicuous door on the north side of the church. From there, they descended a seldom-used flight of steps into a dimly lit basement.

"I must remember to tell the janitor to change out these bulbs," remarked Father. They passed an old confessional and arrived at a tunnel leading from the church to the rectory. "Forgive me, it's a bit damp and chilly in here," he continued, "but it beats having to walk outdoors."

They walked one hundred feet through the burrow before coming to a spot that looked fateful. Bricks and mortar on the tunnel's north wall appeared forebodingly crumbled. "Father," asked Ambrose, "are you sure this passage is safe for travel?"

"City inspectors approved it last month." They continued walking for what seemed like miles until they arrived at the rectory. Once inside, they made their way to Archbishop Auxentius's former study. "I found these letters last week," said Liguria. "The Archbishop had stuffed them in a wine bin down in the cellar." Father scooped then off the desk and gave them to Ambrose to read. "Since you'll be governor in a couple of days, I thought you should know about them. They're all from the Vatican; all of them have the Vatican seal." He looked squarely at Sister. "It seems our Reverend Mother wrote incessantly to remove the Archbishop from his post."

Sister Anne turned away from the churchwarden and gazed down at the floor, smiling. Rather than feel scorned or humiliated at Father's castigation, she felt humbled, and honored that a Vatican theologian had responded to her mail.

"They're all signed by Cardinal Seneca," said Liguria. Ambrose brought the first letter up to his face and began reading:

Most Rev. Claudius Auxentius, Archbishop,

It has come to my attention that you are practicing Arian theology. This subject has long been determined heretical practice. Please desist at once or further action will be required.

Yours in Christ,
Cardinal Seneca

"This is the second one," said Father, handing it to Ambrose. "As you can see it places the Archbishop on probation:

Most Rev. Claudius Auxentius, Archbishop,

It has come to my attention that you are still practicing Arian theology. As I discussed in my previous letter, this is heretical practice under the Nicaea Council. Therefore, this letter serves as notice that you are hereby under probation for your persistence in violating our doctrine. Failure to desist from this unorthodox practice will result in further action, which may include excommunication from our Holy Roman Catholic Tradition.

Yours in Christ,
Cardinal Seneca

"Here's the final one, Mr. Ambrosius. You can see that he received it the day before he took his life."

Most Rev. Claudius Auxentius, Archbishop,

It has come to my attention you are still practicing Arian theology. As discussed in my previous letters, this is heretical practice under the Nicaea Council. Thus, it is my mournful duty to inform you that you are hereby prohibited from performing any priestly duties within the Holy Roman Empire, and you are hereby banished from God's most Holy Catholic church. I pray He has mercy on your soul. Kindly return your Episcopal ring.

Yours in Christ,
Cardinal Seneca

"I found these black boxes in the main-floor confessionals," added Liguria. He picked up a device no bigger than a sugar cube. "I think the archbishop suspected espionage, that's why he used the basement confessionals."

Ambrose looked at Father; the electronics didn't interest him. "How do you know Sister wrote letters to the Vatican?"

"I called them; I wanted to speak to Cardinal Seneca directly, but no one knew how to reach him. I talked with Father Tatius instead. He works at the Office for the Congregation for the Clergy. He told me straight out that he'd read several of her letters; that's what prompted them to monitor the archbishop."

"I've got a right to express my opinion," interjected Sister, "especially when children are being exposed to the ideas around here."

Liguria slammed his fist on the desk. "You've no right meddling in priestly affairs!"

"You've no right withholding Communion!"

Ambrose rolled his eyes. "Um, folks, we have a visitor," he interrupted, pointing toward the door.

Sister Henrietta walked into the room with a frown on her face. "Only fifty percent," she said, gazing down at her phone. She looked up at Sister, and then at Liguria. "Father Palladius didn't make it." Although voters had forty-eight hours to cast their ballots, she knew from experience that the first hour decided everything. After Sister Henrietta left, the mood in the room became subdued. Sister Anne escorted Ambrose back through the tunnel to the massive doors of the empty cathedral.

"Tell me, Sister," he began, "If the Archbishop practiced Arian theology, whatever that is, exactly, and both you and Father disagree with it, then why's he so upset that you wrote letters asking for the archbishop's removal?"

Sister Anne pushed open the doors, "Father Liguria may be a young man, but he definitely has old-school thinking. That's one of the things I admire about him, Mr. Ambrosius. See, our faith thrives when we stick to tradition. On the other hand, that's one of the things I detest about him. See, he believes debating theology is a priestly undertaking, or should I say, a man's occupation. At times, I think he'd like nothing better than for society to resume treating women like chattel—like mindless pieces of property." Sister stared at the empty park across from the church, "Well, good-bye, Mr. Ambrosius, and good luck in your inauguration on Tuesday." She smiled at him as he exited the cathedral, "and thanks so much for your help today."

"What did I do?"

"By insisting I come along, you exposed a wound that would've festered for weeks. I'm truly grateful for your help."

Ambrose brushed snow off his midnight-black Mercedes-Benz SL550 roadster and fired up the engine. He sped north nineteen miles on Interprovince 424, then veered west on Highway 16 for another four miles. He existed onto Hortensi Place and turned left, driving another two miles to Lavinia Townhomes. He kicked off his two-tone wing-tip shoes and walked into the living room where he threw his coat over a black leather sofa, partially blanketing Lava. The feline lay curled up in a corner, fast asleep on the couch. Ambrose sat on his thick, handcrafted Persian rug and grabbed a handful of papers off a coffee table. The documents held the names, faces, and life histories of all thirty-five senators. "It says here, Mauritius, you like bicycling. Who are you kidding? Judging by those jowls, you haven't ridden a bike in years."

After three hours of intense scrutiny, Ambrose lay fast asleep on the floor. Despite a dozen calls from Hermie and other co-workers, including one from Mr. Yang, his former boss, Ambrose slept soundly until six thirty that evening. He awoke with a start after Lava perched herself on his head. "Mary . . . I've got to pick up Mary!" In a panic, he rose to a seated position. After wiping drool from his mouth, he sprang to his feet and darted off to his bedroom for a change of clothes. He put on a fresh pair of jeans but struggled to find a shirt.

"T-shirt . . . too crinkled," he began ". . . turtleneck . . . no, very wrinkled . . . Christmas sweater . . . oh, way out of style!" Lava meandered her way into his room looking for dinner as the lawyer continued searching. After tossing a dozen items out of the closet, he settled on a flannel, green-and-black, plaid button-down shirt, which he wore untucked, partially unbuttoned over an undershirt. He finished the look with a small gold chain around his neck. He brushed his sepia-brown hair and sprayed a waft of cologne into the air beside him. "A couple of mints, put on my coat, and I'm off."

"Meow."

"C'mon, Ambrose . . . try to catch me," said Mary, wearing faded blue jeans with a black peacoat over a black, red, and green Christmas sweater. Her matching hat, scarf, and mittens coordinated well with her dark-chocolate hair, her emerald-green eyes, and her pristine white figure skates. Mary easily sped away from the slow-moving lawyer.

"Hey, I'm not supposed to kill myself before the inauguration," Ambrose said laughing, his ankles collapsing inward in a futile attempt to keep up with her. Ambrose and Mary had had two prior dates—if you could call them dates. Both had consisted of short lunch excursions at the Dio, a casual restaurant in the student center at Cassius College. Although they'd seen one another briefly, both felt that strange, magical chemistry necessary to keep a relationship going.

After sharing a hot dog and cocoa from a street vendor named Guamo, they had rented ice skates and made their way along Lalia Channel. The two-mile, fabricated river channel was aptly named in honor of Lieutenant Governor Hanna Lalia as she had been instrumental in getting it funded and pushed through the Senate. Lieutenant Lalia had been Governor Probus's right-hand woman for twenty years. Recently, however, he began having doubts about her; doubts he couldn't put his finger on.

Lalia channel measured forty-five feet wide. In summer months, its depth was four feet, but in the fall city workers drained it to eight inches before freezing. The channel, cut from the Awanata River, flowed east, dividing the city in half. The channel began at the western edge of Milan and flowed through its southern district in a tortious and convoluted manner, maximizing shops, hotels, parks, and restaurants housed along its banks. Commercial proprietors competed for patrons with brightly colored banners, twinkling lights, romantic lampposts, and inviting brick patios. Near the city's eastern end, the channel flowed northward where it rejoined the river.

At eight fifteen in the evening, snowflakes—considerably larger than those earlier in the day—fell softly to the ground. The temperature, a balmy twenty-four degrees Fahrenheit without a hint of wind, felt perfect for two northern skaters. Snow-covered hedges, which lined the banks of the channel, glowed with millions of twinkling lights extending far into the night. Old-fashioned streetlamps, alternately radiating green and red hues, illuminated sidewalks paralleling the passage. Charming stone overpasses, decorative evergreens, magnificently carved ice sculptures, and a few scattered snowmen completed the scene.

"Whoa . . . I can't stop!"

"I've got you, Ambrose!" Mary grabbed her partner, working her petite frame in an effort to prevent him from falling. After steadying her date, she asked, "Are you sure you want to do this? I mean, we could go elsewhere if you'd feel more comfortable."

"I'm comfortable wherever you are," he replied. Ambrose shut his eyes, knowing his words sounded platitudinous the moment he said them. *She's going to think I'm an idiot! And to think, my parents told everyone I had a honeyed tongue.*

But Mary didn't react that way at all. He had said his words with enough truthfulness and boyish charm that it triggered a moment of passion—of course, being in one another's embrace didn't hurt. "That's sweet of you," she said, looking directly into his eyes, leaning her face closer.

To Ambrose, her words savored like nectar. At that moment, no sounds, no lights, no movements, no worries of any kind came to mind. Time stood still, just two people falling in love. *She's beautiful,* he thought. He closed his eyes and leaned forward, lightly touching his lips to hers, then pulled away to assess her reaction. In that brief interlude, a sensitive man will notice the slightest hint of a woman's rejection. An infinitesimal pullback would have terminated the kiss. Sensing no refusal, Ambrose leaned forward, this time with his mouth ajar and his head pitched to one side. He slowly pressed his lips against hers.

"That was nice," Mary said after they broke it off.

"Whoa," cried Ambrose. A six-year-old skater playing tag with his friends had clipped him from behind. Ambrose crashed to the ice on his butt.

"Oh, Ambrose," Mary said, partially laughing. "Are you all right?"

"I'm fine . . . I guess." Ambrose partially laughed as well. "But would you mind helping me up before that machine runs me over?" Sure enough, a Salimas County Zamboni had just rounded a bend. The company had specially designed the low-lying machine to fit under tunnels. At twenty yards away, it closed in on them fast—at least it seemed that way to a second-rate skater sprawled out on the ice. Mary quickly helped him to his feet, and they skated over to the other side of the channel.

They travelled arm-in-arm for a good portion of the passage. Ambrose periodically gazed up at a hilly area in Milan's northern district where he saw flashing red lights. *That's coming from police cars*, he surmised, although the squads were too far away and the night too dark to see them distinctly.

"Look at that butterfly, isn't it beautiful," said Mary as they skated through Elms Park where artists sculpted elaborate objects from large blocks of ice.

Ambrose quickly brought himself into the moment. "Oh, yeah, Mary, and look at that fancy harp. I wonder how they make strings that thin without breaking them."

"Okay, buster, let's turn around, I sense you're bored with all this." Mary pulled Ambrose into a 180-degree turn. "But on the way back, you have to tell me how things went at your office this afternoon."

"How what went?"

Mary stopped skating. She turned and stared at her partner. "Oh my gosh, Ambrose, you didn't go, did you?"

"Go where?"

Mary threw her arms into the air. "Ahh! I knew I shouldn't have left you alone. Oh, Ambrose, I feel so bad. Hermie called me this morning and asked if I'd bring you to the firm today. But I told her I'd already switched hours with Kiara." The agitated woman looked down at the ice in disgust.

"Mary, what are you so upset about? I only needed to pick up a box; I can do that any old time."

"Oh, you big dope," she replied, half-smiling. "Your firm hosted a party for you—it had nothing to do with a box. I think they planned it as part inaugural and part going away. Anyway, Ambrose, they knew if they told you about it, you'd never show up. Apparently, you're not big on parties!"

Ambrose never heard the last part of her statement. Ordinarily, a person takes offense when referred to as a *big dope*. However, in this case, Mary's phrase took on an entirely different meaning as she spoke her words in such a loving manner. He smiled as a thought came to his mind: *she cares for me.*

"I'll bet you've got a ton of messages if you check your phone." Mary watched him reach into his pocket to retrieve his cell. Just then, five men approached on skates; three of them wore dark suits with long cashmere coats, while two wore Salimas County Sheriff uniforms. Mary spoke first. "Sheriff Crispus, what are you doing here?"

"Hello Mary, it's good to see you again," he replied, before turning his attention toward Ambrose. "Mr. Ambrosius, I think you and I have met before . . . this here's my deputy, Harvey Drusus."

"We've met before, too, Mr. Ambrosius," said Harvey, "but how do you do?"

The lawyer nodded at the deputy, who fumbled to take off his hat. Meanwhile, the Sheriff continued speaking, "and this here is Mr. El—"

"Eligius," interrupted one of the formally dressed men. "Dick Eligius, Secretary of Dionysius Province." The secretary abruptly took over introductions from the sheriff. "This here is Chief Judge John Jupiter—you probably already know him—and to his left is Mr. William Leo, one of Dionysius's Board of Directors.

"It's nice to meet all of you," said Ambrose. "What can I do for you?"

"I'm afraid I have some bad news, Mr. Ambrosius," the secretary replied, darting his eyes from right to left seeing if anyone was eavesdropping. "Governor Probus is dead. Preliminary reports suggest his heart gave out, but we're not sure; it could've been the cancer. He'll undergo autopsy tonight."

"I'm sorry to hear that, Mr. Secretary." The lawyer clung to Mary's arm to steady himself on his skates. "If I recall, he planned to start an experimental medical procedure tomorrow. I trust Ms. Lalia's been informed?"

"Yes, well, that brings me to my next piece of bad news," said Eligius. "Sheriff, do you want to take this one?"

Mr. Ambrosius, Lieutenant Lalia is also dead. She died from a single stab wound trying to protect the governor from a Hun. She and Governor Probus were working together at the mansion this evening when it happened."

"That explains the flashing red lights I saw in the northern district."

Mary looked at Ambrose quizzically. "When did you see flashing red lights?" Without waiting for his answer, she turned herself toward Sheriff Crispus. "Why would a Hun want to kill the governor?"

"I think I can answer that," Ambrose interjected. "See, after Tuesday, Governor Probus will become Mr. Probus—just another elderly man undergoing an expensive procedure to prolong his life. I'm sure Huns viewed that as wasteful."

"We anticipated an attack," Crispus began, "we even hired more guards to protect him. Unfortunately, that strategy backfired; unbeknownst to us, one of the new hires turned out to be the Hun who tried killing him."

"Let me guess," said Ambrose, "Mr. Mariano?"

An astonished look came over the sheriff's face. "How'd you know that?"

"Lucky guess, really. Tiny introduced him to me a couple of months ago when I handled the Llinos case. Mariano mentioned he was applying for a security job at the mansion."

"Yes, well, Mariano is in custody now, and we're questioning Tiny down at headquarters as we speak. I can sure tell you, though, Tiny feels sick about this whole thing. Leonard's going to have a field day when he gets hold of this one."

Ambrose turned his eyebrows upward. "Do you mean, Leonard Thompson, the prosecutor?"

"They had it on the news this afternoon," interjected Mary. "They dismissed all charges against him; he's back to work, Ambrose. They said they didn't have enough evidence against him to prosecute."

"Yes, well, you can bet he'll be after you like an armored tank in heat," said the sheriff. "You'd better watch yourself, Son."

"That brings me to my last bit of cheery news," interrupted Eligius. "William . . . it's all yours."

"Yes . . . well, Mr. Ambrosius," began Director Leo, skating forward to get closer to the group, "it's my job to maintain the by-laws of the province." He pulled out a lengthy document from his briefcase before continuing. "Statute 547, section nine, paragraph two, states that, in the absence of an archbishop, we must swear in a new governor within five hours if neither the acting governor nor his lieutenant is able to serve. This rather obscure law passed twenty-four years ago, Mr. Ambrosius, in the interim between—"

"What he's saying," interrupted the secretary, "is that we're moving your inauguration up to the present . . . to the here and now . . . right here on the ice. Who'd you have in mind for your lieutenant?"

"I'd planned to stick with Hanna."

"That's impossible now, Son; you'll need to select someone else, preferably someone with experience. I think your brother, Satyrus, would make a fine choice if you can drag him away from Trier."

Ambrose looked up at the snowflakes. "His flight's been grounded; he won't get here until Tuesday."

The chief judge spoke for the first time. "Your boss at the firm, Mr. Yang, he'd make a good choice."

Mary spoke up. "What about your friend, Lierchetsky . . . Drew, isn't it?"

Director Leo chimed in. "Senator Mark Mauritius, he might want the job. He's been a forthright senator for some time now."

"You need to decide, Mr. Ambrosius," said Secretary Eligius. "They all seem like resourceful men who know how to get things done."

The lawyer shook his head upon hearing those words. He turned toward his date and asked, "Mary, would you be my lieutenant?"

A shocked look came over her face. "You're asking me, Ambrose? Why, I wouldn't know the first thing about it."

"Mary," he began in a soft, but confident manner, "a wise man once told me, 'this job doesn't require people who know how to get things done. Rather, it needs someone who can move people. Someone who can speak eloquently and motivate others to do things—things they may not want to do.' Mary, you got me on these skates tonight. I think you have perfect skills for the job. Besides, you can still attend college, and you'll be earning a lot more credit than you make at the sheriff 's office."

Mary stared at him. "Oh, Ambrose, I don't know . . . do you really want me?"

"More than you know."

Mary formed a delicate smile; small tears welled in her emerald-green eyes as she gently nodded her head in agreement. She and Ambrose hugged, and then lovingly kissed amidst a flurry of snowflakes. "Ahem," interrupted Eligius, clearing his throat, "if the two of you are ready, we'll commence the ceremony. It's all yours, Judge."

Judge Jupiter reached into his pocket and removed a small Bible. "Now, place your right hands over this book and repeat after me . . ."

After they had both been sworn, everyone, including Mary, bowed their heads and skated backwards to honor the new governor. Ambrose, blinded by flashes from gawkers snapping pictures along the bank, stood alone on the ice. "Whoa," he cried. His feet suddenly slipped out from beneath him, causing him to crash to the ice on his butt.

"Oh, Ambrose," cried Mary, partially laughing, "are you all right?"

VII

PROVINCIAL GOVERNMENT

"Blue-seventy, blue-seventy . . . set, hut, hut . . . hut," barked Joe "Clean-Cut" Terentius, quarterback of the Milan Conquerors. Joe had played in the league for six years, drafted in the first round from Ohio State where he finished runner-up in the College Champion Series his junior year. He used a hard-count to throw off the Liberties amidst a screaming crowd of 150,000 fans at Insubres Colisseum. The stadium, aptly named in honor of one of the oldest and wealthiest families in Dionysius, loomed large on Milan's west side. The structure, only twenty-one years old—sixty-four years younger than the cathedral—needed instant replacement according to affluent fans wearing fancy suits and dresses to gritty athletic events.

The Conquerors were playing the Washington Liberties—the team that beat them in last year's playoffs. After receiving the hike from center, Clean-Cut turned to his right and handed the ball off to his trusted running back, Demetrius "Zip Line" Taylor. Taylor bolted between the center and guard and then changed direction, sidestepping along the line of scrimmage before darting into a small opening made by tackle "Big Pete" Johnson. The Conquerors' offensive lineman stood six foot six, 340 pounds. He spouted steam, blocking Charlie "the Tractor Pull" Williams, the all-pro lineman for the Liberties. Zip Line kept his body low, churning his legs for a couple yards before being crunched by linebacker Tommy Lezetti. The run earned a first down, enabling Milan to continue its drive in hopes of putting points on the board before halftime.

Senator George Symmachus, from Lombardy County, glanced down the row of seats toward Governor Ambrosius as fans graciously applauded the team's efforts. "If they score now," he shouted, "they'll make a game of it." Symmachus bled blue and gold, the Conquerors' trademark colors. He was dressed like an unassailable fanatic, wearing the team's traditional foam hat shaped like a sword. He also wore Clean-Cut's cobalt-blue jersey, number three, under his pinstripe suit, and he waived a yellow hanky donated by Ezekiels, a local bank marketing heavily in its efforts to go national.

The governor remained quiet.

"Atta boy, Zippy," shouted Senator Mark Mauritius from Po County, stuffing popcorn into his mouth. "They're gonna need a touchdown, Sammy, not just a field goal if they want to get back in this one." The large-jowled senator spewed food particles into the air as he spoke.

The score was fourteen to nothing in favor of the Liberties, but no one doubted the Conquerors' ability to come back; they'd been a second-half team all year. Milan had the ball, first-and-ten on Washington's nineteen-yard line—their deepest penetration of the game yet. With twenty-two seconds left to play in the half, Milan broke huddle and ran up to the line of scrimmage. Clean-Cut crouched in drop-back position with four wide receivers: three split out to his left, and one to his right. Joe barked out the signal, "Blue-seventy . . . set, hut." He brought his hands together to receive the snap moments after securing his chinstrap. The quarterback received the ball and faded back a few steps. He pump-faked left, then threw right, letting go of the ball a good hundredth of a second before a blitzing safety pummeled him to the turf.

Fans rose to their feet, erupting in anger, pleading for a penalty. "Late hit, ref. C'mon, throw the flag!" yelled one of them.

The ball sailed away in a tight spiral as if shot from a muzzle-loading canon. Jeremy Jackson III, the speedster from Jamaica—the lone receiver on the right—sprinted eleven yards toward the post, then cut sharply to the sidelines. He fought off holding from one defender and a hand-to-the-face from another. A third defender leaped into the fray and swatted at the pigskin. He missed, but only because his arm was tangled by another Liberties defender trying to intercept the pass. Jackson leaped into the air and caught the ball with his fingers but struggled to pull it in. He felt his arms ripped open and the ball coming loose before he could secure it to his chest. The speedy receiver fell to the turf, landing on his backside without catching the football. However, he fastened his hands around it a few moments later after feeling its tip strike his abdomen. A nearby official blew his whistle indicating a completed forward pass.

"Way to stick with it, JJ. Now that's what I call playoff football!" Symmachus made his remark while taking his seat, staring at the governor. Ambrose fought off a yawn and graciously smiled back at the lawmaker.

It was the second week of January—UP West's championship game. Though Milan had beaten Washington earlier in the year—and held a better regular season record—they found themselves down two touchdowns despite having home-field advantage. Stakes were high; the winner played in the Gildedbowl against the Miami Bull Sharks, who'd beaten the Natalia Natives in the UP Football East championship game—they beat them soundly twenty-three to nothing.

With no time-outs and eleven seconds remaining, Joe lined the team up on the eight-yard line. He barked a quick count, received the snap, and then threw the ball straight at the turf in an effort to stop the clock. Throwing the ball straight at the turf instead of to a teammate normally results in an intentional-grounding penalty. However, in this case—its most egregious example—it does not. "Let's go guys, huddle up," he yelled.

Ephraim Zephyrinus—Milan's head coach—bald, wearing thick black glasses, called the next play into Clean-Cut's earpiece. Joe lined up behind center with tight ends outside the left and right tackles and two running backs in T formation. "Blue-seventy," he shouted, causing the right tight end to go in motion toward the left. "Blue-seventy," he shouted again, after the man in motion crossed behind him, "set, hut, hut." Joe turned to his left after receiving the snap. He faked a pitch, then quickly turned right and threw a lateral to Zip Line. The halfback caught the ball and started running. He appeared to have ample room to run having behemoth tackle Big Pete and a pulling guard in front of him.

Taylor darted past the line of scrimmage, keeping his body low and his lineman in front of him. He got to the four, then to the two, before darting to the outside. As Zip Line neared the end-zone flag, he reached out with his arms to extend the ball over the goal line. A Liberties cornerback smacked at it with his hand causing the ball to drop straight to the ground. For a second and a half, it lay motionless on the turf. Finally, Linebacker Lezetti scooped it up with his hands and ran it out to the thirty-three-yard line.

The referee ruled that the ball never crossed the line, that Taylor fumbled it, and that the Liberties recovered it with no time remaining in the half. The crowd went eerily silent, awaiting a more definitive decision from booth officials. "After reviewing the play," beamed Referee Barnes, "the ruling on the field stands . . ." The crowd booed loudly, never hearing the rest of his speech as they watched sweaty players meander off the field.

Senator Symmachus sucked a succulent Strangford shellfish. "You've got to try these oysters, Governor," he opined. He tossed the shell on the ground after devouring its flesh. "Oh, and these double-deck debbies are to die-for."

"I'll tell you what to eat, Governor," interjected Mauritius. "Try the roast chicken, served whole with matchstick pommes frites—absolutely divine."

"Ladies and gentleman, eat up; we have many delicacies awaiting you," said Extavious Tendenblat, owner of the Milan Conquerors. "Besides, everything here is free!" Tendenblat, a seventy-one-year-old, multi-billion-credit mogul—a star athlete in his day—had been down on the field encouraging his players. After politely waving his middle finger at the refs, he made his way up to the executive suite. "Governor, we've not only prepared an elegant banquet, we've got a splendid half-time show as well. So please, eat more than the watermelon slices," he continued, pointing to exquisite lasagna. "Governor, you must try the pasta cavolfiore—we've the perfect Vignamaggio red to go with it." The elderly man showed off his resplendent suit as he gestured farther along the table. "And for dessert, Governor, don't miss out on the zabaglione. It's my great-uncle's recipe from La Cinzianelle."

"LADIES AND GENTLEMAN, DIRECT YOUR ATTENTION TO THE MIDDLE OF THE FIELD FOR THE FIRST HALF OF OUR HALFTIME EXTRAVAGANZA. WE PROUDLY PRESENT . . . OSAMA!"

A trapdoor on the field opened up at the fifty-yard line, and out came a vicious, five-hundred-pound sub-Saharan lion, snarling, roaring, and swatting as it emerged. The big cat desperately wanted to free itself from its ten-foot chain and shackle.

"You watch," said Senator Mauritius gnawing on a chicken bone and spewing food particles into the air. "Johnson will make mincemeat of that feline."

"Course he will," Symmachus replied after slurping Chianti from a goblet. "I just want to see that scrawny Lezetti get his jugular pierced."

The contest rules were simple. A player from each team, wearing nothing but shoulder pads and a loincloth, had to be within the lion's sphere for thirty seconds and touch the beast twice. Referee Barnes disqualified a contestant if he failed to complete the tasks within three minutes. A successful combatant added three points to his team's total score. Behemoth Pete Johnson of the home team Conquerors went first. "RRROAARR," sounded the lion, its right front paw snapping at Johnson as the big man approached.

"AAHH," grunted the tackle, spreading his arms wide as he stepped inside the ring. The cat hadn't eaten in a while—it had been denied its last meal—and instantly pounced on the man. Its front paws leaned heavily on Johnson's shoulder pads; its claws cut deep into the plastic. Osama's mouth, measuring eight inches vertically with three-inch incisors, tried chomping at Johnson's neck. Using his tremendous strength, the lineman kept the lion's jaws at bay and threw the big cat back. The crowd roared with elation as Johnson stepped out of the ring for a rest. "You need ten more seconds and one contact," shouted referee Barnes.

The lion, sensing difficult prey, lay on the turf after watching the man reenter its sphere. Johnson gestured toward the feline to stand up and fight, causing another round of cheers from the crowd. "Look at that!" shouted Mauritius, spewing macaroon particles into the air. "I knew he'd make mincemeat of that cat." Osama rose up on all fours as Johnson came near. The lion swatted twice, but not wanting another encounter, turned and walked away. Johnson seized his opportunity, slapping the cat's hindquarters before jumping out of the ring.

"Thirty-one seconds and two touches," Barnes yelled. "You successfully completed both requirements." The crowd roared with delight as their eyes shifted to Lezetti, the Liberties' linebacker, set to go next.

"GRRR," he yelled, darting around the ring and entering it opposite the beast.

"CHICKEN!" shouted many in the crowd.

"AWK, AWK, AWK, AWK," shouted others, clucking their arms and dancing in a circle.

Osama walked the perimeter, gradually closing in on its smaller prey. It snarled at Lezetti as it shook its heavy mane. Then, without warning, it lunged at the man, but the nimble linebacker promptly stepped out of the ring. "BOOO," screamed the crowd.

"You need fifteen seconds and two contacts," shouted the referee. Lezetti looked up and waved to the crowd; his smile exuded arrogant confidence. He removed his shoulder pads; defiantly throwing his protection to the ground.

"BIG MAN, LEZETTI . . . LET'S SEE YOU MAKE CONTACT!" shouted a fan.

"HEY, LEZETTI, YOU'VE GOT MORE HAIR THAN THAT CAT!" shouted another.

Lezettti turned toward the lion and began waving his arms up and down. He lunged at the cat several times but remained outside the sphere. The feline became incensed; roaring, it stood tall on its back legs, swatting at the linebacker from an elevated position. Without hesitation, Lezetti dived at Osama's feet, slapped a paw, and rolled out before the beast could lower itself. The move came off slick, appearing to many that he had practiced it for weeks. He could have never made it with shoulder pads on—but unwittingly, it lifted up his loincloth. "Ooh, nice tushie," commented Mrs. Symmachus, holding dainty binoculars up to her eyes.

"Quiet, Judy!" her husband snapped. He didn't want to appear undignified in front of the others, though he dripped red wine on his tie as he spoke.

"I'm with you, girl," whispered Julie Tendenblat, the owner's wife. The sixty-seven-year-old woman wore a blue Egyptian-cotton dress hand-stitched in Italy that ended six inches above her knees. She also wore a gold necklace and three rings made of large, gold-colored diamonds in honor of the Conquerors' colors. Julie sat behind Senator Symmachus's wife; she inclined forward and spoke privately in her ear. "If you ask me, Judy, he's got a damn fine ass; sure beats our husbands'."

After securing the garment around his waist, Lezetti ran around the ring and entered it opposite the animal. He looked up and waved to the crowd, displaying a look of complete and utter confidence. Osama slowly paced closer, swatting at him like it had done earlier. The crowd booed, watching the linebacker nimbly step out of the ring.

"You need eleven seconds and one contact," said Barnes.

"He's doing the same damn thing again," yelled Senator Symmachus.

"Geeez, Sammy, he's making this look easy," shouted Mauritius. He looked down the row. "Governor, I'll bet you a hundred credits Lezetti touches that cat's paw without incurring a scratch."

Ambrose politely smiled and shook his head no.

The linebacker waved his arms up and down and lunged at the beast several times from outside the sphere. Osama became outraged and rose up on its feet. It roared loudly, swatting repeatedly at its scrawny prey. Without hesitation, Lezetti dove at Osama's feet, just as he had done before. This time, however, his right foot slipped out from underneath him. He had stepped on a small towel left behind by one of the trainers. Lezetti stumbled headfirst into the ring. To his astonishment, he lacked the distance to touch the animal's back paw, but to his horror, he lacked momentum to roll out.

Osama crashed down on Lezetti. Its front claws dug deep into his chest; its teeth bit hard into the side of his neck. Blood spurted everywhere as the feline instinctively dragged its helpless dinner to another location. "AAHH," roared Big Pete, who stood idly by. In one swift action, the behemoth tackle charged into the circle, grabbed the lion by its mane, threw it off to one side, got hold of Lezetti's arms, and pulled him from the ring.

"After reviewing the play," began Barnes, "Washington completed two contacts, but still had one second remaining on the clock.

However, due to home-team interference, no halftime points will be awarded . . ."

The crowd booed loudly, never hearing the rest of his speech. Trainers opened the trapdoor, ushering Osama underground while stadium personnel carted the morbid linebacker into the locker room for emergency medical attention.

"At least you got your wish, Sammy," smiled Mauritius, placing a large slab of lasagna on his plate.

"Yeah, he got his jugular pierced all right," replied Symmachus, "but cripes, Maury, I hate losing three easy halftime points like that." The senator sounded disgusted as he set his goblet of fine wine on the crystal table beside him.

"LADIES AND GENTLEMAN, FOR THE SECOND HALF OF OUR HALFTIME EXTRAVAGANZA, PLEASE DIRECT YOUR ATTENTION TO THE EAST END OF THE STADIUM WHERE OWNER EXTAVIOUS TENDENBLAT AND THE REST OF THE MILAN CONQUERORS PROUDLY PRESENT . . . VICTOR ZETSEVA—GLADIATOR TO THE STARS."

Mrs. Tendenblat stood up, pouring spittle from the bottom of her vodka and tonic onto the tiled floor while smoothing wrinkles from her dress. She directed her attention to the senator's wives. "Come on, girls, let's get more drinks. We don't need to stick around for this."

"Dirty dog," shouted Senator Mauritius, slapping his knee. He beamed a wide smile, staring up at the Conquerors' owner. "Is this a last minute add-on?" Before getting an answer, he turned his legs to one side permitting his wife to exit the row.

Tendenblat gazed confidently down at the lawmaker. "Yeah, Maury, the network didn't go for it initially, they'd already lined up a dog and Frisbee show, but they wised up in a hurry. They realized that it wouldn't take long, and that it would bring in a lot of credit. Say, Governor," the elderly man continued, directing his attention toward Ambrose, "you should be interested in this next event."

The governor handed his plate of melon rinds to one of his guards who in turn handed the exquisite porcelain to a scantily clad, well-endowed cheerleader named Molly. Ambrose peered through large black binoculars toward the far end of the field. "Well, well, Mr. Mock, what have you gotten yourself into?"

The province had convicted Michael William Farthington (a.k.a. Mr. Mock or William Keller), and his alcoholic uncle, Darwin Cooper, of the stabbing death of Henry Llinos's wife, Carminea. Both faced the quick-sword if they lost their upcoming appeal. Farthington was attempting to win back his freedom outside the court system by challenging a gladiator inside the colisseum, a legal alternative in Dionysius and other provinces. If he was victorious, Tendenblat promised Farthington a new set of clothes, a sixteen-ounce beer, and a large hot dog with all the trimmings. He could kick back and watch the game in a reserved seat, then leave as though never convicted.

Farthington challenged Victor Zetseva, the most notorious and beloved gladiator on the planet. *Family Tide* magazine had selected the renowned prizefighter as November's gladiator of the month. Farthington chose Zetseva after learning the Russian had a sore right shoulder and could barely swing a sword.

The contest rules were simple. The gladiator wore as much protective gear and utilized as many armaments as needed, while the convict wore a loincloth and carried up to one fifteen-inch gladius.

The prisoner won if he dislodged the weapon held in the prizefighter's hand. The gladiator had equally simple objectives: hold onto his weapon and kill the inmate. "Stand still so we can end this quickly," said Victor in a deep and raspy voice. He wiped his hands on talcum cloth before throwing the rag to the turf.

Zetseva, a big man in his own right, though not nearly as large as Big Pete Johnson, wore a silver-plated helmet with red horsehair down the middle. He had purchased it ten years ago while working as a presidential guard. Zetseva also wore steel-toe caligae to protect his toes; he'd grown weary of amateur fighters jabbing at his feet.

Victor advanced within striking distance of the convict. He raised his right arm, winced in pain, and swung the sword across his body, missing Farthington by a country mile. Farthington, who had soiled his loincloth, retaliated, chopping his armament forcefully against the gladiator's steel. As metal clashed against metal, sparks ignited; glints appeared bright even to those seated in the upper decks. To Farthington's chagrin, however, Zetseva's sword remained steadfast in his hand.

"Stand still so we can end this quickly," Victor said again, advancing toward the prisoner. When he got within striking distance, he raised his right arm, winced in pain, and swung the sword across his body, just as he had done before. Farthington easily moved out of the way and then chopped at Victor's wrist, hoping to strike deep into his opponent's flesh. However, metal clashed against metal again as Zetseva retracted his arm.

"Stand still so we can end this quickly," Victor said a third time. The gladiator glared at Farthington and produced a modest smile. Then, just as before, Zetseva raised his arm, winced in pain, and slowly swung his armament.

Farthington grew impatient with the whole affair. After sidestepping the sword he threw down his weapon and lunged at the gladiator. "Come here," he grunted, "I've got your index finger, now drop your damn sword." However, to his consternation, after prying open several more digits, Farthington spotted a clear plastic strap firmly attaching the armament to Zetseva's wrist. "NOOOOO," the inmate screamed. While Farthington fought to free the handle, Victor reached around his back with his left arm and removed a serrated knife from its scabbard. He brought it around and plunged the blade deep into Farthington's chest. Those seated in the upper decks could easily hear the sound of cracking ribs.

"Good, now you're standing still."

Farthington, in shock and gasping for breath, dropped helplessly to his knees after his rival removed the dagger from his chest. Victor yanked hard, not just to promote bleeding—no, he sincerely wanted his weapon back. He despised ungrateful borrowers who never returned his tools. Victor kneed his opponent after wiping the blade and putting it back in its housing. The act sent Farthington reeling onto his backside.

Farthington, who still had some wits about him, pushed with his legs to slide himself away from the gladiator. He screamed bloody murder after Victor caught up with him and repeatedly hacked at his legs. Zetseva's blows caused a long, vertical gash along the front of Farthington's thighs; the blows broke open the quadriceps and splintered the femurs. Farthington lay motionless on the ground except for muscle spasms and the occasional gasp for air.

Zetseva stood over the prisoner and looked up at the crowd; he liked this moment the best. It was his opportunity to connect with the people, to gain a deeper appreciation for their unwavering hatred for inmates. He stood tall with the tip of his sword dimpling the dying man's chest.

The stadium gathering—a packed house of 150,000, minus those who had stepped out for refreshments—stood chanting: "KILL HIM . . . KILL HIM . . . KILL HIM!" Nearly everyone slammed their fist into their open hand while vocalizing. With a satisfied look on his face, after bringing his audience to frenzy, Victor plunged his sword deep into Farthington's chest, piercing the retched man's heart. Soon, Mr. Mock's gyrations, and the flickering from the vertical scar above his right upper lip, came to rest. Zetseva kicked him, assuring the man's death. A pack of Clannic cigarettes fell from Mock's loincloth.

"Nothing like a good ol' execution," said Mauritius to no one in particular. The senator spoke proudly as he sat down and finished his last bite of pasta.

Senator Symmachus tipped his head back, downing his last drop of Chianti. "He got what he deserved," he said after swallowing. "Wouldn't you agree, Governor?" Upon not hearing a timely response, the senator anxiously peered down the row. "Governor?"

Ambrose looked as white as a sheet. "Mr. Tendenblat," he began, his speech muffled, his head tucked between his knees, "perhaps now's a good time to show me your plans for the new stadium. You can tell me why people living paycheck-to-paycheck should support a billionaire's dream." Senators Mauritius and Symmachus watched Ambrose rise from his seat on unsteady legs. The governor slowly walked across the row, up several steps, and out of the suite, taking bottled water with him.

"Must've been his first execution," Mauritius remarked.

Symmachus looked at his friend. "Would you like some more wine, Maury?"

"Don't mind if I do, Sammy." Symmachus raised his goblet to attract Molly's attention. She ambled toward them holding a half-filled decanter as the senators turned their attention to the blue and gold players meandering back onto the field for the start of the second half.

The governor toured the stadium as promised. He listened to Tendenblat sound off for an hour, and then quietly slipped through a side door with six guards around him. January frost greeted him the moment he stepped out; the cold air comforted his headache and nausea. However, his symptoms soon returned after a pack of pro-gun supporters approached him. Three hundred people yelled and screamed in his ear, parading picket signs with colorful slogans:

"ARMAGEDON WITHOUT THE SECOND," someone wrote.

"GUNS AGAINST HUNS," wrote another.

Ambrose fought his way to the limousine. "The penitentiary," he said to the driver.

The guards, unhappy about leaving the game early, gave one another puzzled looks. "That's not on the agenda," they commented, quarreling amongst themselves. They traveled east along Fourth Avenue South in Milan's southern district, just south of Lalia Channel. Ambrose peered out through dark-blue tinted glass, witnessing the spot where he and Mary had rented skates six weeks earlier. Thoughts flooded back as he remembered how he had crashed into her after an elusive chase, how she had struggled to keep him from falling, the delight of their first kiss, and his grave concerns over the Zamboni. His daydream rudely ended when the limo turned sharply onto Interprovince 35. The vehicle proceeded north across the Awanata River to Stillwater prison in Milan.

"Governor, welcome to our little home," said Master Warden Hensley. "I understand you're here to see one of our inmates. Let me direct you to our visiting area."

"No, Mr. Hensley, I'd like to see him in his cell."

"Certainly, Your Excellency, let me arrange a lockdown, it won't take more than a few—"

"That won't be necessary," interrupted Ambrose, "just show me to his cell." The governor motioned to open the prison doors, then whispered to his guards, "Fellas, stay here; I'll only be a few minutes."

Hensley and three of his men escorted the governor through the main hall, making their way past clusters of glaring prisoners to the inmate's cell on the second floor. "We're retrieving Mariano from the recreation center, Governor," said one of the guards. "We'll have him here in a minute."

Wishing to be alone, Ambrose told them all to leave so he could examine the inmate's possessions. A Bible lay on a wooden shelf, open to Psalm 23 by a bookmark that had come from Governor Probus's funeral. Jade rosary beads lay on a tightly made bed along with a redwood picture frame surrounding Mariano's mother; she smiled and wore a pretty blue dress. Two gold certificates from the Fellowship of Christian Athletes lay crumpled on the floor. Ambrose bent down to pick one up when he heard commotion outside the door. "If you try to harm the man inside, you'll be beaten beyond recognition. Do you understand?" The black man, almost as large as Big Pete, nodded his head at the guards, then ducked his body under the door's arch and entered.

"Michael, please sit down," said Ambrose, motioning him to have a seat on the cot pushed up against the wall. "My name's Ambrosius, Governor Aurelius Ambrosius."

"I know who you are. I met you with Tiny when you was a lawyer; I already got me a lawyer."

Ambrose stared at him intently. "I'm not here to represent you, Michael. I want to know the truth about what happened that night."

Mariano shot him a tired look. "Guessin' I murdered a white woman, ain't that enough?" The big man put a sizeable dent in the cot as he sat. "Man, I doubt no one's gonna believe nothin' else."

"Humor me, Michael. What happened?"

Mariano stayed quiet for several moments, and then shook his head as he spoke. "All right, Governor, you really want to know . . . I be standin' outside the room in the hall—door was open. Governor and Ms. Lalia worked several hours at the mansion. Everything was quiet, there weren't no problems. Then, all of a sudden, I hear a noise inside, the kind that makes you pay attention. Anyway, I look into the room and see the Lieutenant up on the table with one of her hands around his neck."

"First aid?"

"Yeah, right; her other hand be reachin' for a knife to stab him. Man, I come up on her, and we start wrestlin'—she's tough for an old broad. Anyway, the knife drops out of her hand and falls upright into a glass of water. Can you believe that? It falls upright into a stinkin' glass of water! Well, we continue fightin' and I gets to throwing her off to one side. And wouldn't you know it, she falls straight into that knife. Course, as my luck goes, it has to go right through her chest and kill her."

"Was she wearing a colorful bandana, Michael?"

"Not that I remember; colorful sleeves, maybe."

"Was the knife laced with sulfuric acid?"

"I don't know, you got to ask my lawyer."

"What'd you do then?"

"Well, I know the room's secured, so I went runnin' out to the hall to make a call."

"Was the governor alive when you left him?"

"Yeah, I remember him sayin' something, but I don't recall what it was. He was passed out on the floor when I came back a minute later. I tried to revive him, Governor; that's when other guards showed up. They started accusing me of killin' the both of 'em. But I just done my job, Governor Ambrosius, that's all I did; I just done my job!" Small tears formed in the big man's eyes.

A few moments of silence passed before Ambrose spoke up. "Mr. Mariano, are you a Hun?"

"No, Governor, I ain't. I don't believe weak and old folks should die just to save money. I think people should die when God is ready to take 'em back. But Governor, people keep accusing me of being a new breed. I don't even know what that is."

"I only know what I read, Michael," Ambrose began. "It seems younger Huns are more interested in preventing another war than saving resources. They believe religious separatism is killing us, Mr. Mariano. They're seeking spiritual fusion. They want the best of each faith to come forward to form one grandiose religion. They want that to happen before we annihilate one another. So, any prominent individual or group who stands in the way of that merger may be subject to execution."

"That's crazy talk. I am a Christian, Governor. I don't want my faith mixed with no Muslim—or anybody else's religion, for that matter.

A long silence ensued. "Mr. Mariano," the governor continued, "I believe you're innocent, but the evidence against you is overwhelming. You're a black male accused of killing a defenseless, elderly white female. Lieutenant Lalia worked for Governor Probus for twenty years; they hired you only a few months ago. She enjoyed much respect, having the River Channel named in her honor. People only know you as a washed-up athlete who struggled finding a job. How do you propose to defend yourself? Are you prepared to face the quick-sword?"

"I only know the truth, Governor; I just done my job." The inmate held his chin high as he spoke.

Ambrose knelt beside him and whispered, "Michael, between you and me, I recommend pleading guilty to the charges and challenging Zetseva in the colisseum as quickly as possible."

"Now you be crazy. I just seen Willie get massacred on TV!"

"Did you know Michael Farthington?"

"Yeah, he be livin' a couple cells down from me," said the inmate, pointing his hand in an easterly direction. "Just yesterday, Willie be spoutin' off 'bouts how he was goin' to win back his freedom; 'bouts how he was gonna kick back a cold one, get new duds, and sit in a fancy seat inside the stadium. Now look at 'em, Governor, he be deader than dead. I don't think that gladiator even broke a sweat."

"Michael, listen to me carefully: unless your lawyer has awfully good evidence, you'll be found guilty and will die by the quick-sword if you take your chances in court. And, you'll surely die if you try prying the sword from the gladiator's hand like Willie did. But Michael, you still have a chance to win back your freedom. You must chop at the gladiator's arm directly beneath the shoulder."

"But I saw Willie hack at his wrist—that didn't work."

"No, Michael, not at the wrist," Ambrose replied quickly. "You need to amputate his right arm just below the shoulder. He can't reach high enough to stop you. Of course, you'll need to watch out for his left—it's quite dangerous, you know. If you're successful, Michael, he'll lose a lot of blood and fall to the turf. Then you can retrieve the dead arm and pry the sword from its hand. You need patience, Michael; that's something Willie didn't have."

After saying good-bye, Ambrose walked back through the facility and reacquired his guards. He stared aimlessly through the limousine's dark-blue tinted glass as it traveled west on Fourth Avenue North heading home. The Governor's Mansion sat on the edge of Salamis County, nearer to Agnomen than Milan. Built in the late nineteenth century, it resembled the Forks of Cypress—a plantation designed by William Nichols of Lauderdale County, Alabama. That dwelling, designed as a Greek revival, mimicked a style introduced into the United Provinces by Thomas Jefferson and Benjamin Latrobe. The mansion, like the plantation, had been painted magnolia white and featured ornate two-story colonnades around its rectangular perimeter.

Ambrose entered the edifice through a back door, inadvertently missing grade-schoolers from the Barnabas School for the Deaf. He tossed his overcoat onto a radiator, nearly covering Lava, who slept soundly wrapped in a warm winter scarf. "Governor, Father Liguria has been waiting for you," said Melva Hayes in a flurry. Melva was head receptionist at the mansion—as well as its chief cook and bottle-washer—after serving many years there as a housekeeper. "He's waited for over an hour," she continued frantically.

"Thank you, Melva, please direct him into the library." Ambrose looked around the study, barren except for a reddish-brown desk and matching chair on the room's east side and two black leather chairs positioned in front of the windows on the west. Tall oak bookcases lined the room's perimeter. At one time, they had overflowed with texts, treatises, and manuscripts owned by Governor Probus. Now they sat empty but for a few papers stashed in a corner. The governor began thinking, *I doubt I'll overwhelm him with my scholarly appearance.* He shook his guest's hand when he appeared at the door. "Hello Father, it's nice to see you again. Sorry to have kept you waiting."

"That's all right, Governor, I know you're a busy man."

"Please sit," said Ambrose, directing Liguria to the sunny side of the room, suggesting he have a seat in one of the black leather chairs. "If you're here to tell me we have no bishop, Sister Henrietta keeps me abreast with a text every Sunday."

"No, Governor Ambrosius, it's not about that," said Father, staring off into the distance, "but that issue is becoming of grave concern to me." Liguria redirected his attention to Ambrose. "You know, Governor, if you came to Mass once in a while you wouldn't need to rely on her texts."

"You're right, Father, but you didn't come here to talk about that." Ambrose sensed an argument on his hands.

Father Liguria sat forward in the chair. "Governor, I don't know how to put this delicately, so I'm just going to come out and say it: it's come to my attention you're giving same-sex couples the right to marry."

Ambrose responded quickly. "No, no, Father, that's not correct. See, it's my understanding that *marriage* is a religious matter, an act in which God fuses two people together. I wish only to legitimize their *unions*. I'm quite content if they remain side by side. Do you have an objection?"

"Objection . . . yes of course I have an objection," blurted Father. At that moment, the memory of him pounding his fist on the desk in the rectory came to the mind of both men. "I'm sorry," the cleric lamented after regaining his composure, "I don't wish to appear upset, but you must realize these people are an abomination. Their passion isn't natural; it's a perversion . . . an atrocity . . . an ignorance of God's calling. Our Catholic conviction has us well grounded on the subject. Governor, I'm not about to listen to two-bit PhDs fresh from the cradle preaching the ridiculous conclusion that their lifestyle is perfectly acceptable."

Ambrose leaned back in his chair and pondered the priest's words. "I understand your position, Father," he responded, sounding solemn. "All right . . . well, I guess we have room in the warehouse district. We should be able to erect one, perhaps two industrial-sized gas chambers and put them all to death."

"What? Who said anything about killing anyone?"

"Isn't that what the Bible teaches—Leviticus, isn't it . . . chapter twenty something?"

"Well, yes, Governor, but I don't mean to suggest we carry things that far—"

"Smacks too close to Nazi Germany, doesn't it, Father? Well, at any rate, I'll accept that as your admission the Bible isn't foolproof."

"What . . . where do you get off—"

"If the Bible's inerrant, Father, then we don't get to pick and choose which verses we'll accept and which we'll reject. If it's truly spot-on, then every sentence, every word, every comma and period is perfect and must be obeyed. Now, unless you are willing to put same-sex couples to death, I suggest we have a reasonable discussion. Let's not view the Bible as God's literal and final word on the subject."

"Governor, we believe the Bible is inspired, sacred, trustworthy, and reliable, but we've not made an inerrancy claim for quite a while."

"Forgive me, but I needed to know the foundation upon which we were starting our discussion. Now, Father, before we advance, permit me to tell you a story about my youth. You may know that I grew up in Gaul, where my father served as the territorial governor. As a boy, I lived in a well-to-do but remote area close to the Beaverhead River. Shortly after my father's death, my mother moved our family to Milan. While in Gaul, Father, I attended St. Frederick's grade school—a small school with, shall

I say, irascible nuns. The school sat between the towns of Gervasius and Protasius, a good thirty-five minutes from my home.

"I rode the street-train to school with my best friend, Basil," he continued. "Basil was quite a character, Father. I wish I had kept our friendship going, but he went on to a different high school than me. Anyway, I can recall sharing many rides with him on street-train twenty-five." Ambrose began chuckling, "Father, when everyone sat quietly—oftentimes deep inside the Consular Tunnel—Basil would yell out at the top of his lungs: 'GOD DAMN IT!' Oh my gosh, Father, we'd laugh until our sides hurt. Of course, everyone in the car turned around and gave us a dirty look. Then, after about five minutes—after everyone settled down—Basil would yell, 'SHIT,' and the whole process started over. That was a glorious time in my life, Father."

"I hope your friend has cleaned up his act."

"Basil suffered from a rare form of Tourette's syndrome," the governor replied, using an exacting tone.

"I see, and somehow that relates to gay and lesbian marriages?"

"Let me ask you, do you think homosexuals are normal human beings?

"No, absolutely not," Liguria replied. The cleric appeared baffled wondering why Ambrose had asked him such a ridiculous question. "That's precisely why I'm against their marriages, Governor—or even their unions."

"Then I submit you have hatred for these people, Father, and it's clouding your judgment; you're sitting on both sides of the fence. See, you must choose: either they are normal people leading a rebellious, sinful lifestyle, or they have a disorder, like my friend Basil; they're simply manifesting a condition. Which do you choose, Father?"

Liguria felt trapped. "Well, I don't think I should have to choose, Governor, but I lean toward normal leading a sinful lifestyle."

"Yet only a moment ago you fervently stated they weren't normal." Ambrose didn't wait for the cleric to reply; he only wanted to point out the equivocalness in his answer. "Father, I don't think your beliefs are in line with your faith's hierarchy. Pope John Paul II described their condition as an 'object disorder.' "

"I've read his dissertation, Governor. Yes, he viewed their condition as a disorder. Moreover, he said they possessed the same inherent rights as everyone else, but he still rejected their marriages. John Paul considered unions 'a new ideology of evil . . . exploitation on the rights of the family.' Governor, these people are practicing indecent acts of willful disobedience. Should we turn a blind eye because we think they have a medical condition? Perhaps we should look the other way at pedophiles? What about serial killers, Governor—should we let them alone because we think they're manifesting a disease?" Liguria raised his voice as he asked his rhetorical questions. "In your mind, if someone has a condition, then their behavior isn't sinful. We don't see things that way; we judge that what they are doing is evil."

"Father, you above anyone should know we're not here to judge other people's behavior, only to assist them in the ways that we can. Judgment is for God and God alone. The only thing we humans need to decide is whether a person's behavior is so egregious that we should remove him or her from society. Tell me, Father, are we doing the right thing removing pedophiles and serial killers from society?"

"Yes, of course, Governor, it would be preposterous to do otherwise."

"What about my friend, Basil? Should we remove people with Tourette's from society—or at least deny them access to street-trains?"

"No, Governor—"

"And what about gays and lesbians," Ambrose interrupted, "should we remove them, too? I mean, if we're not going to kill them as the Bible commands, shouldn't we at least round them up? And if that's not possible, Father, perhaps we should insert a monitor under their skin. We can raid their bedrooms when they start having relations."

"You're not taking this seriously."

"I'm dead serious, Father. It's my belief that any adult not separated from society deserves all rights society has to offer, which includes the right to have their partnerships legitimized. It's neither fair nor just for someone in authority to inform a whole class of citizens they have the same inherent rights as everyone else and then deny them an interest in their very next sentence."

The cleric shook his head. "Governor, wait a minute. A moment ago, you tried convincing me that Tourette's and homosexuality, both morally offensive, perhaps, deserve the same compassion. I disagree. See, your friend had no choice; he couldn't stop blurting out profanity in a crowded street-train. But homosexuals are different; they're *voluntarily* having sex with one another, *willfully* making a choice to disobey God's directive."

"Father, now let me stop you for a moment," interjected Ambrose. "Let's make sure we're talking about the same set of people. See, Father, many people experiment with their sexuality, either because they are confused or because they are moving through a curious chapter in their life, pushing life's boundaries to the limit. They're not necessarily homosexual, Father. What's more, some of these people find satisfaction on both sides of the fence. They switch from one gender to the other as often as some people switch hats. But they're not necessarily homosexual either, Father. They're desperate; they're looking to lie down with a warm body—someone, anyone, with a heartbeat who will love them. Father, these people may be sinning, as you say, for they *are* willfully exercising a choice. But a true homosexual isn't going through a phase; he is what he is. He's attracted to the same gender as fervently as I'm attracted to the other. Father, he can no more change spots than my friend Basil can stop cussing—for him, there is no choice. You'd have me deny an entire class of citizens because they're sadly mixed in with the inquisitive and frantic?"

"Doesn't matter, Governor, they're still having relations knowing full well that they can't procreate—that's what makes it a sin. See, Governor, part of my job is pointing out people's transgressions. I must insist we do everything possible to prevent them from coming together—well, not monitors, raids, or killing, of course. But we sure shouldn't legitimize their unions!"

"Father, you almost make me wish we had you on our high school debate team. Let me start by saying this: I believe we should advocate for celibacy among all citizens, not just same-sex couples. Sex may be a fundamental right between people, but responsibility is an essential part of our social order. The province and church have a duty to advise everyone to refrain from sex, no matter their orientation, until they're in a fixed liaison. But, Father, life is complicated, and it seems to be getting more so the further we advance into the future. Most people want a secure relationship to help ease their burden, to make life less lonely and more enjoyable. Father, those are valid reasons to legitimize anyone's union."

"Fixed liaisons, as you call them, only occur through marriage, Governor, and marriage is between a man and a woman."

"Father, I understand the church has the right to marry only a man and a woman. But, if I recall from my grade school days, Jesus taught that marriage didn't exist in Heaven. If that is true, then I'm not sure why the church bothers with the subject at all. Perhaps it lines your coffers and pulls quasi-believers into church one more time in their life—rather dubious reasons, don't you think? If Jesus dismissed it, then I doubt the institution can save anyone's soul, which, you may correct me, is your fundamental calling. So, if I were you, Father, I wouldn't waste a moment performing a single ceremony. You'd be wise to leave the whole issue of conjugation to the provinces."

"It's a sacrament."

The governor nodded. "Yes, of course, please forgive me. When I first researched this subject, I read that marriage took hold as a sacrament in the twelfth century—well after the time of Christ. But, I recall Sister Anne telling me tradition is as important to the Catholic faith as the Bible. However, as head of our province, I have no such tradition. I've no right denying a union between same-sex couples. My right to deny them must be based on a rational, secular purpose. Tell me, Father, what purpose shall I use?"

"They've no intent to procreate, Governor. How can that benefit society? It sure doesn't please God!"

"Father, that depends on your definition of procreation. Should we insist upon its narrow definition, meaning 'to create life,' or can we use its broader definition, meaning 'to expand'? Many homosexuals want nothing more than to stop being alone—to come together, adopt children, and multiply into a family. By legitimizing their unions, we are helping to stabilize relationships. Stable relationships encourage less promiscuity, fewer transmitted diseases, and less mental illness. Father, when we no longer treat them like second-class citizens, they'll be more inclined to adopt disadvantaged and orphaned children, which will lessen the burden of our kids rotting away in institutions. Aren't those legitimate benefits to society?"

"Research shows children prosper best in a heterosexual environment."

"Even if that's true, Father, I understand you won't listen to PhDs fresh from the cradle preaching that homosexuality is a perfectly acceptable lifestyle." Ambrose smiled at the cleric. "Did I get that right? Tell me," he continued quickly, "if you won't believe research that looks kindly on them, then why do you believe studies that condemn them—if not for your hatred for these people?"

"I see you're still a lawyer," said Father, standing up from his chair. "However, I think you're wrong, Governor, and I praise God you can't implement your liberal ideas without approval from the Senate. I'll keep praying the Senate keeps a quiet lid over them."

Ambrose stood up from his chair. "I'm aware of the limitations of my office, Father. But know this: whatever you think of me personally, whether a staunch liberal or an absentee churchgoer, I am praying that you find a bishop soon. I believe it's in the province's best interest if I regularly discuss important issues with a learned man of the cloth such as you."

"It's a little late for niceties, Governor, but thank you anyway; your point is well taken. I'll find my way out . . . good day."

Father Liguria had no sooner left the room than Melva reappeared. "Governor, you're late for Senator Leontius's dinner party." She spoke excitedly and appeared somewhat flustered—but then, Melva always spoke excitedly and appeared flustered. "Your Lieutenant called inquiring about your whereabouts," she continued, frantically waiving her arms. "Oh, you do need to get going, Governor."

Ambrose retrieved his coat from the radiator, causing Lava to open her eyes. "Don't get up, girl; I'm on my way out." Ambrose pushed open the side door to the mansion and started walking toward the limo. Halfway to the car, he spotted children boarding a bus heading back to the Barnabus School for the Deaf. His guards seemed confused after he diverted his path and walked toward the visitors. "Hi, I'm Governor Ambrose," he said to one of the chaperons. "I'm sorry I didn't meet you earlier. Would you and the children like to accompany me to Senator Leontius's home for dinner?"

Clara Townsen, a tall, middle-aged woman with thick black glasses, bowed her head in respect for the office. She replied in a trembling voice, "Oh my . . . I . . . I don't have their parents' permission for that."

"I'll take full responsibility for their welfare. You can follow me in the bus and call their parents on the way." The governor looked down at a little blonde girl and signed: "What's your name, sweetheart?"

"Hello, I'm Katie," she said in a moderately hard-to-understand voice. "It's nice to meet you, Governor."

They made their way east on Fourth Avenue North, heading for the wealthy Sheraton neighborhood, situated a mile south and west of the cathedral. Upon their arrival, Agatha, Senator Eugene Leontius's stout, German wife, nearly suffered a stroke. The sixty-nine-year-old woman threw a conniption at seeing a yellow bus with twelve children, three chaperons, and a driver pull up behind the limousine. "Quadruple the batch," she shouted at the servants. Agatha resembled Melva as she raised her arms in a flurry and flew about the kitchen.

Mary met the governor first. She left the confines of the three-season porch and walked out into the pristine white snow of the senator's yard. The sun was sinking fast, now only an orange semicircle in the southwestern sky. Mary embraced Ambrose lovingly, giving him a long, affectionate kiss. Agatha held her hands to her heart looking out the kitchen window at the smooching dignitaries. "Glory be, would you look at that." Then, with rage in her eyes, she looked back at the help. "What are you looking at?" she scolded. "Now get back to work—all of you."

"I missed you so much," said Mary. "Where've you been?"

"Doing what I do best—making enemies." Ambrose reluctantly broke away from her embrace, sticking out his right hand to greet the senator. He'd been slowly closing in behind them.

"Welcome to my home, Governor," said Senator Leontius, shaking the governor's hand.

"It's my pleasure, Mr. Speaker."

"Please, come into my home before we catch our death of a cold." They entered the porch through sliding glass doors, leaving the frosty, crepuscule air behind them. Leontius directed them into his living room before looking back at Ambrose. "Can I offer you something to drink, tea perhaps?"

"Senator, I'd like nothing less than a thirty-year-old, sensuous, Domaine de la Romanée-Conti—nothing weedy you understand. And I'd like it aged in new oak made exclusively from the Troncais forest."

Leontius shot him a perplexed look. "Yes, Governor . . . well . . . I'll see what I've got in the cell—"

"I'm joking, Gene," interrupted Ambrose. "Bottled water will do fine."

The senator let out a sigh. "I'm sure we can accommodate that, Governor."

"And Gene, I brought the children here because I didn't get a chance—"

Leontius raised an arm to stop the governor's speech. Then he directed his attention toward the children. "I hope everyone's hungry—c'mon kids, let's eat." He motioned with his hands toward the dining room as he spoke.

Agatha's meal came off superbly. She had an abundance of meat, potatoes, corn, and rolls left over on the table after they had all finished.

"Mrs. Leontius," began Ambrose, "a group of apostles on some remote mountain would be utterly amazed at how well you just fed the multitudes. A delicious meal, ma'am; the duck was cooked to perfection," he said, pushing himself away from the table.

"Thank you, Governor," she replied, blushing. "I didn't think you'd notice—you ate so little."

"The governor's a light eater," interjected Mary.

"Well then, perhaps I'll give the leftovers to the children."

"Yes, Mrs. Leontius that would be an excellent idea."

"No," countered Ambrose, speaking more harshly than he intended, "I'll take any food you wish to give away—and even some you hadn't intended." He looked directly at Mary; now she had the perplexed look on her face.

Senator Leontius broke the odd silence. "Well, then, if everyone is satisfied, I suggest we move to the living room. We can have some pie while engaging in a lively chat around a fire. Would anyone care for coffee or tea?"

"Thank you Mr. and Mrs. Leontius, and thank you Governor for a very nice evening," said Katie in her difficult voice. The children all said good-bye and loaded back onto the bus.

Mrs. Leontius gave each of them a slice of German chocolate cake to take home to their parents. She watched them drive off before turning her attention to the servants. "Now, I want those plates thoroughly dried before you put them up in the cupboard."

"Governor," began Senator Leontius seated in a Victorian brown leather recliner next to the fire, "I understand you wish to change our welfare system?"

Ambrose sat at the end of a six-foot beige floral couch opposite Leontius, his arm wrapped around Mary. "Senator, I want to make it a maximum five-year program, which includes subsidized housing and food stamps. I won't allow waivers or extensions, and no one may switch into another plan after their time has expired. Oh, and only those with a high school degree or GED equivalent will qualify for cost-of-living raises."

"That's quite harsh, Governor. What do you plan to do with them when their time expires? They don't just disappear, you know; they've got children—often many of them. You don't want them begging in our streets after we've cut off their credit?"

"No, Gene; it's my understanding eighty percent of them leave welfare within five years. We're only dealing with the small percentage that don't, and I won't permit them to make a career of it. Senator, these people and their children will never escape poverty as long as government keeps cracking their shell. However, to answer your question, Gene, when their time draws near, I suspect many will put real effort toward finding a job. Others, I'm sure, will move to another province where benefits are better. A few may become beggars; it will be their choice to live in a cardboard box under some bridge. However, I believe most will transition to charity care where their church will take care of them."

"Their church?"

"Or some other non-profit, Gene. Through private grants and donations, these entities will become the financiers of the chronically disadvantaged. Senator, non-public subsidies come with stipulations—restrictions the province could never impose. If the poor want their money, they'll have to jump through a few hoops to earn it. I'm sorry, Gene, but their days of sitting back collecting a check watching television are over. Senator, I think you'll be pleasantly surprised at how generous the public can be when its wallets aren't being gouged by the government. It'll be good for these people, and they won't lose a penny. Of course, Senator, we'll gradually transition into the new system."

Leontius appeared vexed.

"Don't look so surprised; churches have cared for indigents throughout the ages," the governor continued, "they're good at it, Gene; much better than the province. The province treats everyone alike—like numbers on a page. Non-profits will not only provide financial support, they'll give tailor-made emotional, disciplinary, and spiritual guidance as well."

The senator turned his eyes toward Mary. "And what's your opinion on all this, young lady? Do you agree with your boss?"

Mary smiled as Agatha entered the room with a tray of coffee and tea. The elderly woman preferred to remain busy rather than get involved in politics. She overheard her husband's last question and gave him a disgusted look. "Well, Senator," began Mary, "I suppose Ambrose is my boss, but I choose not to look at him that way. Anyway, we've had lengthy discussions on this topic; we both agree that if we're going to restore the middle class, changes need to be made at the bottom as well as the top."

Leontius looked at Ambrose. "People told me you're politically neutral, Governor. This discussion almost had me convinced you vote Republican. Now, what do you have against our business constituents?"

Ambrose sat up and cleared his throat. "Gene, I remember my father telling me that local government serves two real purposes. First, to establish laws that facilitate civility—of course, that includes auditors, boards, police, and others to ensure good-natured compliance. Second, it exists to appropriate large-scale public projects. Virtually everything else, he'd say, could be handled by the private sector."

"I'm guessing Tendenblat's new stadium doesn't qualify as a *public project*?"

Ambrose shook his head. "Sorry, Gene, not unless Extavius hands over the keys to the province—and even then, I'm not so sure. I believe the province extends enough money to private business in start-up and research funding. Gene, the bulk of taxpayer credit should go toward infrastructure: roads, bridges, parks, waterways, and forests. If Tendenblat wants to further his interest, he'll need to hold a bake sale like everyone else."

"Your decision will cost thousands of jobs, Governor—good construction jobs. People are counting on them to stimulate the economy and get us out of this recession. And you can bet the Conquerors will leave town if they don't get a new stadium; Tendenblat's already made that point clear. Losing the team and the Magra plant in the same year could have detrimental consequences for Dionysius."

"Raising taxes also costs thousands of jobs, but those statistics are more often hidden. And extending gambling to pay for a new colisseum will result in thousands of ruined families." Ambrose crossed his arms in front of his chest. "I'm sorry, Senator, I won't do it."

Leontius gazed at the fire. "We won't just lose a billionaire owner, Governor, but forty-some millionaire players as well. That will mean lost tax revenues."

Ambrose waived off coffee and tea after Mrs. Leontius set a flowered porcelain cup on the table beside him. "Have you seen their returns? With all those deductions, exclusions, and credits, athletes pay more in bail bonds than they do in taxes. But I hope to change that; I want to eliminate a host of shelters and loopholes and introduce a simpler, sliding tax scale. Gene, I want government out of the *incentive* business. The code should be a simple document that raises credit, period! I don't want it being used to reward people for taking this or that action. The wealthy are the only ones who can take advantage of those incentives anyway. Gene, my plan has the rich paying more, but everyone will pay a fairer share of their income."

Leontius kept looking at the fire. "What about other companies besides our team, particularly failing companies, Governor. Will you dismiss them, too?"

Ambrose leaned forward on the couch. "Gene, a stimulus to jump-start failing companies in a recession is fine, as long as it gets paid back in a timely manner. Senator, thousands of CEOs earn millions of credit every year to avoid such disasters. They claim it's worthy compensation for guiding their ship through rough and murky waters. But if government bails them out, then what risk are they taking? They should be earning ten credits an hour like the secretaries who serve them. Gene, I refuse to provide credit to keep them afloat. If Republicans consider themselves capitalists, then they must be willing to fail."

"What about companies too big to fail?"

"That's an anti-trust issue, Gene; it needs to be dealt with before taking on water. Unlike the *Titanic*, large corporations need to have lifeboats onboard for everyone, not just a golden preserver for the captain."

Senator Leontius shook his head side to side and then shifted his weight in the chair, letting out a little gas in the process. "Hmm, why does everyone despise the rich? We should emulate them, Governor, not bring them down. I think you'd be wise to focus your efforts at helping the lower-classes."

Ambrose smiled. "I wish it were that simple, Gene. I believe a sizeable number of wealthy people picked themselves up by their bootstraps. Through hard work, they painstakingly rose up from humble beginnings. Senator, I do not believe for one minute that our American Dream is dead. On the other hand, I also believe that a great many of these people started the game on third base—they had ample access to extraordinary resources, or they possess rare ingenuity or exquisite talent for which society is willing to pay handsomely. Senator, most people in the working classes were born sitting on the bench—they have no assets. Despite arduous labor, they have little to show for their efforts. Gene, I'm not trying to bring rich people down; I'm using my power to level the playing field."

The senator sat with a concerned look on his face. "Without an archbishop you'll need Senate approval. But I'm afraid you've got a rather skewed vision of the Senate." Leontius shifted his weight once again. "See, Governor, we're not here to make sure the province eats its green, leafy vegetables. We only care that our constituents get their desserts. You're going to have an awfully difficult time getting anything passed."

Ambrose remained quiet.

"Governor," Leontius continued, "you were sworn into office off of Governor Probus's appointment. Next year, you'll need to campaign and try your hand at an election. I'd be careful who you piss off."

Agatha overheard his language after entering the room; she shot him another disgusted glance. "I'll try to remember that, Gene," replied

Ambrose. "Well, I should take my leave. It's been a long day, and I have a State of the Province speech to write tomorrow."

The senator stared at his wife but directed his words toward Ambrose. "I hope my language didn't offend you?"

"No, Gene, I've heard worse. Besides, I've overheard nuns using that term." Ambrose stood up from the couch, stretching his back. He straightened his clothing and then offered his hand to Mary. "It's just been a tiring day."

Agatha took hold of her husband's arm and helped him from the recliner; the elderly man let out more gas in the process. "I didn't think young people got tired," he mused. The senator looked at Agatha again; she motioned to him with her German eyes directed at Mary. "Oh, oh . . . of course, I understand, please forgive me, Governor. I'd forgotten what it's like to be young."

Stars twinkled brightly in the cold and cloudless night. Ambrose helped Mary into the passenger seat of his midnight-black Mercedes after clicking on the engine. Then he instructed his guards to follow behind in the limo as he removed his phone from his pocket. "Hey, Drew—would you stop calling me that? What . . . no, I'm still wearing suits; you know I'm not into togas. Listen, I called to say thanks for bringing my car around. Did you find any bugs? . . . Two . . . the feds . . . say again, I didn't catch that . . . Senator Symmachus!" Ambrose shook his head. "All right, so it's clean? Great, thanks, Drew, don't know what I'd do without you."

Ambrose drove north on Twelfth Street, away from the wealthy Sheraton neighborhood. They drove for a while without saying a word before Mary felt compelled to speak up. "If you're tired, Ambrose, we don't have to go to the Point, we can just call it a night."

"I want to go." His words were curt; he continued staring out at the road.

A few more minutes passed; Mary looked at him again, obliged to break the reticence. "I heard you made quite a stir at the game today."

"Not really."

"Mrs. Symmachus said you looked white as a sheet. She thought it might have been your first execution."

"No."

"Maybe you didn't have enough to eat, Ambrose. Mrs. Tendenblat said you only ate a few watermelon slices."

Ambrose began feeling nettled, then roiled; finally, his rage burst forth like a raging river: "MAYBE YOU'RE RIGHT, MAR; MAYBE WE SHOULDN'T GO TO THE POINT. YOU CAN JUST ASK YOUR INFORMANTS ABOUT IT!" They rode in silence for several minutes as Ambrose calmed down and collected his thoughts. He turned onto Interprovince 35 crossing the Awanata River.

Mary spoke up. "I didn't deserve that." Small tears welled in her eyes as she spoke.

Ambrose glanced at her and then back at the road. "No . . . no you didn't, Mar; I'm sorry. I don't know what came over me."

"What's wrong, Ambrose?"

"I don't know, Mar. I just don't fit in. I feel like an odd duck . . . a third wheel when I'm around these people." He stared glumly at the road as he spoke.

"You're not like them."

"Mar, am I wrong thinking government should stick to its job and not try to do everyone else's?"

Mary grabbed hold of his arm, "You're not wrong, Ambrose."

"Should I convince everyone that I thoroughly enjoy biking in the countryside when the sheer size of my jowls says I haven't done it in eons?"

She squeezed his arm harder. "You're not a hypocrite."

His anger intensified. "Mary, should I apologize if I don't enjoy watching a man run with a ball, or . . . or get mauled by a lion, or . . . or get himself hacked to death by a gladiator?"

She began sensing his pain. "No, Ambrose."

"Am I wrong not to give in to people's hatred? Should I cater to men . . . joyous men who discriminate against others, gladly denying the rights of those not removed from society? Learned men who put forth no reasonable explanation for their claims? Holy men who follow their own asinine tradition, which didn't start until well after Christ?" His eyes began welling with tears.

Mary stayed silent; tears began freely flowing down her cheeks, too.

"And these senators, Mar, they aren't public servants; they're deceivers served by the public! How many of them would sidle off to the doctor to treat a hangnail if they didn't have such wonderful insurance? How many of them would fly off to exotic places if they couldn't bill it to the province? And how many of them would spend their own money sitting in a thousand-credit luxury box drinking fine wine if people didn't provide it free to them?"

"You're not like them," she pleaded.

He briefly closed his eyes, squelching his anger before resuming his gaze on the road. In a soft, yielding voice, he uttered, "Maybe not, Mar, but how do I stop myself from becoming like them? How do I work with these people day in and day out and not become one of them?"

"You'll find a way, Ambrose—I know you will!" A few moments passed before Mary completed her thought. "Who knows, maybe God will provide you the answer." Her remark seemed so odd that it made him smirk. Then he grinned; finally, a wide smile overcame him. Ambrose turned toward Mary; both of them began giggling. Within a few seconds, they burst into uncontrollable laughter that brought more tears streaming down their faces.

They huddled in his Mercedes. It took a good minute, but their laughter finally faded. Ambrose turned off the freeway and headed east along Rutherford Avenue. "Gosh, Mar," he began, erupting spurts of joy, "I haven't laughed that hard since my grade-school days with Basil."

As they proceeded, Ambrose took notice of the size of the houses: two-story mansions gave way to Tudors, which gave way to ramblers. "Mar, you wondered why I felt sick at the game," he continued, changing the subject.

"That's okay, Ambrose; I don't need to know. I didn't mean to sound like I was spying on you."

"No, no, Mar, I want you to know. See, it wasn't the blood and gore. I've seen several quick-sword deaths before; they can be just as bad, if not worse. And it wasn't the lack of food, either. Although the disgusting way Senator Mauritius eats would make anyone sick." He looked directly into her eyes. "Mar . . . it was the crowd! The people, 150,000 of them, all shouting and chanting, pounding their fists in a downward direction, all hoping to witness another man's passing. I've had my share of lamentable clients, Mar, but today I fully realized what a brutal, savage beast man really is."

"I'm sorry, Bee," she said, squeezing his arm.

Ambrose looked at her with eyes wide. "You've never called me that before. Only my family uses that name."

"I know." They drove several moments in silence as Ambrose turned onto side streets, making his way into Milan's lower-class district. Mary sat up and looked around at the dismal surroundings. "Bee, this neighborhood is looking seedy. Is my brutal, savage beast still taking me to the Point?"

"I've one more stop, Mar. I received a letter from Sister Anne asking if I would look in on Mr. Mendoza. Apparently, he and his wife are parishioners at the cathedral. He also has quite a few kids at St. George's where she teaches. Anyway, I met Sister Anne the day you called me in church. Do you remember?"

"Of course I remember, Bee; don't be silly—that was the day you became governor."

"You were sworn in as my lieutenant."

"It's the day you missed your work party."

"It's the day Governor Probus and Hanna died."

Mary crinkled her nose. "Ooh, it's the day Leonard Thompson got his job back."

Ambrose smiled. "You know, Mar, out of everything that happened that day, what I remember most is our first kiss."

"Oh, Bee, you remembered! Do you know what I remember most? It's the day you fell on your butt!"

They laughed as his Mercedes pulled into the Mendoza's weedy, rock-filled driveway. Ambrose shut off the engine just as the front door to the house burst open; the glow from a flickering yellow porch light appeared. "*¿Quíen es?*" hollered Fransisco. The drunken man staggered through the doorway holding a bottle of Goose Head beer.

"Hurry, Mar," Ambrose said. "Help me get Agatha's food inside before he thinks we're trespassing."

VIII

FRUSTRATED GRADUATE

Marcellina roused from unexpected, reposeful sleep. She lay nestled under two fleece blankets and an old brown and black Afghan, given to her by Ambassador Binaisa five years earlier. She rolled to her side, flung off the covers, and slowly sat up in bed. She grabbed her phone off a bedside table and looked at its bright, colorful face: forty-one degrees, cloudy skies, and light drizzle. *No, it can't rain today; I've too much to do.*

Marcellina looked around her bedroom. Once adorned in frills, it now looked barren, awash in early-morning blue, an equal mixture of alice and periwinkle. The room sat empty except for a dozen red roses that had arrived in yesterday's mail. The flowers stood tall in a drab-green vase on a white, plastic table next to the bed, providing the room its only splash of color. "AH-CHOO," she sneezed, "AH-CHOO, AH-CHOO, AH-CHOO," she repeated in rapid-fire succession looking out a blurry window at the drizzle. *This miserable cold, how did I ever sleep?*

"Mornin' birthday girl," quipped Jacqueline, peeking in past the open bedroom door. "Can I come in?"

"Only if you want my cold," Marcellina answered her roommate in a nasally, stuffed-up voice, fighting off another sneeze. She reached for a tissue on the bedside table. "AH-CHOO!"

"I've got your shower started, and I put fresh towels in the bathroom. I also put out clean cotton jammies and a robe. I'll have lemon tea brewing on the stove when you're done. Oh, and I picked up a Neti pot, a bottle of vitamin C, and some zinc nasal spray at the drugstore yesterday."

Marcellina looked at her roommate with a sad expression. "What am I going to do without you, Jackie?"

"That's a good question."

After lavishing under a hot shower for nearly ten minutes, Marcellina dressed and made her way out of the bathroom for the rest of her treatment. She walked through the apartment's small living room, sidestepping cardboard boxes packed with clothing, electronics, books, plants, and assorted memorabilia. Marcellina had neatly marked the boxes: "M" for Marcellina—for shipment to New York, and "J" for Jacqueline—for departure to Phi Beta Delta. The sorority, one of the university's oldest structures, stood within a stone's throw from the Lucretius on the northwest side of campus.

Marcellina spoke to her roommate after finding her in the kitchen. "This place looks so desolate, doesn't it?"

"I can't believe how fast this year went," Jacqueline replied, stirring a tablespoon of sea salt into an eight-ounce glass of warm water. "Here, gargle," she continued, handing the tincture to Marcellina.

Marcellina tipped her head and sloshed the tepid brine in her throat before spitting it into the sink. She reached for a towel and wiped the corners of her mouth. "Too bad you couldn't convince Accalia to stay here; it's a decent apartment, Jackie. Do you really think you're going to like living in a sorority?"

"I'll be okay," she replied, twisting the lid off a bottle. "I know most of the people living there already. Amy Butler can be a butt-head, but the rest of them are fine. Anyway, what can I do? That's where Accalia wants to finish out her college." She looked up at Marcellina with a show of toughness on her face. "What's three years of my life?"

"I wonder if Accalia knows how lucky she is to have you. Do you think you two will ever marry?"

"Don't know, Marci, we only hope your brother keeps hounding the Senate." Jacqueline shook her head. "That damn Symmachus always seems to rally votes against us. Here, take this tablet."

"Have you heard anything from Beth?"

Jacqueline bristled curling her right hand into a fist. "I haven't seen or heard anything from that bitch since our fight last week."

"Let's see your eye." Marcellina put her face close, examining the outside corner of her roommate's left eye. "Hmmm . . . looks like it's almost healed, but it still has that indent where she struck you. Does it hurt?"

"No," countered Jacqueline, palpating the dimpled skin on her face, "but that thing better heal, or I'm not kidding; she's toast. You know it came from that big Menorah ring she wears on her finger." The angry woman shook her head. "Jewish my ass; she has as much in common with Moses as I do!"

"But you *are* Jewish, Jackie."

"Well I don't practice," she snapped, "and neither does Beth; she just pretends." Jacqueline reached for the bottle of nasal spray on the counter. "But I showed her, Marci; she looked a lot worse than me after our fight." Jacqueline peeked at the directions on the back of the bottle, changing her tone from angry to apprehensive. "It scares me a little that she's been this quiet. Beth's not one to take defeat lightly . . . I hope she's not planning anything big. Now put your head back so I can spray this crap up your nose."

After taking several sniffs of the mist, Marcellina inquired. "What do the rest of your friends think about her jealousy?" Before receiving an answer, Marcellina lowered her head and sneezed, "AH-CHOO!"

"Bless you . . . should we try this again, sweetie?

"No, just move on."

Jackie placed the cap on the spray. "Well, Brit's too self-centered to care, and Toni, gosh, I never know where she stands. I don't think she's made up her mind yet. And Cardea, you know her, she's such a dear; she never sticks to one opinion. She'll say whatever pleases the person in front of her."

"AH-CHOO . . . AH-CHOO . . . AH-CHOO. Jackie, I sure appreciate all the trouble you've gone to, but I don't think any of these remedies are working."

"Come here and be a good lobster. Now, stick your head over this pot of boiling water." Jacqueline watched her roommate comply with her orders. "That's it, sweetie, now just breathe for a while."

After Marcellina's nursing ended, the women sat together on folding chairs drinking hot lemon tea listening to the pitter-patter of falling rain. Marcellina broke the silence, staring out at their live's possessions all boxed up in the living room. "We had some good times, didn't we Jackie?"

"Hey, don't get all sentimental on me yet," she complained, placing both hands around her steamy beverage. "We've still got lots to do; we have to get through lunch and your graduation ceremony."

"You're taking me to the airport tonight, right?"

"Don't worry; I'll get you there, Marci. But I still think you're nuts wanting to live in New York."

"I've got to go where my dream job takes me." Marcellina blew on her tea before taking a sip. "I still can't believe they gave me the job,"she continued. "Thousands of people apply to the UN social council every year." The grateful woman paused, reflecting on her good fortune. "Just think, Jackie, I get to be part of a committee improving children's education around the world! Doesn't that sound exciting? AH-CHOO."

"Bless you. I suppose so . . . guess that's why you got your degree in the first place. But, Marci, you'd be just as happy if you married Aamir and settled down in Dionysius. I mean, he's a great guy—smart, funny, handsome, and he's got a good job at the university." Jacqueline brought the tea to her face but stopped short of taking a sip. "You could teach religion there—that old geezer can't hang on forever."

"Professor Nero?"

"Yeah, that creep," she replied. "If you did his job, then you and Aamir could buy a big house in Agnomen, put up a white picket fence, and have ten little Muslims running around—doesn't that sound exciting?"

"No, and therein lies the problem; see, Aamir wants kids of his own—lots of them, but I don't. Oh, don't get me wrong, Jackie, you and I have talked about this before; I love children. But I don't want to bring any more into this world. With so many kids in dire need, it's hard to justify adding any more. Besides, Jackie, as much as I love Aamir and want to spend time with him, we're just good friends."

"I wonder about that. I think the two of you make an adorable couple whenever I see you together. I mean, he's a very handsome man—as far as men go—and well, you've got such a cute ass!"

"Hey!"

After finishing her tea, Marcellina got dressed and prepared to leave the apartment. "I put a box of tissues in your backpack," said Jacqueline, "and you should stuff a few in your pocket. Now, here's an umbrella, be sure to use it."

"You sound like my mother." Marcellina smiled at her roommate as she donned a black peacoat over her crimson sweater. "Are you sure you'll be all right when the movers arrive?"

"I'll make sure your stuff gets loaded and they head off in the right direction. Now, are you sure you don't want to take your bed? It's a good piece of furniture; you seem to sleep pretty well on it."

"It's not mine; it's the only thing that came with the apartment." Marcellina opened the door and peered out at the rain. "AH-CHOO!"

"*Gesundheit*—then I'll see you at the Gallus at one."

Marcellina walked away from the only home she had known for the past four years. She stepped over puddles while crossing Palisade Avenue, making her way southward. She traveled across two desolate parking lots, a sidewalk under construction, and a temporary brick pathway situated between the Chemistry and Mathematics buildings. It led to the university's immaculately groomed mall.

She crossed the mall's soggy grass, saturating her shoes, just as a gust of cool wind coiled her umbrella. At that moment, the light drizzle started giving way to a heavy downpour. After running up steps, she used the strength in both arms to open massive doors to the history building. "This meeting with Nero better be worth it," she muttered, glancing back at the torrential rain.

"Ah, welcome Ms. Ambrosius," said the professor. "Come into my office and have a seat. He peered into the hallway, and then locked the door behind her. "Can I get you something, hot tea or coffee, perhaps?"

"Tea would be nice, Professor . . . AH- CHOO!"

"Oh, my dear child, you've got a cold. I'm sorry to have dragged you out in this weather. I'll get your tea right away."

Marcellina studied his office while he busied himself in another room. Christian classics written by Taylor Caldwell, Grace Livingston Hill, C.S. Lewis, George Macdonald, Catherine Marshall, Charles Sheldon, and Charles Williams lined one side of the room. A book by Harold Bell Wright lay open to page forty-eight on an old coffee table next to an older pea-green sofa with matching cushions.

On the opposite side of the room stood Islamic volumes, most noticeably a four-volume set of *Minnat-ul-Munim Sharh Sahih Muslim*, in Arabic only, by Safiur Rahman Al-Mubarakpouri. Beside it lay *Qisas an-*

Nabiyin, or *Stories of the Prophet*, by Abul Husain Ali Nadwi. Marcellina stepped back and took in a panoramic view. Books of all faiths, fiction and non, as well as letters, manuscripts, and documents of varying thickness, lay scattered about in a manner only a genius—or madman—could appreciate.

"Your tea, Ms. Ambrosius," said Professor Nero, returning to his guest. "I'm sorry for the appearance of my office. I just lost my third secretary this month. Please, have a seat on the couch," he persisted, brushing aside crumpled treatises.

"What did you wish to speak to me about, Professor? If it's feedback about your class, I can only say that you were one of the toughest instructors I've ever had. But, at the same time, you taught me a great deal."

"You're most kind, Ms. Ambrosius." Nero wore his customary plaid sport coat and drab olive pants. "May I call you Marcellina?" He made his inquiry while returning a book to the shelf. The reach from his arm lifted his coat, revealing a pair of red suspenders attached to the back of his trousers.

Marcellina took a sip of black tea before answering his question. "I don't know why not, Professor; I'm no longer your student."

"Marcellina, you were my best student in well over a decade, and I appreciate all the hard work you put into my class. But I didn't summon you here to talk about the past. Besides, I've received enough feedback from students over the years to last me a lifetime. It no longer does any good; I'm too old to change. So, let's talk about you; I trust you're employed by the UN?"

"Yes, Professor, I leave for New York tonight." After replying, Marcellina looked away and giggled.

"Did you find my question amusing?"

"I'm sorry, Professor. It's just that I felt a sudden urge to stand up before answering your question."

"Oh yes, yes, I do enjoy imputing a measure of discipline into my classes. No need for that here, though," he continued. "Tell me, to what end is your employment?"

"They've invited me to join a special council; I'll be working on children's education around the world."

Nero sat down on the couch beside her, grunting as his aging body descended. "That's indeed a responsible position, young lady. And whom else, besides me, did you use as references for this salient appointment?" Nero opened his hands wide as he spoke.

Marcellina felt uneasy; perhaps it was his mannerisms, or maybe he sat too close to her on the couch. "Well, you, of course," she began, "and I asked my brother, Aurelius. I tried getting a reference from Dr. Dembe Binaisa, a UN ambassador from Kenya, but he refused. I guess that after all these years he's still angry with me for leaving him so abruptly. So then, I asked Dr. Hankonson in the history department. I didn't know who else to turn to, Professor. I would have asked my brother Satyrus, but they allow only one family reference."

"So, tell me Marcellina, how did you—a new doctoral candidate—get appointed to such a lofty position with such modest references, and no notoriety of your own?"

Marcellina felt uneasy not knowing where he was leading the conversation. But he spoke the truth. Other than her thesis, she had never written anything noteworthy, nothing of any scholarly value. She did not even ace her dissertation; Nero had downgraded it half a point because it lacked original thinking. "Professor, I wouldn't label you or my brother modest references. But to answer your question, I honestly don't know." Marcellina quickly brought the tea to her mouth and took another sip.

Nero formed a cockeyed smile. "Then let me fill you in, Marcellina. See, you look at me and see an old man, a curmudgeon. Oh yes, yes, I know all about what students think of me. You look around this office and think that I must have buried my head in books for the past century. But I assure you, Marcellina, I do get out and about."

Marcellina stayed quiet.

"In fact," he continued, "I'm acquainted with just about every leader on this planet. See, every president, dictator, monarch, or king—they all ask the same questions. How can we expand our country and stay true to our religion? Or, conversely: how can we avoid immigrants promoting their own brand of faith? When trouble strikes—and it always does—the UN comes to me for assistance. See, a serious insurrection never occurs without a religious undertone. And after I tell them what they need to know . . . well, they're hardly in a position to refuse my requests. Make no mistake, young lady, you got your precious job because of me." Nero placed a hand on Marcellina's leg. "And all I'm asking for is a little gratitude . . . a small reward . . . a tiny favor to an old man." He slid his hand further up her leg.

"Please don't, Professor."

"Come now, Marcellina, how badly do you want the job?"

Marcellina stood up and bounded for the door. With hands shaking, she heedlessly turned the handle. "Open up, you stupid door," she cried. Several moments passed before she realized that he had locked it. She quickly turned the latch and retried the handle. After the door finally opened, she grabbed her backpack and bolted into the hallway. Marcellina ran down the steps, through the outer doors, straight into the pouring rain. She didn't stop running until she had sprinted across the mall and arrived at Engineering.

After entering, Marcellina rattled off four sneezes in succession. She sprinted up two flights of stairs to the third floor, entering what was normally a depressing hallway. This time, however, the corridor lay covered in off-white canvas, with five Mexican workers spreading bright orange paint on the walls. Two stood on aluminum ladders painting trim, two rolled a coat standing on the floor, and a fifth slathered acrylic on a cracked, eight-inch baseboard while kneeling on the canvas. Marcellina, doubled over trying to catch her breath, frantically waved at a passing student. "Aamir . . . is Aamir here?"

"You mean Professor Nadif? He's in his office."

Marcellina threaded the cluttered corridor toward the lab. After passing the hard-working painters, she hastened her gait past a bronze folding chair placed outside a room, as well as several bulletin boards bearing outdated messages. As she neared Aamir's office, she took notice of her drenched hair and clothing. *I must look hideous—probably smell like a wet dog.* She peered through an eye-level window on his door, expecting to see him pecking away at his computer. "Oh no," she cried, turning her head aside. Inside, Aamir stood in the loving embrace of another woman.

Marcellina's mind twirled and fluttered—and she hadn't yet recovered from the previous incident. She slowly backed away. *Gosh, I can't disturb him . . . when did this happen? He never told me he started seeing someone else.* Marcellina pondered several questions while walking back down the hallway. Her body felt the inhospitable chill from sodden clothing, but her mind continued probing. *Am I jealous? Is Aamir more than just a friend? For goodness' sake, I'm leaving for New York, did I think he'd wait forever? Did I think he'd always be there for me?* Tears welled in her Persian-blue eyes—just before she knocked over a paint can near the door leading out to the stairwell.

"Marci," sounded a virile vocalization from the littered hallway, "wait up, where are you going?"

Marcellina closed her eyes; she recognized his voice. "I . . . I can't Aamir . . . I'm sorry," she replied, too softly to be heard. Marcellina leaned into the stairwell door, feeling its metal weight give way.

"Wait up; I want you to meet my sister."

The half-crazed woman stopped dead in her tracks. Opening her eyes, she peered down the hallway, tears descending her cheeks. From Marcellina's perspective, framed inside an aluminum ladder, stood the most handsome, most brave, most intelligent man she had ever known—except, of course, her father. Along with Jacqueline, Aamir had become her trusted friend and confidant. "Aamir," she shouted, running at him, sideswiping ladders, leaving orange footprints on the floor. Marcellina thrust herself into his arms, "Oh, Aamir!"

Marcellina swiftly recalled hundreds of cherished moments they had spent together, none more precious than their first date—the day after her ketamine overdose at the Gallus. While nursing a splitting headache, she had asked him sharp and pointed questions. She learned that he had indeed staged the theft of her laptop at the Publius. He did it with the help of his estranged younger brother, Muntisir. Aamir made an unconvincing argument that his brother had thought up the idea. "You're buying lunch, fella," she remembered saying after he'd come clean.

They ate lunch at the Pomona, a popular Greek establishment two blocks from the Gallus. Mrs. Della Bellanca, a native of Karpathos in the southeastern Aegean Sea, owned and operated the restaurant. She traced her ancestry all the way to her country's war against Sparta in 431 BC. Della immigrated to America as a child with her maternal grandmother, starting the restaurant after finishing high school and two years of college. Thirty years later, her *soufflé kounoupithiou* and *kreata me feta* consistently rated one and two in the nation by leading food critics.

Marcellina never ate in her restaurant again. Della befriended Darlene Thompson, Leonard Thompson's wife, who had developed a passion for Greek cuisine. Della and Darlene formed a close relationship. They became so tight, in fact, the restaurateur became rude to anyone remotely connected to the Ambrosius family—fallout from the travesty of the Llinos hearing. "What do you do when you're not stealing laptops?" Marcellina remembered questioning him after taking a bite of cauliflower smothered in creamy cheese sauce.

"I'm an engineer," he replied. "I earned a doctorate in robotics at Dionysius University nine years ago. I emigrated here from Jubaland, the Juba River Valley of western Thrivingi. That's in East Africa, Marcellina."

"Wasn't that area devastated by Huns?"

"No, no, you're thinking of Greuthungi. Ostrogoths live there, along the rocky coastline of the Indian Ocean—near Kismaayo. I'm Visigoth; our people live in Thrivingi on the plains of the Serengeti, inland from Greuthungi. Our nations used to be united, though," he spoke proudly.

"Tell me more about your family, Aamir."

"My father performed well with his hands, Marcellina. He could fix anything. Against his will, they made him janitor in the building occupied by General Mohammed Said Hersi Morpan, one of the early rebels in my country's civil war. They paid my father peanuts, Marci; he meant nothing but slave labor to them. But he was a smart guy, smarter than they realized. By keeping his eyes glued to the floor and his ears more receptive than a satellite dish, he got his revenge."

"Was your dad a spy?"

"Everyone's a spy in times of war," he responded. "But unlike many, my father had useful information to assist the TNF." Aamir looked off in the distance. "He gathered confirmed information that ousted that retched butcher."

"TNF?"

"I'm sorry; that stands for Thrivingi National Front. They have since merged with other tribal groups in the area. My father did many dangerous things for them. He recorded conversations, copied letters, even planted bugs in Morpan's office so the TNF could listen in to what he said. My father told me he worked closely with a young volunteer. I know he mentioned his name, Marci, but it's too bad I forget it. Anyway, in return for his bravery, they promised our family safe passageway to America. So, here I am."

"Aamir, your father was a hero; that's wonderful."

"Yes, Marci, but, unfortunately he passed away from cancer last year. Aamir studied her Persian-blue eyes. "I'm sorry; I've started calling you Marci. Your name's Marcellina; please forgive me, I apologize."

"No, no, that's all right, Aamir; call me Marci."

"Marci, I feel conflicted. On one hand, I do believe my father was a hero, a national patriot whose story needs to get out, but in more detail than I can tell it myself. It would take lots of research and interviews to do justice to his story. For starters, though, I would love to find the man who worked closely with my father." Aamir looked out the restaurant window toward the university campus. "On the other hand, Marci, I'm a scientist. Part of me just wants to move on and not dwell on the past. I want to discover things that will help mankind overcome its physical limitations."

Despite her headache, Marcellina recalled the powerful connection she had felt with Aamir that day as he talked about the rest of his family. Any man who admitted to feeling emotionally torn was miles above the rest in her book. She listened to him talk for half an hour, but as time grew short, she remembered asking him one last question: "Aamir, why did you stage the theft of my computer?"

"You already asked me that."

"Yes I know, but why *mine*?"

"All right, Marci," he had said softly, sensing the meaning in her voice. "Well, for starters, I've accomplished a lot—lots more than most in my country. I've earned a doctorate in physics, I have a good job in the robotics department, and I'm proud to send money back to my people still living in Jubaland."

Marcellina looked at him quizzically. "How does that answer my question?"

He smiled warmly before continuing. "I'm sorry, what I'm trying to say is that having accomplished these things, I feel secure enough with myself to start a relationship with someone else."

"Go on."

"When I saw you in the library, I felt compelled to meet you that day . . . that very hour, in fact." Aamir looked at her hair and cocked his head to the side. "Under the dim light of the chandeliers, your auburn hair radiated passion like a raging fire, incinerating my eyes like a thousand burning embers. And your eyes, Marci, Persian blue if I'm not mistaken, reached out to me like comforting pools of water dowsing your flaming vision. I just had to get to know you; you were my image of Heaven."

Marcellina couldn't recall if her mouth had dropped open, but she remembered feeling her temperature rise. She also remembered taking a big gulp of water about that time. No man had spoken to her that way before. She loved receiving genuine compliments—not ones turned into a joke, or serving as a ridiculous pick-up line enticing her into bed. Most American men didn't know how to do it, but she had frequently encountered men overseas who did; she missed being overseas. From that day on, she and Aamir formed a textbook friendship, seeing each other regularly over the course of her final year at the university.

Aamir withdrew from Marcellina's soggy embrace and escorted her into his office. "Marci, this is my sister, Aarifah."

After entering the tiny office, Marcellina noticed a woman seated in front of Aamir's desk. She had a lovely smile, coffee-brown eyes, and wore a colorful blue-green hijab. "Hi, it's nice to meet you . . . AH-CHOO. Oh, Aarifah, don't get too close to me, and forgive me if I don't shake your hand."

"My brother has told me a lot about you, Marcellina. Thank you for taking such good care of him." At forty-one years of age, Aarifah was the oldest of six children in the Nadif family. She immigrated to America before the TNF had finished working with her father. However, she returned to the Juba River Valley shortly after completing a degree at Loyola University. She did not marry; instead, she chose to devote herself as a nurse caring for Wazigua, descendants of slave refugees from northern Mozambique and northeast Tanzania—her family's tribe.

Wazigua hailed as one of twenty-nine clans in Sunni-occupied Thrivingi. Clans constantly embroiled themselves in civil war beginning many years back—after being freed from foreign rule, first British, and then Italian. The region lacked any government oversight: rarely stable, warlords overran it—military thugs like General Fritigern and General Athanaric.

Athanaric once served in Fritigern's army; he worked as his right-hand man. Now the generals despised one another and competed for power. When they were not fighting each other, Athanaric directed soldiers against the Huns. Fritigern, meanwhile, supervised Visigoth civilians emigrating to the Provinces by way of the American Navy. After civilians arrived in New York—if they were young and healthy enough to arrive, that is—Americans paid little heed to their cultural distinctions. People viewed them as a unified whole and referred to them as "Goths." Aarifah chose not to involve herself in her country's civil war or its conflict with the Huns; she simply gave nonpartisan assistance to those suffering from HIV/AIDS, sickle-cell anemia, malaria, malnutrition—and shrapnel.

Marcellina smiled at Aarifah. "I think we took good care of one another this past year."

Aarifah saw beneath her painted smile; she knew her brother's friend had been crying. "Well, the two of you have much to discuss; I'll take my leave," she remarked. Aarifah directed her gaze at Aamir. "Perhaps we can speak later tonight, brother—over dinner?" She stood up and extended her hand toward Marcellina, then pulled it back. "It was nice meeting you, Marcellina; I hope we meet again. I also hope you get over your cold very soon."

Aamir walked his sister partway down the hallway. He hugged and kissed her lovingly, then said his good-bye. No sooner did he step back into his office than he found himself face to face with Marcellina. "I hate him! I hate him! I hate him," she cried aloud, fists pounding his chest, tears flowing from her eyes.

"Whoa, Marci, what's the matter? What's wrong?" he asked, trying to bring his shivering friend under control. After getting her seated and settled down, Aamir wrapped Marcellina in a wool blanket and brought her a cup of hot tea. He listened to her rant and rave about Nero for the next hour and a half.

"Please, Aamir," she begged, wrapping up their discussion, "don't retaliate against him. He's a tenured professor, and he's got friends in high places; he'll cause you nothing but trouble. Besides, no one else was in his office at the time; we were alone. It's his word against mine; we both know how that would play out."

"We must bring him to justice, Marci."

"Please, Aamir, it's enough you took time to listen to me. I'm feeling much better . . . honestly."

Aamir gazed at her for several seconds with static, unwavering eyes. "All right, Marci, we won't press charges, but I'll keep my eyes on him just the same. Would you like more tea?"

Marcellina declined, setting her cup on Aamir's metal desk, which he'd painted many times over—now a flat green with orange flecks bleeding through it. She pulled the blanket up to her neck; its warmth conveyed the security she felt in his presence. "Thank you, Aamir; you've been a great friend to me this past year. I'm really going to miss you."

"I'd go to the ends of the earth, Marci; you know that. My door is always open whenever you come back."

Fresh tears welled in her eyes. "Promise me you'll come to my graduation this afternoon. You're such a big part of my success here at the university."

"I planned on it; I picked out a nice tie and everything. I don't think I could survive if I missed President Valentinian's commencement." They both laughed upon rising to their feet. She thanked him profusely for the birthday roses adorning her barren bedroom and then embraced him for a good long minute.

Marcellina walked down the hall toward the stairwell, receiving angry stares from painters. She arrived at the first floor, pushed past a heavy door, and made her way out of Engineering. Thick clouds persisted, but the rain had lessened to a trickle. Marcellina walked westward along the mall's northern sidewalk, splashing puddles as she ambled toward the Lucretius. Buds formed on the Alpine currant, thornless barberry, and belle poitevine shrubs outlining the mall's manicured bluegrass. She headed for Lee's Dry Cleaning on Broadway, across the street and adjacent to Phi Beta Delta, Jacqueline's new home for the upcoming season. Marcellina had planned to pick up a red dress for her graduation ceremony.

Marcellina passed by Mathematics, Chemistry, Physics, and Biology—buildings she scarcely knew existed; her curriculum had inluded the humanities, not the sciences. The buildings' white marble and limestone faces, of Greek architectural design, appeared more majestic in the damp, sunless sky then she remembered.

As she neared the Lucretius, a large gathering of people—perhaps two hundred in all—stood listening to a young man speaking into a microphone. He stood on a marble step leading up to the cultural center. In her four years in college, Marcellina couldn't recall a single week when some student wasn't protesting this or that on the mall. Speakers touched on all kinds of topics: the high cost of education, teen suicide prevention, social security, and carbon emissions. Protestors bitterly complained about government legislators and directors and the need to oust more than one of them from office. Every conceivable subject got a voice at the Lucretius. More recently, however, Marcellina began hearing complaints from newly arrived Thrivingi immigrants.

Protests carried little weight with students unless they had received prior billing on websites. If that didn't happen, they walked on by without stopping to hear the complainant. Unadvertised demonstrations were as outdated as dusty books sitting dormant on library bookshelves. Students could care less about them if no one had asked them to come. Marcellina was an exception; she stopped by for a few minutes to hear the young man's objections:

> "MY FELLOW STUDENTS, HEAR ME . . . PLEASE LISTEN TO MY MY PLEA. YOU KNOW MY WORDS ARE TRUE; I SPEAK TRUTHFULLY, AMERICA. THE GOVERNMENT OF THIS LAND IS KILLING FRAIL AND ELDERLY MEMBERS OF OUR GREAT THRIVINGI NATION. THEY DO IT IN SECRET, ACROSS THE OCEANS THAT DIVIDE US. IT'S DONE IN A MANNER MORE SAVAGE AND BRUTAL THAN ANY HUN COULD EVER IMAGINE . . ."

"That looks like Muntisir," Marcellina said aloud, straining to see through the crowd. "Those look like his orange high-top sneakers."

"Praise Allah," a man standing next to her replied, "Muntisir is a wise and gifted leader. He's doing the work of Allah."

Wise and gifted leader? Doing the work of Allah? Marcellina rolled her eyes. *Please, he's nothing more than Aamir's mischievous little brother. Perhaps I should enlighten this crowd and tell them he tried stealing my computer.* Marcellina weaved her way through the gathering to get a closer view. "Excuse me, excuse me please . . . AH-CHOO!"

"Lady, go home if you're sick," yelled one man.

"You're going to infect us all," said another. She ignored their appeal and pressed onward, listening to Muntisir's message:

"AMERICA IS HOME FOR ALL PEOPLE, NOT JUST CHRISTIANS. WE THRIVINGI ARE PROUD MUSLIMS; WE SHALL PRACTICE ISLAM IN AMERICA. THIS COUNTRY HAS NO RIGHT CONVERTING OUR PEOPLE INTO ARIAN DEVILS, NOR IS AMERICA KEEPING ANY OF ITS PROMISES. WE ARE JOBLESS, HOMELESS, AND DISCRIMINATED AGAINST IN EVERY PROVINCE. HEAR US, AMERICA: WE SHALL NOT FIGHT IN YOUR WARS UNTIL YOU RESPECT US. HEAR US, AMERICA, LAND OF THE BRAVE, HOME OF THE FREE, WE WILL NOT FIGHT UNTIL WE ARE GIVEN DEFERENCE . . ."

"Go home, Adoon," shouted one man. "If you're not willing to bleed for this country, then we don't want you here."

"Yeah, Habash, think you know discrimination? I'll show you discrimination," said another, picking up a rock and hurling it at Muntisir. The stone flew well over the young man's head, but close enough to incite nearby Visigoths. One punch was thrown, then another. Soon, a large section of the crowd was embroiled in a scrap. Students yelled and screamed, slugging one another with fists. The masses soon ran in all directions after knives, machetes, daggers, and swords appeared.

"Muntisir, Muntisir!" screamed Marcellina, trying to get his attention. However, the commotion from the mob caused too much noise for him to hear her. She tried again, but then saw a man hit Muntisir from behind with the flat of his blade. Muntisir dropped his microphone and fell headfirst down the steps of the Lucretius. Marcellina screamed, continuing to fight her way through the crowd. Upon reaching him, someone viciously struck her in the head, sending her tumbling to the ground. "Are you all right Muntisir?" she asked with fading breath, just before passing out.

Marcellina regained consciousness moments later. She lay woozy on the ground, deliberately groped by ruttish men who had fallen beside her. Before lodging a complaint, however, she felt herself hoisted into the air by strangers in black uniforms. Squads of Agnomen police, who were painstakingly patrolling the university in preparation for Caesar's arrival, descended upon them. "Put her ass in the second van," said one of the officers. "I saw her trying to talk to the speaker; she's probably one of the organizers."

Marcellina had no recollection riding to the police station. She sat quietly on a bench looking out at fifty other people in a holding room as barren as her apartment. "AH-CHOO!" Her sneeze sent a pang to the back of her tender skull.

"I'm sorry you got involved in this, Marcellina," said Muntisir. The youth took a seat beside her. "It's Aamir who should be here, not you."

Muntisir was the youngest sibling in the Nadif family. At twenty-one years of age, he appeared every bit as tall and handsome as his six-foot-three-inch older brother, Aamir. Very dark skinned, he had a muscular physique with kinky, black African hair. However, Muntisir shied away from family; he was a lone wolf, and his siblings knew little about his reclusive nature. In fact, no one in his family knew where he lived most of the time, or how he paid his way. No one even knew his college major, though he had only one exam remaining in his final year at the university.

Marcellina looked straight ahead, holding both sides of her head with her hands to control the pain. "Aamir's a scientist, Muntisir, he's trying to make the world a better place, not incite riots."

"I, too, am trying to make the world a better place. But good cannot proceed until evil is rooted out."

Before Muntisir finished speaking, a black man stood over him, "Nadif . . . Mr. Muntisir Nadif, may I have a word with you?" Marcellina watched the men walk off toward a corner of the room.

"Nadif, my name is Colonel Dirie, Aashif Dirie," he said in a peaceful manner. "I came to the Provinces last year with my daughter aboard the *George P. Sanford.* General Abdul Kareem Fritigern elevated my rank and put me in charge of Visigoths immigrating to this country."

Muntisir's face lit up with excitement. "Colonel, I've heard of you. I'm so happy to meet you."

"Quiet, you fool." The colonel barked out his order using a muted voice. "Listen to me, Nadif; I've watched you closely over the past few months. Although I appreciate your passion, we're not ready for riots just yet. We must treat the Americans with respect for now."

Muntisir's expression turned serious. "But Colonel, I didn't cause the riot; I only spoke the truth."

"Truth as you and I know it, Nadif." Aashif scanned the room for eavesdroppers; he witnessed Marcellina sitting quietly on the bench with her head still cupped between her hands. "But not the truth America is willing to hear." The colonel redirected his gaze at the youth. "I could use an enterprising man like you, Muntisir, but you must be patient; you must learn to temper your words."

Marcellina looked at the men conversing in the corner and then reached for her backpack to grab a tissue. She suddenly realized her pack was missing. Her mind flooded with questions: *Did I have it with me when I came here? Did I leave it on campus? Did someone here take it?* Her anxiety energized her stupor. *My creditizer is in there; how am I supposed to pay for my dress at the cleaners? And my phone,* she thought, *Jackie probably called wondering why I didn't meet her for lunch at the Gallus.* Marcellina rose to her feet, her head still pounding. "Officer, officer," she shouted, making her way to the agent.

"Get back in line," uttered an angry voice.

"Yeah, lady, wait your turn," said another.

Marcellina sat back down on the wooden bench trying to reenact her steps. After reflecting for what seemed like a few moments, she looked toward the corner in search of Muntisir. She wanted to ask him if he had seen her pack, but he was gone. "I don't see him," she mumbled, looking around the room. "When did he get processed?" She closed her eyes and shook her aching head. *Oh, wake up, Marci . . . how long have I been out?*

Suddenly, a tall set of legs in brown trousers appeared in front of her. She looked up and gazed at her savior. "Aamir," she shouted, smiling at her friend. "Oh, and you've got my backpack, too!" She rose to her feet and gave him a hug.

Aamir sat on the bench beside her. "Muntisir called me and said you were here. That's the first I've heard from him in quite a while. Anyway, Marci, as I walked toward my car, I noticed police standing on the steps of the Lucretius. Then I noticed the bomb squad surrounding what looked like a green and white package. As I got closer, it seemed to fit the profile of your backpack. You should have seen their expressions when I walked up, excused myself, and carried it off."

Marcellina looked deeply into his brown eyes. Any man who remembered the details of a woman's backpack was miles above the rest in her book. "Oh, Aamir, I'm foolish for leaving you. I don't know what I'll do without you."

"Our dreams make us do foolish things," he replied, looking into her Persian-blue eyes. "But we're meant to pursue them," he continued with a smile. "Don't worry, Marci, I'll find some ugly hag who wants to bear my ten children. Now, your graduation is about to start, when can we get out of here?"

Marcellina didn't answer; she lowered her sore head on his shoulder and closed her eyes. Another hour passed before the Agnomen police released her. She squinted in the sunlight and bathed in its warmth as she and Aamir exited the station. *It's windy, but at least the sun is popping through*, she thought, seating herself in his car. A clock perched high atop the station's outer wall read half past five o'clock in the afternoon.

Aamir drove a seventeen-year-old, rusted-out, four-speed Toyota. They drove slowly in rush-hour traffic along Quintus Avenue South, seeming to catch every red light on their way back to the Lucretius. Marcellina reached for her phone from the depths of her backpack and read a short text from her brother, Satyrus.

"Oh my gosh, Aamir, my mom's in the hospital." Not waiting for his response; she nervously pressed the call button with her fingers: "Sy, its Marci, what's going on with Mom? Why is she in the hospital?"

"Calm down, Marci. Mom's okay; she collapsed in the kitchen about ten o'clock this morning. I'm here with her at St. Clemens; she's in the emergency ward, but she's resting comfortably. The doctors have been running tests on her all day. I tried texting and calling, but you never answered. Where've you been?"

"It's a long story, Sy; I'll fill you in later." Marcellina suddenly remembered being with Professor Nero about ten o'clock. "Sy, tell me more about Mom, do they know what happened? Do they know why she collapsed?"

"They've ruled out a stroke, or anything to do with her heart. The only thing they have discovered so far is a bad case of pneumonia—and a nasty bruise above her right eye from the fall. You know Mom, she's always on the go with her book club, her lady's aux—"

"Is Bee with you?"

"No, he came earlier and stayed for a couple of hours. I'll give you three guesses who he brought with him."

"President Valentinian?"

"Yep! And holy cow, Marci, do they ever take unscheduled trips seriously. I mean, they had this place crawling with police, secret service, FBI—you name it. If they wore a badge, they scoured the hospital checking things out."

"What'd you think of the president?"

"He's all right, I guess, but I'll say one thing: he wasn't dressed nearly as well as I imagined he would be. I mean, he wore a drab, ill-fitting toga; utterly bland, and entirely too small for him. He needed one three sizes larger—he's not a little guy. Even his shoes looked old, Marci; you could tell he hadn't polished them in weeks. What can I say, he just didn't look presidential."

"He needs someone like you to take care of him, Sy. Did he say anything?"

"Well, he was never at a loss for words, Marci, and he's got a pretty good sense of humor. He told us this story about how a timberwolf freakishly jumped through a window at the Chalet Aspenia last year. He said the mangy beast killed an FBI agent and that blood spattered everywhere. In fact, two of his best guards were so scratched and mauled they had to retire from service. He told a sad story and all, but the way he portrayed it had us all rolling in the aisles. Still, I find him a little disturbing. All I can say is I wouldn't want to be on his bad side."

"How's Bee doing?"

"You know, our little brother's becoming one cool customer. I'm really proud of him."

"What do you mean?"

"Well, most local politicians get down on their knees and grovel whenever a higher official comes into town—but not Bee. Oh, don't get me wrong, Bee is cordial enough, but he acts like he's bored with the guy, like he's had enough of his bull already. You don't often see other politicians acting that way around nobles. They're usually busy putting on fake smiles."

"That's our Bee, a straight shooter." Marcellina smiled; pleased to see traffic moving faster as she redirected the subject. "Sy, are you going to make my graduation?"

"Afraid not, Marci; I need to stay here with Mom. But if you get one of your friends to video it, I'll look at it later."

"That's all right," she chuckled, "I'll pass on that. Anyway, I'm probably going to skip it myself; I'm late as it is."

"Will you visit Mom before you leave?"

"I'd like to," she replied, looking across at Aamir. "Maybe I can ask my friend to drive me there. Oh, but St. Clemens is clear across town. I'd be cutting it close to get to the airport on time." Just as she considered asking Aamir if he wouldn't mind changing directions, another revelation popped into her head. "Sy, I can't see Mom; I've got a bad cold. They'd never let me in if she's got pneumonia."

"Sorry to hear that, Marci. Well, if we don't see you, have a great birthday and congratulations on your graduation. You worked hard getting your doctorate; we're all very proud of you. Make sure you call me after you get to New York. Oh, and when you're at the university, remember to look up—"

SCREEEECH! Aamir slammed on the breaks to avoid broadsiding a white Magra Commando running a red light at the intersection of

Quintus and Third Street. Momentum from the stop sent them both reeling forward. Though their seat belts held preventing any personal harm, the sudden halt sent Marcellina's phone crashing into the dashboard, smashing into pieces.

"Are you all right?" asked Aamir.

"I think so, but now the back of my neck feels as bad as the back of my head."

Horns honked as Aamir tried restarting the engine. "Come on baby, come on, you can start for me," he pleaded. His old, rusted Toyota struggled to turn over. After what seemed like an hour, it finally roared back to life; its two occupants gratefully continued their journey on down the road.

"Sorry, Marci, you can use my phone if you need to make a call."

"It wasn't your fault, Aamir," she said, putting a hand on his shoulder. "Jackie left two messages, but I'll talk to her when we get to the Lucretius. What concerns me most is that I received a call from my supervisor in New York. I don't have her number memorized; I wonder what she wanted?" Marcellina stared out at the buildings lining the road, "and I wonder who my brother wanted me to look up?"

"Look up, Marci," shouted Aamir. Turning left onto Sextus street a quarter mile east of the university, they observed plumes of black smoke billowing high into the sky. Flashing lights and blaring sirens from police and fire units seized their attention. People of all shapes and sizes littered the sidewalks, gazing up at the raging spectacle. "Marci, I don't think I can get you to Lee's. They've got the entire street blocked off."

"Forget about my dress, Aamir, they're probably closed. Just try getting us back to your parking lot." Marcellina examined the sinister sky. "Oh my gosh; I bet something huge is on fire at the university. Can I still borrow your cell?" Marcellina texted Jacqueline after he handed her the phone.

"Law steps," came the prompt reply.

After parking the sputtering vehicle, Marcellina and Aamir walked past the Publius and Language Arts buildings heading toward the

Lucretius. Marcellina stopped abruptly at the History building. "It's all right, Marci," he said, "I'm here to protect you. Put Nero out of your mind."

She took hold of Aamir's arm as they walked past the frightful building. Marcellina felt short of breath, but managed a gratuitous smile. As they continued walking, they saw hundreds of people dressed in fire-engine-red caps and gowns—some with gold honor cords made of rayon and cotton. Everyone mingled about on the mall's damp enclosure watching a historic edifice go down. Marcellina ran up to her roommate after spotting her sitting on the steps. "Jackie, are you all right?"

Jacqueline quickly stood up and embraced Marcellina; tears streamed down her face. "Two people died, Marci," she began, sniffling, "including Amy Butler." Jacqueline was visibly shaking. "I may not have cared much for her, but I didn't want her to die!" Jacqueline clenched Marcellina tightly as she spoke.

"Its okay, Jackie, it's not your fault." Marcellina peered down at Accalia sitting quietly on the steps. "Do you want to join us, honey?"

Aamir stood idly by as the three women embraced. He watched thirty-foot flames surging high into the sky through the windows of Phi Beta Delta. Flames engulfed the four-story edifice, a structure nearly as old as the university itself. Hundreds of firefighters with ladders and pickaxes worked tirelessly to extinguish the blaze. Aamir watched the men spray the building with water shooting out from six-inch diameter hoses. Due to a strong northwesterly wind, angry smoke made its way across the road to the Lucretius. University officials cancelled the graduation ceremony and warned students to stay outdoors and not get any closer.

"Everything I own was in that house," Jacqueline lamented. "And to think, I just moved in today!"

"I'm so sorry, Jackie. Do they know how it started?"

"I haven't heard," she replied, still sniffling.

"Did you see my brother?"

"No, but I'm sure university officials escorted him and the president out a while ago."

They all stared at the carnage in silence. Suddenly, Aamir spotted a de Havilland Tiger Moth flying low to the ground encircling the campus. The biplane pulled a ninety-foot banner. "Look up again, Marci," he shouted.

"Welcome . . . President . . . Valentinian," she read aloud, squinting her eyes at the print on the streamer.

"No, read the next part."

"Congratulations . . . Marcellina . . . XXX & OOO . . . Sy & Bee." Tears welled in her Persian-blue eyes. "What am I going to do with my two goofy brothers?"

"Your family loves you," Aamir exclaimed. "You deserve to have your accomplishments shouted from the hilltops."

"Congratulations, Marci," said Jacqueline, still sniffling. "Me, too," interjected Accalia, softly.

"Thank you . . . thanks to all of you," Marcellina said, looking around at her friends. "I don't know how I would've gotten through this year without you." More tears flowed from her eyes. Then she looked down at her silver-plated Timex and took note of the time. "I guess we'd better be going, Jackie." Marcellina turned and looked lovingly at Aamir. She gave him a hug followed by a kiss on the cheek. "I'm going to text you every day, and I want you to text me back, you hear?"

"Right after I change my tenth child's diaper."

Marcellina inscribed his image in her mind. The three women remained silent, walking toward Jacqueline's car still parked near their old apartment. They headed for the Dionysius International airport.

"What do you mean my flight has been changed?" argued Marcellina.

"I'm sorry, ma'am," replied the agent, "but we have you down for tomorrow morning, Flight 763 to Kismaayo."

"Kismaayo? I'm supposed to fly to New York!"

"I'm sorry, ma'am; your flight was changed this afternoon."

Marcellina closed her eyes and lowered her head. She knew what it meant; it meant she was no longer part of the UN Social Council, no longer part of a committee developing strategies to improve children's education around the world. Her dream job had ended before it started. It meant Professor Nero had made a call. "Thank you," she replied, "What time does that flight take off tomorrow?"

"Seven, ma'am."

"I'll bet that rat bastard caused this," began Jaqueline. "He did this, didn't he?" Jacqueline spoke with fire in her eyes.

"It's okay, Jackie; I'm willing to put in my dues."

"That co—"

"I mean it, Jackie; I don't want the job if I have to sl—"

Jacqueline appeared stunned. She heard the start of the s-word—enough to cause her mouth to drop open. "Are you telling me that pervert hit on you today?" she interrupted. "I'll kill him, Marci; I'll kill that son of a bi—"

"No, Jackie, let it go. Besides, we have a more pressing matter. Where do you want to sleep tonight?"

Jacqueline stared angrily at passengers boarding Flight 89 to New York. "I've still got a key to the apartment," she said, trying to bring her wrath under control. "The new people don't move in until next week."

After eating a light dinner, Marcellina and Jacqueline, along with Accalia, drove back to their old apartment. The women reminisced for a while before hopping into bed. They lay nestled under two fleece blankets and an old, brown and black afghan given to Marcellina by Ambassador Binaisa. Marcellina rolled to her side and looked lovingly at a dozen red roses standing tall in a drab-green vase on a white table next to the bed. Aamir had given them to her for her thirty-eighth birthday, providing the barren room its only splash of color. "AH-CHOO . . . AH-CHOO . . . AH-CHOO!"

"Bless you," her roommates said.

IX

ISSUE ASCENDANCE

"In other news today," said Henry Llinos to his radio-listening audience, "Michael Mariano, the former Vespids football player, was found dead in his apartment from multiple stab wounds early this morning. Mariano, a long-time Dionysius resident, lived near the swamps in Messalla. You may recall that the province convicted him of killing Lieutenant Governor Hanna Lalia last January. Rather than appeal, he took his chances in the colisseum. He miraculously released the sword from Victor Zetseva's hand, winning back his freedom and preventing his own quick-sword execution. He did so by biding his time, eventually amputating the gladiator's arm near the shoulder. Police have no suspects in custody but are questioning Russian immigrants with close ties to the renowned prizefighter. We go live to Steven Harper who has Sheriff Maurice Crispus standing by . . ."

"Poor bastard," said President Valentinian to no one in particular. Caesar, alone in his bathroom, listened to Llinos while shaving his beard with a Broon Series 4 electric razor. At that moment, his phone began ringing.

"Talk to me, Larry. . . . What's that? Oh yeah, Milan is a picturesque place, but way too many Arian Christians living there for my tastes. Tina would fit right in, though; they're her kind of people. What's that? . . . Yeah, the recession hit Dionysius pretty hard. They closed the Magra plant in Milan, you know. What's that? . . . Well, Ambrose seems to have his act together. He's a charming fellow when you get to know him—so is his brother, Satyrus. But, geez, Ambrose is trying to do some strange things there, Larry. I mean, get a load of this: he sent some Latino kid—some drunk, a punk laid off from the plant—to go talk to those bastards in Japan. Yeah, like that beaner has a chance in hell changing their minds!

"The senators all tell me his plans for the province are ludicrous. Geez, he wants to legalize homos and completely overhaul tax and welfare legislation. And, get a load of this: he wants the churches and other non-profits to manage chronic welfare recipients. What's more, Larry, he won't spend a dime on big business. I don't know how he intends to create jobs with that attitude. What's that? . . . Well that's the crazy part, Larry; the people and the board all seem to love him. What's that? . . . No, I had to cancel my speech at the Lucretius; some idiot set fire to a sorority next door to it."

"Val, are you ready?"

The president ignored his wife and kept talking. "Get this, Larry: Police escorted Ambrose's sister to jail for inciting a riot just before I arrived. I never met her; she must be the recluse in the family. Anyway, now I'm hearing reports about this Mariano character being murdered in his apartment. I tell you, things are not looking swell in Dionysius.

What's that? . . . No, they still don't have a bishop—and that concerns me, you know. Thanks to my idiot brother, many Muslims are moving into that province. That region just might become a religious hotbed if the right person isn't in charge. I'm beginning to think Ambrose is in over his head. He could use some ecclesiastical guidance."

"Val, are you ready?"

The president kept talking to his advisor. "Damn it, Larry, if governors like Probus—God rest his soul—don't start replacing themselves with experienced businessmen, then they ought to at least appoint someone with religious qualifications. Larry, if I know that an official is serious about Christ, I'll approve his application in a heartbeat. In fact, draw up a proclamation to that effect and I'll sign it. Have it sent out to all the governors and directors. What's that? . . . Oh, yeah, I met the governor's girl; she's also his lieutenant. Wowza, Larry; let me tell you, she's a knockout. She is one fine-lookin' babe. If Tina gets any saggier, I'm thinking of stealing his old lady. . . . What's that? How should I remember . . . oh, let me see, her name is Mary . . . Mary something . . ."

Justina walked partway up the steps leading to the second floor. She had no choice; Caesar hadn't responded when she shouted to him from the chalet's ground floor. "C'mon, Val; I want to get going!"

"Coming, dear," he shouted back. "Look, Larry, I've got to go. I told Tina we would drive to the new White House in that vintage '48 Buick . . . what do you mean? Sure, I've still got it; it purrs like a kitten. I tell you, Larry, it's going to be great getting out of this hole; this place never had a good feel to it. What's that? . . . You bet, Larry, you're welcome to stop by the new place and have a cold one. What's that? . . . No, as far as I can tell I have nothing wrong with my hearing. Why do you ask?"

Augustus descended the stairs wearing a tight-fitting, double-breasted, grey pinstripe suit. He wore a white-collared shirt and a narrow black tie to accompany it. Jenkins handed him a solid grey, smooth-felt fedora when he reached the bottom of the steps. Justina's eyes grew large, and she smiled broadly as he donned his hat. "Oh darling, you look positively gangster," she said, bringing her hands to her mouth.

Caesar gazed lusciously back at his wife. "And you, my dear, look positively ravishing." Justina wore a wartime, deep-purple velvet tea dress with ruffle trim. She had a matching purple hat with the brim turned up, the left side tilted higher than the right. "And what do we have under here?" he questioned, grasping her dress in the front at the V-neck pulling the material away from her succulent breasts.

Justina's eyes grew wide. "Stop that," she scolded, brushing his hands away from her bosom. "Not until we move into the new house. Besides, you don't want to do it in front of the help!"

They drove out of Chalet Aspenia's parking lot in their metallic maroon-and-white convertible. It boasted 150 ponies up front from a 320.2 cubic in-line eight-cylinder engine. The car had become famous for being one of America's first motorcars to feature automatic transmission. Against the advice of field agents running alongside the vehicle, the Valentinians meandered down the road with the roof pulled back so their loving fans could adore their period outfits.

"Wave to everyone, Tina."

"I can't, Val; I'm too nervous. You need to stay in the middle of the road; you keep veering to the right. You nearly clipped that poor man on my side." Justina pointed to a Secret Service agent on a motorcycle slightly ahead and to the right of the motorcade. "Are you sure you've got a license to drive?"

"What'd you say, baby?"

Justina wagged her head side to side. "Honestly, I think you're losing your hearing," she muttered. "STAY IN THE MIDDLE OF THE ROAD," she shouted. After giving her husband an exasperated stare, Justina began waving to the crowd. *Just get me there in one piece,* she thought to herself. She had just started relaxing when she received a call on her phone from an unidentified number. "Yes?"

"*Buen dia, Señora Justina.*"

"Maximus," she shrieked. The First Lady quickly changed to a muted voice, turning her head away from her husband. "How did you get this number?"

Magnus Adolfo Muñoz Maximus was former President Adalberto Rodriguez's playboy nephew. Following Rodriguez's mysterious death thirteen years ago—when his plane suddenly lost power investigating immigration travesties along the Mexico-Arizona border—a fierce political battle began for his replacement. Senator Maximus, who hailed from the New Allegiance Party, unexpectedly became the winner. Most people believed his victory was flawed, but no one brought forth any evidence against it. People observed that the young leader rose inexplicably fast through the ranks after forming relationships with Los Zetas and the Gulf Cartel, two rival gangs competing for drug trafficking into Texas.

Justina had been Maximus's first real love despite being President Rodriguez's wife at the time. They frequently snuck off to exotic villas in Punta Mita whenever Rodriguez travelled on business. She had shown Maximus how to please a woman. "Now, place your fingers here," she would say, "and push down gently . . . not so hard, Maximus; we're not made of metal, you know!" Though Maximus had married and divorced twice since Justina's departure, he still longed for her embrace—at least that's what she thought.

"Mexico's calling; it wants you back, Tina. It's time you left your murderous husband and came back here where you belong."

"That's impossible, Maximus; you know I can't return to Mexico."

"Then I cannot guarantee your safety. We have proof your husband killed my uncle, and I plan to avenge his death."

"Maximus . . . please, you do not want to kill Val!"

"And after I kill your precious husband, Señora, I'll take over the southwestern provinces—consider it payment in full. My lady, well over half the people living in those provinces are Mexican citizens. They'll fight for us when the right time comes."

Justina shut off her phone and sat dumbfounded, blankly staring out at the crowd lining the road as the Buick rounded a bend leading up to the White House. *What am I supposed to do with that? I can't tell Val that Maximus spoke to me directly; he'll suspect an affair. If that's the case, he won't trust me anymore, and . . . he'll find a way to dispose of me. But, if what Maximus told me is true and I don't tell Val, the country may be in peril. I can't risk the lives of millions of innocent people, even if most of them are merely locals.*

"There she is, baby," proclaimed Caesar, pointing straight ahead.

"Oh my gosh, Val, it's beautiful; it's simply magnificent." Justina's mouth dropped open as she gazed out at the impressive structure.

Their new home, enormous and exquisite, mimicked Austin Hall, a classroom building at Harvard University for students studying the law. Architect H. H. Richardson, in a unique Romanesque Revival style, built the law building in 1882–1884. Similarly, the center portion of the new White House had two stories with matching wings on each side. A glass-enclosed, hundred-meter pool with surrounding conservatory extended rearwards from the center of the building. When viewed from above, the pool gave the property a T shape. Three oval arches, made of light-colored stone—mostly Ohio sandstone—greeted visitors as they arrived at the front. Ornate reddish stone around the perimeter formed most of the exterior surrounding the magnificent edifice.

"Do you really like it, baby? I chose it out of respect for Joe since he and I were best friends at Harvard—and because he recommended me for president if anything happened to him. I thought I needed to do something to pay my respects. That red brick sure looks stunning in these Colorado trees, don't you think?"

"It's gorgeous, Val," she said as the motorcade came to a stop in front of the arches. "Oh, I love it; I can see you put a lot of effort into it. But honey, if it's mostly red, can we still call it a White House?"

The emperor shut off the engine and waited for his guards to come round before exiting the coupe. He looked at Justina with a proud look on his face. "Call it whatever you like, baby."

A group of handpicked reporters assembled in front of the house; everyone else stayed behind a wrought-iron fence five hundred feet away. Augustus gave a short speech and cut the ribbon using an oversized pair of scissors. He carried Justina over the threshold, entering their new home amidst lofty applause and camera flashes. Two exuberant boys, Gratian and Ian, greeted them at the door, outfitted in royal-purple swimming trunks, snorkels, and flippers.

"The pool's great, Father," said Gratian. "Will you join us?"

"Daddy, they've got a dinosaur tongue for a diving board," said Ian, tugging repeatedly on his father's pinstripe suit.

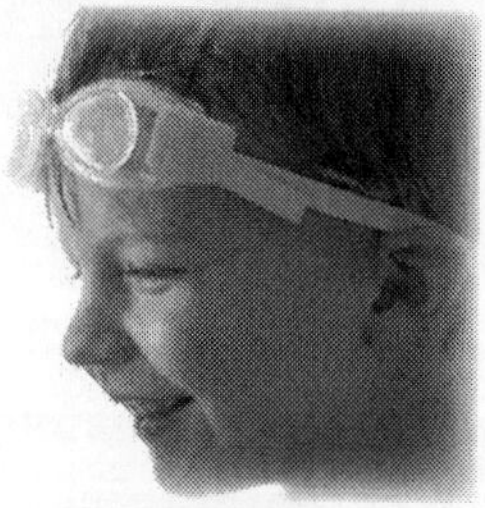

"In a minute, boys . . ."

"Whoa, I know what that means," Justina interjected, gazing deeply into her husband's eyes. "Now, Val, you go with them; today is family day, remember? I'll be shopping with the girls; you need to spend time with the boys."

"All right, dear, but you stay in that dress until I wriggle you out of it." Before she could respond, he had grasped the front of her dress and pulled it away from her succulent breasts just like he had done before. Caesar had a broad smile on his face.

Gratian walked chest deep in the ninety-two-degree water. The pool resembled a small lagoon tucked into the farthest reaches of the Australian rainforest. Ginger, dwarf harpullia, ferns, native jasmine, and orchids were just a few of the hundreds of plants surrounding the pristine water. At the pool's deep end stood a sixty-foot-tall, scaly green tyrannosaurus rex emerging from the flora. One of its knees, a hand, and its tongue all served as diving platforms of varying heights. Gratian tossed a tennis ball at Augustus. "Father, who is Procopius?"

Ian splashed the water excitedly. "Gratian said pee, Gratian said pee!"

"Stop that," hollered the president, reaching with his left hand to catch the ball. He looked over at Gratian. "Who mentioned anything about him?"

"Uncle Jules talked about him a couple of weeks ago."

"Well, I guess you're old enough to understand the truth." Caesar cocked his right arm and threw the ball back at Gratian, landing well short of the mark. The president soon discovered he had no strength in his arm.

"Daddy, you throw like a girl," said Ian.

With concern on his face, Caesar tried several times to raise his right arm. He soon became more anxious after tingling and numbness appeared in the limb.

"What's wrong, Father?" asked Gratian.

"Nothing . . . nothing, Son," he replied, "just an old shoulder injury I got in the war." Caesar squeezed his arm tightly, trying to instill life into the useless extremity.

After a minute passed, the president sighed in relief, feeling strength and sensation returning. "Ian, go tell Mr. Jenkins daddy needs a cocktail. Tell him to make it a strong one." After Ian left, and after submerging his body underwater to conceal quivering muscles, Caesar began telling Gratian about Procopius—his story took all of two minutes. "So there you have it, Son; Procopius is President Julianus's cousin, his one and only heir. He had every right to succeed him to the presidency."

"But Uncle Jules says he's an imposter, Father. He says President Julianus had no heir."

"Uncle Jules says those things because that's what I tell him to say. See, your half-witted uncle may be our nation's eastern president, but on certain matters, he still takes orders from me."

Gratian splashed himself with water, desperate to clear the confusion playing out in his mind. *If Procopius was President Julianus's heir, then he should be president—not Father. His family should be in this house—not ours—not me.* Gratian looked at his dad after water stopped dripping from his face.

"Father, why are you telling Uncle Jules to lie? And why are you deceiving the American people?"

"Grow up, Gratian," the president snapped. "Truth isn't something that is. It's not a singular reality; it's not an absolute. It's not anything that exists out there," he continued, pointing toward the plants. "It's something you make, a perception you create. Everyone has a unique way of looking at the world, Gratian; everyone designs their own truth in their head. You need to come to grips with that if you ever hope to be president one day. You must learn to fight for your truth over the purported truth of others."

Gratian turned his back on his dad and began exiting the pool. He turned his head around and remarked, "None of us have any right to be in this house, Father. Mr. Procopius should be here instead."

"That's enough," the president hollered. "Stop acting like a righteous little snot and get back in this pool until I dismiss you!" Caesar watched his son slink his body back into the water. Tears welled in Gratian's brown, youthful eyes—infuriating Augustus even more. "Now listen you virtuous bastard," the president continued, "I did what I did for the betterment of this nation, and don't you ever forget that! What do you know about anything? You sit in your room all day playing video games! The truth is, I helped President Jovianus. Yes, Son, I helped my friend Joe become president of this beloved nation despite knowing Procopius had every right to it. We knew he was Julianus's maternal cousin, but—"

"But what?"

The president loathed interruptions, but he chose to ignore it this time—at least Gratian was taking part in the conversation. "Procopius is a patriot," Caesar continued, losing the sting in his voice. "He's also related to former President Constantine—third or fourth great-nephew, I believe. The Constantines hold considerable power in this country, you know." The president looked off in the distance, gazing up at the green scales on the tyrannosaurus rex. "However, if I'm not mistaken, he's currently dating Maxima, one of Leonard's great-granddaughters.

People are questioning whether that's even legal." Caesar returned his stare at Gratian. "In any case, boy, Procopius happily served our country in Afghanistan and never came forward to assert his right to the presidency—until now.

"Didn't anyone tell him?"

Augustus smiled. "Not when they believed him dead, Son. See, Jovianus and I faked his death." Caesar looked up at the big dinosaur again. "Damn we were good. We wrote up papers and sent a grotesque body back to his family. Digging up a corpse isn't easy, Gratian. Luckily, a friend of ours who worked for Marty's Landscaping donated some heavy equipment." Caesar looked down at the youth. "We did it so they had someone to bury, you understand. Why, we even convinced his company commander that the sergeant he had in his unit was pretending to be Procopius. Damn we were clever!"

Gratian looked horrified. "How could you do that, Father?"

Caesar ignored his son's reaction and continued speaking matter-of-factly. "In retrospect, we should've just killed the bastard. It would have made things a lot simpler today. But, if I recall, we didn't want his death on our conscience. Boy, were we naïve. Gratian, Joe and I knew Procopius was pagan. He didn't give a rat's ass what religion folks preached or believed in—and that kind of thinking didn't square with President Constantine's ideology for a unified nation. Procopius would allow Muslims into this country today if we let him be president—just as that apostate Julianus did before him. They both had that same cockeyed vision that we would all be better off if we just melded together. Poppycock!"

Gratian remained quiet, his tears slowly drying.

"Admittedly, Gratian," Caesar continued, "people once came to this country and incorporated themselves into our American Dream. They shed their old customs and became . . . well, American. But that doesn't happen anymore. Immigrants today staunchly maintain their old way of thinking. They want to live in America, but they don't want to become American. When that happens, our country becomes a mosaic, a patchwork quilt—not a melting pot nation. President Constantine—God rest his soul—recognized that fact and wanted no part of it. Leonard refused to let us become a collection of separatists because he knew it would weaken us. Son, Procopius may be a distant Constantine, but he doesn't think at all like Leonard. If Jovianus and I had allowed him the presidency, Leonard would be turning over in his grave. We did what we did, Son, not to better our station, but to preserve an ideology President Constantine started some thirty-odd years ago."

Gratian crossed his arms in front of himself; he had difficulty swallowing his father's words. "Father, Uncle Jules is letting Muslims into the country. Why doesn't that bother you?"

"Your uncle is an idiot—and I've told him that to his face. He's doing that because he believes I took too many troops when I moved here to Colorado. But I've told him time and again that Mexico is an imminent threat—that moron just won't believe me. Anyway, Gratian, he's letting Goths into the country to bolster his legions. But he's going about it the wrong way. He thinks he's doing them a favor, saving them from the Huns. In reality, he's just pissing them off. He's killing off their elders and converting the remainder to Christ."

Caesar gazed out at a grove of apricot orchids. "Geez, Gratian, he's converting most of those poor bastards into Arians just to appease his god-awful wife! It's gotten so bad, no Goth will fight for America," Caesar returned his gaze to his son, "except one . . . oddly enough. I know of one Visigoth colonel—I don't know his angle, and I've forgotten his name—but he's acting strangely cooperative. For some reason, he's convincing those beggars to enlist in your uncle's army."

Gratian was still not convinced of his father's innocence. "Father," he began, "I understand why you helped President Jovianus succeed Julianus to the presidency over Procopius's rightful claim. But what I can't understand is why you killed Jovianus—the man you claim was your friend—and after he'd served in office for only eight months."

Caesar's hair bristled; the question caught him off guard. He thought nobody knew about his private little murder. He paused several seconds and looked directly at Gratian. "Well, I see you've become a man, haven't you. Do you realize I killed an FBI agent and two of my best guards for knowing that information?" Caesar began circling Gratian in the pool. "Yes, I killed President Jovianus. I killed my best friend, Joe. I killed my ally at Harvard and my closest companion in the war. I killed him despite the fact that he was renewing Christianity as our nation's sole religion. I killed him despite the fact that he was ousting wretched Muslims from our homeland. And I killed him, Son, despite the fact that he was restoring Leonard's vision for our future."

Gratian felt his heartbeat surge as his father hastened his pace around him. "But it's not what you think," continued Caesar. "Joe's popularity plummeted after he sold Alaska and Hawaii to the Chinese to pay down our debt. Joe wasn't just an unpopular president; he'd become the most hated man in America. It was just a matter of time before someone took him out. My friend had a bull's-eye pinned to his chest, and no one could do anything about it. Even our defense agencies felt helpless to prevent his assassination." Caesar rolled his eyes as another thought popped into his mind. "Now that I think of it, I thought your Uncle Jules might be the one to kill him."

Gratian waded toward the deep end of the pool. He swam much better than his father. If his dad attacked, he stood his best chance if their feet never touched bottom.

"So, as you've come to learn," continued Caesar, "I did indeed kill President Jovianus. But Son, I did it for two very important reasons: First, I had confirmed reports that The Covenant, The Gladius, and The Arm of the Radicalist—a Christian militant group, better known as the Cigars—planned to kidnap him and nail him to a cross. I couldn't let my friend die that way, Gratian, not a terrible death like that. So, I made sure he died peacefully in his sleep. I asphyxiated him with poisonous gas through a ventilation duct at the Manhattan Commons Hotel."

"And?"

"Don't think you can escape me, boy!" The president clung to the side of the pool as he resumed his speech. "And I couldn't leave the timing of Jovianus's death up to chance. I didn't know when the Cigars would strike—sooner or later." He gestured with a hand back and forth as he spoke. "I had to kill my friend and assume the presidency before Procopius returned from the war—before the Constantines discovered he was alive. Son, the public despised Joe so much they would have replaced him with Procopius in a heartbeat; they would have insisted that heathen take up his rightful place in the White House. Oh, don't you get it, Son? The public admires me, or should I say, Jules and me. Except for this recession, we've led an exemplary administration. The public won't expel us for Procopius as long as we maintain that he's a fraud."

"Why don't we just kill him, Father?"

Caesar stopped dead in his tracks. "What did you say?"

Gratian looked forthrightly at his father; he had no more tears in his eyes. "I said, why don't we just kill Procopius. If his death means safeguarding President Constantine's vision, then I want to be part of it. Besides, you wished you'd done it earlier, remember? You said it would have made life simpler. Well, Father, let's simplify life."

The president gazed into his son's brown, youthful eyes. "You mean that, don't you, boy," he said softly. He stared at his son's face for signs of equivocation. "You get it," he continued, "you really get it; you understand." Then, in a booming voice that would have made a live t-rex quiver, he shouted, "OH MY GOD, GRATIAN; YOU'RE READY!"

The emperor let go of the side of the pool and swam out to congratulate his heir; he gave his teenage boy a warm, affectionate hug. "You know, Gratian, killing a man isn't easy, but I always knew you had it in you. Oh, Son, you don't know how long I've waited for this day—you know we named you after my father," he continued, giddy with excitement. "He'd be so proud of you—I'm so proud of you! All right, come to my office after you've showered, and I'll show you how Uncle Jules and I plan to dispose of Mr. Procopius."

"Daddy," whined Ian, returning to the pool, both hands holding a crystal goblet, "Mr. Jenkins says this is gin and 'ic on the rocks. But I don't see any rocks."

Caesar grabbed the cup from his youngest son and flung the liquid into the flora. "Go back and tell Jenkins to break out the champagne. Tell him to bring it to my office. Oh, and tell him we'll need two goblets."

After showering, Augustus slipped into an unpretentious green-and-white toga. He entered his office on the second floor for the very first time and closed the door behind him. Looking up, he noticed a charcoal-stenciled mosaic of the twelve provinces decorating white ceiling tiles, and a large gold-plated chandelier hanging down in the middle. Twelve-foot-high walls, elaborately robed in French Victorian wallpaper, supported four-by-six-foot oil paintings of every American president.

Each painting, enclosed in an ornate russet frame, included a short insignia touting that person's legacy: President George Washington, *Against All Odds*; Thomas Jefferson, *Against All Tyranny*; Abraham Lincoln, *All Men are Created Equal*; William Jefferson Clinton, *Prosperity to the People*; George Walker Bush, *Admonish All Oppressors*; Barack Hussein Obama, *Restoring Faith in America*; Leonard Constantine I, *Autocratic Christian Guidance*; Flavius Claudius Julianus, *Religious Freedom to All*; and Flavius Jovianus Augustus, *One Land, One People, One God.*

Three windows towered in the southern-most part of the room; milky-white satin curtains draped over them and flowed down along their sides. Stained glass illuminated the president's desk with red, blue, yellow, and green colors while surrendering a striking view of the forested landscape. Caesar sat down in his brown aniline-leather chair for the very first time. *Not bad,* he thought, swiveling himself in a circle. *I wonder what they'll say about me on my canvas.* He brought his chair to a halt and removed his phone from his pocket. "Valens on-screen," he texted Ms. Clarkston.

"Jenkins here," she replied.

"In."

The door to his office swung wide as an aged man appeared. Dressed in all black, he had a small white cotton towel draped over his forearm. Jenkins entered the room carrying several items: a bottle of

Dom Perignon White Gold Jeroboam Champagne, a silver-plated bucket filled with ice, two tall, fluted crystalline goblets, and a stack of four-by-four-inch coasters stolen earlier in the day from Chalet Aspenia.

"Where would you like me to put this, sir?"

"Hmmm," replied Caesar, his eyes straining as he clung to his phone.

"Excuse me, sir, I didn't catch that?"

"Hmmmm," the emperor replied again, motioning for him to leave.

Jenkins quickly placed the items on the desk and hustled toward the door. "Yes sir, I can see you have an important call; I'll take my leave right away."

No sooner had he left than Ms. Clarkston sent another text: "okay?"

The emperor sat motionless in his chair, trembling from fear. His ability to speak, though still impaired, was gradually improving. Caesar steadied his hands and formulated a reply to his secretary: "Fine," he typed—but it took him three tries to do it. After wiping slobber from his mouth, the president leaned back in his chair and closed his eyes. He took several deep breaths, attempting to regain his composure.

"Rutherford here," Ms. Clarkston texted a few minutes later.

"Beer," the president texted back. After a few minutes, Larry Rutherford, Caesar's chief advisor, entered the rectangular office holding a frosty glass of Aspen Light. "Hey, hey, Larry," said the president in a spirited voice, rising from his desk. He walked over to greet his consultant. "I'm glad you made it," he continued, forgetting the linguistic troubles he had experienced a moment ago.

"How's it going, Chief?"

"Fine, Larry, it's my first day in this glorious new red house," he began, raising an arm, pointing in all directions. Then he stroked his chin. "Hmm, you know, Tina was wondering what to name this place. I think I'll call it the Red House. Oh, and I drove the Buick today, but I think I told you that this morning." The president looked around the room as if someone might be listening. "And Larry, Tina's wearing this fabulous purple dress that's open in the front . . . if you know what I mean." He elbowed his advisor in the side after speaking. "Oh, and I had a terrific talk with Gratian in the pool this afternoon. Guess what, Larry; he's on board with everything we're doing. You'll get a chance to talk to him and see for yourself; I'm expecting him any moment. Gosh, Larry, I'm so proud of him I'm bursting at the seams; Gratian is really coming into his own. After he learns to kill, he'll make one hell of a president. How's the beer?"

"I found him here when I came to pull back the sheets, my lady," said a Red House maid.

"Thank you, Dorothy, I'll take it from here," Justina replied. "Oh, I have packages downstairs; would you kindly bring them up and put them in my room." After the housekeeper left, the First Lady cautiously approached her stepson. Gratian lay curled in a fetal position on his bed; he had tears in his eyes. Justina sat down beside him, still wearing her deep-purple velvet tea dress with ruffle trim. "You know, honey," she began, stroking his hair and speaking softly, "I first met you when you were six. We all flew kites in the park that day on an Easter weekend. You had that big black kite, a shark. Do you remember?"

Gratian stayed quiet; he slowly turned over and looked up at his stepmother. "I remember your string broke," she continued, placing a hand on his shoulder. "It wasn't your fault, Gratian; things like that happen. But I remember you ran after it like there was no tomorrow. I enjoyed watching you run; you're so fast."

"I never caught up to it."

"I know; the wind was blowing pretty hard that day. I think we found it stuck in a tree the next morning."

Gratian nodded. "Father's a murderer."

"I know that, too, honey. See, as a leader, your father has to do whatever is best for this country. Sometimes that means killing people; are you prepared for that?"

Strain appeared on his face; his whole body shook with fear as new tears welled in his eyes. "I can't do that, Mom," he said in a terrified voice, "I just can't do that!" Gratian turned and looked away from his stepmother.

"It's okay, honey." She resumed stroking his hair, trying to calm him down. "Nobody is asking you to be your father. You don't have to follow his example. Oh, honey, you can be whatever you want."

"But Father expects—"

"I don't care what your father expects," she interrupted. "Gratian, we just want you to be happy. Oh, honey, don't cry. If you want to lead this nation, then fine; if not, then that's okay too. Just know that we'll always love you."

They remained quiet for a moment before Gratian finally spoke up. "Will I go to hell if I kill someone?"

Justina stared into his brown, youthful eyes. "I don't think I can answer that. Whether you choose to take someone's life, like your father, is strictly a personal matter. I think it hinges on your intent—what's in your heart at the time. If you're doing it for anger, spite, or personal gain, I'm guessing it's wrong. However, if you're doing it for the betterment of others, especially an entire nation, then it might be all right. I just don't know, Gratian. Perhaps you should speak to a bishop about that."

"His speech is going to start any minute, Larry," said the president. "Can I get you another cold one?" Caesar texted Ms. Clarkston on his phone concerning the whereabouts of Gratian while awaiting his advisor's response.

Rutherford took his last gulp of beer. "No, Chief, one is plenty for me."

Several moments later, the president's phone went off. "I can't talk now, baby; Procopius's speech is about to start."

"I heard you were summoning Gratian," said Justina. "I finally got him settled down; he's been crying in his room since you left him. What did you guys talk about?"

"He's what?

"Forget it, Val . . . we'll talk about him tonight."

"Tonight, huh?" Disappointment shone on Caesar's face as he looked across the desk at his adviser; then he looked down and lowered his voice. "Say, baby, are you still wearing that sexy dress?"

"Go listen to your speech, honey." Justina clicked off her phone.

"Well, I've enjoyed the day up until now, Larry; scratch what I said about Gratian. Ian will be ready before he is."

"Sorry to hear that, Chief."

"It's my fault, really," the president continued, looking around the room. "I spent too many hours working and not enough time with him. Marina spoiled him rotten."

"Do you still keep in touch with her?"

"Oh, god no, Larry; I wanted nothing to do with her after I found out she's a switch-hitter in bed. But Gratian still visits her a few days each month."

"Pardon me, Chief, but isn't Justina bisexual? I mean, wasn't she the one having sex with Marina?"

"It's different with Tina, Larry—by god, that woman was born for sex. I couldn't take my eyes off her at President Rodriguez's funeral. Cripes, Larry, after I brought her back to Washington, I had to stop taking her to football games. The lions would get an erection and stop mauling the players. The Liberties lost out on some easy halftime points."

Rutherford chuckled. "Well, Caesar, perhaps we should change the subject. However, I do have one more item to discuss regarding the First Lady. We learned that she received a call from Mexico this morning. Do you happen to know who she talked to?"

"I'm the president, Larry," he snapped, "course I know who she talked to; it's my job to know. She conversed with Mr. Magnus Adolfo Muñoz Maximus, her former lover."

"President Maximus?"

"No, Larry, *Presidente* Maximus! I know all about their sordid affair—you're not my only adviser."

"Of course not, Caesar, I didn't mean to insult—"

"Those Mexican bastards think they're so clever, Larry," the president interrupted, leaning back in his brown leather chair as he spoke. "They dress their soldiers like civilians, and they've started using narcos."

"I'm not familiar—"

"Cheap tanks . . . beefed-up trucks, really. They fortify pick-ups and SUVs with steel plates and then mount small canons on them. Drug czars use 'em all the time."

"Why would their military . . . oh, I get it; their military is building something there, aren't they? But they want to make it look like it's nothing more than a struggle between warring cartels, right?"

"Bingo, Larry. Our intelligence revealed plutonium shipments across the Texas border. I think they're building an underground nuclear missile facility. And guess who they'll be aiming at in the future?"

"Why us?"

Caesar formed an anguished look on his face. "Well, Larry, maybe 'cause I killed their former president."

"You killed Rodriguez?"

"By accident! I was trying to kill Maximus at the time. That bastard playboy began shipping drugs into Texas with help from Los Zetas. We thought Maximus was going up in that plane, Larry, not the president. What can I say; our intelligence got it wrong! We heard that beaner planned to inspect one of his heroin shipments across the border. Instead, the president went up to inspect the bridge into Roma. It's a crying shame, Larry. Rodriguez had my deepest respects."

"Do they suspect—"

"Well, you'd think so . . . that happened thirteen years ago, Larry. I wouldn't be surprised if Maximus tried avenging his uncle's death. But then again, maybe that squirt is just looking for more power. Whatever the reason, Larry, he's chosen to build south of the border because he knows that territory so well."

"How soon before they're operational?

"Who cares; I'll annihilate that bastard before he gets one rocket into the air." A broad smile replaced his anguished appearance.

Rutherford stepped back. He looked inquisitively at the president, and then in a sheepish voice, he asked, "Are we operational?"

Augustus leaned forward. "Five of 'em, Larry; five of 'em are set and ready to go. All I have to do is push these buttons," he said, pointing to the console on his desk.

"When did they come online?"

"Three days ago—the last space mission put the final pieces together. Those babies are armed, Larry; they're armed and ready to launch at my command. And in another year, we'll double that number to ten. Just think of the precision; I can destroy a shed without nickin' the garage, or I can wipe out all of Mexico City. Star Wars is here, Larry; it's finally a reality. I know President Reagan would be pleased. I know I'm sleeping better knowing those babies are up there. So, if Maximus tries anything stupid, he won't know what hit him."

"Fantastic, Chief, but has Justina said anything to you about Maximus?"

"No, and she won't, either, not if she knows what's good for her."

"Mr. President, I have your brother on the screen," said Ms. Clarkston into the intercom.

Caesar gazed at a sixty-inch screen that lowered from the ceiling ten feet in front of his desk. "Geez, Jules, you look like hell. Are you getting any sleep?"

Flavius Julius Valens, affectionately known to his family as "Jules," was Caesar's younger brother by seven years. At five foot eight, 140 pounds, he had a considerably smaller physique than Augustus. Valens had grown up on his family's orchard in Fredericksburg, Virginia, where he worked picking apples until his early thirties. A quiet man, he had a good head for numbers and assisted with the plantation's bookkeeping. He wasn't a half-bad handyman, either, getting most of his knowledge talking to patrons at Pete's hardware store a few blocks west of the orchard.

Valens had moved off the woodlot and into a cottage after marrying Albia Domnica, or "Al" for short. He met his wife while buying okra, radishes, carrots, and other organic vegetables at a nearby earth market. Al, a truncated, redheaded woman, had initially presented herself as having a pleasant demeanor and a fine sense of humor. Unfortunately, she bestowed her fiery temper after their wedding. She took after her father, Petronius Domnica, an Arian Christian and county prosecutor. Though a mere local, he behaved like a noble, caring as little for the innocent as he did for the guilty.

During their tumultuous marriage, Al behaved like an unappeasable bitch. She constantly complained about their tiny bungalow and her husband's unwillingness to ameliorate his station. As a child, she had grown accustomed to seeing her father socialize with the biggest and brightest the province had to offer. She felt embarrassed by her husband's steadfast alienation; he pretty much kept his nose in the plantation's books. Begrudgingly, Al bore Valens two plain and homely daughters, Carosa and Anastasia. From the start, she taught them to loathe their father, lest he change his sequestered ways. Much later, she produced a male heir, Valentinianus Galates—whom she willingly conceived—but only after Jules promised to convert to Arian Christianity.

Valens felt lost, misplaced, as if his life had gone astray before Caesar offered to share his presidency. He jubilantly accepted the invitation to become the United Providence's eastern leader more so to escape his ill-natured wife than improve the nation's welfare.

"Where do I sign up?" he had asked. However, as ill prepared as he was for marriage, Valens felt even less prepared for the labors awaiting him as president. "I won't get any sleep until Procopius is dead, and you stop stealing troops out from under me," he had said.

Augustus didn't know what to make of his brother. They were as different as their age and physiques. Val, a soldier all his life, led a more obstreperous life than Jules. He'd been, by most accounts, a boorish, controlling, and highly competitive man—a scheming militant who craved power. Although ill-mannered—incapable of holding a fork—he didn't pride himself on being refined, but on out-hustling, and out-muscling, any man alive.

Jules, on the other hand, had grown skittish and cheap since his marriage to Al. Though cultured and refined—he knew the names of fine wines—he had become an excitable twit whose only passion in life, other than dodging his wife, was watching his money advance. Valens nickel-and-dimed his way through life, a trait he had arduously developed overseeing the books. Though just as mean-spirited as his brother, he lacked the prowess to confront people directly. He possessed the capacity to kill—a necessary trait for any American president—but he needed an agent to do the work for him.

"Would you calm down?" snapped President Valentinian. "Look, Jules, I've already explained this a hundred times; we need troops in the west to guard against a Mexican invasion. Maximus is crazy, Brother. Besides, aren't Visigoths enlisting in your army?"

"Yeah, well, they're not exactly swelling the ranks."

Caesar stared hard at the screen. "Really, I can't imagine why not. You're only killing their grandparents and dumping their dead bodies into the ocean. You'd think those Bantu would be jumping for joy to join forces with you. What a bunch of ungrateful bastards."

The president turned his head and whispered to Rutherford, "Larry, my brother's a whiz with numbers—and by God, he'll get us out of this recession—but when it comes to soldiering . . . well, he's got peach fuzz upstairs."

"Yeah, well, I'm not doing anything the Huns wouldn't do."

"Jules, you idiot," hollered Caesar, "Visigoths are trying to escape the Huns. That's why they asked for our help in the first place. Besides, Huns don't ask favors once they've killed someone's relatives!"

"Yeah, well, we can't afford to take in their sick and dying. We have a recession here, you know. I think I made that pretty clear to their leader." Following his remark, Valens stood up and began walking out of his office. "You explain it to him, Theo."

"Hello, Mr. President, this is Brigadier General Theodosius at your service. It's nice to see you again, sir." The general sat in President Valens's chair looking straight into the camera. A strapping man with a dreadful temper, Theodosius had once served as one of President Valentinian's generals. He moved quickly through the ranks until a year ago when he lost two legions of soldiers at the battle of Al Mukalla, Yemen.

American troops went there to oust President Ali Abdullah Temani on grounds of government corruption—proposing to limit the people's rights under their constitution. The campaign should have taken a few days at most, and no American soldiers should have been lost.

The general, however, suffered a nervous breakdown after his father, Theodosius the Elder—a senior military man in Valentinian's army—got embarrassingly drunk at a White House party. The Elder made a pass at Justina, and Val had quietly executed him two days later. After learning of his father's fate, Theodosius suffered onerous grief and depression. As a result, he made tactical errors invading the port where Temani and his men held out.

Caesar jumped at the sight of his former commander. "Theodosius, what are you doing in Washington? Didn't I fire your miserable ass? Last I heard, you were shoveling manure in Barcelona. Now get Jules back here!"

The general watched Valens close the door behind him. "I'm afraid that's impossible, Mr. President," he replied, turning to face the camera. "Your brother has a migraine; he's gone off to lie down for a while."

"Don't tell me you're in command of this operation?"

Theodosius ignored Caesar's implication and gently nodded his head. "Mr. President, Procopius's speech has begun. Contact will occur at precisely twenty-thirty hours. Do you wish to view the feed?"

"You screw this up, you donkey, and I'll have your head on a platter—OF COURSE I WANT TO VIEW THE FEED!" A few moments later, they saw their archrival looming large on their respective screens. Procopius stood tall in front of Lincoln on the grounds of the National Mall. They also saw Maxima Constantia standing behind him in the background. Two-million cheering fans—the most ever since Dr. King's famous speech in August, 1963—came to hear Procopius speak on his entitlement to the presidency.

> "I, TOO, HAVE A DREAM THAT FRAUD AND CORRUPTION SHALL BE UNCOVERED AND ROOTED FROM ITS CORE. THE DECEIVERS IN THIS ADMINISTRATION, WHO CLAIM TO SERVE AND PROTECT YOU, SHALL BE EXPOSED AND BROUGHT TO JUSTICE. MOREOVER, I, THE TRUE HEIR TO THE THRONE, SHALL CLAIM MY RIGHTFUL PLACE AS YOUR ONE AND ONLY PRESIDENT . . ."

Augustus kept one eye fixed on the screen, the other on his watch, "Three, two, one . . . there it is . . . there it is, Theo; I saw it, hot damn, I saw it." Valentinian jumped up with excitement. He forgot all about his anger toward the general he once fired. "Did you see it, Theo?"

"I saw it, Mr. President; it came off just as we planned."

"Hot damn," said Augustus again, this time slapping his knee as he sat.

"What, what'd you see?" Rutherford asked his question standing to get a closer look at the screen. "I didn't see anything. I don't get it, what happened? Procopius is still standing; he's still speaking!"

"Theo, can you play it back for Larry?"

Theodosius ordered a technician to replay the video. "We'll have it up in a minute, Mr. President."

"There, Larry," said Caesar. "Did you see him slap his neck?"

"Yeah, Chief, I saw that before; he slapped at a fly or mosquito, so what?"

"That was no bug, Larry. One of our field agents shot him with a ricin pellet using a modified camera."

"You poisoned him? How long before—"

"Theo, what's the time frame?"

"He'll feel ill in two hours, Mr. President. In three, they'll be calling the paramedics."

"We've got our paramedics standing by, Larry," interjected the emperor. "Theo, tell Larry what they plan to do once he's inside the van."

"They'll remove undissolved shell fragments from his neck, of course, and then they'll—"

"They'll shoot him up with heroin," interrupted Augustus. He stood up from his desk and started pacing. "By the time he arrives at the hospital, Larry, he'll look like an ordinary junky. It's the heroin that'll kill him."

"Won't they discover the ricin?"

"Theo, tell Larry why we don't care if they discover the poison."

"This is a Bulgarian method of killing, Mr. Rutherford. It may also be a KGB—"

Caesar grew impatient with the general's answers. "Larry, we're holding a Bulgarian extremist in custody as we speak. If they find the ricin we'll bring him forward, if not, we'll set him free."

"What about the Constantines?" asked Rutherford. "Isn't Procopius related?"

The president smiled. "They won't have anything to do with poor old Mr. Procopius after learning he's an addict. . . . Say, Theo?"

"Yes, Mr. President?"

"Welcome back ol' friend."

The president raised the screen and said goodnight to Rutherford, who arranged to sleep in a guest bedroom near the pool at the rear of the Red House. Caesar remained at his desk and worked steadily until eleven thirty that evening. He took casual sips of the champagne that had been delivered earlier by Jenkins. "Can't let this go to waste," he said to no one in particular. After examining several proposals and signing one last document, it suddenly dawned on him: *I wonder if Tina is still wearing that dress*?

Caesar walked toward the door, but then turned around. He gave his new office a final glance before switching off the lights. "Well, it's not oval," he mumbled. "Guess I'll have to come up with something else."

He politely nodded at two guards as he made his way down the hallway. He turned right and headed toward the east end of the building. "Mmm, I love that new carpet smell." Augustus arrived at the master bedroom where he paused outside the door. He cautiously peered inside, curious as a schoolboy, to see whether Tina was inside. "Psst, baby, are you in here?" he whispered.

"In the lady's bath, Val, I'll be with you in a few minutes."

Augustus entered the bedroom and walked into his private lavatory. "STAY IN THAT DRESS," he shouted. After a brief wash, he emerged wearing nothing but a baggy pair of boxers. He quickly climbed into bed and clicked on the television.

"We go live to George Washington University where Amy Scottsdale is standing by. . . ."

"Thanks, Peter. Self-proclaimed president, Procopius, fell ill hours after giving his speech on the grounds of the National Mall. He's been taken to George Washington Hospital where he is listed in critical condition. Doctors aren't saying much . . ."

"See you in hell," remarked Caesar.

Justina emerged from the bathroom. "Is this what you waited for, baby?" She asked him in an erotic, titillating voice after removing her bra and panties, and loosening her wartime, deep-purple dress, making it easier for him to take off. She'd splashed herself with Wonderworld's *Flomme des Gardons* in honor of the Aspen woodlands, and stood tall in three-inch heels in front of the bathroom door. Her feminine shape came alive with a light shining behind her. She looked at him through ocean-blue eyes while keeping her back extended—projecting full-size, succulent breasts. Justina lifted the hem of her dress revealing two magnificently shaped, golden-brown thighs. "Well, baby, what do you think?"

"Hmm," the president uttered, rolling onto his side staring out at his delicious meal.

"Oh, Val," she complained, "how many times have I told you: if you want the food, you have to set the mood!" Justina left her suggestive pose to walk over and shut off the television. Then she made her way to the bedroom door where she dowsed the lights and clicked on overhead music. Frank Sinatra's "The Way You Look Tonight" began playing. Justina swayed to the music, shaking her hips side to side. She slid under the covers and cuddled up close to her man. She made sure to brush his chest with her breasts while draping her top leg over his. "I'm all yours, baby . . . you can wriggle me out of my dress. Oh, honey, make me beg," she pleaded. "AAHH!"

Dr. Ornuf Caecilius had gathered the family in the main-floor parlor. "I'm sorry," he began, "he died of a massive cerebral hemorrhage—a stroke. Did any of you notice anything unusual about him today, anything at all?"

Larry Rutherford spoke first. "Well Doctor, he seemed to be hard of hearing this morning when I talked to him on the phone. However, I chalked it up to a bad connection. I didn't notice anything unusual about him tonight."

"He drove from the Chalet to here," said Justina, sniffling. "He kept veering to the right. I just thought he drove badly. He doesn't drive much; he gets chauffeured most everywhere he goes."

Gratian spoke next. "Dr. Caecilius, he couldn't lift his right arm to throw a tennis ball in the pool this afternoon. Father claimed he had an old war injury."

"Daddy throws like a girl," interjected Ian, stirring in Justina's lap. "Mommy, when's Daddy coming back from Heaven?"

Justina handed Ian to Dorothy. "Please take him back to bed." Then she looked at her daughters. "Girls, you should head back as well."

Jenkins spoke next; he waited to speak until the children toddled off to bed. "The president seemed distraught when I brought champagne to his office this afternoon. I thought he ushered me out of the room because he had an important phone call."

"Yes, well, these events could easily have been transient ischemic attacks," the doctor began. "They're known as TIAs, or mini-strokes.

They often precede a major clot or hemorrhage. Folks, they can be very difficult to recognize, so none of you should blame yourselves for his death. Well, I'll let you get on with your grieving. We'll take his body to the hospital for autopsy tonight. Tomorrow, you can begin making funeral arrangements. Once again, it's been my honor to serve him, and I'm truly sorry for your loss."

One by one, everyone gave condolences to Justina and departed from the parlor. Only the First Lady and Gratian remained. They sat together on a brown leather couch, crying and holding one another's hands.

"Your father loved you very much, Gratian. He was so . . . so proud of you, my son."

"He loved you too, Mother."

"Thank you, Gratian, and I loved—" Justina had difficulty finishing her sentence. The thought of making love to Maximus found its way into her head.

"What's wrong?"

Justina wept bitterly. "Nothing . . . nothing, Son," she said, after regaining her composure. "It's all in the past anyway. Oh, Gratian," she continued, trying hard to change the subject, "I know you didn't want any of this. But despite everything, you and Ian are president-elects. The directors might approve both of you, or they might approve only one of you."

"I'll be fine, Mother. I'll accept whatever decision they make."

"Are you sure, Gratian?" She gave a penetrating look into his brown, youthful eyes. "If you're approved, you don't have to rule like your father. You're free to do things your way, and I'll help you as much as I can."

"Thank you, Mother. I'm sure I'll need your support. What about you? You didn't ask for any of this either."

They sat silently for a while. Justina couldn't answer; she stared down at the floor. Finally, she looked up. "I don't know if I can stay here. This house is gorgeous and all, but after what happened to your father tonight, I don't think—"

"It's all right, Mother, we don't have to stay." He brushed her hair away from her eyes. "We can go wherever you want. Is there a place you had in mind?"

"I'd like to go to Dionysius. Oh, Gratian, Milan is such a beautiful place, and many Arian Christians live there, too. It'd be the ideal place for me to grieve." Justina looked at her stepson more deeply. "Oh, but they don't have a bishop; they have no one for you to ask about killing."

"That's all right, Mother; Milan it shall be."

X

VISIGOTH CONFLICT

The *Aigneis*, a handy-sized tramp container owned by Captain Riley, motored half a foot below its plimsoll line. The ship arduously sailed past the port of Obbia on its way to Mogadishu. Three men occupied its pilothouse: Riley, his first mate, Abbas, and Colonel Alavivus—a militant Visigoth loyal to General Fritigern. Each looked westward toward the Gruethungi coastline, a country still occupied by Huns. The ship traveled southward where land peaks and ridges gradually gave way to flats and undulated plateaus.

Captain Riley, a member of the East-African Merchant Marines, charter partied his way up and down the Eastern Seaboard of Africa. He traveled from Kuwait to Kismaayo transporting rooibos and honey bush teas. He also shipped brocade, mudcloth, and kente fabrics and laces as well as njangsa, groundnut, mbongo, chobi, bush onion, nutmeg, and black pepper spices. He shipped exotic plants and animals on occasion, making his way along the shoreline. This trip was different than most: he transported arms from Yemen purchased by General Fritigern.

In the past, Captain Riley had transported guns, canons, and other

ammunition from one place to another. Military officials routinely asked merchant captains for assistance during times of war, but in this case, Fritigern never asked. The general had commandeered the *Aigneis* and abducted its physician, Dr. Lynch. He also withheld the fifteen hundred credits he had promised Riley for nursing him back to health.

Riley leaned forward, whispering into Abbas's ear, "Laddie, reminds me never to save the likes of anyone ranked higher than captain."

Colonel Alavivus overheard the comment. He quickly turned his attention away from the landscape toward his hostile companions. "Quit your yappin' and find a way to make this garbage hull go faster."

"Perhaps the colonel would be interested in strokin' a wee oar in the water," replied Captain Riley.

Alavivus didn't hesitate; he plugged the captain with a right cross, sending him headlong to the deck. "Smart off to me again, Captain, and I'll put a bullet through your head."

Riley grunted as he rose to his feet and spit out a tooth. "Cost me a dental bill, ye did." He looked at Alavivus, who sat in a chair stroking a Taurus revolver fastened at his waistline. "Beggin' the colonel's pardon," he continued, "but we be arrivin' at a checkpoint in 'bouts an hour." The captain wiped blood from the corner of his mouth with his sleeve, spitting on the deck just after he spoke. "You might be interested, Colonel; we be drawing a bit o' suspicion from the Huns seein' we're a bit under the waterline."

Alavivus looked over at Riley and produced a dry smile. "Maybe we should throw your first mate overboard."

The captain quickly defended his helmsman. "No doubts me Abbas would make a tasty morsel for the creatures below, but I doubt his scrawny absence would lessen our tonnage. And I doubt you'd enjoy bouncin' your pretty face off the rocks once he's gone."

Alavivus stood up; he made a motion to strike the captain. "Your solution, sir?" He asked his question while losing his smile and placing a hand near the revolver. "I must get this shipment past those wretched Huns!" The colonel stared hard at Riley. "And you'd be wise, Captain, if you made that your priority as well—if you ever hope to see your precious doctor again!"

Captain Riley took a few moments to ponder a solution, then directed Abbas to steer the ship toward shore. After anchoring the *Aigneis* for several hours, the captain resumed a southerly course toward the mouth of the Juba River.

Colonel Alavivus tried hard not to breathe. "Allah be praised, did you have to take on so much manure?"

"Ahh, Colonel," the captain replied, taking in a big whiff of air, "the stench will ensure safe passage past the Huns, and short lay day once we've arrived at port. Of course, we be travelin' a wee slower now, but I finds the smell comfortin' to yours."

†

General Fritigern, now mostly healed after the armory's explosion, disembarked the *Aigneis* before it sailed for Yemen. He wore a short-sleeved cotton t-shirt and plaid boxers under polyester/cotton twill camouflage fatigues. He prostrated himself, praying silently in front of his father's mausoleum. His loyal soldiers had built the crypt—a twelve-by-seven-foot, African-beige granite columbarium—from rock found less than a mile down the road. *Father*, he prayed as he had prayed a hundred times before, *I'm sorry I let you down. I only wanted help against Huns; you saw how those barbarians devastated our Ostrogoth comrades. Father, I knew enlisting Americans would anger some of my men, but I never dreamed Athanaric would try killing me over it. Oh, I know, I know, Father; I should have seen it coming.*

If only I had been the one to negotiate terms with President Valens, he continued. *Leaving important issues to Colonel Saphrax was a colossal misjudgment. He was much too inexperienced to handle such delicate matters. But, Father, I was weak, not up to the task. Yes, Allah gave me strength to survive, but it took a lot of time to get back on my feet. Oh Father, please forgive me! None of this would have happened if I'd recovered from the armory sooner. I'd never have agreed to bring our people to America under such deplorable conditions. Father, but for my weakness, you'd still be alive!*

Father, about half of our people have emigrated to America—but to what end? Their Navy kills off our elders and dumps their bullet-ridden bodies into the ocean. The general paused out of respect for his father; small tears began welling in his eyes. *Father, our youth has no means of support amid America's recession. They are given menial jobs if they're given any at all. As a result, Father, I've instructed Colonel Dirie to enlist our people into their military; it's our only chance for survival. Oh, but Father, what's the use? Priests are converting our Visigoth soldiers into Arian devils in every conceivable province . . . save one, a place called Dionysius—the place you were heading before being brutally murdered aboard that carrier. But it's my understanding they are letting us practice Islam only because they've appointed a novice governor, and they have no Catholic bishop.*

Oh Father, please forgive me for decimating our homeland. The Huns hover over us like annoying cats toying with innocent mice, waiting for the right moment to strike. Those of us who stayed behind are nothing but vassals to General Athanaric. He's a cold and merciless ruler, Father. He purloined my power, and he stubbornly believes our fractional army can overcome the Huns without anyone's assistance. He's wrong; our people are doomed under his irrational principles.

Oh Father, know that I've buried you on your side, facing our most holy city—and in the clothes of your demise. I ask only for your forgiveness. Father, in my dreams, you bear witness to no God but Allah. He giveth life, and He taketh it away—and none of us is fit to question His wisdom. Father, I've burned the flesh of the Hun responsible for your death. I sprinkled his ashes around your grave that he might serve you into eternity. However, the time has come for me to strike fear into those more responsible. To be sure, that strong-minded youth played a role in your death, but it's presidential revenge that I want. Now that Emperor Valentinian is dead, I'm most anxious to kill his brother. Oh Father, I pray upon your grave for strength to help me destroy the flesh of President Valens!

Fritigern ended his prayer and rose to his feet, hearing chatter and commotion from children entering the compound. The place consisted of nothing more than an old, uninhabited farmhouse and shed. The buildings lay deep inside the Juba Valley, situated twenty miles north and east of the river's union with the Shebelle. The general had fortified the complex using cement blocks stolen from an abandoned construction site five miles down a lonely stretch of road. The only credit he spent on the place went for guns purchased from Yemen and mortar to construct his father's mausoleum. The camp wasn't difficult to break into or out of—it was simply hard to find.

"Get going you mangy, dog-eared puke," hollered Saphrax, kicking a boy in the rear with his shiny, black leather boot as they entered the gate. The boys—fifty-two in all, ranging in age from six to nineteen—stood shoeless and chained at the ankle. Most of them hailed from the Wazigua tribe.

Fritigern walked over to greet them. "Colonel, I trust they're healthier than the last batch of boys?"

"Yes, General," replied Colonel Saphrax, "all except one." He pointed to one of the older boys who appeared to have trouble walking. "I've kept my eye on him, sir; he's a bit sluggish and lacking in color."

The general hated wasting resources. However, the thought of AIDS, sickle-cell anemia, malaria, or other serious diseases invading the camp was more than he could bear. He pulled out a Taurus revolver and shot the youth in the head. The rest of boys flinched at the sound of the gun. Their eyes became saucers as they watched their friend collapse to the ground. "Drag it behind the shed and burn it," said Fritigern, "then report back to me at once."

Fritigern, a methodical man, had been a soldier all his life. He ordered their shackles removed and that they line up in five columns of ten rows deep. He hollered at them several times until their patterns lined up right.

"Boys, my name is General Fritigern," he began, eying black smoke rising behind the shed. "I'm your savior," he shouted, walking among them. "You're deplorable in Allah's eyes—not for what you've done, but for who you are. You're defective; Allah can't stand the sight of you in your present condition. You're death to Him. Your souls are corpses covered in worms. Your mothers gave you up to me in hopes that I can restore you. If I can't, she'll spit on your grave; she'll renounce before God that your soul should be damned forever." The general continued his speech until Colonel Saphrax rejoined him.

"Done, sir."

Fritigern nodded. "Now, boys," he continued, "your savior needs credit to save your despicable souls. It costs money to cleanse your filthy spirit. Therefore, I'll assign some of you the task of selling pharmaceuticals. Others will get a chance to solicit donations from vessels passing by our coastline. Any of you so martyred for our worthy cause shall receive nothing less than eternal life. What's more, Allah promises you seventy-two virgins in the afterlife," he said with a smile. "Boys, a woman never before touched is one of the greatest gifts Allah could bestow on ingrates like you.

"But, as you've observed, if anyone becomes sick, he'll be shot. If anyone tries to escape and run back to his mother, he'll be shot. And if anyone tries to ask me a question, or speak to me in any way, he'll be shot. Your flesh will burn behind that shed, and your soul will be damned forever." Fritigern pointed to the area where black smoke arose. "Now, does anyone have a question?"

One of the younger boys began crying. "I want to go back home to my mom," he said sniffling.

The general pulled out his revolver and shot Colonel Saphrax in the chest. His loyal soldier dropped to the ground in a fetal position gasping for breath. Fritigern ignored him, staring at the crying child. "Be thankful my colonel took a bullet for you, young man—my father prefers his death to yours."

The general walked over and spit on the soldier. "Stupid negotiator," he muttered. Then he raised his head and looked around at his newest recruits. "Listen to me, men," he shouted, "never cross my words again; you'll get no more second chances."

The general began walking toward the farmhouse when he turned around and called for Captain Alatheus.

"Sir?"

"Unshackle the ship's doctor and have him patch Saphrax if he can—if not, burn both of their bodies behind the shed."

†

Marcellina stood beside her desk analyzing safety reports and surveillance photos handed to her by a low-ranking UN soldier. A ceiling fan hummed above her, creating a modest breeze insufficient to prevent her skin from becoming clammy in the 104-degree heat. She had a disgusted look on her face as she threw the documents aside. "Ambassador, can you tell me who is doing this?"

"Don't be so hard on yourself, Dr. Ambrosius," replied Ambassador Chavez. Dr. Montoya Chavez, a seventy-year-old native of Mexico City, sat in a brown leather chair in the corner of the sultry room, dressed in an ivory suit and tie, as always. He was leaving the UN and retiring to Porta Viarta after forty years of managing peacekeeping missions around the world. He had agreed to stay in Kismaayo for a month until Marcellina got herself situated. "You only arrived here a few weeks ago," he continued. "You'll find Thrivingi a fascinating place, Doctor, but she gives up her secrets slowly."

"Meanwhile, people are dying, Ambassador." Marcellina sat in her chair with a stupefied look on her face. "It's got to be a fishing vessel, yet we've checked them thoroughly up and down the coast. They all leave in the morning at about the same time, and they all return at night—yet nobody sees or hears anything about pirates killing people off our shores. Then I get reports like these telling me that someone has attacked three more ships this month. What am I supposed to do?"

"Well, warlords may be subsidizing the fisherman for their silence, Dr. Ambrosius, but that would require a sizable operation. As you'll learn, many chieftains live in this area, but most are small, and none of them share their wealth with others. Perhaps the one person capable of doing this is General Athanaric."

"I've heard what a sweetheart he is."

"Be careful with him, Doctor. In all my travels, I've encountered none viler than him. He'd just as soon kill you as give you the time of day. If you should cross him, you could find yourself beaten beyond recognition: bones broken, lying facedown in a pool of vomit at the bottom of a remote, flea-infested garbage bin surrounded by worms and swarms of biting flies. You'd be praying for death, Marcellina. He knows exactly how badly to beat you so you'll painfully linger a couple of days."

Marcellina smiled. "Sounds like a wish I once had for a professor." Chavez looked at her quizzically.

"Never mind," she replied, shaking her head. "Tell me, Ambassador, who commanded this region before Atharanic?"

"Fritigern . . . General Abdul Karim Fritigern—hatched from the same sewer as Athanaric, I'm afraid."

Marcellina wiped sweat from her face. "What ever became of him?"

"No one knows, Dr. Ambrosius. He was as powerful a warlord as Athanaric at one time, perhaps even stronger. Some people think he still lives in this area with his father, others say he feared the Huns and immigrated to America. However, most people I talk to think he's dead."

"Any idea as to who may have killed him?"

"Nope, could have been Athanaric—or Huns—who knows?"

"Can we find out?"

"In due time, Doctor; Thrivingi gives up her secrets in time." The ambassador grunted as he rose from his chair. "Well, I must be leaving. I must get to the airport by noon or I'll miss my plane. I understand you're driving up the Juba this afternoon."

"That's right, Ambassador," Marcellina replied. She got up from her desk and grabbed hold of the elderly man's arm, helping him walk to the door. "A friend of mine back home has a sister living in the valley. She grew up there and works as a nurse."

"How nice. Well, good luck, Dr. Ambrosius," he said, donning his hat. "Be sure to stay on the main roads; it's easy to get lost."

After waving good-bye, Marcellina returned to her desk and studied the photographs. "That's strange," she mumbled, wiping more sweat from her brow, "these fishing boats left port with a dinghy, but they didn't return with one."

"Your vehicle is ready, Dr. Ambrosius," said a soldier, peeking his head past the door.

"Thank you, I'll be with you in a moment."

The UN sport-utility vehicle kicked up considerable dust as Marcellina drove over dry, bumpy patches of gravel. She was headed for a small village near Buaale, one of three districts in the Juba River Valley. The temperature approached 111 degrees, and it hadn't rained in months.

Charlie Lipton, a World Food program director, had told Marcillina about the drought minutes before she left. "That area is the most fertile in all Thrivingi," he began, "but it's got a black cloud over its head. Some years it gets too much rain. When that happens, excess water flows down from the Ethiopian highlands; the Juba floods the entire area. Other years, like this one, there is a drought. Sadly, when nature does get it right, warlords move in and steal the harvest."

The road stayed close to the river for most of her route. The terrain displayed rolling pastures of tropical grassland dotted with low-lying trees. Dartmouth-green patches from *Acacia senegal*, candelabra, jackalberry, umbrella thorn, and whistling thorn rose above an earthy yellow carpet of Bermuda and elephant grasses. Foliage contrasted sharply with the cornflower-blue sky.

Terrain west of the road dipped slightly, allowing Marcellina to make out a container ship nearing the mouth of the Juba—just before the road veered in a northwesterly direction. Marcellina surmised it held a weighty cargo because the ship carried itself low in the water. "Gosh, I hope they don't get stuck on a sand bar," she said quietly to herself.

Marcellina passed several remote villages, most of them deserted. Chickens pecked at the ground while wild dogs panted intemperately in the shade. *Where is everyone?* she pondered, driving past schools, small stores, and abandoned wooden shanties. Signs hung crooked or were missing, paint appeared badly chipped, and everything seemed to rest on cracked foundations.

Marcellina spotted an intersection ahead and redirected her gaze to the road. The region had no stop signs or lights. Fortunately, she approached the road with caution, for a military vehicle came zooming past her from a ninety-degree angle. *Was that Athanaric, or the allegedly dead General Fritigern?* After driving another hour, Marcellina finally arrived at her destination.

Aarifah spotted the vehicle and ran out of the hospital with open arms. "Welcome, Dr. Ambrosius."

†

Prize II, a ninety-six-foot topsail schooner, heeled seventeen degrees to portside. The ship broad reached from Antananarivo to Kismaayo; it traveled twelve to fifteen nautical miles per hour in southeasterly trade winds. Its mother ship, the *Prize*, had capsized in eighty-knot winds 250 miles north of San Juan. The Norwegian tanker *Jorun* saved part of her crew; unfortunately, Captain Trudeau hadn't been among them.

Almost two and a half years later, the Navy commissioned *Prize II*. Designed by Thomas Flankston, the vessel served as goodwill ambassador, promoting business and tourism near Maryland. However, President Valens had recently called on her for a loftier mission.

After bargaining in good faith with Colonel Saphrax, who seemed eager to strike a deal, Valens had accepted Visigoth into the United Provinces. He did so in exchange for their military and religious allegiance. However, the president wasn't an idiot, despite his late brother's contention; he had anticipated difficulties with the accord.

"I think they'll denounce Islam and accept Arianism once they hear it from our bishops," he had told one of his advisors, "but they may not comprehend why I must dispose of their elders." Thus, he had dispatched *Prize II* on a journey to Kismaayo in hopes of keeping the Visigoth alliance on positive terms.

Four full-time crew and several on-call sailors—all of them abrasive—managed the ship's day-to-day activities. None of them, however, not even Captain D'Angelo, qualified as worthy ambassadors. Thus, President Valens commissioned Extavious Tendenblat, the Conquerors' owner, to satisfy that purpose. "I'd be honored to serve my country," he had told the president, "as long as I can do it in the off-season."

Tendenblat, who had kept his team in Milan despite receiving no gubernatorial approval to rebuild his stadium, had made arrangements soon after the Conquerors lost to the Liberties in the playoffs. He recruited several prominent people for the voyage: Ephraim Zephyrinus, the team's head coach; Joe "Clean Cut" Terentius, the team's quarterback; "Big Pete" Johnson, the team's behemoth tackle; running back Demetrius "Zip Line" Taylor; Jeremy Jackson, the speedster receiver from Jamaica; football fanatic and lawmaker, Senator Mark Mauritius and his lovely wife, Cindy; former Liberties linebacker, Tommy Lezetti, who sported a keloid scar on the right side of his neck after being mauled by Osama; and a few notable cheerleaders, including the ever-vivacious Molly.

The only people he had failed to enlist were Senator George Symmachus and his wife, Judy. They declined for personal reasons; she got seasick easily, and he had developed chronic diarrhea.

"It's going to be a wonderful experience," Tendenblat had told his recruits, "and you'll be doing your country a great service."

Although Captain D'Angelo had ultimate responsibility for making safe passage, he allowed his guests to perform many routine nautical functions. "Don't fall off the wind, Mr. Terentius," he shouted, standing near midship, "you'll jibe the sails."

Clean Cut stood swaying at the helm. After faintly hearing the instructions, he popped the top off his fourth can of Goose Head beer. He looked down at Zip Line. "Did he just tell me to fall off the ship?"

Taylor, half sloshed himself, sat on the leeward side of the cockpit, soaking up the sun. Molly, wearing an undersized red-and-white thong bikini, sat on his lap, gently swaying her hips to rock music playing in her earphones. "I don't know, Bro," Taylor replied. "Maybe the man wants Moll's top to fall off." He slid his hands up her ripped abs toward her enormous bosom. Without opening her eyes, or missing a beat, she grabbed his hands and pulled them back to her waistline.

Julie Tendenblat appeared in the companionway holding a vodka and tonic. She wore a white one-piece swimsuit with yellow trim and a matching wide-brimmed bonnet. "Everyone's fast asleep down here," she said, "they're louder than a chainsaw convention." Molly held her drink while she climbed up a ladder leading from the galley to the cockpit. "Thank you, dear," she said with a smile, peering over the top of her sunglasses.

Mrs. Tendenblat would easily pass for a woman in her forties. She'd had more than her share of tucks, lifts, sucks, and fortifications along the way—after all, she'd been married to a billionaire for the past thirty-one years. Besides her youthful appearance, Extavious gave her everything she wanted—everything, of course, except his time.

Julie filled his absence by flirting with the men around her—men talented enough to earn a spot on the football team. She wouldn't allow them *much* past first base; their compliments and sexual innuendos usually got her through weeks of lonely nights until her husband returned. "Do you need help back there, Joe?" she asked, steadying her balance on the boat.

"I could use a little help filling my sails, Mrs. T," he answered, flapping the front of his shorts.

Mrs. Tendenblat smiled, ambling toward the back of the cockpit. Unlike the lifeless brutes snoring below, Clean Cut knew how to play her game. *Joe knows what I want,* she thought to herself. She quickly slid her body between him and the helm. "Ooh, you have such strong hands, Joe."

"How do you keep yours so soft, Mrs. T?" The ship and its complement sailed merrily on for the next half hour. They could readily see Africa's coastline, but they still had three hours to go before making port at Kismaayo. Suddenly, the boat felt lifeless in the water; it leveled itself and stopped heeling—an eerie sensation came over the unskilled sailors. The ship's sails no longer filled with air, luffing noisily in the breeze. Joe stopped kissing Mrs. Tendenblat's neck. "What's going on?" he asked. Before anyone answered, however, the boom tore across the cockpit to the other side of the craft.

"Jibe ho," shouted several professional sailors in unison.

The sails caught wind on their opposite side, sending the boat lurching toward starboard. The sudden pitch caused Julie to lose her balance. "I got you, Mrs. T," said the sure-handed quarterback, "you're not getting away from me that easily."

"Oh, Joe, you sure know how to react fast under pressure."

Molly, however, wasn't as fortunate. The boat's motion sent her head over heels to the opposite side of the cockpit. To everyone's relief, the cheerleader wasn't injured. However, to the men's gratification, her breasts had dislodged from their holster. To Zip Line, they appeared gargantuan enough to catch wind and make the boat sail faster. After taking a moment to gawk at the half-naked woman, he looked up and over at Clean Cut. "How'd you do that, bro? You're a heck of a sailor, man!"

Joe ignored his teammate's kudos. He leaned over and whispered into Mrs. Tendenblat's ear, "I bet yours are better."

Julie beamed a wide smile. "Oh, go on, Joe."

†

Victor Zetseva—once renowned Gladiator to the Stars, now a one-armed, used-up Russian—lay supine on gold dandelion heads and other assorted weeds inside the Thessalonica prison. The province had charged him with the murder of Michael Mariano—the security guard found guilty of killing Hanna Lalia, Governor Probus's former Lieutenant. Zetseva listened to the sounds of protesters outside the penitentiary walls.

"He's too good to have done it," shouted some.

"We're gushin' for the Russian," shouted a group of teenage girls.

Mariano had fought Zetseva in the colisseum following his murder conviction. He did so at the urging of Governor Ambrose to win back his freedom and avoid a quick-sword execution. During the contest, which occurred during halftime at a Conquerors football game, he successfully hacked off Zetseva's arm near the shoulder. After the Gladiator had succumbed to blood loss and shock, Mariano had retrieved the dead arm and pried the gladius from its hand, cutting through a tough plastic band in the process. Mariano became the only man to beat the gladiator, and the only convict in over a decade to beat any prizefighter.

Immediately after the match, Tendenblat had given Mariano a new set of clothes, a sixteen-once souvenir cup of Goose Head beer, a stadium dog with mustard and onions, and a reserved seat in the stadium. Michael had proudly sat in the stands and waived to the crowd as he watched the second half of the contest. Incidentally, the Conquerors won that day, edging out the Norsemen by three. Thus, despite being convicted of murdering one of the province's most beloved politicians, fans accepted Mariano back into society as if he had done nothing wrong.

For the next four months, Mariano's life was turned upside down. News reporters interviewed him constantly and splashed his face over tabloids. Radio hosts, like Henry Llinos, couldn't stop talking about him. Movie producers begged to make a film of his life, and single women wouldn't stop calling. That's when he had met Akwasibah, a wonderful woman who eventually became his fianceé. She'd convinced him to marry her because her name meant "born on Sunday," the same day that he'd won back his freedom.

Mariano's fortunes soon ended, however, as he lay dead in his apartment on the morning of his wedding, nearly six months to the day he had terminated Zetseva's career. Someone had pried open his door and found his body lying prone on the bed with multiple stab wounds. Investigators found no signs of a struggle, and Akwasibah testified she couldn't recall a single enemy that he may have had.

Messalla's police had rounded up Victor and other Russian immigrants with ties to the former gladiator. Prosecutors had charged Zetseva after forensics revealed the knife he kept behind his back fit the size and shape of the wounds found on Mariano's body.

However, the public seemed unconvinced; they loved Victor. To them, he was more than a brave and gritty gladiator, more than just an entertainer—he had become their representative. A courageous man, he stood in their place, crushing the bodies—nay, the spirits—of every sexual predator, pervert, serial killer, or other loathsome criminal who dared challenge him. He wasn't just a circus performer; he had become their god; a god who exacted justice.

The public's affection for Zetseva did not escape the prosecution's attention. Normally, defense attorneys remove their case another county when they perceive that the media has influenced the jury to hate their client. In this case, however, the opposite happened. Prosecutor Thompson asked the judge to remove Victor's case to another venue. He chose Thessalonica in hopes of finding a town that didn't adore him.

Colonel Aashif Dirie stood by as Warden Rogers looked out at the Thessalonian people. "Warden," he began, "you must calm the crowd before they storm the penitentiary; otherwise, I can't guarantee anyone's safety."

Warden Blake T. Rogers served as the prison's head constable. He had held that position for the past nine years after marrying Brigadier General Theodosius's sister, Helen. The general wasn't particularly fond of his brother-in-law, especially after he had joked about Theodosius the Elder's flirtatious behavior with Justina. However, Theodosius treated him justly out of respect for his sister. "Well, if he's the best you can do, Helen, I guess I can live with that," he once remarked. The Warden jotted down a few notes on paper before making his way out of his office to address the crowd.

After watching Rogers leave, Dirie disappeared into an office and closed the door behind him. Brigadier General Theodosius had placed him—and a company of two hundred Visigoth soldiers recently inducted into the UP Army—at the Thessalonian penitentiary to guard against riots. Theodosius chose them because Dirie had begged him for the chance to display Visigoth talents. "Let me prove to you that Visigoths are good soldiers," he had told the General in a hallway, moments after a White House staff meeting ended. "Visigoths are brave, General; we're loyal to America."

Dirie moved to a window and peered out at the crowd. He removed his phone from his pocket and began speaking, "General, everything's going as planned."

The general sat at a table inside a farmhouse looking out at his father's mausoleum. He watched to make sure none of his young soldiers played on the columbarium, which he'd built out of stone in the center of his compound. "Excellent, Aashif," Fritigern replied.

††

The *Aigneis* finished its southerly course down the coastline of Africa, passing guards stationed at the Juba River's entrance. After the ship veered a northwesterly course, Colonel Alavivus came out of hiding. "That happened too easily, Captain; they didn't look into any bins. What did you say to them?"

"I let our stench do most of the talkin', Colonel," began Captain Riley. "I merely points out they'd be eatin' our fruits in a few months' time if they kindly let us pass on to the farmers. But you may take an interest, Colonel; the men I convinced wore an endearin' shade o' green, nary a colorful headband."

"They weren't Huns?"

"I be sayin' they had shapely heads and no scars, Colonel; scraggly beards as lovely as yours."

Colonel Alavivus pondered the captain's words. *Did the Huns pull out? Are Ostrogoths back in command of their coastline?* The colonel removed his Taurus revolver and pointed it directly at Riley. "You're lying."

Captain Riley remained calm and directed his attention at Abbas. "Aye, mate, kindly makes yer pass in the heart of the channel. We're ridin' a wee low in the water, you know; wouldn't want to get too close to the banks." After displaying a puzzled look, Abbas corrected the ship's course to the middle of the river.

"Now Colonel," continued the captain, moving within a foot of the pistol. He paused for a moment, took hold of a rail, and then looked down at the shiny black gun. He thought about what he might offer in exchange for the firearm if it ever became his to sell. He glanced up at his captor. "Colonel, it makes no sense for lies; I cares neither for Huns nor Goths—only credit. Besides, what do I gain if I lose me doctor?"

Alavivus began responding just as the ship came to a precipitous halt. It had struck a sand bar in the middle of the channel, sending him flying forward—straight into the fisticuff of Captain Riley. The smack sent him reeling in the opposite direction, head over heels onto his backside.

While Alavivus lay dazed on the deck, Riley confiscated the gun and made it his own. Following his boss's command, Abbas broke away from the helm and assisted the stunned soldier back to his feet.

"Did you lose a tooth, Colonel?" asked Riley.

Alavivus checked his mouth with his tongue. "No . . . no, I don't think so, Captain; I seem to have them all."

Riley smiled, and then struck the Colonel smartly in the mouth with the butt of the gun. The blow sent the man, and several of his teeth, hurling back to the deck. "How's 'bout now, Colonel?"

After reversing engines and working tirelessly for several hours, Captain Riley and Abbas freed the *Aigneis* from the bar without calling for assistance. Then they set their minds on restoring their full complement of crew. Colonel Alavivus refused, however—even under threat of death—to reveal the location of General Fritigern's compound. Without that information, Riley had little chance of finding his doctor. They hoisted the stubborn soldier overboard in the center of the river. The mark on the leadline read half, which meant three feet deep, but the river raged on either side. Alavivus shouted expletives as the *Aigneis* traveled southeasterly toward the ocean. "Head for Kisi," said Captain Riley. "We'll sell these arms to the Americans—enough to settle yer wages and affords me a tooth."

"What about Dr. Lynch?"

The captain stared at the landscape on either side of the river. "Aye, he's out there, laddie, and we've nary a lead; even the bloodhound in you couldn't find 'em. After we dispense these wares, we'll find a waterin' hole where lesser men chew more than khat."

††

A blazing hot sun beat down on Fritigern's arid and quiet compound. All but a few of the youngsters had left for the day, dispensing pharmaceuticals to drug-addicted natives or collecting credit from ships passing near the coastline. Dr. Lynch, drenched in sweat, pried deep inside Saphrax's chest using a pair of needle-nose pliers he'd boiled in water. "That's the last fragment," he said, pulling shrapnel from the groaning man's body.

Captain Alatheus looked at the exhausted physician. "Doctor, can I inform my general he'll live?"

Lynch smacked his dry lips. "Are you insane? The worst is yet to come. I've removed the fragments and stopped the bleeding, but he's going to develop a raging infection." He looked down at his blood-soaked hands, "and I don't have any means to prevent it."

"We have many fine plants in the valley, Doctor. Would they be of any use to you?"

Lynch stared up at his captor. "Perhaps." Soon, he and Captain Alatheus opened the gate and went in search of flora with antibacterial properties. They returned with specimens of black pepper, clove, geranium, nutmeg, oregano, and thyme. They showed the plants to children arriving at the camp and instructed them to go out, under guard, and bring back as many as they could find.

Lynch boiled the leaves and then ground them into a paste to release their oils. He packed the medicine deep into Saphrax's lesion. After removing the residue with boiled instruments, he rinsed the wound with water. He performed this routine every 120 minutes for the next seventy-two hours. Captain Alatheus kicked Dr. Lynch in the foot to wake him. "Well, Doctor, what do you say now?"

Lynch rolled over, displaying lumps of pus that he had removed from Saphrax's body. "I can't keep up with it," he muttered.

The captain looked disappointed. "That's too bad," he began, "General Fritigern's orders are to burn the colonel's body behind the shed. So, please, get on your feet and start dragging."

Dr. Lynch slowly complied. After rising, he grabbed hold of Saphrax's arms and started pulling—all the while wondering why Alatheus had said "please."

"Faster, Doctor."

Lynch gave the impression of trying harder. However, his foot stumbled in a rut made by a vehicle after a rain. The slip caused him to fall to the ground on his backside. "I'm sorry, Captain, I can't move this man any faster."

Alatheus displayed his un-holstered revolver. "Get up!"

Lynch rolled onto his stomach and secretly stashed a stone three inches in diameter in his pocket before ascending to his knees. After rising to his feet and brushing dirt off his trousers, he resumed dragging the dying soldier's body to the shed. "Keep your pants on, Captain, we're getting there."

Upon their arrival, Alatheus instructed Lynch to hoist Colonel Saphrax onto the grill where he would be fatally shot, doused with petrol, and burned. The captain failed to apprise Dr. Lynch that an identical fate awaited him after the colonel's business concluded.

After laying Saphrax on the frame, both men suddenly heard jeeps, trucks, SUVs, and other military vehicles entering the compound. Rapid-fire shots from semi-automatic weapons soon followed. The sounds startled Alatheus, who took his eyes off Lynch for a moment—enough time to give his prisoner a chance.

Lynch retrieved the stone from his pocket and hurled it at Captain Alatheus. The rock struck him square in the forehead, causing him to collapse to the ground. "Take that, you hypocrite," muttered Lynch, retrieving the pistol from the officer's hand. He quickly inspected the weapon; to his surprise, the chamber held no bullets.

"Go . . . get out of here," said Alatheus in a weak voice. "They'll kill you if they find you."

Lynch stared at his former captor. He knew the Arabic word *jihad* meant different things to different people. For most Muslims, it meant defending one's thoughts and actions against the corruption of personal temptation. For others, it meant a collective defense of their faith against paganism and unbelievers. And for a few, it meant mounting an offensive strike against those who refused to believe in the Islamic tradition.

At that moment, Dr. Lynch knew Alatheus wasn't the latter. If it came down to shoot or be shot, he would happily accept a bullet rather than confront Allah with an unclean spirit. In that moment, Lynch took back every mean thing he had thought about him. "Allah be praised, and peace to you, Captain. I see now you're one of the children, a slave in Fritigern's compound." He said these words just before hoisting himself over the five-foot concrete wall and running off into the Serengeti.

The invaders—General Athanaric and his soldiers—quickly descended on the men behind the shed. "General," they shouted, "we've got Saphrax and Alatheus." Athanaric walked around the corner of the building; his black mustache appeared limp in the heat.

As the warlord made his approach, Colonel Saphrax opened his eyes and spoke. "General," he said in a faint and feeble voice, "I've seen writings of the Companions."

The dying man's utterance surprised Athanaric. "Colonel, what do you know about those sacred documents?"

"The museum . . ."

Athanaric stood tall and began thinking. *Of course, they must be in that tiny room with the winding staircase.* He ordered several men to make haste to the repository in search of the sacrosanct letters.

"No," said Saphrax, speaking with a diminutive voice, "moved." The air proceeding from his lips would not have curved a feather.

The general brought his face closer. "Where? Where were they moved?" After receiving no answer, he lifted Saphrax by the scruff of his shirt and repeated his query more strongly: "WHERE? WHERE WERE THEY MOVED?"

"Mo . . . mo," uttered Saphrax, giving it his all. Unfortunately, his spirit left him before he could finish.

"Damn," muttered Athanaric, staring at Saphrax's remains. "Burn it," he told one of his men. Then he looked down at Captain Alatheus, still dazed and seated on the ground. "Burn him, too."

The general promptly walked away from the shed toward the middle of the complex. A large number of youths had returned from work and were crying for a bowl of gruel. "Children," he shouted, "all of you work for me now. Have any of you seen General Fritigern?" No one dared say a word. They had learned their lesson the first day arriving at camp. Athanaric's mustache twitched, a sign that their discipline pleased him. "It's all right, boys, you have my permission to speak."

"He took off in a black SUV," said one of the older boys. "I heard him say something about Dishu."

Dishu, huh? Maybe I've finally driven that traitor to America.

††

Marcellina exited the UN vehicle and proudly embraced the exuberant woman. "Please, call me Marci."

"And you may call me Aarifah," the woman answered with a smile. After making small talk in the scorching heat, Aarifah directed her companion into the hospital. Aarifah began the tour by discussing one of her favorite topics: Aamir. "My brother thinks the world of you," she said. "He tells me you nearly got raped by one of your college professors," she continued, passing by a middle-aged man with AIDS lying on a cot, his body covered in lesions.

"Aamir's such a dear friend, Aarifah. I remember the day you're referring to, though. I celebrated my birthday on the day you came to Dionysius." Marcellina let out a chuckle. "At first I didn't know who you were. I thought you might be a new girlfriend when I peeked into his office."

"Oh my!"

Marcellina smiled at her reaction. "I wasn't thinking clearly; I remember having a bad head cold. I was crying, sneezing, feeling wet, and shivering, all at the same time. After you left, Aarifah, Aamir gave me a blanket and a cup of hot tea. He listened to me rant and rave for over an hour about the despicable behavior of Professor Nero. Then he offered to help bring him to justice, but I told him no, that I just wanted to forget about it."

"I don't know what my brother told you, Marci, but he doesn't forget many things, and he certainly doesn't take no for an answer. He's a Visigoth, Marci, a proud Wazigua, a gallant and brave Thrivingi Bantu. We've dealt with more than our share of evil people over the years; we've learned how to get even.

"That same evening I met Aamir for dinner," Aarifah continued. "He asked me, since I live in close proximity to UN officials stationed in Kismaayo, if I'd ask someone to produce a list of names of every UN employee who had attended Dionysius University in the past thirty years."

"Oh my gosh, Aarifah, he asked you to do that?"

"Dr. Montoya Chavez was most helpful, Marci."

"Oh my gosh, Aarifah, he's the man I'm replacing!"

"He gave me a list of ninety-two names, seventy of them women."

"Aarifah, I talked to Ambassador Chavez this morning. Why didn't he mention anything about this?"

"Because I asked him not to; Aamir is following up on the names as we speak. I'm confident he'll discover your college professor took advantage of at least some of those women. Hopefully, he'll find one or two of them willing to come forward."

The women walked in silence. Marcellina began crying after passing two juveniles suffering from severe malnutrition; their projecting ribs were their most prominent feature. Marcellina spoke after drying her eyes with her sleeve. "Aamir needs to be careful, Aarifah; he could lose his job if Nero finds out what he's doing."

"My brother is aware of that, Marci, and he's willing to take that chance. Aamir is talented enough to find another job, but he worries the credit he sends us could get disrupted. He's paid for most of the things you see here in this hospital."

As they passed a dozen more patients, it suddenly made sense to Marcellina why Aamir, a respected engineering professor, drove a seventeen-year-old, rusted Toyota. She did not think her admiration for him could get any higher, but it just had. Tears still trickled from her Persian-blue eyes.

"Are you all right, Marci?" The UN ambassador didn't answer, finishing their hospital tour in silence. When they got outside, Marcellina took a big breath of air and then asked to see the school. They made their way along a dirt road, up a steep incline, to a hutch stationed a block north of the hospital. Marcellina listened to Aarifah speak about recent events when she suddenly spotted a boy, about six years old, peeking at her from around a corner. He had a wonderful smile, but his front teeth were missing.

"A lot of families are missing," Aarifah continued, "we expect depletion during a drought. When families can't find food here, they usually migrate to Kenya or Kismaayo. But this absenteeism seems excessive, Marci; it's as if someone's kidnapped the children."

Marcellina made a funny face at the youth before speaking. "Have you asked the children where their brothers and sisters went?" She pointed in the direction of the boy staring at her from around the corner.

Aarifah smiled. "I don't think he's ever seen a white woman before," she said. "But to answer your question, yes. We have made many inquiries.

I know lots of families went to America, but that doesn't explain what happened to the children of those families who stayed behind. I thought the Huns may have taken them, but they appear to be leaving.

"Huns are leaving?"

"Yes, Marci, from what I can tell, Ostrogoths are back in control of their coastline. It makes perfect sense that the Huns should leave. They stuck around to determine whether to wage war against us. But since our civil war is over—"

"Your civil war is over?"

"Yes, Marci, from what I can tell, we now seem at peace. The people of one mind moved to America while those of another stayed behind."

Marcellina contemplated her words while strolling through the schoolhouse. After a few minutes, she spoke up: "I feel so useless, Aarifah. As a peacekeeping official here in the valley, I should be telling you this information, not you telling me."

"You've just arrived, Marci. You'll find Thrivingi gives up her secrets quickly once you know where to look."

Marcellina shared a few hours with Aarifah before returning to Kismaayo. She drove over bumpy gravel roads, kicking up lots of dust in the process. Vegetation became abundant as the road veered closer to the river. Suddenly, Marcellina witnessed a man emerge out of nowhere; he staggered out of the bushes and crossed the road where she traveled. Fortunately, she stopped the vehicle in time before hitting him.

Marcellina sat trembling. The middle-aged man that she nearly killed seemed to be sweating profusely; he also appeared haggard, as if he'd been walking for days. His clothing appeared tattered, and he had numerous small cuts on his skin. "Help me," cried Dr. Lynch, collapsing onto the road. "I've been bitten."

††

Clean Cut cracked open his sixth Goose Head beer as he tenderly kissed Julie on the neck. "Hey, is that a small boat out there?" he asked. He pointed with his hand that held onto the beer; his other hand fondled her breast.

Mrs. Tendenblat didn't answer his question. She urged him to forget about anything he saw. "Trust me, Joe, you have no one to throw a ball to out there; just pay attention to me."

Molly ignored him, too. She rolled onto her six-pack abs and adjusted her thong, eager to sun her backside.

"What do you think, Zip, does that look like a boat to you?"

Taylor, who had downed seven beers by now, looked out over the water. "Can't see nothin', bro; sail's in the way. Don't this rig have a big ol' crows nest to get a better view? Besides, I got all the view I need," he said, slapping Molly's ass.

Captain D'Angelo and the rest of the professional sailors had spotted the small craft a half hour ago. They kept abreast of its position as it steadily made its way toward *Prize II*. When it came within five hundred yards, the captain came to the cockpit. "I'll take it from here, folks," he said, eying Joe and the billionaire's wife suspiciously. "The dinghy appears to have kids aboard; we'll need to bring our ship around for a rescue."

The captain powered up the diesel and drove the vessel thirty yards downwind and to the left of the dinghy. He turned ninety degrees starboard and proceeded on a beam reach bearing. As he neared the small craft—bobbing heavily up and down in the water—he turned his vessel once more to starboard. *Prize II* came to a gradual stop alongside the dinghy. After securing the two vessels together, the crew helped the children aboard.

Noise from luffing sails woke everyone sleeping below. "Hey, what's going on?" asked Extavious Tendenblat.

"Yeah, who's disturbing the peace?" moaned big Pete Johnson, sleeping in the v-berth with Tommy Lezetti.

Six children—mostly Wazigua ranging in age from ten to fourteen—sat sniffling and crying. While eating a hearty meal of meatballs and spaghetti, they tearfully explained to the crew how their dinghy had been marooned in the ocean. After finishing off lemon pie for dessert, each withdrew a Taurus pistol from a holster secured under his vest. The children aimed their revolvers directly at their hosts.

Big Pete responded first. "You're kidding?" He sat dumbfounded, staring into the angry eyes of a twelve-year-old boy.

Jeremy Jackson went next. "Give me a break, man. You kids ain't going to hurt us; those guns ain't even real." He made a strange contortion with his fingers in an attempt to communicate with the boys. "Besides, man, we brothers. We cool."

Mark Mauritius interjected his two cents. "Now look here, boys, I'm a senator . . ."

Just then, one of the boys spotted Mrs. Tendenblat calling for help on her phone. He aimed his pistol and shot her point-blank in the chest. The bullet pierced her heart and dropped her like a stone. Big Pete rushed the youth; the boy quickly shot the Conquerors' tackle right between the eyes. He too, dropped like a stone.

Suddenly, pandemonium engulfed *Prize II* as sounds of yelling, crying, screaming, and gunfire filled the sailing vessel. Adults ran in all directions in an effort to avoid the children. But they couldn't hide; they had nowhere to go. One by one, the kids picked off each of the crew until they had all perished. Clean Cut and Zip Line died last, shot in the back of the head, execution style.

The ordeal lasted less than ten minutes. The goodwill ambassadors to Thrivingi died in the blink of an eye; all that they were, or had ever hoped to be, vanished in an instant. Their schooling, their training, and long gridiron practices; their travels, their enthusiasm, and lonely nights without husbands; their anxieties, their lusts, and dreams for the future—all snuffed out by a band of wet soldiers.

The children meandered about the ship and stole whatever credit they could find. Then they doused the vessel with petrol, lit it on fire, and climbed back into their dinghy.

"Ayuub," a younger boy began.

"What?"

"Do virgins have boobs?"

"Supposin' so."

After conversing for the next half hour, they gave praise to Allah before nodding off to sleep. Their small craft bobbed heavily up and down in the water, waiting for a fishing vessel to come pick them up in the morning.

††

Victor lay on gold dandelion heads and other weeds inside the Thessalonica prison. After patiently listening to protesting voices from outside the correctional facility, he stood up and started pacing as Warden Rogers spoke into the microphone: "FOLKS," he began, "I KNOW THAT YOU ALL LOVE ZETSEVA FOR THE ENTERTAINMENT HE HAS PROVIDED. MOREOVER, I KNOW THAT YOU ALL THINK HE'S INNOCENT OF THE STABBING DEATH OF MICHAEL MARIANO . . ."

At that moment, Colonel Dirie looked out a slender window at the spectacle. He estimated the gathering at five thousand, a 25:1 civilian to soldier ratio. He motioned to someone in the crowd with a trifling wave of his index finger. Suddenly, a shot rang out, sending Warden Rogers plummeting to the floor. The bullet killed him instantly—a bullet to the left side of his head from a Taurus revolver.

The crowd, however, showed little reaction. Colonel Dirie stood pondering. *Were they stunned? Perhaps no one witnessed the tragic event that had just transpired. Perhaps no one believed that Warden Rogers lay dead—or perhaps that's what they wanted.* He questioned whether the fatal incident occurred too quickly.

Many in the throng had recently emerged from a large tent that volunteers had set up to shade them all from the blistering sun. Johnny "Mustang" Clampert, who owned the biggest car dealership in town, had donated the tarp for the cause. "Since nobody's buying cars in this dreadful recession, I might as well advertise where the people are," he once commented.

Whatever the reason, Colonel Dirie concluded that he needed to do more; killing the warden had proven insufficient to incite a riot. With another small gesture, one of his men, dressed in plain clothes, took hold of the microphone and addressed the assembly. "I SAW THE ASSASSINS GO INTO THE YARD. THEY ARE GOING TO KILL VICTOR. WE MUST ALL TRY TO STOP THEM!"

The message stirred the crowd into action; thousands began storming the penitentiary in hopes of saving their representative. Colonel Dirie called Brigadier General Theodosius at his office in Washington. "General, the warden has just been assassinated. The crowd is overtaking the facility; they are helping the prisoner escape. What would you have me do?"

"Maintain a defensive position, Colonel."

"But General, they killed your sister's husband . . . your nephew's father." Dirie tried hard to goad the general into anger.

A moment of silence ensued on the phone. For Theodosius, the thought of losing his brother-in-law wasn't painful, but the thought of Helen being alone—and not finding another suitor—made him angry. Then the battle of Al Mukalla popped into his head. He recalled losing soldiers because he didn't act decisively to oust President Temani from Yemen. At the time, he was grieving the loss of his father, Theodosius the Elder—and he was not about to let the gravity of that incident rule over him again. "Kill them! Kill them all, Colonel," he shouted into the phone.

Dirie sprang into action, herding everyone into the penitentiary before locking the doors behind them. Then he ordered his troops to unsheathe their swords and lay waste to the entire assembly. Soon came shouting and screaming, crying and gnashing of teeth as soldiers plunged and hacked their way through the crowd. Bodies lay stacked: some prone, some supine. Others lay twisted with gaping holes in their necks. Some tottered about from missing limbs before they collapsed. The soon-to-be corpses gasped for breath like dying fish while shades of red permeated their clothing. Colonel Dirie watched the carnage unfold from a monitor inside a room. "My general will be most pleased," he muttered. "I've not lost a single soldier."

After twenty minutes, one of Dirie's men knocked on the door before entering. "Colonel," he began, "we've completed our mission; we've successfully killed all seven thousand."

Aashif raised a brow; *had my calculations been that far off?* "Private, does that include everyone inside the pavilion?" The soldier nodded. "And the inmate?" The private's face displayed a quizzical expression—before he ran out of the office to dispose of Zetseva.

Colonel Dirie retreated to Rogers's former office and sat in his black leather chair. He put his feet up on a large mahogany desk, speed dialed his comrade, and then began watching world news reports on overhead televisions. "It's happening, General; strikes are happening all across the nation. And the best part is, most of them are being ordered by American officials!"

"Excellent, Aashif," replied Fritigern, sitting in the passenger seat of an SUV heading east across the Juba. "That will permit us a few more attacks before they figure things out."

Just then, Fritigern caught sight of a container vessel riding low in the water. Its stench caused him to think of General Athanaric. "I've changed my plans, Aashif; I'll have to forego raising credit and come straightaway to America. I'm heading for Dishu International Airport."

"I look forward to your arrival," Colonel Dirie replied, lighting a Padilla cigar he had found in the top drawer of the bureau.

After crossing the river, Fritigern's vehicle kicked up dust traveling tortuous gravel roads. After passing houses and abandoned wooden shanties, he snarled at a UN vehicle yielding at an intersection. An astonished look came over his face when it appeared a woman drove the truck. "Aashif," he continued, "did all the attacks come off as planned?"

"All but one, General; from what I can gather, nothing happened in Milan, Muntisir's territory."

Aashif called Muntisir on the phone, and General Fritigern laid into him harshly. "Allah will set fire to your flesh and supplant your brains with worms. He'll pack you into a homo's ass where you'll dine on feces and sperm!"

"But General," the young man replied, "I can't rouse our people to anger. They are treating us well here, much better than in any other city. Our people are content with Governor Ambrosius's promises."

"Promises," Fritigern interrupted, "Thrivingi Bantu are content with promises? Muntisir, did you tell them what happened to their elders? How Americans slaughtered them, dumped their lifeless bodies into the ocean?"

Muntisir pleaded his case. "Yes, General, but people know that the governor had nothing to do with that. They're aware that Governor Ambrosius isn't a noble—or a bishop—and that he can't make laws on his own. I've heard him speak, General; his words are like nectar. He has the people's will—including our own. But that's not enough; he needs Senate approval to carry out his wishes."

"Don't lecture me on their cockeyed political structure, Muntisir. I know all about Senates; it takes them decades to approve anything—everything except their own pay raises." Fritigern paused for several moments, and then spoke softly, "I'm disappointed in you, Muntisir. You showed real promise starting a riot on the day President Valentinian went there to give a commencement. Now, I've half a mind to replace you with somebody else."

"Please General, I'll do anything you ask; just give me another chance."

Fritigern ended the connection with Muntisir and redirected his words to his lieutenant. "Aashif, tell him to wait for our call. If he screws up again, I want him dead."

Part Three

The Ensuing Summer Till Year's End

XI

CHILDREN'S FUTURE

Thine eyes so green; so radiant a sparkle
Hair dark brown midst lips so tender
Thy heart so sweet; o' innocent confection
Hold my hand and show affection

Lava hopped up on the king poster bed and sprawled across several pages of handwritten poetry. The feline ducked her head partway beneath the sheets while her paws batted a crumpled piece of paper.

"Hey, girl, how am I supposed to finish this verse with you lying on top of it? You know, I promised Mary I'd write her more poetry." Ambrose looked at the cat a little more closely as he petted her soft, textured fur. "You look like a cloistered nun with that sheet over your head. Are you praying, sister, or are you practicing idolatry?" Ambrose picked up the feline in his arms and held her close to his chest.

"Meow."

"I know," he said enthusiastically, "I've something to show you." Ambrose set Lava down and walked over to an old-fashioned chest of drawers. "I bought this at Apollo's yesterday, what do you think?"

Lava sniffed at the container, then at the contents inside. The box held an antique, platinum, filigreed, one-carat diamond engagement ring. The jewelry had a sleek band, a circular diamond in its center, and cut diamonds along the sides. The feline pawed at it before turning her nose away.

"What's the matter, not big enough for your finger?" Ambrose removed the ring from its box and gazed lovingly at its glitter. "Well, I think it's perfect," he continued, turning it about in the light. "Besides, I want it to showcase Mary, not the other way around."

"Meow."

"Oh, you don't like it because you can't eat it."

"Meow, meow."

"All right, give me one last try; third time's a charm, you know. You don't like it because you're jealous. You think I'm bringing home another feline to take your place."

The cat rubbed herself up against Ambrose. "Prrr," she sounded.

He stroked Lava's head and scratched under her collar before setting the ring in its box. "Don't worry, girl, I'll always have room for you in my heart." He closed the lid and set it on the bed when he heard a disturbance in the hallway.

Melva Hayes appeared at his door. "Hey, Melva, where's the fire? You do know it's early on a Sunday morning?"

The woman appeared frantic, but then again, Melva always appeared frantic. "I'm sorry, Governor—"

"No, Melva," Ambrose interrupted, "I'm begging you; please, do not tell me someone is calling on me at this hour."

"I'm sorry, Governor, Mr. Jacobson is here to see you. He says—now let me get this right—he says 'there are no days off in a campaign fight.' "

Ambrose lay back on the bed and covered his face with a pillow. After a few moments of reflection, he gave her the universal okay sign with his thumb. He followed it with two flashes of his open right hand.

"Very good, sir, I'll put him in the study and tell him you'll be down in ten minutes." Ambrose flashed the okay sign again and then flopped his arm down on the bed.

"Well, Governor," began Jacobson, "he's officially entered the race. I think he had planned to wait until after the Zetseva trial to make a formal announcement, but since the gladiator's dead, he has no reason to delay."

"When did Leonard make his announcement?"

"Last night, at the Switzer Hotel. I saw quite a few senators there, Governor. It didn't take him long to start blasting you."

"Did he talk about the issues, Chris, or did he keep it strictly personal?"

Jacobson smiled. "Evenly split, I guess." Ambrose's campaign advisor leaned forward in his chair, as if to convey top-secret information. "Don't take him lightly, Governor," he said in a soft voice. "You might be leading in the polls now, but after Thompson starts running negative ads, you'll be surprised at how fast he catches up."

"That may be, Chris, but I've made it clear the types of ads I'm willing to run. I don't care if they are negative, so long as they're truthful—and no marginal half-truths, either—nothing out of context, understand? Chris, if I lose this election running a constructive campaign, then so be it. I made a good living as a lawyer, and I've no qualms about returning to it."

Jacobson appeared exasperated. "Governor, we can control our ads, but we can't control the special interests. If they want to lie or tell half-truths about Thompson, we've no power to stop them."

Ambrose stood up and began pacing the room; he missed pacing on the Persian rug in his old townhouse. "Sure we do, Chris, we'll denounce any group that wrongfully criticizes Leonard."

Jacobson peered over his glasses. "Let me get this straight, Governor. It's not enough to limit yourself to Boy Scout publicity, now you want to defend the guy, too? Governor, has anyone told you your idea is insane? Thompson will be trying his best to eat you alive, and you want to protect him?"

"Why not, Chris, we think he's an animal—let's just pretend he's on the endangered species list!" The men remained silent for about a half minute. Finally, Ambrose spoke up after sitting down in his chair. "Chris, did he name a lieutenant?"

Jacobson responded quickly, "No—not that I know of. Look, Governor," he continued, standing up, "you're right; this probably is a bad time to discuss the election. Maybe we should take the day off and start fresh tomorrow."

"If you think that's best, but I thought you told Melva there are no days off in a campaign fight?"

"Forget what I said, besides, I'm not sure we're in a fight anymore." Jacobson donned his solid-blue sport jacket after closing and locking his briefcase. "Don't get up; I'll see my way out. Good day, Governor."

No sooner had Jacobson left than Melva reappeared. "Governor," she said frantically, waving her arms in all directions, "you have an urgent call on line one. It's Father Liguria from the cathedral."

Ambrose nodded at the hysterical woman. Then he looked around at barren shelves lining the walls of the study as he arose from his chair near the windows. *I really should start filling this room with books.* Ambrose walked across the carpeted floor and sat in his reddish-brown leather chair next to the desk. "Good morning, Father—it's going to be a scorcher—what can I do for you?"

"Good morning, Governor Ambrosius," came the cleric's reply. "I know this is early, and I'm calling on short notice, but I need your assistance at the cathedral today. I fear for people's safety, Governor, and I could sure use your help settling them down. Governor, I'm mindful of our past disagreement; I wouldn't be disturbing you if I didn't think it was urgent."

Ambrose sensed dread in his voice. "Father, slow down. Now, tell me the exact nature of the problem."

"As you know, Governor, Dionysius has no bishop. We have lacked one for some time now. But what you may not know is that our diocese is equally split between Arian and Nicene Christians."

Ambrose immediately thought of a subject to add to the bookshelves. "I know a little something about that issue, Father," he interrupted, "but, please, continue."

"Yes, well, you're also aware of the recent massacre at Thessolonica, and the vicious attacks that have occurred in other provinces."

"Yes, of course, Father, I went to Thessolonica personally. I can tell you firsthand the experience sickened me. Upwards of seven thousand people lost their lives that day. Father, as I've already told the media, I'm holding Brigadiere General Theodosius responsible for what happened, at least until my sources tell me otherwise. He ordered his soldiers to kill all those people. But, if I may ask, what does that have to do with your situation at the cathedral?"

"Governor, you may blame the general, but my parishioners aren't convinced. Around here, people are blaming each other; Nicenes accuse Arians of terrorism and vice versa. Governor, many people hold the Goths responsible for what happened at Thessolonica—and since many of them are converting to Arianism by way of President Valens's accord . . . well, you get the picture. Anyway, Governor, these groups don't get along in the best of times, so when you start mixing in fear they go for the jugular."

"Father, no reported attacks have occurred in or near Milan. Thessolonica may be in our province, but it's still a long ways away. And, as I've said in my recent broadcasts, we've elevated our security level to red; we've every available defense agency working overtime."

"People are still afraid, Governor; I see anguish and fear in their eyes. Many believe Milan is the next target. And without a bishop, I could sure use your help settling them down. Why, last night alone, I broke up two fights in the church's parking lot and one in Orchard Park next door. Sister Anne informs me children as young as six are fighting in the halls at St. George's."

"I should think a man of the cloth, such as yourself, would be far better suited than I to comfort a troubled congregation."

"You're very modest, Governor, but I've listened to your campaign speeches. I may object to some of your ambitions, but you do have a mellifluous tongue. You know how to get a point across—how to drive home a message. To be quite honest, Governor, I've never heard anyone persuade people better than you."

"Thank you, Father. I see your own persuasive skills have improved. However, the campaign is what concerns me. See, people may think that I'm using your pulpit to springboard my political messages. I don't want churches used in that manner, Father; not to mention, my opponents will roast me over a fire for tying it."

"Governor, I don't want churches used in that way, either. But there must be something I can do to convince you." Silence came over the phone before the priest resumed speaking. "Governor, what if I turned the cameras off and promised not to broadcast your speech over television and radio? That would convince them you are not doing this to benefit yourself. Of course, you'd only be speaking to people inside the church, but they're some of our worst offenders."

Ambrose chuckled. "All right, Father, you win. I'll come to church and calm your parishioners. But I warn you, I may be bringing a little surprise of my own." The governor paused for a moment. "I'm sorry, Father, I should know this, but what time does Mass begin?"

After closing out the conversation, Ambrose called his friend. "Hey, Drew—would you stop calling me that! Now listen, I know it's early, but we have to change our plans. After you pick him up from the airport, don't bring him to the mansion. Take him straightaway to the cathedral instead. Oh, and one more thing: get him a nice suit if you can."

Sister Angela tapped her cane as she paced back and forth under the cathedral's great dome. She no longer required cotton balls over her eyes, but she still did not have vision. Doctors had informed her that the experimental surgery had failed. She remembered one of them saying, "I'm sorry, but your optic nerves are necrotic; they lost their minute circulation. They died. We'll need to take them out before an infection develops."

Sister felt naturally disappointed, but not agonizingly so. "I don't miss what I've never had," she would repeatedly tell others—before going off to her room to cry. After hearing the main doors to the church open wide, she implored, "Hurry Reverend Mother, parishioners are arriving."

"Calm down, Sister, I'm going straightaway," replied Sister Anne. She gave Angela a contemptuous look before making haste down the aisle. Sister Anne greeted Mr. Schmidt, who made his way toward the front of the church wearing his customary sneakers, dirty tan trousers, a ball cap, and a dusty, brown leather jacket. A large, dirty red ribbon remained fastened to his lapel. "Good morning Mr. Schmidt."

Clarence beamed a wide smile. "Did you come for the beer, young lady? We have a wonderful assortment today: a pilsner, an incredible stout, and oh, you must try our fabulous new brown ale. Please, come try them all, you'll be thoroughly impressed."

"Thank you, Mr. Schmidt, perhaps some other time. I think you want to go up another five . . . let's see now . . . five more pews," said Sister. Clarence still had not missed a Sunday Mass in all the years she had known him.

The elderly man fumbled around in his pocket. "I've got an opener here somewhere—oops, that's my old army knife." Clarence set his cane down and reached into his other pocket. "Here it is," he proclaimed a moment later. "We don't use fandangled twisty-tops on our bottles. No, sir, we make sure our caps stay tight so our beer stays fresher, longer. Yes, sir, young lady, Goose Head beer is the finest in the entire province. I should know; I'm their head brewmaster."

"I'm sure it is, Mr. Schmidt." Frightful images of a fall-down drunken mother and two staggering brothers arose in Sister's mind. She recalled one night when she was about eighteen: she had put her inebriated brothers to bed after one of them had gotten sick and thrown up on the furniture. "Come on, Phillip; up you go," she remembered saying, wiping vomit from his chin.

"Annie, come to bed with me," he'd slurred. "I've got a hard package . . . I know you want it." Sister closed her eyes and shrugged off the wretched image. She stayed with Clarence, walking him to the third pew until he had comfortably seated himself. Mr. Schmidt sat in his usual spot, where years of friction had removed nearly of all the varnish and stain.

Sister Anne resumed walking toward the vestibule, passing forty rows of near-empty pews. The heels of her black Oxford shoes clicked against the myrtle-green marble floor causing a loud echo throughout the church. No wind greeted her on this steamy August morning as she pushed opened the massive doors at the back. The sticky, muggy air felt unbearably stifling; even crickets and grasshoppers didn't dare move. However, that didn't stop a group of energetic boys playing a game of baseball at the far end of Orchard Park. Sister watched one of the boys run around the bases after hitting a home run.

As the doors swung wide, Lareyna Mendoza, along with her six children, Antonio, Miguel, Mario, Rafael, Elsa, and little Yesenia, ascended the concrete steps. Mario and Rafael raced past Sister Anne in an effort to be first inside the church. "*Buen día, Madre Superiora*," said Lareyna.

"*Buen día*," replied Sister, "you look beautiful, as always, Lareyna. Did your mother make your dress?"

Lareyna wore a lovely floral-print cotton sundress with a tieback waist. "*Gracias, Madre Superiora*; no, I made this myself."

"It's darling. Now tell me, how's the family?"

Lareyna remained quiet, lowering her eyes to the ground as they began filling with tears. After a few moments, she looked up at Sister. "Madre Superiora, Pancho is still away; I haven't seen or heard from him for two months. He doesn't answer my calls." The young woman burst into tears. "I'm so afraid that something awful has happened to him."

"Was he drinking the last time you spoke?"

She nodded her head. Sister took her by the hand and led her into a small room inside the cathedral. She found Sister Angela and arranged for her to greet parishioners at the door. "I'm not asking, Sister; I'm ordering," she said in a displeasing tone. "And I don't care to hear any more about your predilection for the dead!"

Then she found Sister Martin and ordered her to take the children outdoors. "Sister," she began, "run off their energy, but don't let them get too sweaty. Oh, and before I forget, have you seen Naeem Williams?"

Bells chimed in the steeple as Sister Martin stooped to tie her tennis shoes. "Naeem said she'd be in Washington, D.C. this week. You should have seen her, Reverend Mother—she was all smiles telling me about Tavius's transfer into a military band. She seemed so relieved he'd be out of harm's way from the Goths." Sister Martin took Sergio by the hand. "Oh, Naeem also said to watch for him; Tavius will be playing the trumpet in a televised parade."

After the cathedral's pipe organ began playing, Father Liguria, dressed in a solid-green chasuble with gold stitching, marched out of the sacristy and onto the altar along with two deacons and six servers. Despite his appreciation for parishioners, Liguria preferred serving as churchwarden rather than its governing cleric. Apparently, people felt the same way about him—he had never come close to getting the necessary votes to become bishop; twenty-one percent was his highest tally.

Father Felix was next to audition for the position; he registered halfway down Liguria's list. However, Felix had canceled his performance after winning an identical office in Zion, a province located east of Dionysius. Therefore, Liguria had quickly emailed Father John from Kenya to try for the billet. Sadly, his transfer got fouled, then postponed for a while, then cancelled outright due to maddening bureaucracy. Thus, Father Liguria took to the altar, serving once again as Dionysius's unsanctioned bishop. "I'm technically the highest ranking man in the province, but I haven't a lick of power," he once commented.

Walls reverberated as 1,500 parishioners and another thirty-two choristers stood tall singing the opening hymn, "Hail, Holy Queen

Enthroned Above." Hermann of Reichenau, a parylitic cripple, or Adhémar, bishop of Le Puy, are said to have authored the canticle—an eleventh-century adaptation of "Salve Regina:"

> ♫ Hail, holy Queen enthroned above, O Maria.
> Hail, Queen of mercy and of love, O Maria.
> Triumph, all ye cherubim,
> Sing with us, ye seraphim,
> Heaven and earth resound the hymn:
> Salve, salve, salve Regina!

The altar came alive with colorful ruby-red, fairway-green, and mustard-yellow banners hanging from four enormous, black marble pillars. Tapered beeswax candles too numerous to count burned brightly in front of the altar. Large crystal vases with bouquets of white dendrobium orchids dotted the front of the stage. The blooms stood upright as a tall welcome along the wrought-iron railing partitioning the priest from the people. The immense oil painting depicting the Last Supper—with its rich browns, blacks, and ruddy-reds—served as a blatant backdrop. And as if the hot, sultry air wasn't enough, syrupy smoke from sacred incense smothered the sweaty congregation like a weighty blanket.

"The Lord be with you,"† boomed Liguria, facing the people with his arms extended, as if to embrace them all.

"And with your spirit,"† they replied.

Mass proceeded without a hitch. Father Liguria performed soundly, even if he couldn't emotionally connect with the people. After the Gospel ended, parishioners sat down on old mahogany pews to listen to his sermon.

"Brethren," he began, "I've invited a guest speaker. Governor Ambrosius has kindly agreed to speak about recent events happening in and around our province. It is my hope he can drive some of our fears away and reunite us as a congregation. However, in order to dispel any idea that he is using our pulpit for his own political gain, he's agreed to speak on one condition: that our television cameras and radio microphones be turned off. Therefore, we will do that at this time. We will reunite those of you watching or listening at home after the governor's talk has concluded. Now ladies and gentlemen, I give you Governor Ambrosius."

The two men nodded at one another, exchanging places at the pulpit. The people, not used to demonstrative action in church—save for the occasional wedding—gave a paltry round of applause. The governor looked out at the crowd and adjusted the microphone.

"Thank you, Father Liguria," he began. "Fear is a dangerous thing, ladies and gentleman. It spreads like wildfire. It begins as a flicker of confusion—then anguish stokes the coals as all hope seems lost and despair blows into the embers. Today, I'd like to take away your despair. I want to offer you hope and stomp out your confusion. To that end, I've brought a special guest of my own.

"The man I am presenting today has been with this congregation for the past several years. You've seen him, you know who he is, you've supported him and his family. You have come together despite any theological disagreements among you. You have loved one another, and you've devoted yourselves only to the bonds that unite you. In return for your love and devotion, he's seen fit to honor us all."

Ambrose signaled Lierchetsky, who waited patiently at the back of the church. Heads turned as the tall, lanky investigator urged the honoree forward. The young man walked slowly up the aisle. Although his scuffed brown shoes didn't match his new blue suit, the boyish Latino looked nice all the same. His hair lay flat, neatly combed, his face, clean-shaven—and he hadn't had a drop of liquor for months.

"The man I give you is your own Francisco Mendoza," said Ambrose, extending an arm in his direction. "The man you see before you, the man whom everyone doubted, the man whom no one believed could possibly change the minds of the Japanese moguls. This man, who's had to oversome his own personal demons, this man, who stands before you under the dome of the this glorious cathedral, this man single-handedly brought the Magra plant back to Milan!"

The congregation rose to its feet in thunderous ovation to the sounds of the governor's words. All eyes stared at Francisco as the crowd roared with elation. They knew what it meant: it meant jobs! It meant hope! It meant a return to happier days! It meant an end to their foreclosures and bankruptcies, an end to their stress and the constant bickering that inevitably came with it. It meant, by the grace of God, the beginning of the end of their wretched recession!

After hearing her husband's name, Lareyna tore out of the tiny room where she and Sister Anne sat talking. "Pancho, Pancho," she shouted. She raced down the aisle and lept into his arms, hugging and kissing him like there was no tomorrow. "Oh my gosh you're back, Pancho; I can't believe it. Oh, I love you so much . . . I've missed you; I've missed you," she cried over and over.

The crowd continued its thunderous roar. Ambrose looked up at Father Liguria from his place at the pulpit. Like many, Father was bursting with smiles. Father looked down at the governor from his perch on the altar. His smile seemed to say it all: *You have a gift, governor; what an extraordinary talent!*

Ambrose spotted Sister Anne standing in the doorway. Like many, Sister had tears in her eyes. She glanced over at Ambrose and produced a warm smile. Her smile seemed to say it all: *You've only been here twice in your life, Governor Ambrosius. Yet each time you've come, you've brought miracles.*

Ambrose looked on at the gathering and motioned for everyone to sit down and be quiet. He stared out at the blissful crowd and thought, *perhaps I should quit while I'm ahead.*

However, just as the thought of saying something more came to his mind, a six-year-old girl seated in the rear of the church spoke up: "Ambrose, bishop." Katie, the girl from the Barnabas School for the Deaf, who regularly attended 10:30 Mass with her parents, wasn't aware that the sound of her voice had carried. Although *shushes* came from persnickety folks nearby, enlightened people in Katie's vicinity began seriously contemplating her message.

"You know, she's right," said one parishioner. "Ambrose should be our bishop."

"It was his idea to send Mendoza to Japan," said another.

Murmurs from the back of the church spread forward; talk grew louder as more and more people chimed in. Vocalizations elevated to such a high level that Ambrose caught wind of their proposal. "No, no, folks," he began, waving off their idea, "I can't possibly be your bishop. Please, let's all be quiet now," he continued, trying to hold up a smile. "Please be seated, I have a few more things I'd like to say."

But sound in the church grew louder. Soon, the entire congregation broke into chorus: "AM-BROSE, BI-SHOP . . . AM-BROSE, BI-SHOP . . . AM-BROSE, BI-SHOP . . ."

The governor pleaded for cooperation as he waved off their chanting. "Please, folks, everyone calm down," he begged, but everyone ignored him. Ambrose sensed an odd feeling taking hold in the church. The feeling was, well, Christmas-like. He blinked twice, trying to rid images of angels flying about, casting glittering snowflakes over the congregation.

This is hot, steamy August, he reminded himself. Then he began hearing Christmas prose. *Is this 'the Night before Christmas'? Have we gone back to using the Julian calendar?* Ambrose glanced back at Father, who sat there beside him—the man had a stymied look on his face. "Say something, Father," he yelled about the matter. "Please, Father, plead for my case!"

Before Father could react, however, Sister Henrietta walked up the cathedral's main aisle. She positioned herself directly beneath its great dome. Standing under its high ceiling, she too saw the angels that flew over her home. In Christmas prose, Sister stood grandiloquently addressing the fold, staring at numbers that lit up her phone. "Forty-nine . . . fifty . . . fifty-one," she cried out. "HE'S DONE IT! HE'S DONE IT EVERYONE," SHE YELLED THROUGH THE HALL. "THE GOVERNOR IS OUR NEW BISHOP—YULETIDE TO ALL!"

The sounds of her words brought a thunderous roar. The jubilant throng exploded for more. Cameras were flashing from cellular phones;

people soon texted their loved ones at home. Reporters ushered in whilst they danced in the aisles, "We can't believe it, they said," their faces all smiles. The bells from the steeple rang out with a clatter; the boys from the park came to check on the matter. They ran through the church as they shook off their dust. "It's Christmas," they shouted, "it's Christmas in August!"

Ambrose stared out at the pandemonium. *They're delirious; the heat has gotten to them,* he surmised. He glanced over at Sister, still standing in the doorway, her arms crossed in front of her. He gave her a puzzled look; she returned one filled with contempt. Ambrose turned his eyes back to the assembly. *This can't be happening—Lava, Melva, please wake me up.*

The congregation kept cheering. "Please everyone, Mass is over," he said quietly, "go in peace now . . . go home . . . just go . . . " Just then, he felt vibration from his phone.

"GET OUT," Drew texted.

The governor responded with a text of his own. "Bring car to rectory, meet in tunnel." Ambrose quickly nodded at Father before running off into the sacristy.

A few minutes later, Ambrose met up with Lierchetsky in the damp, subdued lighting of the burrow. "I didn't know this place existed; I had to ask directions," said the investigator, looking around at the grey concrete enclosure. "These walls look like they're ready to cave in."

Ambrose ignored his whining. "Hurry, switch suits with me," he said.

The men undressed and exchanged their formal clothing. Fortunately, both of them were thin, having nearly the same waistline dimension. However, Lierchetsky stood three inches taller than Ambrose. "Well, I'm ready for the floods, Father."

"Don't even presume to think that's funny," Ambrose replied. "Now listen, Drew, go to the sacristy—my guards are there—they'll surround you as you walk to the limo. But crouch down and keep your head low. Once you are in the car, keep the windows rolled up. Tell them to drive you around for a couple of hours, and then they can drop you off at the mansion. You can use my Mercedes to drive home. Oh, and if you'd do one more thing," he said, "call Mary and tell her I'm all right."

"Where are you going?"

"I don't know, but I'm taking your car."

Ambrose drove aimlessly around Milan for several hours in Drew's old rusted Impala. He had initially thought about going to Mary's house but decided against it. *That's the first place they'll look.* Then he thought about going home to visit his mother. *Oh, they'll look there, too, and with her health, she doesn't need the aggravation. Maybe I should drive all the way to Trier. I'll tell everyone I went to visit my brother, that I needed his advice on the upcoming election. He's survived two of those ordeals before.*

Just as Ambrose settled into the idea of visiting Satyrus, he drove past the Barnabas School for the Deaf. He thought about the day Katie and her classmates came to visit him at the mansion. Then he thought about the evening they had spent together at Senator Leontius's home. "That's it," he shouted, "I'll hide out there. No one will suspect it; everyone knows I don't get along with the Senate."

Ambrose bowed politely after his hosts came to the door. The elderly couple returned his bow, receiving him into their home. Afterwards, Leontius closed the sliding glass doors of the three-season porch and pulled the drapes shut to save on air conditioning costs. Before fully closing the curtains, he peered out at the Impala parked in the driveway. "Bit of a step down, isn't it, Governor?"

Ambrose smiled. "We all have to do our part in a recession, Gene."

The senator ignored the retort and slowly walked his guest up a short flight of stairs. "I'm surprised you came here; thought you'd be halfway to Trier by now. Please, have a seat in the living room . . . or would you prefer more privacy in the study?"

"The living room will do fine, Senator."

"Forgive the mess, Governor, I wasn't expecting company at his hour. As you can see, I enjoy tossing newspaper sections on the floor after I've read them."

Ambrose sidestepped papers as he walked toward the back of the room. He purposely avoided the Victorian leather recliner next to the fireplace. He knew from experience that Leontius favored that spot. Instead, he sat at the end of the six-foot beige floral couch where he and Mary had sat before discussing politics with the lawmaker.

"Thank you, Gene," he said, lowering himself down, "this will do fine; it's quite comfortable."

The television broadcast the Yankees and Cardinals in an interleague baseball game. Leontius stood staring at it: "There's a line drive hit into left field," began the announcer. "One run will score, and we're tied up at two runs apiece."

The senator turned his attention back to Ambrose. "I'll turn it off so we can chat, unless you prefer to watch the game?"

The governor shook his head.

Leontius picked up the remote and clicked it off. "You'll be happy to know, Governor, I bought some of that fine wine you asked about earlier. I think it's called, Rome-is-Calling?"

"Romanee-Conti."

"Ah yes, that's it," the senator replied. "I tried a glass of it last week; good stuff. It has a rich maroon color; it tastes good and deep. If you'd like, I can have Agatha rustle up some food to go with it."

Ambrose mused at his host's descriptive vocabulary. He looked up at Leontius and waved off the suggestion. "No, Gene, water will do."

The senator motioned to one of the servants to fetch bottled water and then lowered himself into his favorite chair, passing some gas in the process. "Governor," he began, "I'm not totally ignorant of your situation. The television has already broadcast the news, and for a while, my phone would not stop ringing. I must say, though, I'm a bit surprised by your reaction. Most of the male colleagues I know in the Senate would give their left testicle to be Bishop of Dionysius."

Mrs. Leontius appeared in the doorway with a tray of Brazilian coffee and prosciutto sandwiches. She arrived just before her husband had made his remark. Agatha set the tray on a coffee table after giving her husband a disgusted look for using vulgar language.

"Pardon me, Governor," said Senator Leontius, looking into Agatha's angry eyes, "would you care for some coffee and snacks?"

Ambrose directed his attention to the elderly woman. "No thanks, Agatha, but everything looks delicious."

Mrs. Leontius politely smiled back. "Well then, Governor, I'll leave these things here just in case you get hungry and change your mind." She turned around to exit the room. "I'll see what's taking the help so long with your water."

Ambrose replied to the senator's assertion soon after she left the room. "Gene, I'm aware of a bishop's political power; from that perspective, I can understand why people would covet the position. But," he continued, leaning forward on the couch, "what about its theological side? I have no religious training whatsoever. Senator, I'm not qualified to be bishop, or even an altar server for that matter."

"Yes, well, the issue of your eligibility did come up in my earlier conversations." The senator paused to take a sip of coffee. "Ooh, that's hot," he said, setting the cup back down on the table. "Governor, that's why I invited Father Liguria from the cathedral, I figured he'd be able to tell us whether or not you qualify for the position. We may be fussing over something that's not even possible."

"You invited Father?"

"Yes, Governor . . . oh, but I did it before you arrived," he replied apologetically. "I didn't know you were coming."

The men remained quiet for a few moments, contemplating each other's words. Leontius spoke up. "Governor, over thirty years have passed since President Constantine reunited church and state in this country. But in all that time, we've yet to find a balance."

"What are you saying, Gene?"

"What I'm saying is that even if Father Liguria qualifies you under episcopal law, you may not qualify under our federal laws. In other words, Governor, the directors may not approve your new office even if the church ordains you. That's why I invited Secretary of State Eligius and Director Leo here as well."

"You invited them?"

Senator Leontius tried another sip of coffee. "Yes, as well as a few other senators, and—"

"And?"

"Your fiancée. Oh, I know you haven't made a formal announcement, but everyone knows you're in love with her. Even I know that, Governor, and my wife tells everyone I'm not observant about such things."

"You invited Mary?"

"Governor, you must understand, you've been gone for several hours; no one knew where you were. We had to inform your Lieutenant that she might have to take over your duties for a while."

"Gene, when does this party get started?"

"In a few hours; you're free to take a nap in the guest bedroom if you like. Oh, and I may be able to find you a better-fitting suit."

"That's all right, Gene, but if I may, I'd like to use your study to make some calls. And Senator, I'll take a small glass of that fine maroon wine you talked about earlier. Heaven knows Jesus imbibed before He was crucified."

Ambrose peered through the drapes of the sliding glass doors, anxiously awaiting Mary's arrival. "Governor, come join us," said Secretary Eligius. "We're having a spirited debate over healthcare insurance."

"Thank you, Dick," he replied, "I'll wait for your summation." Moments later, the governor saw a pair of headlights pull up in the driveway. *It's my Mercedes!* Ambrose slid the doors open and ran into the yard. He met Mary as soon as she exited the vehicle.

"Hold me, please," he said, folding his arms around her.

The distinguished couple embraced for nearly a minute. "Oh, would you look at that," cried Agatha under her breath. She stared out through her kitchen window at the two swooning dignitaries, placing her hands over her heart. Then she looked back at the help. "What are you gawking at?" she scolded. "Now all of you get back to work."

"Are you all right?" Mary asked, still in his embrace.

"I am now, Mar. Look, why don't you head into the house; I'll join you in a minute after I talk to Drew. I'm confident we can figure a way out of this mess if we both put our heads together." Ambrose watched her stroll across the yard and into the house.

Then he turned toward his trusted investigator. "Thanks for bringing her here, Drew. I don't know what I'd do without you."

Lierchetsky smiled. "You're a lucky man, Ambrose; she's quite a gal." The governor nodded in agreement.

"And your car isn't half bad either," Lierchetsky continued, "but I found a few more of these in it." He reached into his pocket and pulled out three black boxes no bigger than a sugar cube. "Somebody's interested in your thoughts."

Ambrose stared down at the receivers. "If I don't get out of this predicament, Drew, they'll be even more interested. Did you bring the ring?"

"Sure did." He reached into his other pocket and produced a small silver box. "I was lucky to find it, though. Your cat had it on the floor; I found her batting at it with her paws. If I'd have come any later, she'd have had it hidden under a radiator."

Ambrose looked puzzled—and mesmerized by headlights off in the distance. "I thought Lava was on board after our little chat this morning," he said. "Gosh, felines can be fickle."

"You had a little chat . . . with your cat? And the good people of Dionysius seriously want you as their bishop?"

Ambrose smiled as he snapped out of his trance. "Thanks, Drew," he said, taking the box from his hand. "Here're your keys. I'll return your suit after I've cleaned it."

"Keep it; God knows I'm keeping yours. You're famous now, pal."

The governor peered off into the distance again. "You'd better get out of here; looks like the media got wind of our location." The two men stared at a mile-long line of cars exiting the freeway.

"Everyone be quiet . . . please, quiet down now," said Dick Eligius, taking charge of the discussion. "We'll let Father speak first. Father, from the church's perspective, is Governor Ambrosius eligible for the office?"

Liguria stood up to address the assembly. "Well, Canon 378 lists the requirements for an episcopal candidate. First, he must have a good reputation—"

"There, you see; you can all go home now," interrupted Leontius, "the Senate will never vouch for his laurels." Chuckles arose from the group, but Mrs. Leontius looked unamused. She gave her husband a wicked glance and then looked down to see how much wine they had drunk from the bottle. "I'm sorry," he said, "please go on, Father."

"Yes, well, the candidate must have morals, piety, wisdom, prudence, human virtues, and a solid faith—"

"There you go," sounded Ambrose. "I don't have a solid faith. Father Liguria can attest to my absence from church."

"That's true everyone; I've only seen the governor there twice. Unfortunately, that doesn't prove anything. Many of our best parishioners don't attend Mass regularly. We're trying to make it more appealing—"

"Yes, yes, Father," interrupted Eligius; he had grown impatient with the whole conversation. "Isn't there something more legal in your document?"

"Only that the candidate be at least thirty-five years of age."

Eligius stared at him with a dumbstruck expression. "That's it? You mean to say the church doesn't require a candidate to have a doctorate in theology, or that he serve as a diocesan priest for so many years before applying for the position?"

"No, there's nothing else here, nothing else on the paper," Father replied, flipping the document over several times. "Quite honestly, Mr.

Secretary, I don't understand it myself. But I do know the Vatican faxed me this letter today after I specifically requested it. See, I needed to know that I had the most recent law and that it came directly from the horse's mouth. Like you, Mr. Secretary, I thought for sure there'd be more. But that's all I see on the page."

"Have them fax over another copy," said Eligius. "That just doesn't seem right." The secretary turned himself toward Ambrose.

The governor sat disturbingly quiet on the floral couch, holding Mary's hands, studying the delicate curves of her fingers, wondering how they would look with his ring. He periodically released his grip, but only to wipe sweat from his palm.

"How old are you, Governor?"

"I turned thirty-five last month," he said without looking up.

"All right then," said Eligius. "We should move on. Bill, what does federal law say about his eligibility?

Director Leo stood up to address the assembly. "Our by-laws don't address the issue, Dick; it's a matter of first impression. This topic has never come up in any other province. But I do have a proclamation signed by President Valentinian. Emperor-Appoint Gratian faxed me a copy earlier today. He told me that he found it amongst his father's possessions—one of the last things he signed. I won't bother reading it all," he continued, flipping through the pages. "He strongly encourages all governor-elects, public appointees, and other high-ranking officials to prepare themselves for an Episcopal position, especially those lacking in business experience."

"That's it?" asked Eligius.

"Pretty much."

An awkward silence ensued. Finally, Eligius stood up to address them. "All right folks," he began, "assuming Father Liguria receives nothing more from the Vatican, it appears federal law is silent on the matter, and that our former president expressed delight in public servants assuming a religious office. Of course, as you all know, our local law only requires fifty-one percent of the people's tabulation."

"Excuse me, Dick," asked Mary, "what was the final tabulation?"

"Eighty-three percent—no bishop-elect has ever received a higher percentage."

"And don't think the Senate didn't take notice of that little fact, Lieutenant," interjected Senator Symmachus. "We know that if he becomes bishop, the people will get everything they want."

Mary stared at the senator before redirecting herself at Eligius. "Dick, don't you think people were giddy about the Magra plant reopening? I mean, their enthusiasm must have crossed over into their vote. If we poll them next week, maybe they'll be more reasonable; maybe they won't vote the same way again."

Ambrose glanced over at Mary. He felt comforted knowing she worked hard in his corner.

"That doesn't matter, Lieutenant," said the secretary. "The law doesn't allow do-overs because some people weren't in their right frame of mind. No, Lieutenant, I'm afraid everyone has lawfully weighed in on the subject. Everyone, that is, except Governor Ambrosius." He looked straightaway at Ambrose. "Well, Governor, the job appears to be yours if you want it. It's your decision."

Another awkward moment came upon them. This time, Ambrose broke the silence. "Please, everyone, would you clear the room? Lieutenant Peterson and I would like to discuss the matter in private."

People reluctantly stood up to exit. "I don't see why we have to leave," barked Senator Symmachus. Another guest proclaimed, "He just needs to give us a simple yes or no . . . what's there to talk about? Who wouldn't want the position?"

Senator Leontius was last to leave the room. He required help from Agatha to get up from his recliner, passing a little gas in the process. "Take your time, Governor; don't give up your left testicle too quickly."

"Sorry to displace you in your own home, Gene." Senator Leontius gave an insouciant wave of his hand as he departed the room.

Ambrose and Mary sat on the couch in silence. She turned to look into his Egyptian-blue eyes while he kept his gaze on her fingers. She finally spoke up. "Bee, I heard it was Katie—you know, the little deaf girl—she's the one who spoke up in church and put this whole thing in motion."

Ambrose shook his head. "I can't be bishop, Mar, have you seen the strange hats that they wear? And what about that long wooden stick they carry around with them—what's that all about? Are they really trying to convince people they're tending a pitiful bunch of sheep?"

"No, Bee, I—"

Ambrose kept talking, quickening the pace of his argument. "Can you picture me putting a host on someone's disgusting tongue? Cripes, Mar, I don't want to plan church music with some blue-haired organist named Millie. Oh, and my gosh, Mar, the wine—have you tried it? It's revolting!"

"Bee, I—"

The governor continued his insurgence; grounds against a religious life gushed from his lips in a flurry. "Mar, I can't pronounce half the names in the Bible. I routinely fall asleep in church. And my knees, Mar, my knees still hurt from those blasted kneelers. Did you know that place has no air-conditioning? Did I ever tell you how much I hate bingo? And what about all that incense? It'd be a great class action if we discovered it caused cancer! Mar, I feel like killing myself when babies don't stop crying. I never got along very well with the nuns at St. Frederick's . . . and I just got over wondering about the color of their hair. Mar, infected people will be kissing my ring. And what about demons? Does Satan really turn people's heads in a circle?"

"BEE, STOP," said Mary. "Just stop," she repeated more softly. "Now, I know you well enough to know you're hiding from the truth. Please, Bee, tell me the real reason you don't want to be bishop."

Ambrose kept silent; tears welled in his eyes.

"Please, Bee, just say it; I need to hear it. Do you love me?" Ambrose turned his head and looked into her emerald-green eyes.

"I love you with all my heart, Mary; I don't ever want to lose you." Then he said softly, "The beauty in your features is unsurpassed in a thousand worlds. I yearn to hold you on dark and stormy nights and feel your frightened embrace when life turns chilling. Your touch awards me the strength of a thousand men; I want to hold you through all eternity. . . . Mary, you consummate my soul; I've grown to love you more than you could imagine."

"Your words are beautiful, I can tell you've been working on your poetry," she said, wiping tears from her eyes. "But I won't always be this lovely, and we won't always feel this way about one another. My hair will grey, my breasts will sag, and I'll complain incessantly about hot flashes, incontinence, and leg cramps. Then I'll turn my vengeance on you and complain about your potbelly, watching too much television, and the gas you'll pass when I help you up from a chair."

Ambrose stared into her eyes. "You don't feel the same way about me, do you?"

She stayed quiet.

"Gosh, Mar, how could I have misjudged our relationship so badly?"

"No, that's not it, Bee. I think you're fooling yourself; you want what other people have. I think you're afraid to face your destiny."

"You don't love me!"

His words cut her deep—down to her very core. "Damn it, Mister, I love you with everything I've got," she screamed. "Don't you know how badly I want to wake up with you by my side in the morning? How badly I want to plan our day on a porch that needs painting? How badly I want to fix your tie before you head out for a meeting?" Tears streamed down her face. "I want to yell at you for dripping mustard on your shirt when you come home in the evening." Mary began slapping him on the arm. "God, Bee, don't you know how badly I want your child kicking inside my belly?"

Ambrose took her into his arms and embraced her tightly. She kept crying, hitting him on the back with her fists.

"I'm sorry," he said. "I'll never doubt you again."

She slowly regained her composure. They stared lovingly at one another, drying their eyes with their sleeves. Mary spoke first. "I love you, Bee," she said sniffling, "and I always will. I just needed to speak up for the Katies of this world. Who will fight for her future? She wasn't excited about the Magra plant when she cast her vote. I doubt she even knows what it is. She just knows you're someone she can trust, someone who isn't so self-absorbed, so filled with hate and greed. I think many people in the province feel that way. That's why they want you as their bishop, why they want to make it your destiny."

Ambrose stared at her fingers, then reached into his pocket and pulled out the small silver box. He opened it and knelt down beside her. "Mar, I meant this as an engagement ring, but I'm calling it a *permission* ring instead."

She gazed at the shimmering diamonds. "Oh Bee, it's lovely. Did you pick it out yourself? It's so beautiful, but I don't understand—"

"Mary, I love you. But I can't marry you if I'm going to become bishop. If you accept this ring, then I have your permission to hug you and kiss you on the cheek no matter whom you might marry in the future."

"Oh no, Bee, please."

"Mary, if you accept this ring, then I have your permission to think of all the wonderful things we could have done had we stayed together." She began crying profusely again, putting her hands to her face.

"Please, Bee . . ."

"And Mary," he said, "if you accept this ring, then I have your permission to try to love Him as much as I love you."

"I hear music coming from the living room," said Father Liguria.

"Someone should take a peek inside and see what they're doing," Symmachus replied.

"They're dancing . . . dancing cheek to cheek," Secretary Eligius said after cracking the door open. "I also see a beautiful ring on Lieutenant Peterson's finger."

Director Leo spoke up. "What does that mean? Dick, go ask the governor if he has made his decision. We can't wait here all night."

Eligius started walking into the room, but he stopped abruptly after hearing his name called out in a forceful manner.

"Dick," Senator Leontius began—he had gotten out of his chair all by himself. "This is still my home, and I have a say in what goes on here. Now, I want you to close that door and let those two alone. If you want to be useful, then go tell the press we have a new bishop." As soon as he finished speaking, he glanced over at Agatha. She had a proud smile on her face and a small tear trickling down her cheek.

XII

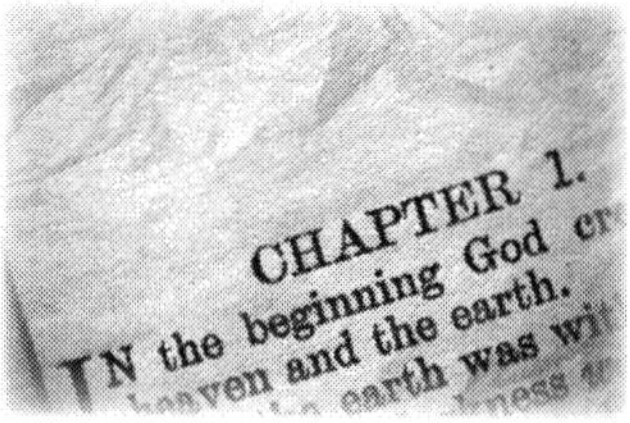

PRIESTLY PREPARATION

Ambrose sat alone on an old wooden pew beneath the cathedral's great dome. Five dreadful days had passed since he swapped his fiancée for a ghost. It was six in the morning, the sun barely peeking over the eastern horizon. Yellow light passed through St. Jerome's stained-glass window, causing colorful rays to cascade into the hall. The altar, however, remained in tenebrous shadows, appearing dull, lifeless, and grey. Unlighted candles stood like insipid soldiers. Church volunteers had removed all the colorful banners and flowers—supposedly making way for new arrivals—but nothing had yet been delivered.

Ambrose felt as dreary as the stage. He sat reading a book by Origen, pondering why the Christian scholar, who had castrated himself for the sake of the altar, believed in the preexistence of souls. More precisely, he wondered why the ludicrous guy even cared.

What possible use could that knowledge be to anyone? Ambrose sighed as he placed the book on his lap and looked out upon the chamber. Milky-white hands affixed in an open embrace, which projected from the twenty-foot metamorphosed statute of St. Mark, caught his attention. *I need to be more like him; I need to care about these things. I'm not a casual guest here anymore. Next to God, I'm the brain-trust of this establishment.* Ambrose looked down at the floor, its myrtle-green color just starting to emerge. *I feel like such an imposter . . . a fraud; gosh, I don't belong. How will I ever make this place come alive? I don't know the first thing about any of this. My god, what have I gotten myself into?*

An encased pipe organ burst into song atop the cathedral's balcony; treble pierced the silence—Ambrose nearly fell out of his pew. The startle caused him to speak unintelligibly while his book fell from his lap to the floor. The blue-haired organist heard his cry and stopped playing.

"Your Grace," she began, looking over the terrace to the rows of seats below, "I didn't know anyone was here. I didn't mean to startle you. Let me introduce myself; my name is Millie."

Ambrose composed himself and exchanged pleasantries with the woman. Soon, he heard footsteps approaching. Sounds grew louder as hard rubber soles clicked against the marble floor. The forthcoming person suddenly stopped, but his echo resounded through the church for several more seconds. "Good-bye, Mr. Ambrosius, I wish you luck," said Father Liguria.

Ambrose scooted over on the bench. "Please, Father, sit down if you have a moment. You've hardly spoken a word to me since last Sunday evening."

The cleric sat down on the pew next to Ambrose, leaving his luggage standing upright in the aisle. "You know my thoughts on this matter, Mr. Ambrosius. It's either a scam or a sham, but either way, I'll have no part of it."

Ambrose felt miffed. "A scam? Father, do you think I meant for any of this to happen? Do you think I told that little girl what to say?" His voice got progressively louder—and angrier. "Father, do you really think this is my sinister way of taking over the world? I LOST THE LOVE OF MY LIFE IN THIS FIASCO! AND YOU CALLED ME, REMEMBER!"

"You didn't have to accept the position."

"Oh really, Father," continued Ambrose, still feeling vexed. "Tell me, how long would my marriage have lasted to someone who thinks I'm too scared to face my destiny? And how long would it have lasted to someone who thinks I cared more for my happiness than a deaf girl's future?" His eyes moistened making his last remark. "I didn't lose Mary when I accepted the position, Father; I lost her when you declared me eligible!"

"I'm sorry, Mr. Ambrosius, but you can blame the Vatican for that. I called them three times and talked to three separate people. I even spoke to knowledgeable people in their legal department. Everyone told me the same thing: before consideration, a bishop candidate must have a doctorate in theology, must have graduated from an approved Catholic college, and must have at least five years of experience. However, after they told me that information, Mr. Ambrosius, none of that stuff appeared on their documentation—only the stuff about having a good reputation, being moral, and being pious. Well, you know the rest. I tell you, the world has gone mad, and I'm sorry to say you've been sucked into it."

Ambrose sat quiet, his emotions still churning.

"You're free to go there," Liguria continued. "No one is stopping you, Mr. Ambrosius. You can have a Vatican clergyman type out their rules on letterhead paper if you like. They will even sign and seal it on the spot. When you return, you can declare your ineligibility and get your lady friend back."

Ambrose lost his anger listening to Liguria's words. "She wouldn't want me back, Father. She'd never look at me the same way again. She'd wonder why I went to such trouble to defeat a child's future, why I couldn't just look a gift horse in the mouth."

The cleric smiled. "Mary sounds like an extraordinary woman, Mr. Ambrosius. I think you're quite remarkable, too. You don't look at things the way other people do. You have a unique perspective on life. I admire that about you. And, I must admit, you've given me some interesting things to ponder over the past year. However, let me see if I can give you some advice.

"You once reminded me that there is no marriage in Heaven, so why should the church bother with it on earth? Well, I suspect your Mary asks that question, Mr. Ambrosius. That doesn't mean she doesn't want you; on the contrary, I think she wants you now more than ever. But she doesn't want a chain around her neck; she just wants to be by your side. I know you can't have relations, and she can't bear you children, but that doesn't mean she's going to stop loving you. I'm sorry your romantic love came to such an abrupt end, but now you have a chance to grow into a deeper, more lasting relationship. Do the work of the church, Mr. Ambrosius, and you'll win Mary's love for life."

Ambrose stared into Liguria's eyes. "I take back what I said about you, Father; I really wish you'd been on our high school debate team."

Liguria smiled, standing up from the pew. "Well, I need to leave if I'm going to catch my plane. My mentor, Archbishop Auxentius, worked in El Savador as a missionary priest. I want to experience that life. More importantly, perhaps, I need to get away from all the petty turmoil around here. You'll soon discover that Arian versus Nicene fighting gets a little old after a while. I want to help people with real problems."

"Be careful what you ask for, Father."

The cleric nodded as he began pulling his luggage down the main aisle. The echo from his rubber-soled shoes resumed. "It's awfully good of your brother to quit his position in Trier to serve as your churchwarden," Father said. "Although I must admit, Mr. Ambrosius, I'm a little skeptical about the two of you working together. I mean, two former politicians invading the church's domain."

Ambrose walked alongside Liguria, heading for the back of the church. "My brother is also an extraordinary man, Father; he's not your average politician. He's a virtuous man who knows how to get things done. Once he gets settled here, he'll take care of my mother in addition to assisting me. She hasn't been in good health lately."

Nearing the back, they heard two honks from a taxi outside the cathedral. "I'm sorry to hear about your mother, Mr. Ambrosius; I hope she gets well very soon. Well, this is our final good-bye," he continued, extending his hand. "I wish you luck, especially for your first Mass on Sunday; you've got a lot to learn in a very short time. If you have any questions, call Father Palladius; he's a street-priest here in Milan. He works with the homeless on the city's east side."

"I do have one question, Father."

"You'll have to make it quick."

"Can I say Mass if I haven't received any sacraments?"

Liguria's eyes lit up and his mouth dropped open. "What?" His singular expression pierced the warm, muggy air starting to veil the church. "I thought you said you attended St. Frederick's grade school in Treverorum? You know, that whole shtick about your friend Basil with Tourette's."

"I did, Father; my parents sent me there for the discipline. You know, nuns have a unique way of infusing guilt into any youth they encounter. They are not afraid to hit you, or run around after you—my sister will attest to that. But my folks played it smart; they left it up to me whether I wanted the sacraments or not."

"And you declined?"

"Naturally, Father," Ambrose replied straightaway. "I mean, from the very beginning, those infernal sisters tried convincing me that I'd done something wrong just for being born. What a crock of—"

"I get it, Mr. Ambrosius," interrupted Liguria, pinching the bridge of his nose with his fingers; he felt a headache coming on. "Look, I'll give you emergency baptism, but you'll need to call Father Palladius to get the rest of them completed. But you need to be careful of him. He's Arian; he'll try persuading you that the Father created Jesus, and therefore, Jesus holds a subordinate position in the Godhead."

"That brings up another question, Father. How does Jesus fit his whole body into that tiny host?"

"Just dunk your head into that drinking fountain, Mr. Ambrosius."

Ambrose watched the cab drive out of sight, then made his way toward the rectory, staying outdoors, basking in the early morning light. He walked on freshly mowed grass along the northern side of the cathedral; the lawn appeared lush, still wet from morning dew.

He stopped to look at a bed of *Agapanthus orientalis*, better known as "African lilies," "lily of the Nile," or "Aunty Aggy's pants." Each flower had six clear-blue petals. Some wilted and drooped on the plant while others stood erect in full bloom. The leaves exhibited a shimmering green, broad and fleshy, and nearly one meter in length.

Unfortunately, Sister Anne had ordered their removal. Sister Henrietta hadn't realized their poisonous nature when she first ordered them from a catalogue. Sister Anne had told her to rip them out after several boys from St. George's got sick. Apparently, two of them had put stems to their mouths; they blew air past the shoots trying to make whistling sounds at pretty girls.

"Good morning, Father Ambrosius," said a mysterious figure.

Ambrose turned around, startled by the vocalization. He had thought he was alone. He didn't recognize the man's voice, or his face—partly because the sun shone back in his eyes. However, Ambrose could plainly see that the intruder dressed like a man of the cloth. He wore an ornately embroidered gold dalmatic that ended well past the knees. Ambrose guessed at his guest's identity. "Father Palladius?"

"No, I'm Cardinal Seneca; from the Vatican."

"Cardinal Seneca, I wasn't informed of your arrival."

"No, Father, I came unannounced. I prefer to see firsthand how people are doing before they have had time to prepare. Father Ambrosius, I've been told we made a mistake in your case, that you shouldn't have been ordained. Is that true?"

Ambrose remained silent. The query seemed simple enough on its face, but it caught him off guard. How he wished someone from the church would have posed that question earlier—five days earlier in fact. Ambrose wanted to cry out a thousand times over, "Yes, yes, Cardinal Seneca, why hasn't my relief come sooner?" However, Ambrose sensed something odd, something strange, even frightful. He sensed the cleric's question probed beneath the surface; it pried at his very soul.

"Well, Father, did we make a mistake?"

Ambrose felt his insides churning. *He's not releasing me from this assignment; he's denying my excuses. This man knows my thoughts. He knows that my happiness stands in direct opposition to President Valentinian's proclamation, against Mary's idealistic vision of a deaf child's future, and in stark contrast to the Vatican's thrice-scripted errors. His question isn't about mistakes, or who may have made them. He's asking me if I willingly accept God's commission despite my misgivings, whether I prefer going my separate way or choose Christ in my life. It's not enough that I'm here by default; he needs to know that I care.* The cleric's question tore at the young man's heart.

"I'll ask you one more time, Father. Are you ready to do God's will?"

Ambrose nodded. "Yes, Cardinal Seneca, I'm ready."

The cardinal smiled. "Well then, let's not waste any more time. Tell me, Aurelius—oh, may I call you Aurelius?"

"Certainly, Your Excellency."

Cardinal Seneca took hold of Ambrose's arm as they walked over damp grass on the church's northern garden. "You may call me Giovanni when we're alone," he whispered. "Now, tell me, Aurelius, do you know how to pray?"

"On my knees."

The cardinal smiled. "Yes of course, Father, but do you know the *Pater Noster*, the Lord's Prayer?" Ambrose shook his head.

"It begins with, 'Our Father in Heaven.'[3] That simple line says a lot about our faith. What do you suppose Jesus meant by the word *our*?"

Ambrose shook his head again.

"Aurelius," the cardinal continued, "in the beginning God created man and woman; he did so whole, without evolution. We don't know much about them, other than that they were made sinless in God's image and lived virtuously in Eden. We affectionately call them Adam and Eve. Father, you and I, and the rest of humanity—past, present, and future—are remnants of those blessed creatures. Now, what do you suppose the word *Father* means in the context of this prayer?"

"That we're paternalistic?"

Cardinal Seneca smiled again. "You should kick back and enjoy it, Aurelius. In a century or two, women will control the church."

Ambrose looked at him quizzically.

"Just kidding," he replied, pulling on Ambrose's arm. "Oh, I am going to miss chatting with you when our time is through. Yes, Aurelius, I suppose we are paternalistic. More importantly, though, the word denotes three concepts: First, since no one can have more than one father, it's saying that God is but one God. Everyone prays to the same God, Aurelius; there is no other. Second, since most of us have a personal relationship with our fathers, it denotes that we also have one with Him. It's saying that He's not some static, distant object, some remote cosmic machine. Rather, God is a living being who interacts with us. Finally, since a father most often serves as head of a family, it's saying that God has authority over us and serves as our protector. Now, dare I ask your views about Heaven?"

"I guess it's the place we all aspire to, Giovanni. But most of us, it seems, aren't in a big hurry to get there."

"Hmm, perhaps it's best you call me Cardinal Seneca. I can certainly understand why the Father commissioned you," he said, rolling his eyes.

"Aurelius, Heaven is a magnificent place, a stunning, verdant curtilage. Think of the most gorgeous place on earth and then multiply that by infinity. God calls this place home, and, unlike our own universe, it has no boundaries. It's also mankind's new home, but I'll discuss that later."

The men stopped walking to view a grove of variegated hosta. Morning dew clung tightly to their eight-inch wide, green-and-yellow leaves. Reddish-blue flowers sprang up from the distal half of three-foot cylindrical stems, making each plant look patriotic, as if it held a flag. Ambrose almost remarked on their beauty when he spotted a car roaring past the cathedral. It was Mary. She and her guards sped past the church heading for the rectory.

"Do you wish to go to her, Aurelius?"

Ambrose held his tongue, squeezing Origen's book. "No, Cardinal Seneca, I'm okay if we continue." He had a chastened look on his face, as if he'd been castrated.

"All right, then, let's move on to the second line of the prayer. What do you suppose 'hallowed be Thy name' means?"

Ambrose kept looking toward the rectory. "I think it's a lot like these hostas, Cardinal Seneca: their beauty and magnificence are simply too great for words."

"Yes, well, that would be Heaven," the cleric replied. "We've already moved past that one, Son." The cardinal gazed at him intently. "Your mind appears to be elsewhere, Father." He looked over at the rectory and saw Mary exiting the car. "She's quite lovely, Aurelius. Are you sure you're here by your own volition?"

Ambrose stood quietly for several moments; he turned his head away from Mary and stared disgustedly at the ground. "I'm trying, Cardinal Seneca. Please know that I'm trying as hard as I can. Do you think Jesus would've accepted the cross if He'd been less than a week into his ministry?"

A big grin swept over the cleric's face. "Well now, Father," he began, "that's more like it; that's the spunk I was told to expect from you. If you wish to go to her, Aurelius, perhaps we can finish later."

"No, Cardinal Seneca," Ambrose insisted. "If I'm ever going to love Him, then I need to learn all that I can."

Mary ran into the rectory and came upon Sister Henrietta seated at a desk in the lobby. The nun was comparing landscaping companies on her computer. *Wow, Marty's will pull out all those flowers at half the cost of the others. I wonder why they're so cheap?*

"Please, Sister," Mary entreated, appearing agitated, hysterical, and winded. "Take me to the bishop; I'm told he's dying."

"Dying, who in the world told you that, Governor?" Sister asked her question while bowing her head; she politely turned her eyes away from the pretty stateswoman.

"My receptionist told me to rush over here right away. Her exact words were: 'he's dying; you must come see him in church before he croaks.' "

Sister Henrietta let out a hoot, and then she sat back in her chair with a broad smile on her face. "Governor, it just goes to show you how fouled things can get when our people start talking to yours. Now that we have a bishop again, we'll need to get better acquainted so we can communicate properly with one another."

"What are you saying?"

"I'm saying he's fine, Governor. I called the mansion this morning and spoke with a . . . a Melva Hayes. She must be your receptionist. Now, I have no idea why, but she sounded frantic on the phone. Anyway, I relayed the bishop's exact words: 'I'll be crying if I don't sip coffee with her on the porch.' "

Mary sat down on the edge of a chair and closed her eyes. Her whole body shook with fear; tears trickled down her cheeks. "Thank God he's all right," she whispered. After a few moments, she looked up at Sister. "Did he really say those words?"

Sister stood up and peered out a window. "He's walking outside alongside the church; perhaps you'd like to join him?"

Mary stood up; her knees still trembled. She walked over and peered out the same window as Sister. "He looks so animated, doesn't he," Mary said with a sniffle. "It's like he's talking to someone; like there is someone walking out there with him. You know, when I worked for the county, prosecutors used to tell me they would find him rehearsing in empty courtrooms before a trial. I imagine he looked just like that," she continued, pointing at Ambrose from the window. More tears erupted in her eyes. "Oh, Sister, I'm afraid I pushed him into something he doesn't want to do." She stood weeping and shaking as more tears ran down her cheeks.

"There, there, Governor," said Sister Henrietta, putting an arm around her. "You may have played a part, but trust me, you didn't do this to him. God commissions his servants when they're ready. He does this in his own way, in his own time, and for his own purpose." The nun walked back to her desk. "Will it cheer you up if I show you his Episcopal ring? We haven't had a chance to give it to him yet; it arrived by courier last evening." Sister opened up a drawer and retrieved a small box and a basket.

Mary gazed at a large amethyst, *fleur-de-lis* gold ring. "It's beautiful, Sister—did those portabellas come with it?"

Sister chuckled putting the shimmering band back in its box. "Governor, the Vatican sent this ring to Bishop Felix by mistake. He's the new bishop of Zion—he almost auditioned here, you know. Anyway, he had already gotten his ring, so when this one arrived he kindly forwarded it here along with this compliment of mushrooms."

"Sister, may I give the bishop his ring?"

A troubled look came over Sister Henrietta. "I hate to say no, Governor, but we had planned a little surprise party for him later today, after we return from taking our sister to the hospital."

"I hope no one is ill."

"No, Governor; Sister Catherine just turned ninety-eight—she's healthier than the doctors. But every year she feigns an illness and spends all day at the infirmary. Honestly, Governor, you've never seen anything like it. She ruthlessly scorns the women but has an utterly delightful time with the men."

Mary smiled. "All right, Sister, I won't ruin your party. It sounds like you'll need some cheering after your work is finished."

"Oh no, that's not the reason, Governor; see, it took us two days to get permission for this party from Sister Anne—she's our Reverend

Mother. She is not exactly on board with all this. I mean, Reverend Mother made it clear she would much rather have a middle-aged Nicene who had risen slowly through the ranks. Governor, to put it mildly, she's not very pleased with the man you see out there."

"You know, Aurelius, they say good composers leave the best verse for last. Do you know the last line of the prayer?"

"I think so, Cardinal Seneca," Ambrose replied, "I believe it's, 'but deliver us from evil.' " Ambrose had no sooner answered the cleric's question when he asked one of his own. "Does use of the word *deliver* mean that we are already in Satan's grasp? Is that why we treat each other so badly?"

"Let me dispel some myths about Satan," began the cardinal. "To begin with, he's not a fallen angel or a fire-breathing dragon. And he's certainly not a red-skinned creature in the likeness of a human. He hasn't any claws or fangs, nor does he carry a two-tined pitchfork, either. That's Lucifer, man's personification of Satan. Oh, I suppose no harm comes in giving it a personality—even Jesus' scribes did that—as long as you recognize that Satan is not a *he*: he's an *it*. Satan is a force, a product of nature.

Ambrose looked confused.

"Let me explain. When God created the universe, it began as a point of matter no bigger than an atom. In other words, Aurelius, it started out as a frozen, motionless dot. God exploded that dot billions of years ago, sending particles of matter spewing into motion. It's the motion that's important to our discussion. See, our bodies are made from the particles, but our minds derive from their movement."

The cardinal reached down and picked up a stick, drawing a line in the dirt alongside a hosta. "Aurelius, if a point moves along a line going east, does it not also have the potential to go west? If I flip it so it travels up, can it not also go down? Every positive direction has an equal and opposite bearing. Satan is merely the cumulation of every wrong direction, every erroneous heading our minds shouldn't travel. Our thoughts, our choices—they must all be directed toward Heaven. Aurelius, every deplorable idea leading away from God results in evil.

"So to answer your question, yes, we're in Satan's grip. Like gravity, or the fabric of space, none of us can escape it until we get where we are going. No one walks in the sunlight without dodging shadows. As long as we're embodied in this universe, our minds will always have the potential to move in the wrong direction."

Ambrose thought it best to save further Satanic discussion for another day; rotating heads still twirled in his mind. "Tell me, Cardinal Seneca; was Jesus's death more important than his life?"

"Well, now, Father," the cardinal replied, "I'm finally starting to hear intelligent questions from you. New priests I encounter are mostly concerned about tripping on the altar, or saying something that offends their parishioners. But you, Aurelius, you have a sharp mind. Now, to answer your question, his life and death were equally important. Are you familiar with man's five ascents?"

Ambrose shook his head.

"Well, for man's first ascent, he simply gained an awareness of God's presence. Remember a moment ago when I talked about that exploding dot no bigger than an atom?"

Ambrose nodded.

"That was Eden, Aurelius, Adam and Eve's home. See, before God exploded it, He fashioned it as a gorgeous hunk of real estate, an exquisite rainforest that He created out of nothing—and in six days, mind you. Adam and Eve, in their glorified bodies, ruled over it in a blissful, loving embrace; everything felt peaceful and sublime. However, after they sinned, everything changed; Eden became a nightmare. God subjected them and their descendents to death; and indeed, Aurelius, they died, leaving behind only their glorified genetic material.

"God imploded Eden to the size of an atom, condensing it into a minuscule freezer in order to preserve their lionized substance. Then, He shattered it into trillions of burning, hurling, spinning particles after its pressure rose to an unsustainable level; shards of Eden burst forth to create our finite universe. Father, our universe is one popped kernel in a big round bowl; the only difference is that the fabric of our space is black, not yellow. See, God did this in order to separate their genetics into different parts of the classroom—for a reason I'll get to later."

Ambrose didn't dwell on the image; he tried understanding the nature of man's preexistence—at least he understood why it had fascinated Origen. "Cardinal Seneca, no self-respecting cosmologist today would believe such an improbable story."

The cleric smiled. "Aurelius, after the big explosion, inert matter was quite content moving outward toward cosmic expansion, never caring if it ever collided with another particle. But, life requires contraction; it demands molecular interaction. Thus, a few hundred thousand years after the explosion, when the universe was still in its infancy, the gravitational force that once held Adam and Eve together began asserting its influence again. It clumped the elements into gasses and eventually reformed their genetic substance. So you see, no cosmologist will ever fully explain the bizarre motion of those early atoms unless he or she takes life into consideration—but I think we are getting off topic . . ."

Ambrose lowered his book to his side and lifted his eyes toward the cleric. "Are you saying life existed before the big bang, that man's fêted genetics recovered, and that earth is a reconstituted chunk of Eden? Is that why God wanted two creation stories recorded in Genesis?"

"Seneca nodded. "And don't forget about Noah. His story concerns God's creatures starting over once Earth's waters receded and the planet became inhabitable. See, that bang dispersed the celebrated remains of many plants and animals. Lots of glorified material reformed after the explosion. Peptide chains from millions of species impregnate comets and planets all over this expanding universe.

However, none of that special material remains on earth; here, everything has either sprouted or died. For a creature to survive today, it must pass on one to another. Of course, that could change if the right comet struck us again. Oh, and don't worry about what has been lost or destroyed; God does everything by intelligent design. He doesn't take chances with natural selection.

"Now, when our planet's environment finally took hold," the cleric persisted, "seedling material started germinating: first plants, then animals. Man slowly emerged after millions of years, going through many changes. All species undergo environmental variation, but none evolves into others; chimps don't become men no matter how long you give them. Father, man ploddingly appeared because he's complex, not because he derived from some other species. He is virtually the only animal that functions without instict; he must learn as he goes, or he dies. It's hard for his kind to take hold in the wild; surviving years before reproducing is infinitely more challenging than what a fruit fly endures.

"After *sapiens* took hold, God began putting a soul in each of their bodies. The soul is what gives them higher thought and morality. It is what separates us from the other animals; otherwise, we'd not be much different. God seeds each *sapien* at conception; beauty and the beast are married—a marriage whereby the two become one—which is why no one should ever take abortion lightly. Do you have any idea where souls come from?"

Ambrose shook his head.

"Every soul inserted into a *sapien* once served as a living cell in Adam's or Eve's glorified body. The soul that resides in us is one of trillions of life forces that once animated them and their children. See, after the fall, God did not punish each of them as a singular entity; He punished their components. Each cell played an important roll in coaxing its host in a Satanic direction. Father, our souls are guilty as sin. God keeps them in Purgatory until He is ready to impregnate a *sapien*. He keeps them in a holding tank sullied with Adam and Eve's transgression. Once impregnated, our *sapien* serves as a catalyst, neither created nor destroyed, returning to Eden's substrate after its work is finished. It bonds with the soul, Father, dragging it through mud to wipe clean the stain that defiles it."

"Cardinal Seneca, I thought we were discussing man's ascents?"

"Hold your collar on, Aurelius. When impregnated *sapiens* initially arose, they behaved as ignorant beasts, having no awareness that God existed. It took them thousands of years to come to that realization, for their brains to develop and make that connection. Aurelius, early man discovered God when he learned about physics, when he understood cause and effect; religion and science were born together. That is how humanity's first ascent happened on this and most other hospitable planets. Of course, things are a lot easier today; if we want an awareness of God, we just have to ask our parents."

"Cardinal Seneca, Hindus believe that man, and indeed all God's creation, is good. Why does Christianity make the world sound so odious and dreadful? If I may ask, how does our faith square with them?"

"Our faith mostly agrees with theirs, Father. See, God shattered Eden and created this universe for one solid purpose—to scrub clean our blemished souls. From his perspective, creation is good. It works wonderfully; it accomplishes its goal. And, I might add, His perspective is the only perspective that matters. Now, we also agree that our minds and bodies are one with the universe, for everything physical arises from Eden. But our souls are quite separate, Father; that's where we differ. Our souls are unique, spiritual entities that God created. Now, may I continue?"

"Certainly, Cardinal Seneca, I'm sorry for the interruption."

The two men resumed walking arm in arm. "You're doing quite well, Father. I realize this is a lot of information in a short time. Now, where was I? Oh yes, after man achieved his first milestone, he foolishly glorified everything in sight. Now, our Jewish friends—and we can all be thankful—recognized the one, true God. Because of their insight, *sapiens* no longer paid homage to the sun, moon, and stars. Man gave devotion only where devotion was due. Man achieved his second ascent when he singled out God."

Aurelius remained quiet. He didn't wish to upset the cleric with another interruption.

"Now that *sapiens* have become aware of the one true God," Seneca continued, "our next milestone is to accept Him. That is where humanity struggles today. What I mean is, we must want Him in our life. God gives us that choice, you know. Many people do not want to include Him."

"If God is so great, and Heaven's so wonderful, why do we reject Him? I consider myself a prime example."

"Don't be so hard on yourself, Aurelius, you're further along than you think; after all, God has commissioned you. Nonetheless, you make a good point—why do people choose Satanic directions instead of ones leading to Christ? Let me start by saying there are as many ways to reject Him as there are people rejecting Him. However, people usually fall into one of three camps. Actually, people in the last camp accept Him, Aurelius, but they do so under false pretenses. They're actually our worst offenders."

Ambrose looked puzzled again.

"Let me explain. Life for those in the first camp is terribly stressful. These people continuously search for someone or something to divert them from the cortisol that ravages within them. They become addicted to drugs, sex, work, sports . . . anything, Aurelius, anything that douses that awful feeling inside them. They often try God, but find him wanting. But God doesn't exist to comfort us, at least not directly. He has never made that promise. God doesn't care if we are agitated or stressed—in fact, he needs us to feel alone and abandoned. But folks demand comfort; they get discouraged when He won't pacify them.

"The second group," the cleric continued, "consists of intellectuals. These people reject God because they spurn the people who revealed Him. They believe ancients were too primitive to put forth an objective truth. They correctly maintain that Jesus's disciples believed the world to be flat and that they had no concept of germs, genes, quarks, or black holes. Furthermore, these people forever searched for someone to deliver them from foes. Intellectuals rightfully question how such naïve people could possibly have gotten it right. They ask: why doesn't God reveal himself today so we can verify their testimonials?

"But Aurelius, religion isn't about revealing God's nature. It wrestles more with man's relationship to Him. And for that reason, ancients were as qualified then as we are today. In truth, intellectuals reject God because they can't wrap their minds around Him. They can't slice Him or dice Him—they can't neatly file Him away into their computer. They're too egotistical to understand that man is a mere speck of dust in a near-infinite universe, and that our entire universe is but one popped kernel to God."

"What about the third category, Cardinal Seneca? You said something about them being our worst offenders."

"The last group claims to love him, Aurelius, but they do so under a misguided perception. See, these people believe God exists to fulfill their wishes. They believe that if they pray long and hard enough, or with enough sincerity, He'll grant their requests. They act as if He's a cosmic genie, a heavenly Santa Claus.

"Aurelius, nothing could be further from the truth. God isn't our servant—we're his! He cares not a wit if our country wins a war, not a wit if our team wins a bowl, not a wit if we marry, divorce, or crash into bankruptcy. He doesn't care if we live homeless under a bridge, have an aunt dying of cancer, or stain our new tie with mustard before our big interview on Tuesday. None of these things matter, Aurelius—none of them count! Yet, people pray, hoping for a positive outcome. They are worse than the people who reject him; like whiny children, they want everything in sight. Father, they don't love Him for who He is; they love Him for their greed!"

Ambrose stood quietly for a moment; he had a shocked look on his face. "What *does* He care about?"

The cleric smiled. "Aurelius, if we pray for his help making sound Christian decisions, He'll answer us every time. If we beg for forgiveness—or for scraps on our table—He might bend an ear toward us. However, if we pray for credit, or to tip odds in our favor, we should expect a cold shoulder. God's only concern is that we get our asses into Heaven. Forget about this life—it's temporary. He loves our souls. He loves them so much that He's willing to drag them through mud! He wants them cleaned and pressed, united with Him in Paradise. He doesn't view this mired life as our entirety; that's man's shortsightedness. This world is nothing more than a purifying process, a succinct moment in our eternal existence."

"How does that happen? How do we purify ourselves and get our souls into Heaven?"

"Each of us must pass the five ascents. Each of us, one by one, must learn to accept God for who He is, and not for what He will do for us. To accept Him, we must distill our hearts; each of us must learn to be his servant. To that end, we must endeavor to negate the discord running within us, the strife that divides our thoughts and our actions. How many of us are sweet and pleasing on the outside, yet angry or panic-stricken on the inside? Moreover, how many of us have loving dispositions on the inside, yet find no time to help others on the outside? We must temper our discrepancies—become sanctified on both sides of our cup. Once we've subdued that dragon, we are no longer so susceptible to Satanic directions. Finally, we must learn to praise God regularly and help fellow *sapiens* in ways that we can. It's not rocket science, Aurelius—it doesn't require a doctorate in theology. But it does require a commitment to excellence."

"Cardinal Seneca, after a person purifies his heart, what then?"

"It's affectionately called *Confirmation.* After a person cleans up his act, God comes into his being as surely as night follows day—we call this *grace*; grace is the first step in the validation process. Jesus's disciples found out about grace on Whitsunday, when they received the Holy Spirit in the form of a flame. But no one can summon God's arrival; no one has power to move Him in the least little way. Nevertheless, He comes, Aurelius. He comes in his own time, in his own way, and for his own purpose."

"Is that different than being in our midst?"

"God is always in our midst; He's always available to help us out and show us the way—if we pray for the right things, that is. However, He only crosses the threshold of those with clean hearts. Once within, He commissions a favor—the second step in the validation process.

It may be something easy, or it may be quite difficult. It all depends on the person's gifts and the circumstances that surround him. Know that whatever God asks, it'll aid others into Heaven and won't be for some superfluous reason." The cleric smiled at Ambrose. "Trust me, Aurelius, He'll never ask you to put a puck in the net, I've heard about your skating."

Ambrose smiled as he continued walking with the cleric. "Cardinal Seneca, I remember my teachers telling me that faith alone saved us. Now you're telling me that works must be done."

"Excellent, Aurelius; see, the work a man does on his own, no matter how righteous, will never save him. He can walk blue-hairs across the street until he himself needs assistance, but that alone is not enough. God's commission is different. He designs it to test our love for *Him,* not as a charitable contribution to others. God desires to know if we will use our gifts to complete a task that He's assigned and not one we picked out on our own.

"Like any test, it encompasses a few unpleasant elements, forcing us out of our comfort zone, causing us to stretch. Jesus once remarked, 'a person must be born of water and Spirit.' Water signifies our purified hearts—why God graces us in the first place. But once inside, He wants to know if our love for Him is real, whether it's sprouted roots, or whether it will wilt on the vine at the first sign of drought. The Holy Spirit proctors the test. He alone confirms whether we've satisfactorily completed the project, or whether we've squandered our time."

"What's the last ascent, Cardinal Seneca?"

"It's called *Judgment.* For practical purposes, Aurelius, souls completing Confirmation regain the Father's favor. God allows them into Heaven after they have showered off their mud. Of course, they are still answerable to a few questions, but it's more of an exit interview, really.

"Moving through the five ascents is what life's all about, Aurelius, and it's what Jesus's life was about. First, He satisfied ascents one and two when He became aware of the one true God through conversations with his parents. Then He went on to step number three, working hard to lessen the discord between His thoughts and His actions. "Though repeatedly tempted in the desert, Jesus never knuckled to Satanic directions. And during His ministry, He praised the Father frequently and taught people sound rules to live by.

After sanctifying His heart, He moved on to step number four when the Spirit came round to confirm Him. Thus, in the middle of the night, in the garden of Gethsemane, God commissioned Jesus to die on a cross. As you know, Aurelius, Jesus accepted and fulfilled that request and confirmed his love for the Father. Need I say He breezed past Judgment?"

"Cardinal Seneca, what happens to—"

"The losers," he interrupted, "souls that aren't confirmed. Well, if they're lucky, God sends them back to the holding tank where they'll await another chance at absolution. But know this, Father, God doesn't play around; He takes all of this quite seriously. If a soul can't come clean being dragged through the mud of God's cosmic cleansing machine, he'd best be prepared to pay dearly."

Ambrose shook his head, taking in all the information. "Father, if Jesus's life revealed the way to Heaven, then why did He die?"

"Only his *sapien* died—his Essence lived on. Aurelius, all *sapiens* die when a vital organ no longer complies with nature. At that moment, the mind stops twirling and the body starts turning to ashes, but its widowed soul survives. However, to answer your question, Jesus's death served two important purposes . . . hmm, perhaps I should break them down. Tell me, how many Gospels does the Bible record?"

"Four."

"Very good, and do you know the order of their appearance?" Ambrose shook his head.

"Mathew is first, Aurelius. Now, what did he record as Jesus's last words?"

Ambrose crinkled his brow, thinking hard about the answer. "Something about being forsaken?"

"That's right," Cardinal Seneca replied. "He said, '*Eli, Eli, lama sabachthani*?' 'My God, my God, why have You forsaken Me?'[4] Those are a dying man's words—they are not to be taken lightly. In that moment, Jesus's spirit is speaking through his *sapien*, telling the Father what He feels, what we all feel, Aurelius—abandoned, plain and simple.

"Now, Jesus didn't have to say anything, or He could have said a thousand other things. However, his Spirit chose those words. He chose those exact words because that is what the Father needed to hear. The Father needed to learn if his punishment had succeeded, to know if humanity felt sufficiently vanquished. He needed to know if the inscrutable sands of Eden had adequately cleansed our souls. If Jesus hadn't felt enough suffering, the Father would know that his punishment had failed, that it hadn't broken man's spirit—and if that were the case, He'd never have let our souls into Heaven."

"Couldn't He have just learned that from us?"

"Come now, what parent asks their child if they've been sufficiently punished? The answer is always yes. Aurelius, every parent must decide that on his or her own. And to that end, God took on a *sapien*'s mind of his own. That's why Arianism fails, Aurelius," he continued in a softer tone. "The Father couldn't create a being for this purpose; He couldn't just fashion a messiah. He needed to incarnate someone living in the Godhead; someone He loved and trusted. Not a separate being, Father; a separate office of Himself. Love within the Godhead is so great, so pure, so refined, that one can *always* get a truthful answer. The task was too important to leave it to a lesser being."

"Where did we go wrong? I mean, it had to have been more than eating a forbidden apple."

"We're getting to that," continued the cardinal. "So, let's continue our journey through the Gospels. Mark is the next one in the series. Unfortunately, he recorded the same words as Matthew when Jesus uttered his final sentence. Of course, it could have happened the other way around—many people think Mark's Gospel came first. Some people believe this duplication is a form of attestation while others consider it plagiarism. If you ask me, though, I think one of those sources was relieving themselves in the bushes the moment Jesus uttered his final thought." The cardinal beamed a wide smile. "What? Don't give me that look, Aurelius; you know life happens." The cardinal jabbed Ambrose in the ribs with his elbow. "But wouldn't it have been something if the bushes were burning!"

Ambrose rolled his eyes.

"Let's move on to the third Gospel in the series. Do you know what the physician records as Jesus's final words?"

Ambrose shook his head again.

"Jesus cried out with a loud voice: 'Father, into Your hands I commit my Spirit.'[5] No one has ever spoken finer words of contrition. He's apologizing—giving himself back to God—not just for Himself, but for all mankind. See, our souls *willfully* disobeyed God. We, the breathing cells of Adam and Eve, imposed our will over His. Aurelius, man commits many mistakes. We're clumsy, so we drop things. We're naïve, so we think nothing of touching a hot stove. And we're simple, so we say foolish things. However, none of these things warrants punishment, at least nothing severe. Still, one behavior deserves attention, and every responsible parent will guard against it—and that is *willful* disobedience. Adam and Eve didn't just eat a forbidden apple; they tried to run the show! Jesus, in his dying breath, proclaimed humanity's readiness to come back under God's authority.

"Aurelius, the moment our souls turned against God, Satan came into the world. A serpent didn't create it, we did. It didn't exist until we opted to please ourselves over Him. It's our child, our offspring—our baby. God merely brought it along when He made his batch of popcorn—when He created His cosmic cleansing machine. He clothed Satan around us, in the mud that surrounds us; it twirls inside our heads every day. Every thought has the potential to move up or down. God wants to know which direction suits us, which master compels us. He needs to know if our love for our progeny usurps Him. Now do you understand why He commissioned Abraham to kill his son Isaac? Aurelius, the Bible bases its entire theme on that question. It's the golden thread that runs through its books!"

Ambrose remained quiet.

"Why do you suppose we have Old and New Testaments?" the cleric continued, without waiting for an answer. "Because that legendary story had two sides to it: the Old Testament answers the Biblical theme through Abraham's eyes, the New through Isaac's. Isaac may not garner the same respect as his father, but God commissioned him in Moriah all the same. That spirited boy willingly laid down his life for God. Do you honestly believe that energetic lad couldn't have escaped his one-hundred-year-old dad if he had wanted?

"And like Isaac," he continued, but in a softer tone, "Jesus freely laid down his life for the Father; He literally became the sacrificial lamb. Did He not tell everyone His Father was greater than He? Do you suppose Christ meant that literally? No! Jesus spoke in parables. He said those words in keeping with the Biblical theme. His love in the Godhead is so unselfish, so magnanimous, that He gladly became subservient to the Father. Aurelius, if we ever hope to reach Heaven, we must learn to have greater love for God than anything else in our life, including our offspring, our Satan, or ourselves. See, there is nothing a man can make, nothing he can be, say, do, think, or create that warrants greater love than the love he must have for God. If a soul can understand that tiny fact, get his pointy head wrapped around that idea, then he'll be well on his way to Heaven."

Ambrose shook his head, feeling a bit overwhelmed. "How do we know God accepted our apology?"

"Take a look at the final Gospel. What does the beloved disciple, John, record as Jesus's final words?"

"'It is finished.'"[6]

"Yes," the cleric replied. "Jesus chose those words because He'd restored our relationship. He felt our pain and accepted our contrition. As a result, God promises to remove the blemish from our souls and welcome us into Heaven. Of course, Jesus merely paved the way; each of us must still do our part. But, now you know the Gospels' importance," continued the cardinal. "Each writer, save one, heard Jesus say something different at the moment of his death—something that explains our restored affiliation with God. Aurelius, the Gospels may be alike in many ways, but they differ where it counts. Together, they tell a miraculous story."

"If Jesus's death restored our relationship, then why did He rise from the dead? What was that all about?"

"These are wonderful questions, Aurelius, please keep them coming. You see, others rose from the dead before Jesus. People of that generation were no longer very impressed with that little miracle. Jesus rose from the dead in order to fulfill scripture and to display a glorified body. He showed people of that time a glimpse of how we used to be before Eden exploded." Seneca smiled. "It gave everyone encouragement—something to shoot for; it helped boost his followers' faith and launch the early church."

"Cardinal Seneca, Muslims tell me Paul corrupted the church's teachings. They say he compromised Christian precepts to conform to Roman paganism. Is that true?"

The cardinal looked shocked. "Well, I'd say you've done some reading in the last few days. Aurelius, all religions, including Islam, turn sour to some degree. Even if Muslims pray in their original language, eventually that language dies out, or its words change meaning over time. Furthermore, priests and clerics of all religions gain notoriety by wrongly suggesting new meaning in scripture. Depending on their persuasiveness, they carve out a new denomination, or they die on the vine.

"The more often men try to interpret the Word, the more corrupt it becomes—that's simply the nature of man. But, to answer your question, Father, if Paul compromised Christian values, then it did him no good, for he spent many years in prison, and we're quite certain he lost his head."

Ambrose stood thinking as he shrugged off the image. The Cardinal's answers seemed logical; they appeared scholarly and carefully thought out. "Giovanni," he began, "please don't think badly of me, but I'd never forfeit my head for this cause. Tell me, how do I learn to love Jesus? How do I leave this classroom behind and make it real enough to sacrifice my life?"

"That's an excellent question, Father, one I seldom hear. See, Paul was an extraordinary fellow, a maverick, a tiger. If he lived today, he would be the lead soldier charging up the hill. But I suspect you're more like Simon Peter. Peter hung out with Jesus for nearly His entire ministry. He'd heard the sermons, witnessed the miracles, and gazed out at the crowds.

"Yet, at that moment when Jesus needed him most, he couldn't perform; his fear outshone his faith. Why, I bet Peter went to bed trembling most nights, wondering who was out to get him. But that's who Jesus chose to head His church. He preferred that scared little runt to the robust tiger. Aurelius, you'll discover that the power of a bishop is his weakness.[a] It isn't necessary to supersize your faith and become obnoxious to your neighbors. You just need a mustard seed's belief to complete the Father's commission." The cleric looked up at the morning sky, "Well, I should be going now. I think you've heard enough for one day."

"Please, Cardinal Seneca, one more question. As bishop, I'll need to defend this faith. How do I know ours is superior to others?"

"They're not in competition, Aurelius. Think of all monotheistic traditions as different forms of music. One might be jazz, another blues, still another, god forbid, rock 'n' roll. They are all God's Word, all tools designed to help humanity get into Heaven.

"However, as you know, they all come with different rules and regulations—guidelines that oftentimes overshadow the true meaning of the tradition. That was certainly true of Pharisees and the problem they had with Jesus. Pharisees wanted everyone to obey the rules—rules that had greatly multiplied since the time of Moses. They wanted all Jews to conform in order to please God, so God, in turn, would send them a messiah to deliver them from Romans.

"But Jesus didn't conform. See, He didn't come to save his countrymen from oppression, but to model our five ascents into Heaven. He didn't follow all their rules—not because He had anything against them. He simply had to make the point that man's ascents were more important.

"Aurelius, don't get fixated on rules," he continued. "If one religion foregoes pork and another despises beef, so be it. If one demands five prayers a day while another sets no conditions, who cares. Do as the traditions require; societies are free to set their own rules for worship. However, remember this: rules can never supplant the five stages of ascent. Everyone must ascend them in order. Rules and rituals that accompany the journey are the bridesmaid, Aurelius, never the bride."

"The next time I'm in Rome, Cardinal Seneca, I'll do as the Romans do."[b]

The cardinal smiled. "So, to answer your question, Christianity is the best tool for those of us wishing to glorify Jesus. For those that do not, they will have to go it alone or find some other music. Personally, I think they are foolish, but no one can force them; they must want to exalt Him on their own. I think it makes sense to pay homage to Christ for all that He's done for us. I know for myself, glorifying Him helps sanctify my heart like no other practice. And that's all I'm after—a sublimated conscience. I want a soul that loves God, one that is acceptable to Him. I desire only to become a servant worthy of commission. Father, my goals in this life are simple: get my ass into Heaven, and point as many people as I can in the right direction."

"Bee! Bee!" shouted Mary, running down a steep hill from the rectory.

Ambrose heard her voice and looked lovingly up in her direction. He embraced her after she met up with him alongside the cathedral. "Mary, I've missed you so much," he said, wrapping his arms around her. He released his grasp after hugging her for a good half minute. Then he put a hand to her cheek while he stood gazing into her emerald-green eyes. "Mar, why are you crying?"

She sniffled several times. “Oh, for different reasons, I guess. Don’t worry about me, Bee; I’m okay, honest.”

They walked arm in arm toward the vicarage when Ambrose suddenly remembered Cardinal Seneca. “Gosh, where are my manners?” He quickly turned around and looked for the cleric.

“What’s wrong Bee?”

Ambrose kept turning, desperately searching. “He was here a moment ago.”

“Who, Bee? Who was here a moment ago?”

“Cardinal Seneca . . . from the Vatican.”

“Bee, are you all right?” Mary asked her question while taking Origen’s book from Ambrose’s hand. “Are you sure you’re not losing it? I mean, you seemed very animated when I watched you from the rectory. Are you nervous about your first Mass on Sunday?”

Ambrose stopped searching and turned his attention toward Mary. “I was, Mar; I felt very anxious a short while ago. But the cardinal set me straight; he took away all my concerns. I feel surprisingly calm now.”

“Bee, look down,” Mary commanded. “If somebody else was here, then where are their footprints? Why are there only yours and mine in the wet grass?”

Ambrose took notice of the depressions in the lawn. After shrugging his shoulders, they continued arm in arm toward the rectory. Mary spoke up as they neared the door. “Thank you for inviting me for coffee on the porch.”

“I hoped we could plan our day together.”

She smiled. “I’d really love to, Bee, but I have to get back to the mansion. I’m meeting Chris Jacobson this morning to go over our campaign strategy. I can’t tell you how much I hate this election. Are you sure you don’t want it back?”

“Let me guess, Mar, Chris is telling you ‘there are no days off in a campaign fight’—am I right?”

Mary laughed. “That’s exactly what he’s telling me. But you know, Bee, he’s probably right. Ever since I took it over from you, Thompson has been gaining ground. We're almost neck and neck in the polls." Mary looked up at Ambrose; she posted a serious look on her face. "Bee, Chris wants me to start running negative ads. What do you think?"

"What have you told him?"

"So far I've said no. In fact, I told him I'd denounce any special interest running inappropriate ads against Thompson. You should have seen the funny look on his face after I told him that. He started muttering about two peas in a pod. Anyway, Bee, what do you think?"

"I wouldn't change a thing, Mar; your strategy is right on target. The people of Dionysius will love you in the end—just don't quit on them."

Mary squeezed his arm. "Thank you, Bee. I wish I felt as confident as you do about this upcoming election. Tell me you're coming to my debate at the capitol tonight?"

"I'm sorry, but I won't have time. I need to meet Father Palladius this afternoon; he'll be administering my sacraments. Then I need to greet the Valentinians at the airport. They're due in at six thirty."

"No!" she exclaimed, tugging on his arm. "It's my first debate. Besides, aren't the Valentinians coming next week?"

"They changed their plans at the last minute, Mar. I found that out last night. That's one of the reasons I invited you here this morning. See, they're keeping their travel plans flexible due to recent problems with the Goths."

"Why wasn't I informed?"

"They're grieving. Lady Justina doesn't want anything to do with politics right now. She only wants the church's help to mourn the loss of her husband. But listen, Sy is due in at four this afternoon, and I'm sure he's itching to tell us all about his dreadful trip to Africa; he almost died there, you know. Anyway, I'll send him straightaway to the capitol. He will be more than happy to assist you; after all, he's been through several debates before. I don't need him to take me to the airport, I'll ask Sister Anne instead. She and I need to bond; we have a few speed bumps to smooth over concerning my election to the clergy."

Mary thought about delving into his problem with sister but decided against it. "Bee, Sy's doing a wonderful thing leaving his mayoral seat in

Trier to become your churchwarden. Are you positive he won't mind coming to the capitol?"

"A gaggle of gladiators couldn't keep him away."

She smiled, staring into his eyes. "Are you okay with all of this?"

"I will be, in time." Ambrose put his hands on her shoulders. "You know, Mar, we're already acting like an old married couple."

"What do you mean?"

"Neither one of us has time for the other."

Tears welled in her eyes as she put her arms around him. "I love you, Bee."

"And I love you, Mary."

A few moments passed before they released their embrace. Mary brought her hands up to his neck. "I know you don't wear a tie, Your Grace, and you've already gone out the door, but let me adjust your collar."

"I told you I had fungus growing in my stomach," blurted Sister Catherine.

"Oh, you do not—you're as healthy as a horse," fumed Sister Anne, slamming the limousine door shut. It was six in the evening; they had just gotten back from the hospital after arriving at eight that morning.

Sister Anne raged, "Every year for the past ten years you've put us through this; we waste a whole day for nothing!" After taking a moment to compose herself, she looked across the top of the car at Sister Henrietta. "Please stay with her until she is safely inside the convent." They both watched as the elderly nun negotiated a tiny sidewalk crack with her walker.

"Sister Henrietta," Anne continued, "you'll have to postpone your surprise party for what's-his-name today; there's simply no time for it. You can give what's-his-name his ring tomorrow." Sister Anne walked hastily around the vehicle. "I'll be taking what's-his-name to the airport to greet the emperor's family. I should be back in a couple of hours."

Sister motioned for the chauffeur to scoot over. Mr. Peters, a timid, middle-aged man, reluctantly complied. "I'm driving tonight," Sister said; she had an angry smile.

Sister laid tire tracks after revving up the engine and speeding the short distance from the convent to the rectory. She was upset over Ambrose's election to the clergy. "It's not right," she said, looking over at Peters, "he's had no ecclesiastical training whatsoever. I've worked too hard on my faith to take orders from that imposter." Sister narrowed her eyes at the middle-aged man, pondering her preference for Archbishop Auxentius. *Perhaps he would do us all a favor and return from the grave to resume command of the altar.*

Ambrose stood waiting for her when she arrived. He politely greeted them and then sat quietly in the backseat of the car. "Buckle up, Your Excellency," Sister said, turning a sharp corner.

Ambrose sensed her frustration while he gazed out at the passing scenery through a blue-tinted window. *They guarded me with six sword-wielding behemoths as governor. Now that I'm bishop, they supply me with one angry nun brandishing a rosary.* He shook his head and smiled at no one in particular. *I'd call that even.*

"Don't worry about me, Sister," he shouted over the engine, "just get this bucket moving."

Sister weaved in and out of lanes; she drove irascibly through one red light after another. Mr. Peters anxiously huddled in the corner clutching his hat, the grip from his fingers tearing the fabric. "Are you okay, Your Excellency?" Sister asked her question while swerving to avoid a BMW.

"Fine, Sister, but could you speed it up? I'm in a hurry."

Sister hissed and scowled, peering at him through the mirror. *You want speed; I'll give you speed.* She leaned forward in the seat, adjusted her sunglasses, cracked her knuckles, and bore down on the pedal. She drove onto the ramp leading onto the interstate. Once there, she quickly whizzed past all the other vehicles. Her two male companions violently jostled as she veered in and out of traffic. Mr. Peters slumped in his seat, shielding his eyes with his hat. "How's that, Your Excellency?" she shouted.

Ambrose calmly twirled his ring; it had a menorah symbol on it and was too big for his finger. Father Palladius had given it to him that afternoon when he had found time in his busy schedule with the homeless to administer the sacraments to Ambrose. In truth, Palladius wouldn't have missed it for the world—his foremost opportunity to indoctrinate the bishop into Arian theology. "This will have to do," Ambrose recalled the Arian priest saying. "It's yours to keep until your Episcopal ring arrives from the Vatican."

The ring had fallen off Ambrose's finger several times and had nearly gotten lost in the limo's upholstery. Ambrose yawned, peering forward at Sister. "We'll be late if we continue at this rate of speed."

Sister Anne bristled. "All right, buster, all gloves are off," she said under her breath. "I'll show you that you can't just waltz in here and proclaim yourself sovereign. Don't think you can flaunt your fictitious dominion over me." Sister pressed hard on the horn and floored the limo. The speedometer on the car read 122 miles per hour. She bumped other vehicles, rattling the car's windows as lane markers blurred in her vision. Just then, they heard sounds of police sirens closing in from a distance.

"Perhaps you should stop," said Ambrose, looking serenely at the foaming nun through the mirror.

Sister ignored his suggestion and heedlessly sped several more miles. Finally, she came to her senses and slowed the vehicle to a trickle. She pulled the car over to the side of the road a quarter mile short of the airport; steam rose up from the engine. Sister sat motionless, her head resting against the steering wheel; tears dribbled down her cheeks.

Police approached the vehicle from behind and tapped on the bishop's window. "Sir," open up," one of them yelled. The officer continued speaking after Ambrose complied. "Your Excellency, there's been an explosion at the capitol. Several people are dead, and hundreds are wounded; you need to come with us." Dread crept into Ambrose's mind as he exited the car and made his way forward to inform Sister Anne of the circumstances.

The nun lifted her head off the wheel and shamefully peered out the window at Ambrose. The glass had shattered; most of it had fallen out in pieces during their journey. Tears flowed from her eyes, "I'm sorry, Your Grace," she began. "I hope you'll forgive me. I've no idea what came over me."

Ambrose gazed down on her kindly. "Sister, you did what I asked and I'm grateful. If it hadn't been for you, we'd have never arrived here on time. I don't know what I'd do without you." Ambrose glanced at the police officers before turning his attention back to the driver. "But if you don't mind, Sister, I've another favor to ask you. Please go the rest of the way and greet the Valentinians for me. Inform them that I'm not coming. Tell them I'm attending to more important matters."

Sister sat sniffling. "They're nobles, Your Grace, are you sure you want me using those exact words?"

"Would you prefer I asked Mr. Peters?"

Sister glanced at the man huddled on the opposite side of the vehicle. He had passed out. His eyes were closed, his mouth gaped open, and his mangled hat lay flipped upside down on the floor. A big smile swept over her. "No, Your Grace, I'd be happy to comply with your order," she said, sitting up straight in the seat.

Plumes of smoke billowed up from the capitol. Black emissions ascended high into a darkening sky, muddying the air with ash; its residue smelled for miles. Ambrose looked out through the squad's tinted window, noting the entire front-center of the building was missing. A bomb had demolished the capitol steps and the gubernatorial stage where the debate was to have taken place.

Firefighters on ladders sprayed water over the wreckage while their comrades below worked with pickaxes, shovels, and hoses. No fewer than fifty police and fire units and umpteen ambulances animated the twilight with copious red and blue flashes. Sirens, shrill and piercing, penetrated the air as more rescuers kept coming.

Harried people scurried in all directions: some screaming, some crying, some kneeling on the ground beside those who were dying. No sooner did Ambrose exit the squad than a medic asked for his help. "Father, come quickly."

The bishop hustled over, gasping at the appearance of a man in his twenties. The victim lay conscious; his eyes teared, his lips quivered, but no sound emerged from his mouth. The skin on his right arm and face looked mangled and charred to the bone. A crimson stain drenched the lily-white sheet that lay over him.

Ambrose brought his fingers up to the dying man's face to administer Extreme Unction. He soon realized, however, that he had no oil. The bishop checked his shirt and pants pockets, and then looked at the paramedic, who was busy adjusting an intravenous line. "Excuse me, would you happen to have some ointment?"

The medic reached into his smock and pulled out a packet of vinaigrette he'd put there from lunch. "Will this do, Father?"

Ambrose ripped open the container, blessed its contents, and dribbled the liquid over the tips of his fingers. He brought his shaking hands up to the victim's forehead. After making the sign of the cross, he spoke, "Through this holy anointing, may the Lord—"

The paramedic reached out and grabbed the bishop's arms. "He's gone, Father; you can stop." Ambrose retracted his hands and stared at the decedent. The man's lips remained motionless, no longer quivering. Ambrose backed away, his mind aflutter. *Did I cost this man's soul its rightful place in Heaven?* Soon, another medic begged for his help, cutting his self-brooding short. Ambrose hustled twenty paces over, sidestepping wounded who lay groaning on the pavement.

"Hold your hands here while I fix this syringe," said the paramedic, directing the bishop to apply pressure over a deep laceration. Ambrose, not wishing to cause harm, pressed lightly with his fingers over the victim's carotid. Suddenly, blood shot into the air in violent pulses as insufficient compression no longer contained the artery. Spattering sanguine humor drenched the cleric's hands, face, and clothing.

"Press harder," screamed the medic, glancing down at a monitor. Ambrose complied, pushing zealously on the blood-soaked dressing. "You can let up, Father," he said. "She's gone."

Ambrose backed away holding his bloody hands in the air, not noticing that his over-sized ring was missing. He mindlessly stared at his strobe-like surroundings while walking aimlessly about the grounds as twilight sky gave way to darkness.

Ambrose tried to make sense of it all, but life no longer held meaning. *Lord, why let them die before You've confirmed them? Give them a chance if you want them in Heaven! Father, what would have happened if Jesus had died prematurely? What if He had ducked under a tree in a storm and gotten struck by lightning?*

Religion seemed so easy when taught by a learned cardinal, so natural in the early morning dew of the cathedral's northern garden and utterly delightful when death wasn't looming. "I can't do this," he said, looking up toward Heaven. "I cost this poor woman her life!" Then he came upon the gubernatorial stage and saw volunteers dragging out two bodies.

"You're too late for this poor fellow, Father," said one of the workers. "He never had a chance."

Ambrose looked down at the decedent; a lump in his throat developed. The explosion had destroyed Leonard Thompson, the former Salamis County prosecutor and current gubernatorial candidate, who had spent millions on negative ads to rise neck and neck in the polls with Mary. Ambrose recognized Thompson's face, but the rest of him lay a twisted, mangled heap of broken bones rising from gnarled and char-hardened flesh.

Ambrose recalled a statement that Thompson had made in Judge Devoe's office: "I'll have your sweet hide for this when it's all over, Ambrose . . . go to hell."

The bishop stood staring, wondering where the man's soul had gone. He doubted it went to Heaven, but did it go to Hell—did that place even exist? Pergatory, perhaps? Would God give him a second chance?

Ambrose pondered whether Thompson, the endangered species, took notice that his campaign was over.

"Here's the next one, Father," said a rescuer. "I'm afraid you're too late for this one, too. But at least he's not all mangled."

The bishop recognized his brother instantly. Ambrose felt numb, paralyzed; he closed his eyes and bowed his head. He immediately felt the dread that had swept over him when the police first informed him of the tragedy.

Tears formed in his eyes as he stroked Satyrus's hair with his hands. "Sy, I'm so sorry," he began. "Can you forgive me? I took you away from Trier and brought you here to your death." Ambrose placed his head on his brother's chest and sobbed. "Sy, I love you so much," he said repeatedly.

Several minutes passed before the bishop regained his composure. "I'm going to miss you," he continued. "Marci's going to miss you, too. Thank you for being my brother. And thanks for being my churchwarden—at least for a few hours." Tears flowed freely again as he looked away and gazed out at the carnage. "Oh, Sy, I don't know how I'm going to break this to Mom!"

"We have one more victim," yelled a rescuer.

Ambrose heard the call. He shut his eyes and clenched his fists, bracing for the worst. *No,* he prayed, *no, God; I beg you: don't take Mary away from me, too!* He concluded his prayer by saying: "but let Thy will be done."

"It's the governor; she has a faint pulse." Other paramedics rushed over to see what they could do.

XIII

HOMEWARD BOUND

"In other news today," reported Henry Llinos to his radio-listening audience, "tenured professor J. Celsus Nero, who taught religious studies at Dionysius University, was charged with thirteen counts of sexual assault. Steven Harper has more details."

"Celsus Nero," began Harper, "who is currently seventy-two years old, graduated summa cum laude fifty-one years ago from Lynchtown College in Virginia. Nero devoted his life to ancient history. He'd become a leading authority on comparative religion, which he has taught at Dionysius University for the past thirty-one years. Prominent heads-of-state consulted the professor, while the United Nations recognized his expertise on matters of civil unrest, particularly where religious insurrections were at issue.

"Agnomen police arrested the professor at his dutch colonial home early this morning. The province charged him with thirteen counts of criminal sexual assault dating back twenty-two years. Two of the assaults are first degree, carrying a maximum sentence of thirty years in prison. Nine women have stepped forward. All are current or former members of the United Nations who claim that Nero propositioned them in his office after he secured their employment with the agency. Nero's attorney, Harold Aegidius, declined to comment on the allegations. Salamis County Prosecutor, Stan Amica, stated: 'we're confident we can bring him home to justice.'

"Of passing interest," Harper continued, "Nero requested an attorney from the law office of Agrippa, Leontius, and Drusus to defend against the allegations. The firm refused, however, citing a conflict of interest. Marcellina Ambrosius, sister of Bishop Aurelius Ambrosius, is one of the women testifying in the case. The bishop, you may recall, was a former partner in the Agrippa firm. Marcellina, who graduated summa cum laude from Dionysius University several months ago, works for the United Nation's peacekeeping division in Thrivingi, East Africa—"

Marcellina sat in the back of a limousine listening to Harper's report. From her position in the middle, she reached over Jacqueline and shut off the radio. "I can't listen to that," she said. She turned to her right. "No offense, Aamir, your personal sacrifice bringing him to justice is admirable. I can't begin to tell you how grateful I am for all the work you've put in. It's just that I can't deal—"

"I understand," he interrupted, grabbing hold of Marcellina's hands, "you need to focus on your brother."

"Nero's an asshole," interjected Jacqueline. "I'm glad you're testifying against him."

Marcellina glanced at her former roommate but remained quiet. The threesome rode in silence, having left St. Joseph's church located in the heart of Trier. The city lay in the far northwest region of Dionysius; travelers from Milan could reach it in eight hours by car.

They headed for the Gallia Belgica Cemetery, thick woodland found in Trier's northern suburbs and the final resting place of Marcellina's brother. His family had cremated him after his public viewing where mourners packed the church for two solid days.

The burial ceremony, on the other hand, was private. Only four cars trailed the hearse, each a black stretch limousine displaying an orange cross on the driver's door panel. Marcellina and her friends rode third in line.

President-appoint Gratian rode in the lead vehicle. He sat alone in the back while six sword-carrying guards sat up front. Gratian, along with stepmother, Justina, his half brother and co-president-appoint, Ian, and his three half sisters, Justa, Galla, and Grata, had all recently moved to Dionysius. They occupied the governor's mansion—at least until the directors voted to build them another Red or White House.

Gratian knew nothing about Satyrus. However, having recently lost his father and being a sound Nicene Catholic, he felt compelled to visit Satyrus's grave and offer his condolences to Ambrose. Justina would have come too, but she felt offended that the bishop hadn't personally met them at the airport. In her words, "What do I care about a silly bombing? He should have come in person to greet us. He had the audacity to send a haggard nun in his stead."

Ambrose and his mother occupied the next car. Mrs. Aurelianis, now in good health after her bout with pneumonia, talked incessantly about her eldest son's accomplishments. "Bee, do you remember when his Cub Scout car won the Pinewood Derby? Oh, and how about when Sy made that tremendous save in his high school soccer tournament? Bee, didn't your brother look handsome the day they swore him in as mayor? Oh, and my goodness, I'll never forget the day he showed you how to tie your shoelaces . . ."

The bishop nodded. He listened patiently and smiled occasionally but remained deep in thought. He felt sad for his mother; he knew she hadn't accepted her son's death. How could she? Sy had been her favorite—and so little time had passed since the capitol's bombing. She had looked with fond anticipation to Satyrus's arrival and had planned to spend a lot more time with him now that he would be living at the cathedral.

Ambrose hoped that she didn't blame him for Satyrus's death. *It really was Sy's idea to be my churchwarden,* he continued. *What can I say; he didn't want me looking unkept like President Valentinian. But I'll never convince her of that. Still, I hope she doesn't blame me for sending him to the gubernatorial debate that evening. Even if I hadn't asked Sy to give Mary pointers, he'd have still gone on his own. Mom must have known about his insatiable appetite for politics.*

As the limo drove on, Ambrose continued pondering. He stared out at a pasture and observed a collapsing red barn. Time had decayed its foundation; it leaned heavily to one side. He considered what Satyrus might have been like had he lived to old age. Then he thought about children—and a distressing thought came to mind. *We have no one to carry on our name. Marci is our last hope, but she's starting to get old; I wonder if she's planning to adopt?*

Then he thought about names he would prescribe to his children if he had them. He'd select Aemelia for his daughter and Philo for his son. He soon speculated about how he would feel if he lost one of them prematurely. *It's terrible when one of your children die early. The feeling must be very sad . . . very empty. I guess that's how the Virgin Mary must have felt.*

The last car transported the Benedictine sisters of the cathedral. One or more of them always accompanied Ambrose since his brother's death had left him void of a churchwarden. Sister Anne, who had gained a remarkable appreciation for the bishop following her speeding incident a week ago, sat in the front, offering the chauffeur some guidance: "You're going too slow . . . you're falling behind . . . you're going to miss the light if you don't hurry!" The driver looked at her strangely; he had consternation written all over his face.

Sister Henrietta sat by herself in the long row of seats behind the driver, researching hardy perennials on her phone. She had hired Marty's Landscaping to remove the poisonous *Agapanthus orientalis.* They had done a thorough job, digging much deeper than they had to—and at half the cost of the others. She searched for harmless plants to replace them and all but decided on *Aconitum.* Sister marveled at their spiked, steely-blue flowers. *I can't wait to see the Reverend Mother's face; she'll be so pleased with my selection.*

Sisters Angela, Martin, and Catherine sat quietly in the long row of seats on the passenger side of the vehicle. Angela stared out the window thinking of the best time to set an eye appointment to remove her necrotic tissue. Sister Martin hummed to herself after listening to Sister Catherine fret for an hour about her fungal gastritis. The elderly nun, having yielded to fatigue, slept soundly after laying her head on the apprentice's shoulder.

The air smelled fresh; a light fog obscured faraway vision. The hearse and the accompanying limousines turned into the cemetery entrance and traveled past a stretch of Lombardy poplars. The gathering looked out at hundreds of marbled tombstones stretching in straight white lines over rolling hummocks.

The newest markers—short, rectangular, and identical—greatly outnumbered the older ones that stood ten feet tall, shaped like lions, horses, and other strong creatures guarding their denizens. After the vehicles stopped and everyone had strolled over to the grave, they all sat on metal folding chairs, except Ambrose. The group directed their gaze at the urn, perched on a flag-draped table in front of them, while the bishop began his eulogy.

"Nothing among things of earth, dearest brethren, was more precious to me, nothing more worthy of love, nothing more dear than such a brother.[c] To this must be added I cannot be ungrateful to God.[d] I must rather rejoice that I had such a brother than grieve that I'd lost a brother; the former is a gift, the latter a debt to be paid.[e] You who are rich, weep; by weeping, prove that riches gathered together are of no avail for safety, since death cannot be put off by a money payment.[f] The last day carries off alike the rich and the poor . . ."[g]

Gratian bowed his head after hearing Ambrose's words. He reflected on his father's insatiable drive for wealth and power, and his casual attitude toward killing—how utterly useless all that expended energy had been. He recalled the words of his old catechism teacher: "People will do anything to have their names etched in history, Gratian. However, after the earth passes away, they will all be forgotten. Only those living a pious life shall be remembered."

"You that are old, weep," continued the bishop, "because in Him, you fear that you see the lot of your own children.[h] And for this reason, since you cannot prolong the life of the body, train your children not to bodily enjoyment, but to virtuous duties."[i]

Mrs. Aurelianis closed her eyes—her tears flowed as droplets of joy, not sorrow. "Thank you for those kind words, Bee," she whispered. "That's exactly how I raised my children."

Ambrose continued speaking after carefully looking at his audience. "And you that are young weep too, because the end of life is not the ripeness of old age . . ."[j]

Jacqueline perked up at his words. Tears welled in her eyes as she pondered how petty she had been over the past year. She had obsessed about marrying Accalia and living in the mellifluous bonds of matrimony. After regaining her composure, she gave serious thought to her future—her future beyond the grave.

"Oh deceitful joy," continued Ambrose, "oh, the uncertain course of earthly affairs![k] We thought that he who was returned from Africa, restored from the sea, preserved after shipwreck, could not now be snatched from us. But, though on land, we suffered a more grievous shipwreck . . ."[l]

Aamir closed his eyes. Before Satyrus died, Marcellina had spoken to him about her older brother's trip to Kismaayo. She informed him that young pirates, kidnapped children who murdered and plundered on behalf of Thrivingi warlords, had capsized his vessel.

Aamir shook his head, wondering how Satyrus had survived that ordeal, only to return home and get himself killed in a bombing attack at the capitol. *I can't believe my people are doing this. Don't they know killing is wrong? Despite our deplorable conditions, retaliation is cowardly thinking. I pray Muntisir isn't involved.*

Ambrose continued. "Any time there was a discussion between me and my sister on any matter, as to which was the preferable opinion, we used to take you as judge, who would hurt no one, and anxious to satisfy each, kept to your loving affection . . ."[m]

Marcellina began crying, remembering a conversation between Ambrose and herself when they had attended grade school. They had debated whether the Reverend Dr. Martin Luther King Jr. or Mahatma Karamchand Gandhi was the world's greatest humanitarian. Marcellina had chosen King for his bloodless leadership advancing civil rights around the globe. Ambrose had chosen Gandhi for being Dr. King's predecessor and for his nonviolent leadership in securing India's independence.

Their argument had waged until they turned to Satyrus for help. "Well, let's see now," she remembered him saying, "they were both men of peace who opposed oppression and discrimination, both showed exemplary courage against insurmountable aggression, both were assassinated, and both were humble enough to have nominated the other for this distinguished award. Still, I'd give the nod to Gandhi."

"Why?" she remembered asking.

"Because he made his own clothes."

"That's what I told her," Ambrose interjected. Marcellina remembered watching the two of them walk off together—her two inseparable brothers.

"He made him Jesus," continued the bishop, "Him, that is, who received the name in his bodily nature; He made Him of whom also the patriarch David writes, 'Mother Sion shall say, a man, yea, a man is made in her.'[n] But being made man He is unlike the Father, not in Godhead, but in his body; not separated from the Father, but differing in office, abiding united in power . . ."[n]

Sister Anne graciously bowed her head; small tears formed in her eyes. *Thank you, Jesus; our new bishop believes wholeheartedly in the Trinity. Lord, he may not have risen up through the ranks as I had hoped, but I'm forever grateful he's not Arian.*

Ambrose looked out at his audience. "Why should I weep for you, my most loving brother, who was thus torn from me that you might be the brother of all?[o] For I have not lost, but changed my intercourse with you.[p] Before we were inseparable in the body, now we are undivided in affection; you remain with me, and ever will remain."[q] The bishop paused for a moment to regain his composure; he wiped tears from his eyes before speaking further. "To You, I offer my sacrifice; accept favorably and mercifully the gift of a brother, the offering of a priest.[r] May his soul, and the souls of all the faithful departed, through the mercy of God, rest in peace." Ambrose knelt down and kissed the urn, then sprinkled it with holy water. "Please everyone, the ceremony is ended," he said upon arising. "Go home to love and serve the Lord."

Sister Henrietta approached the urn to retrieve the flag that lay beneath it. After folding it tightly, she presented it to Mrs. Aurelianis, who now wept uncontrollably; Satyrus's mother no longer denied his death.

"Mrs. Aurelianis," whispered the nun, "your son was a true patriot, an honorable American. But even more importantly, he was a child of God, a servant to Jesus. We know he purified his heart and did the work of the Spirit. Weep not for him, ma'am, for his soul resides in Heaven. Your son has found his way home."

The gathered stood up from their chairs and began mingling. Marcellina smiled at her brother. "I'll stay with mom until she's ready to leave." Then she promptly added, "Bee, thank you for the lovely eulogy."

Ambrose returned her smile, but his attention soon turned toward the people standing beside her. "I've heard you talk a lot about your friends, Marci, but I don't believe I've ever met them."

Jacqueline spoke up before Marcellina could introduce her. "Hi, I'm Jackie; it's nice to meet you." She walked toward the bishop, extending her hand, but cut short her introduction—she didn't know how to address him. She couldn't call him "Bee"; only his family used that name. "Your Grace" or "Your Excellency" sounded too formal—after all, he was her roommate's little brother. She also debated kissing his ring. Being Jewish, she didn't know Catholic protocol.

"Hello Jackie," he replied, "it's nice to meet you, too. Please, call me Bishop Ambrose," he said, shaking her hand.

"Bishop Ambrose, I couldn't help notice the ring on your left hand. May I ask where you got it?"

Ambrose looked down at his oversized ring; it had a menorah symbol on it. He wore it despite wearing an Episcopal ring on the right, which he had received a few days ago during a surprise party given to him by the Benedictine nuns at the cathedral. Strangely enough, Sister Anne had been the most exuberant person at the party.

"I've received this ring twice," he began, twirling it on his finger. "Father Palladius gave it to me when I received the sacraments. However, due to its large size, I lost it after assisting paramedics at the capitol. One of them found it inside a deceased woman's body and kindly returned it to me the next morning."

Ambrose glanced up at the overcast sky. "I took it as a sign God wants me to wear it. It reminds that even though no Jew is a Christian, every Christian is a Jew. Does it hold particular significance for you, Jackie?"

Jacqueline stepped closer to inspect the ring. "You said a colleague of yours gave it to you, Bishop Ambrose. Do you happen to know how *he* got it?"

Ambrose surmised it held significance. "Yes," he replied, "Father Palladius held a prayer service for university students at Phi Beta Delta the morning after it burned. He said he found it amidst the building's ruins. He put a month's notice on the school's website, but nobody came forward to claim it. Then, because my Episcopal ring hadn't timely arrived, he gave it to me on the day of my sacraments—so I'd have something to wear for my first Mass, you understand. Does it belong to you, Jackie?"

"No, but my partner's former lover has one just like it. It even has that sharp edge at the base of the candle. It couldn't possibly be hers, though, she had no reason to . . . be . . . at . . . that . . . sorority." Jacqueline's words slowed as a terrible thought came to mind. She looked at Marcellina, wondering if she had concluded the same.

Marcellina didn't infer anything at first. Instead, she examined Jacqueline's eye to determine if the ring had permanently scarred it. "I don't see a mark any more"—she suddenly stopped speaking; Jacqueline's terrible thought came upon her. "No, Jackie, don't even think it. You told me Beth wanted revenge, but she wouldn't go that far. She'd never burn down a building, would she?"

Ambrose looked at them quizzically. "Is there a problem, ladies?"

"Nothing, Bee," Marcellina replied, "Jackie and I just had the same preposterous idea—forget it, it's nothing." She quickly changed the subject. "Bee, did you know Jackie is getting married in a couple of weeks?"

"Congratulations"

"Thank you, I owe it all to—"

"Oh, Bee, I'm so sorry," Marcellina interjected, before turning to Jacqueline. "Jackie, my brother was proposing marriage to the governor on the day he was elected bishop. I'm so sorry, Bee," she continued, redirecting herself toward her brother. "The whole idea of marriage must be very painful."

"I'm getting over—"

"All I wanted to say, Marci," interrupted Jacqueline, "is that I'm grateful to him for approving same-sex unions." She directed herself toward the bishop. "I've read your articles, Bishop Ambrose. I'm sorry, but I don't agree with you that we have a biological disorder—even psychologists don't understand it—but I'm thankful you don't discriminate against us. And I'm pleased that you can now implement your ideas without approval from the Senate." Then she smiled and added, "Bishop Ambrose, you're welcome to come to my wedding. I have decided to have it at my synagogue. I need to start going there more often. If you come, you can watch Marci holding up a leg of my chupa."

"Thank you, Jackie; I'll do my best to make it." He smiled at her, and then shifted his gaze toward Marcellina. "You know, Marci," he said, making a devilish grin, "we could have lots of fun if I held up another leg." Without waiting for a reply, he redirected his attention to the man they had left out of the conversation.

Aamir stepped forward. "It's nice to meet you, Bishop Ambrose," he said, extending his hand. "My name is Nadif, Aamir Nadif."

"Nadif . . . now where have I heard that name?"

"I work at the university in their robotics department."

"Hmm . . . no, that's not it."

"You might know me as the man who bailed your sister out of jail on the day of her graduation."

"I do remember that, Mr. Nadif—and I'm grateful—but no, that's not it either."

"Perhaps you've heard my name in connection with my younger brother, Muntisir." Aamir began speaking more softly. "I fear he may be involved in the recent attacks on our province. He may have played a role in the bombing at the capitol."

"I'm sorry to hear that, Mr. Nadif, and I trust you've given your information to the authorities." Ambrose stroked his chin. "But it seems to me I've heard your name in connection with another matter. Oh, I know," he said excitedly, snapping his fingers. "You're the guy who stole Marci's computer in some crazy scheme to date her."

Marcellina shot him a malevolent look. Aamir lowered his gaze to the ground. "Yes, sir, that would be me."

"Well, I think you and I are going to become good friends, Aamir," said Ambrose. The bishop put an arm around him as they began walking toward the limo. "Aamir, would you join President Gratian and me on the way back home to Milan?"

Sixteen days had passed since Satyrus's funeral. At 10:30 on a Saturday evening, Lierchetsky sat slumped in the seat of his old rusted Impala. He was parked in the shadows between flickering street lamps five houses from Beth Mizrahi's apartment, his fourth night investigating the lesbian's nocturnal habits. He was tailing her at the request of Bishop

Ambrosius, who had a strange notion she may have set fire to Phi Beta Delta. "Where does he get this stuff?" he muttered. "He must have had another chat with his cat."

Tonight was an especially important night—the eve of Jacqueline's wedding at the Akiba Synogogue, located six miles east of the cathedral. "The way Jews are bad-mouthing Catholics, Drew, I wouldn't care if their temple burned to a delicate crisp come Sunday evening. Just don't let it go up in smoke before Jacqueline's wedding in the morning," he recalled the bishop saying.

"There she is," the investigator mumbled, watching Beth emerge from the complex. She wore cowboy boots, faded blue jeans, and a muscle shirt under her denim jacket. She walked to an adjacent parking lot and hopped inside a silver-grey Magra. "Not bad if you like 'em tough," he mumbled again.

The detective followed ten car-lengths behind, weaving through traffic on the way to the Gallus. *She's a creature of habit, I'll give her that.* He backed his car into a space on the street across from the pub. For the past several nights, he had remained in his car and waited several hours until she emerged. Tonight, however, he opted to follow her into the establishment. The tall, lanky man looked up at an advertisement. *No kiddn', the Balba Stuarts are playing. I haven't heard them since I broke up with Jen.*

Lierchetsky sat at the bar nursing a single-malt scotch. He kept his eyes on Beth, who had positioned herself near the band. She met up with three other women—two of them pretty brunettes, the third a manly, brutish looking lady, if you dared to call her a lady. *I wonder what she sees in that ugly one,* he pondered, watching them saunter onto the dance floor.

Cummings, the band's lead guitarist, played an array of lively songs. The detective took another sip of his drink and tapped his foot to the music. Lierchetsky raised his glass to toast the lesbian ensemble. "Keep drinking and dancing ladies, then go home and sleep it off," he said to no one in particular.

Lierchetsky downed his fifth whiskey just before two in the morning, yearning to hold one of the brown-haired women in his arms as Cummings slowed the music. *The one in the red is gorgeous,* he thought, staring directly at Britannia. *I'd give anything to have her pressed up against me right now.* He shook off his lust and looked around at the patrons. Their youthful faces started him thinking, *Drew, you old-timer; you're not twenty-one any more. Playing the field is how you lost Jen.* "God, I wish I had J . . . Jen back," he stuttered. Tears welled in his eyes while caliginous circles formed beneath them. He motioned at the bartender. "Coffee; I'll take it black."

He had taken two sips of the hot liquid when his target, and the women with her, stood up to leave. He turned himself toward the bar and ducked his head low as they passed within inches behind him. He followed them closely, keeping his eyes glued to Britannia's ass as they made their departure.

The night air felt refreshing, welcome relief from the malodorous, smoke-filled emporium. The women walked toward the parking lot while the inebriated detective staggered across the street and fired up his Impala. Beth tore out like a Grand Prix racer, driving erratically south on Fourth Street. "Sh . . . she ain't going home," he stuttered aloud to himself.

Lierchetsky tailed her to the synagogue. Neither the adrenaline rush from the high-speed chase nor the breeze from his open window did much to sober him up. He parked his car around a corner and watched two other women pull up in a green SUV behind Beth. The women emerged from their vehicles and walked toward the front of the church, carrying several bags and a large spray canister.

Lierchetsky cautiously exited his vehicle, tiptoeing toward the west side of the temple, hoping to get a better view of their movements. As he crept along the side of the building, he spotted one of the women spraying liquid along its foundation. Just then, he heard a voice behind him.

"Can I help you, creep?" Britannia asked.

Lierchetsky jumped a foot in the air, wheeling around to address his would-be attacker. "Whoa," he exclaimed, "you almost gave me a heart attack, lady." He stared at the brown-haired woman in red; she held a canister of pepper spray in her hand. Suddenly, he no longer felt the urge to have her pressed up against him, nor did he care much for her ass. Nonetheless, Lierchetsky remained calm; years of training had taught him to focus his mind on the right course of action. Meanwhile, the other two women came running up to the scene.

"I found this creep spying on us," said Britannia.

"This creep's been spying on me all week," Beth replied.

"He was in the bar tonight; I saw him," Antonia interjected.

Lierchetsky remained composed, needing to act slowly with no sudden movements. He knew that if he stayed calm the situation would defuse. *These women are reasonable,* his fuzzy mind surmised, *they'll talk it through; we'll all have a good laugh when it's over.* The detective began talking, slurring his explanation. "L . . . ladies . . ."

Unfortunately, the stubble on his face, the fumes from his breath, his blood-shot, dark-circled eyes, and his unremitting tottering, made him resemble a hostile animal, a combative, bibulous predator. Before he could complete a sentence, Britannia shot him with aerosol.

The irritant sent him reeling to his knees as he covered his face with his long, lanky fingers. "AAHH," he shouted, trying not to rub the agent in any deeper. Lierchetsky's eyes screamed with fire. Feeling them swell, he tried desperately to open them. Just then, the women pushed him to the ground and kicked his back, sides, and stomach in a seemingly endless barrage. Things got fuzzy after they hit him in the back of the head with a metal object. A second blow just like it caused Lierchetsky to forget all his troubles.

Houses, trees, fences, and other familiar objects replaced mystical figures as Lierchetsky slowly regained consciousness. He didn't know how long he'd been out—darkness still encircled him—but he wasn't sure it was the same night. He sat up; a sharp pain shot through his side. "Ohhh," he groaned. Upon standing, his body hurt less—but then his head started throbbing. "Oh geez."

He walked slowly, dragging his feet to the side of the building. *Thank God it's still standing.* Then he staggered along a walkway to the front of the edifice to determine if the women still lingered. Lierchetsky moved sluggishly, not keen on taking another beating. Upon arriving, he noticed that their cars were missing. He could see rows of flowers newly planted on opposite sides of the entrance; a sweet fragrance arose from the foundation. "They wanted to make it look and smell nice for the wedding," he said beneath his breath. "Geez, I'm so glad they went home."

Lierchetsky groaned, wriggling into his Impala. Once seated, he glanced into the rearview mirror and winced in pain at the site of his eyes. *Oh, geez; it hurts just to blink. The last time I looked this bad three burly men in a biker bar had beaten me; now all it takes is three little lesbians.* He closed the door, started the engine, and drove away from the side of the road. *I'm never touching booze on the job again; you can be sure of that!*

The detective drove five minutes away from the synagogue when he reflected on something he had thought about earlier. *Did I say all it took was three little lesbians?* He slammed on the breaks. "Shit, I remember a fourth one being at the bar," he said aloud, "and she was damn ugly." Lierchetsky made a 180-degree turn and pushed hard on the accelerator. He headed back to the temple. "I sure hope what I think happened didn't just happen."

Flames shot up the north wall of the Akiba, reaching its tiled roof. Lierchetsky dialed 911, then exited his car as fast as his aching body would permit him, determined to douse the combustion. He spotted a hose on the south side of the building—too short to reach the escalating fire.

He looked about again and found a bloodstained spade, upright, leaning against the temple's west wall. He grabbed it and began frantically shoveling soil over the flames near its foundation. "I wish I'd saved this for evidence," he muttered, half out of breath, rubbing the back of his head after taking a short rest.

He worked intensely for five more minutes before the fire reduced to a flicker. Then he looked out at the adjacent streets. "She's here . . . somewhere." Sirens sounded in the background as he spotted a manly, brutish looking lady—if you dared to call her a lady. She stood a block away under a flickering yellow street lamp, smiling sweetly while stepping into a silver-grey Magra. Lierchetsky shook his head. He limped back to his car and arduously drove himself home.

"It's up to you, Jacqueline," said Rabbi Abiah later that morning, "and your fiancée, Accalia, of course. The marshall estimates twenty-thousand credits' worth of damage to the building. But he says it's perfectly safe to occupy, as long as you and your guests don't mind the smell of ash. Look at it this way," he added, "with the hole in the roof, we'll be pleasing some of our stricter parishioners."

"How's that, Rabbi?"

"There'll be nothing above the chupa except clear, open sky," he replied with a smile. "Besides, you'll be a beacon to others that we Jews press on no matter what life throws at us. Of course, Jacqueline, I'll understand if you and Accalia choose to delay your wedding until we get it fixed."

Jacqueline returned his smile. "If it was just the roof, Rabbi Abiah, I'd go ahead with the ceremony. But I have a much more serious problem."

"Oh, and what's that, my child?"

Tears began welling in her eyes. "One of my dearest friends, Marci Ambrosius, didn't arrive at the airport yesterday. I can't contact her, Rabbi; she doesn't answer her phone. She came here a couple of weeks ago for her brother's funeral but then returned to East Africa. She's an ambassador with the United Nations in their security department. Marci had arranged to come back and hold up my chupa. Oh, Rabbi Abiah, it's not like her to miss an important engagement. She's the most responsible person I know. Oh, Rabbi," she cried again, "I'm so afraid that something terrible has happened to her."

Abiah laid a hand on Jacqueline's shoulder. "There, there, child, don't go jumping to conclusions." He looked squarely into her eyes and asked, "Are we talking about the bishop's sister, a Catholic?"

Aamir landed safely in Moqdisho at 11:30 that morning. He'd flown African Express Airways red-eye Flight 821, arriving on the day of Jacqueline's wedding. Jacqueline had called the bishop's office the previous day asking if Ambrose had received any news from Marcellina—to which Ambrose replied no. After their conversation had ended—and after his own attempts to reach his sister had failed—Ambrose had called Aamir.

The engineer immediately called his sister, inquiring if she had heard any news about a high-ranking official missing in the area. Aarifah got little to no information from agency officials, but her own sources convinced her that something was wrong. Her informants agreed that General Athanaric seemed more agitated than usual. That was all Aamir had needed to hear before purchasing an airline ticket. He had immediately called the bishop and spoke of his plans to visit Thrivingi. Aamir convinced Bishop Ambrosius to stay home, that his presence would only delay him. Then he had called Aarifah again. "I'll see you in twelve hours."

Aamir walked arm in arm with Aarifah through the Wazigua Hospital. "We've made outstanding purchases with your credit," she said, pointing at five new cots and a cabinet full of medicine. "But I'm afraid too many people are still dying from starvation. Poor Labaan," she continued, watching a nurse pull a white sheet over the bony man's head.

"Sister, about our discussion on the phone yesterday, do you have any information on Marcellina?"

"Only what I've pieced together. Muntisir showed up unexpectedly after you called me."

Aamir's eyes lit up. "Muntisir is here?"

"He didn't stay long, brother; he's already come and gone. Strange, he seemed very upset and wanted to know if I knew anyone connected with the United Nations stationed in Kismaayo. Naturally, I told him about Marcellina, but that was the extent of our conversation. After that, he flew out the door—presumably heading for Kisi. I wish he hadn't left so abruptly, I had a large doll with hazel-brown, marble eyes wearing a lovely pink dress that I wanted to give him."

"A doll?"

Aarifah didn't answer him directly. "Another strange thing happened yesterday, Aamir. Missing children from our community suddenly reappeared. They said General Fritigern had held them under guard at his compound—we all thought that man was dead. Then they said General Athanaric drove Fritigern off and kept them all hostage for himself."

"How did they get free?"

"They said a doctor escaped from the camp. They didn't know his name or where he came from, but they presumed he went for help."

"I'm guessing he went to the United Nations," Aamir surmised. A gruesome picture formed in his mind. "Marcellina and her team would have raided the compound." He lowered his gaze at a sickly man laboring for breath before finishing his thought, "and she may have gotten hurt—or killed—in the process."

"I pray that's not true, brother," said Aarifah, squeezing Aamir's arm tightly. "Marcellina is such a nice person."

Aamir patted her arm. "Aarifah, if they captured Marcellina, then how did the children get here?"

"They said they ran for hours before finding the river. A ship finally rescued them." Aarifah chuckled. "They said the vessel stunk to high heaven, but that the captain seemed really nice. He had an unusual accent; they all joked about the way that he spoke. They also said he offered to sell them manure at a good price. They thought he was kidding until he opened a bin and showed them inside. Apparently, he offered them a deal because he couldn't find a buyer this late in the season."

Aamir stayed focused. "You said something about a doll?"

"One of the boys had it with him when he returned. It had hazel-brown eyes and a lovely pink dress, except the dress was quite dirty, and parts of it were torn. The boy said he found the figurine in a dumpster near the compound and that he planned to give it to his sister." Aarifah strengthened her grip on Aamir's arm. "He said he'd found it partially hidden under a dead woman's body."

Aamir shook his head and lowered his eyes.

"But I got to thinking, Aamir, why would a doll be at a warlord's compound? So I asked the boy if I could borrow it. I wanted Marcellina to see it, to see if she could make sense of it—but at the time, I wasn't picturing her being the one in the dumpster. I cleaned it up and sewed its tattered edges together. I had planned to give it to Muntisir after he inquired about the United Nations, but he left in too big a hurry. I've since sent the doll through the mail for delivery to Kismaayo. Aamir, how does our little brother fit into all of this?"

"I don't know, Aarifah, but I have a bad feeling he's working for General Fritigern. If Athanaric drove him off like the children said, then that horrible man is probably living in America, probably under an assumed name. Sister, terrible attacks are occurring throughout the provinces, and I'll bet he stands behind most of them. I texted you earlier that seven thousand people died at Thessolonica and that someone recently bombed our capitol, do you remember?

Aarifah nodded. "Of course."

"Marcellina lost her brother in the capitol bombing," he continued, "and our governor remains in a coma. Things are heating up so much, it wouldn't surprise me if America declared war on our people." They walked along in silence before a thought popped into his mind. "Aarifah, could the children direct me back to the compound?"

"They're much too young, Aamir; none of the older ones returned."

Sadness swept over his face. "Then I'll need to find that doctor; he can show me the way. Did the children say anything more about him?

"Only that he worked on a ship. Perhaps you'll find him on the docks of Kismaayo. Aamir, I pray you stay longer than Muntisir; much time has passed since you've been home."

An orange globe in the western horizon soon darkened as Aamir stepped foot in Kismaayo. He strolled through shipping yards, passionately talking to anyone not wearing a uniform. Despite his best efforts, no one knew anything about any doctor escaping one of Athanaric's compounds. Thus, Aamir went in search of an illegal tavern. He supposed that a watering hole had to be nearby, where lesser men chewed more than khat.

Aamir entered a smoke-filled, run-down establishment. After making inquiry at the counter, he walked down rickety steps to the basement. From there, he made his way through a maze of crowded chairs to the front of a crepuscular bar. He smiled at the man standing behind it. "Do you serve tea?"

A bald, burly man, sporting a mostly black beard stood wiping the grain's surface with a rag. He smiled back at Aamir, revealing a mouthful of disagreeable teeth. "Yep, to zenanas," he replied.

Aamir wasn't rattled; he kept smiling as he stroked his finger along the counter. "Then I'll gladly pay you double for the inconvenience of serving a male." After receiving his herbal beverage, he turned around to address his pixilated audience. "Does anyone here know where I can find a doctor?"

A masculine voice rose up from the end of the bar, "I'm a doc—"

A strong kick to his shin cut short his words. "Now don'ts ye go spewin' yer words without mind," whispered Captain Riley to his besotted physician. "I'm in no haste to lose ye again. Let's see what this gent's got to offer."

The captain lifted his eyes and looked across the bar at Aamir. "Laddie, do you think it wise presenting yerself sick to a group of workin' men?"

"I'm not ill; I'm looking for a special doctor—"

"Lynch is a special doctor," interrupted a man seated at a ramshackle table. He pointed his finger directly at Murray Lynch. "Damn good one, too."

"Be mindin' yer concerns, Clyde," interjected the captain. Riley directed his gaze at Aamir while patting Dr. Lynch on the shoulder.

"What me shabby friend means, laddie, is that he *was* a good doctor. See, me inebriated physician here, he done lost his license a couple years back. Seems he amputated the wrong body part; 'twas a crying shame, really, but it wasn't his fault. The nurse's red lipstick made the man's danglin' chimes look more inflamed than his leg."

Aamir remained steadfast. "I'm looking for the doctor who recently escaped one of General Athanaric's compounds."

"Well, now, laddie, 'tis always a fine day hearin' of generals missin' a thing or two," continued Riley. But, I'm afraid me doctor's never been out of me sight. All I can offer ye is me dentist. I ain't seen him in a while, but I plan to visit soon. I aim to mends me tooth after I pay me mate, and me ship's been scrubbed clean of her stench. Yer free to ask him if ye want the likes of his name."

Aamir felt desperate; he would have to reveal all if he hoped to make any progress with this group. "I'm from the Provinces, and what I'm trying to understand is what happened to a high-ranking United Nations official. She may have had unpleasant dealings with General Fritigern, or General Athanaric; I need to find their compound."

Dr. Lynch roared back to life. "I met a UN offi—"

Another strong kick to his shin cut short his words. "I'm sorry, laddie, we be no use to yer cause," said Riley. "If you'll kindly excuse us, I needs be escortin' me sack-carve'n doctor back to the ship. He's partook a bit much as you can see. It was a pleasure meetin' ya, Mr. . . ."

"Nadif, Aamir Nadif."

Captain Riley hoisted Lynch off the stool and assisted him up the stairs. "I hope ye finds yer doctor, Mr. Nadif, and yer lady friend, too."

Aamir downed his tea and left the establishment soon afterwards. The air smelled clean; it felt good to be out of that smoke-filled, murky basement. He walked along the side of the dilapidated building, bricks and mortar crumbling in thousands of places.

Suddenly, a man pulled Aamir into a dark alleyway next to the tavern. "Just listen, Mr. Nadif," whispered Abbas, holding a serrated knife to the American's throat. "The captain believes your story. Come aboards the *Aigneis* at pier three in an hour—and comes alone."

Aamir arrived at the wharf on time. Two men soon came upon him and blindfolded his eyes in a cloth smelling of diesel. They escorted him down several long hallways and a short stairwell and then shoved him into a room and told him to remain there. He wasn't scared; he smelled a stench aboard the ship. He deduced the *Aigneis* had transported the children up the Juba and back to their Wazigua tribe. He remembered Aarifah saying the children had all thought the captain was nice. *He must be doing this to protect himself,* he surmised.

An hour passed before the door to the room opened wide. Two men escorted Aamir out of the ward and into another. He squinted from the light of a flickering bulb after Abbas removed his blindfold. Then he heard the captain speak. "I regret puttin' ye through this, Mr. Nadif, but we couldn't risk ye bein' followed."

Time was of the essence; Aamir had no desire wasting it by protesting his conditions. "Captain, please, if you have answers for me?"

Riley looked over at Lynch. "Doctor, now ye may spew yer words."

Dr. Lynch sat at a table slurping black coffee—though coherent, his head still felt lethargic. "Mr. Nadif, I believe you've come all this way looking for me. I also believe your female official is Dr. Ambrosius. So, let me start at the beginning. General Fritigern commandeered this ship a short while ago, after we foolishly nursed him back to health in hopes of procuring a modest credit." Lynch glanced over at Captain Riley, who tipped his head taking a swig of Irish whiskey.

"Fritigern hijacked this vessel to retrieve arms from Yemen," he continued, "while holding me captive in one of his wretched compounds.

He ordered my death after I failed to restore one of his officers—a high-ranking soldier that he personally shot instead of one of the children. Fortunately, my guard was God-fearing and chose not to kill me. I escaped and wandered around for a day and a half, no idea which way to turn after I'd leapt over the wall. I failed to find the river, Mr. Nadif; I had no water after thoroughly baking in the sun. I became delirious, and then a black mamba bit me while I searched for liquid in the roots of some shrubs. I thought my time on earth was over, when suddenly, I crossed a road; there she was, Mr. Nadif, an angel sent from Heaven.

"Dr. Ambrosius kindly transported me to a hospital in Kisi. The doctors never thought I'd make it, but I gradually pulled through. I slowly regained my strength. Dr. Ambrosius returned a week later and wanted to know more about my condition. Naturally, our conversation drifted to the children imprisoned at the compound." Dr. Lynch took another sip of coffee. "Mr. Nadif, there's no doubt in my mind your lady friend organized her staff to free those kids from that despicable warlord."

"I've reason to believe General Athanaric has taken it over."

"Pity; from what I've heard, he's worse than Fritigern. But even if that's true, Mr. Nadif, I think Fritigern still holds an interest. See, he built a mosoleum to honor his father; he may have stashed treasures inside it."

"Could you direct me to the camp?"

"Within a few miles, perhaps, but that still leaves a lot of ground to cover."

"Aye, laddie," began Captain Riley, looking directly at Aamir. He set his whiskey aside before folding his arms across his chest. "If ye be planin' to use me crew fer yer business, then I insists upon a say in the matter."

"I can pay you, Captain, but know that the credit comes from a fund helping the Wazigua tribe in Thrivingi."

The captain smiled. "Aye, Mr. Nadif, ye got flair for a man who paid twice for his tea. But I won't be negotiatin' for credit. I figure me doctor is indebted to yer maiden, and if she's as bad as we've bargained, then she'd gladly assign her favor to thee. No, Mr. Nadif, I'm proposin' we sends me mate to search for yer lady. Abbas has a nose like a bloodhound; he'll find her much faster than ye."

Aamir hated giving control of the mission to strangers, but what else could he do? He didn't know the area well anymore; he had spent too many years in the Provinces. Nor could he enlist Aarifah's help; the mission had grown too dangerous. "All right, Captain, we'll do things your way; what do need from me?"

Captain Riley smiled again. "Aye, laddie, I needs ye to roll up yer sleeves and grabs ye a mop. Neighbors been complainin' of our stench for weeks. But to be fair, Mr. Nadif, I'll throws in a wage."

One day passed, then another, when news of Marcellina finally arrived. "The captain says to present yourself," said one of the crew, looking down on Aamir standing knee-deep in foul-smelling stool. Aamir climbed out of the tank. He quickly showered, shaved, and dressed himself in normal attire. After giving thanks to Allah, he ran up two flights of steps to the pilothouse. "You have news for me, Captain?"

"Aye, please sit, Mr. Nadif," began Riley, pealing and devouring a banana. "I'm pleased to say we found yer lady, and her breath still flickers a candle." Then he looked down at the floor, hesitating to go on.

"Please, Captain."

"She be beat'n beyond recognition, laddie. Me mate found her facedown in a pool of vomit at the bottom of a flea-infested bin. Many of her precious bones be broken, Mr. Nadif, and she be surrounded by worms and swarms of bitin' flies; her breath be a fraction of the true. Me mate says her tremblin' lips reveal she'd been prayin' for death lo these past couple days."

"Will she survive?"

"Me Abbas is bringin' her back to the ship as we speak. We'll do whats we can, but we's terribly short supplied; the *Aigneis* wasn't due for leavin' yet a month." Captain Riley dug into his pocket and produced several gold coins. "Here be yer wages, Nadif; I thanks ye kindly fer cleaning me vessel."

Aamir looked down at the money; he hadn't seen currency in quite a while. "Captain," he said, "this is much more than you promised!"

"Aye, Mr. Nadif, some of the extra comes from me doctor. Seems he's not only grateful to yer lady for savin' his skin, he's also indebted to yer father for givin' him purpose. In his youth, Dr. Lynch worked closely with the likes of yer dad; says he's a hero, a national treasure. Lynch has hundreds of stories 'bouts how yer father risked his life gatherin' proof against Morpan. He wants nothin' more than to discuss the matter further, once yer maiden is safely aboard me ship. He thinks ye's all can write a book, if yer willin' to work together."

"Dr. Lynch honors me, Captain," Aamir replied, bowing his head, "but I can't accept this money."

"I won'ts be tellin' ye how to spend it, Mr. Nadif, but it seems to me yer maiden will be requirin' airliftin' to Germany. If her resolve be anything close to yours, she'll be finding her way home from there."

XIV

SELECTIVE TOLERANCE

Lady Justina emerged from the bath feeling clean and refreshed. She wore a champagne-colored, dragon-embroidered, mulberry silk robe handcrafted from one of the finest textile houses in France. The robe draped her perfume-scented body, secured by a tie wrapped snugly around her delicate waistline. She wore fine-crafted slippers and an oversized tree-cotton towel encircling her frost-colored hair. After leaving the bath, Justina quickly made her way into one of three walk-in closets in search of a pair of diamond-studded, Secret Carnival jeans. "Whose are these?" she asked, cautiously lifting a pair of ordinary denims.

"Sorry, my lady," said Dorothy. "They must belong to the governor. I thought we'd removed all her things."

Justina's face soured as she examined the size of the slacks. *I'd sure like to see her fit into these after she's had four kids.* The empress dropped the jeans on the floor and asked, "By the way, Dorothy; how is that poor dear?"

"Still in a coma as far as I know," she replied, folding a pair of Italian, black linen slacks over a wooden hanger. After a short pause, the attendant pointed to no fewer than ten diamond-studded jeans in the third row of the closet—the second of twelve shelves from the top. "Are those what you want, my lady?"

"No, I want a darker shade, Dorothy; ones with gold-embroidered pockets. Those are faded and terribly unstylish. Oh wait," she said again, "those are the ones I want; I remember tossing the other ones out to the locals."

"I'll get them down." Dorothy ascended a stepladder and retrieved a 3,000-credit pair of neatly pressed jeans from the shelf. She handed them to Justina. "Now, don't forget about the bishop; he's been waiting for over an hour."

"What do I care? Let him wait. He's not important; he's a mere local. I'll see him when I'm ready, and not a moment sooner. Oh, for a pity's sake, where is Jean-Luc with my polish and Jenkins with my bubbly?"

Two hours passed before Justina presented to Ambrose. "I'm terribly sorry to keep you waiting, Bishop . . ."

"Ambrose, my lady . . . Bishop Aurelius Ambrosius."

"Sorry for the delay, Bishop Ambrose; it's just that I've had such a difficult time motivating myself since my husband's death."

"I can sympathize with you, my lady. I, too, feel the weight of my brother's absence."

"Yes, well, that's the reason I summoned you, Bishop . . ."

"Ambrose, my lady," he said, completing her phrase with a smile. The bishop knew that ordinary people forgot names due to nervousness or self-centeredness. He also knew older nobles sometimes forgot a name due to absent-mindedness. But in his experience, royals in the prime of their life, particularly women, never forgot a name unless it served a purpose—flaunting their power.

Justina appeared tired and bored sitting at the reddish-brown desk in the mansion's study. She mindlessly shuffled papers. "Bishop Ambrose," she began, without looking up, "you had a lengthy talk with my stepson on the way home from your brother's funeral." The empress smiled prophetically, burning her eyes upon him. "Gratian is quite fond of you, you know, and you told him exactly what he wanted to know." Justina raised her voice. "You convinced him—falsely, I might add—that the Nicene Creed is the favored tradition!"

"I convinced him of nothing, my lady," Ambrose said calmly. "He firmly believed in that doctrine before I ever spoke to him. However, though I've no quarrel with his religion, I am troubled by the Christian Prince's mental disposition. I fear he will react badly if he suffers any more rejection. I am worried he may harm himself, or others, if the directors vote to limit his presidential powers. My lady, I believe he has a strong discord running through him."

"Rubbish! Gratian has been loved his whole life; he has had no conflicts to contend with whatsoever. Why, everyone who knows him has nothing but fond things to say. Why, he's even started dating Maxima, one of the Constantine daughters—everything is going fine for him. Besides, Gratian has assured me he will accept whatever direction the directors choose to vote on the matter. What's more, I've assured him many times over that he needn't act like his father; his presidency needn't involve killing." Justina hesitated for a moment. "By the way, what did you tell him about killing?"

"I told him God carved no exceptions on the tablets."

A corner of her mouth lifted. "Anyway, if my stepson appears confused, it's because he's still a boy; after all, he's only nineteen."

The bishop stayed quiet.

"Now," she continued, "I never want to hear you or Gratian speak of the Nicene Creed ever again in my presence. That ridiculous belief must end. Who ever heard of a God with multiple natures? As far as I am concerned, there is one supreme God—and He created the Christ! So, Bishop . . ."

"Ambrose, my lady, Bishop Ambrose."

"Yes, yes, Bishop Ambrose," she said, still burning her eyes upon him, "I'm ordering you to speak to Gratian. You will convince him that Arianism is the only true doctrine. Then you will march your tuckus into your basilica and tell your parishioners the very same thing. Do whatever it takes to persuade them. After all, I came to Dionysius to be among Arians. I shall not grieve among heretics."

"I must refuse, my lady. See, the Father did not create Jesus out of thin air, as Arians would have us believe. Jesus was begotten, not made; He pre-existed with the Father. We glorify Christ because He manifests a distinct function, an independent purpose, a separate office. But make no mistake, Jesus is consubstantial with the Father, united in power and spirit in the Godhead. I'm sorry, my lady, but I shall not entertain your misguided thoughts of polytheism; to do so would set mankind back thousands of years."

"Look around you, Bishop Ambrose. Do you see all of these books?" Ambrose looked at the impressive display of titles, manuscripts, and journals perched on the shelves of the study. He compared their lofty numbers to the paltry collections that had occupied a small corner of one shelf when he lived at the mansion. *Gosh, when do people find the time to read all of this stuff?* "Astonishing," he replied.

"Nearly all these texts vindicate Arian theology," she said with an arrogant look on her face, reaching for a volume.

"Be careful, my lady, your nails aren't dry!"

Justina coiled her hand. Her face bore an ominous expression after realizing that he had played her. "Get out of here, Bishop Ambrose, and do exactly as I say or you'll face dire consequences. Acting the tyrant will only get you killed!"

Ambrose walked toward the door. Before leaving, however, he turned around and said, "My lady, if you demand my person, I'm ready to submit; carry me to prison or to death, I will not resist. But I will never betray the church of Christ."[s]

The bishop sat quietly in the cathedral's white limo traveling east on Fourth Avenue North. He and Sister Anne headed for the capitol. They sat in the back watching the news on television while Mr. Peters drove arduously slow.

"Yesterday," began the anchor, "Rabbi Frank Abiah, from the Akiba Synagogue, formally accused Catholics of setting fire to his church early last Sunday morning. As you can see on your screen, the blaze caused considerable damage to the north wall and roof of the building. In a letter to Bishop Ambrosius, the rabbi named four female witnesses claiming they saw a man dressed in black, who appeared excessively drunk and who staggered near the blaze. Wakened neighbors said the inebriated man looked like a priest. The bishop denied the charge and reiterated that the wrongdoers were female parishioners of the synagogue. In another top story . . ."

Ambrose clicked off the monitor and stared out the blue-tinted window. Sister Anne, eager to converse with him, spoke up. "Have you heard any more news of your sister's condition, Your Grace?"

The bishop continued staring off in the distance. "They airlifted Marci to Landstuhl, Germany using a C-17 cargo plane," he finally replied. Then he smiled while looking over at Sister. "According to Nadif, she's making gradual progress, coming along little by little. He sends me text updates nearly every day. I sure appreciate what he's done for her, Sister; he's been a godsend."

"Is Nadif the man who was with her at your brother's funeral?"

Ambrose nodded. "He stole . . . her heart, in college. I got to know him on our way back from Trier. Did you know he's a robotics engineer at the university?"

Sister shook her head. "Is he Catholic, Your Grace?"

"Muslim." Ambrose laid his hands over hers after seeing her shudder. "It's all right, Sister; he may listen to different music than us, but he's working to purify his heart all the same. He'll be commissioned and confirmed, and will secure his place in Heaven." Ambrose reflected on his words. "Come to think of it, Sister, Nadif may be fulfilling God's charge as we speak."

Sister Anne looked bewildered. "How can that be, Your Grace? He's never been baptised, and he doesn't proclaim Jesus our Lord and Savior. His view of Jesus is that of a man, just another prophet in a long list of oracles."

The bishop sensed an argument lurking; he knew how formidable she could be. "Sister," he began, "it's not the creed that flows past a man's lips that saves him, but the righteous sentiment flowing through his heart. Did Simon Peter not deny Jesus three times and then go on to build God's empire?"

Sister remained unconvinced; her greyish-brown eyebrows remained thoroughly knitted. "Proclaiming Jesus our Lord and Savior is too important to be ignored, Your Grace."

"Sister, permit me to defend my position. I'll tell you a magnanimous tale of two men. One proclaimed Jesus his Christ and Savior but lost his soul; the other bore witness that He was mortal and won over God's favor."

"There's no such example, Father."

"Sister, who else died alongside Jesus?"

Sister Anne crossed her arms, entrenching her posture. She knew how formidable he could be. "There were two criminals; one on his right and one on his left."

"Do you recall what they said? Remember, Sister, these men were dying; we mustn't make light of their words."

"Well, not exactly, all I recall is that one of them believed in Him and the other didn't. If I recall, the robber who shunned Him also abused Him, like those walking by, and the soldiers who cast lots for his clothing."

"No, Sister, both men abused Him. Mathew's Gospel records, 'The *robbers* were casting the same insult at Him.'[7] He wouldn't have used the plural if he only meant one. Now, Luke goes on to say that as time passed, both men proclaimed faith in Him. The first one said, 'Are You not the Christ? Save Yourself and us!' "[8]

"But he wasn't truthful, Your Grace. His words were a lie."

"Sister, that man's proclamation, standing alone on its merits, rivals the finest Christian passage. The words that passed by his lips would impart a cosmic smile on the most stoic and unemotional Catholic. Luke even capitalizes *You*, *Christ*, and *Yourself*, so we'd all know that man believed in Jesus."

Ambrose smiled as he continued, "But you're right, Sister, we all know what that robber meant, for Luke included the context. Luke let us all know that that man had a beastly heart; he cued us it was an insult. He told us this man's inner disposition did not match his creed, that he only wanted Jesus to save his earthly being. But I submit to you, we know his words insulted Jesus only because Luke tells us so; by themselves, they harbor no ill will at all. Luke gave away the story to teach us all a moral. The man's creed didn't kill him. It wasn't the words that ran past his lips, but his hardened heart beneath it!"

Sister sat silent.

"Now, let's move on to the second robber. Sister, this man, too, hurled abuse at Jesus. However, Luke tells us that he softened his heart a short while later. Nonetheless, in his refined state, he referred to Jesus as a man when he rebuked the other robber. He said to the effect, 'we're receiving what we deserve, but this *man* has done nothing wrong.' Sister, this robber's creed was only half-right, or half-wrong depending on how you want to look at it. Yet, Jesus accepted him on the spot because of the righteous sentiment flowing through his heart."

Sister wouldn't dream of going down without a fight. "I'll admit, the second man's testimony needed fine-tuning. However, you and I know he believed in Jesus—he had 'the right sentiment flowing through his heart,' as you put it. He would not have asked Jesus to remember him in his glory if he didn't. Your Grace, that's the belief poor Mr. Nadif is missing. If I may speak plainly, your admiration for him is clouding your judgment. Your tolerance for him goes too far."

"Sister, Muslims aren't wrong—nor are Jews. Like us, they believe in one Lord and the coming of God in his Kingdom. The difference is that they honor God's united power without distinguishing His components."

Ambrose thought of an analogy outside the Bible. "Sister, if God was a factory, and Muslims and Jews gazed upon Him from a distance, they'd say His building had no windows. Without windows, Sister, they claim they can't peek inside and make heads or tails of His workings. But, Sister, our faith sees windows. We've been priviledged to peek inside and identify some of God's functions. So far, we have identified three important operatives: Father, Son, and Spirit—but in truth, there may be trillions. It's not unreasonable to think God has as many components as man; after all, we were made in His image."

Sister remained quiet.

"Sister," he continued, "God doesn't require that we see inside His Being; that's privilege of being a Christian, not a prerequisite for saving our souls. What matters is that we understand and accept how Jesus lived, that we take up His teachings, His principles—His cross. Jesus taught us all how to ascend into Heaven, by first purifying our hearts and then fulfilling God's commission, confirming that our love for Him surpasses all others. That's what He stood for; that's what matters. Luke tells us that everyone—even a hardened criminal boasting that Jesus is mortal—can still save his soul if he's willing to take up Christ's instructions.

"That's the difference between them," he continued. "It's not that one criminal hurled abuse while the other didn't, or that one believed in Him and not the other. It's that one took His teaching to heart; one lifted his eyes to Heaven as Jesus commanded, while the other kept his eyes fixed on earth. Sister, regardless of whether we get our creed right or wrong, if we take Jesus's precepts to heart, then we're showing our love for Him. Nadif accepts Jesus's teachings; he is living the life that He taught us. So as far as I'm concerned, the only thing wrong with Nadif is that he suffers from a bad case of nearsightedness. One day, after his soul shakes off its mud, he'll see God's windows; he'll peer into God's factory and discover His inner workings." Ambrose smiled. "Now, you wouldn't begrudge a man needing glasses, would you, Sister?"

Sister stayed firm. "So what are you saying, Your Grace? Are you belittling our Catholic doctrine?"

"No, Sister, I'm saying that all monotheistic faiths have a place in God's Kingdom. They are all God's Word, all tools—tools for making us worthy to receive his commission. Sister, we're not meant to fight over them, to try to determine which one is best, or to ascertain which of them God favors. And neither are the Huns correct, for they want to fuse them, meld them into some incomprehensible conglomerate. God gave us these doctrines separately; let each man hear the one that moves him.

"But know this," he continued, "a man's creed can't save him. A creed unto itself, right or wrong, is useless. It's only when we use our creed in a laudable attempt to put our lives together, to think and act justly no matter the consequences, that action invites grace; it's grace that ultimately saves us. Sister, the second robber's creed needed fine-tuning, but he used what he had to soften his heart and infuse it with Jesus's teachings. Even so, he would have been hung out to dry and fallen short of Paradise if the Holy Spirit hadn't confirmed him."

"There wasn't time for all that!"

"You and I know that justification is normally a drawn-out process, beginning with baptism; it slowly advances through the sacraments. However, no one dare say it can't happen in the blink of an eye. Sister, a lot happened behind the scenes that day as dark clouds rolled over the skull. While Jesus was saving humanity, the Father commissioned the second robber to enlighten the first—to soften that man's heart and give him one last shot at redemption. God assigned a difficult task—remember, Sister, these men had been hanging from a cross for several hours. By that time, one's instincts are to remain quiet, to save one's strength and cling to life as long as possible. The mere fact that he spoke up earned him God's favor; that's why the Spirit confirmed him, why Jesus told him He'd meet up with him later."

"But that's what I'm saying, Your Grace: faith in Jesus is the only way to prepare ourselves for God's commission."

"Sister, you know from educating students at St. George's that a best way exists to teach mathematics—or any subject for that matter. However, the best way is never the only way. Stalwart teachers deviate from accepted practice using different methods to get the results they want from students. That is what God has done. He doesn't use the same tactics on everyone; not everyone is at the same level of understanding. He's handed down different messages throughout recorded history, helping people where they are at."

"I admit teachers use different approaches," countered Sister. "And people's understanding certainly varies, but in the end, one plus two must equal three. People must come to accept the Trinity. Why are you defending those who can't count?"

"Because, Sister, everyone counts. God is dry-cleaning everyone's soul, whether he or she believes in the Trinity or not. Nonetheless, we can't force people to Christ; we can only love them. And we can't judge them, for that domain belongs to God alone. A wise man once told me that our bodies derive from Eden's particles, and that our minds evolve from their motion. Our spinning world has fashioned 360 degrees of opinions on every conceivable subject—including religion. We live on a rotating planet that God created; He knew we'd not all think alike. Sister, we need to rely on faith that things are proceeding according to plan, and that He will take care of those believing differently than us. Our only concern is to sew the seeds of our faith and put up with those sailing another vessel. I'm not defending them, Sister, but nor will I criticize them. I'm simply finding ways to make tolerance easier, to make relationships smoother with those passing leeward of our ship."

Sister Anne uncrossed her arms.

"Now, with that said, Sister, I take a much harsher stance with those daring to call themselves Christian. We have a right—nay, a duty—to oust those on board who do not believe Jesus shares equally in the Godhead. We have an obligation to keep his most Holy Catholic doctrine pure and intact. Sister, no one will swim in our waters if we get it muddied; no one will recognize our ship if we raise more than one flag. So, my admiration for Nadif has not clouded my judgment. If he came onboard our Christian vessel without learning to count, I'd make him walk the plank in a heartbeat. I'd throw him overboard, Sister, not because his creed is wrong or because he's failing to put Christ's words into action. No, I'd discharge him to the sea because of his nearsightedness. His inability to see God's components, to count no higher than one, to devalue Christ, would make things harder on the rest of us. His limited vision would hamper our desire to peer into God's windows."

"Is that why you started proceedings against Father Palladius?"

The bishop nodded. "It breaks my heart calling together a council," he said softly. "Wulf works tirelessly with the homeless, and he took time to administer my sacraments; he even gave me the ring off his finger. But, he's married to Arianism and won't change his mind. I can't let him defile Christ's church any longer." Ambrose looked over at the Benedictine nun. "I'm afraid he and his chess board will have to go elsewhere."

Sister sat back in the seat and contemplated his words. She let out a chuckle. "Your Grace, I remember a short while ago you didn't know what Arianism was." After pausing, she thought of one more question to ask him. "This morning, didn't you chastise Rabbi Abiah and refuse him credit to rebuild his synagogue? And don't fool me, I know you didn't refuse him because you think his parishioners set fire to the church. I'm mindful you denied him because he daily blasphemes our faith. Your Excellency, if you tolerate Jewish doctrine, you certainly didn't show it with the Rabbi this morning."

"Sister, I see now why Father Liguria pounded his fists on the desk; he was no match for you. Yes, I chastised the Rabbi this morning. I'm not charitable to anyone who openly criticizes our beliefs. Like I said, God didn't intend for us to fight over his messages. Knocking another man's faith—faith that has undergone centuries of critical analysis—only stirs the fire and accomplishes nothing. I want to move people toward Heaven, not lay waste to the tracks."

Sister nudged herself closer to Ambrose and clasped her hands around his. "I'm glad I never faced you in court, Your Grace, and I thank you kindly for including me in on a theological discussion—that's something Father Liguria would never permit. You've come a long way, Bishop Ambrose. Perhaps in a few years you will become a Pastoral Doctor of our Catholic Tradition. Oh, and by the way, you did convince me of one thing today—I should try to be nice to Nadif."

Upon their arrival at the capitol, Mr. Peters got out of the car and opened the bishop's door. "Please, watch your head, Your Grace," he said louder than needed, all the while glaring at Sister Anne getting out by herself on the other side of the vehicle.

Ambrose and Sister donned jackets and traversed an eastern sidewalk before walking up twenty marbled steps. They stood for a moment, watching construction workers wearing hard hats and orange vests maneuver cranes, scoops, bulldozers, dump trucks, and other heavy equipment. The men and women repaired damage to the capitol's center section. Ambrose glanced at the site where paramedics had found Satyrus and Mary. "I sure hope they finish soon," he commented. "Daylight is getting shorter."

Upon opening a massive door amidst twirling wind in the mid afternoon, they slipped through a side entrance into the three-story, white-marbled building. They headed for the Senate Chambers. Workers had roped off a large section of the building's interior, making passage slow. They groped their way through a maze of plastic sheeting before arriving at their destination. Senator Symmachus paced near his desk when they arrived; he patiently waited to address his fellow lawmakers.

"Hold it, George," said Speaker Leontius, striking his gavel three times on a golden oak table before him. "ALL RISE," he continued, "the Most Reverend Aurelius Ambrosius, Bishop of Dionysius, is now in Chambers." Everyone stood up and bowed respectfully toward the cleric. Ambrose scanned the room, and then motioned for everyone to be seated. No one did, of course, until he sat down first. Sister Anne smiled; she adored the entire spectacle.

Leontius spoke into the microphone, "Your Excellency, would you like to address the assembly?"

"No, Mr. Speaker, I'm only here to understand Senator Symmachus's proposal."

"Very well, Your Excellency," Leontius replied. "Senator Symmachus, you have the floor."

"Thank you, Mr. Speaker. If you recall, ladies and gentlemen, President Valens dispatched the ship *Prize II* on a goodwill mission to Kismaayo. He did this a while ago in hopes of keeping the Thrivingi alliance on positive terms—"

"Mr. Speaker," interrupted Senator Wiley, "will Senator Symmachus yield?"

Symmachus nodded his head. "Senator Symmachus will yield," the Speaker replied.

"Thank you, Mr. Speaker. Senator Symmachus, I don't believe we have authority to vote on this matter. After all, this bill didn't come down to us from the governor. I'll yield to Senator Symmachus."

"Senator Symmachus, you have the floor," said Speaker Leontius. "Thank you, Mr. Speaker," began Senator Symmachus. "Senator Wiley, I realize this bill didn't come to us from the governor. We have no acting governor—or lieutenant governor, for that matter. However, I submit this is old business; we have dealt with these issues before. Under Article 9, Section 4, subsection (b)(2) of our statutes—"

"Mr. Speaker," interrupted Senator Henderson, "will Senator Symmachus yield?"

Symmachus nodded again. "Senator Symmachus will yield."

"Thank you, Mr. Speaker. Senator Symmachus, isn't it true that Article 9, Section 4, subsection (b)(2) of our laws pertains only to past appropriations bills cleared by the tax committee? I'll yield to Senator Symmachus."

Ambrose shut his eyes. He reached over and grasped Sister's hands, squeezing them tightly. Sister Anne squeezed his in return. "I know just how you feel, Your Grace," she said shaking her head side to side. The bishop had finally had enough. After listening to useless arguments for ten minutes, he rose to his feet and addressed the Speaker.

"The Chamber recognizes Bishop Ambrosius."

"Gene, I'm not getting any younger. Could we please just hear the Senator's proposal? You can debate its foundation later."

Speaker Leontius looked over the assembly. "Senator Symmachus has the floor—and he'll not yield to further interruptions."

Symmachus rose to his feet. "Thank you, Mr. Speaker. If you recall, ladies and gentlemen, President Valens dispatched the ship *Prize II* on a goodwill mission to Kismaayo. He did so a while ago in hopes of keeping the Thrivingi alliance alive. However, as you all know, the mission failed miserably. Pirates killed everybody on board; they stole everyone's credit and burned the ship till it sunk. What you may not know, however, is that a team of divers rescued artifacts from that wreckage and brought them back to Milan. I have a few items with me today," he continued, holding up a canvas duffel.

The senator reached into the bag and removed a pair of black Italian shoes; he held them high for the assembly to view. "These shoes belonged to Extavious Tendenblat, owner of our beloved Conquerors." He reached into the bag again and pulled out a ball. "This is a football thrown by Joe Terentius. I have reason to believe he used it in a playoff game against the Liberties. If you look closely, you can see the chalkline where the referees robbed Zip Line of a touchdown." He dug into the bag once more and pulled out a large piece of fabric. "I'm not sure how this survived the ocean," he said, holding up a bra, "but it must have belonged to Molly."

"Excuse me, Senator," interrupted Ambrose, "exactly what do you plan to do with these items?"

"The floor recognizes Bishop Ambrosius," the Speaker said, late. Leontius sheepishly looked around the room and then struck his gavel hard on the desk. "The floor recognizes Senator Symmachus."

"Thank you, Mr. Speaker. Your Excellency, I plan to build an altar in the shape of *Prize II* and place these items inside it. I thought about erecting it here in the assembly, but I know the perfect spot near the vestibule of the cathedral. I'll call it, the Altar of Victory. Just picture it, Your Excellency, parishioners entering the church can stop by and pray to the men and women who died aboard that ship—after all, they are now saints. You will recall, these people were not only prestigious members of our province, but heroes martyred in honor of our great country. When parishioners pray to them, Your Excellency—and the things that they cherished—they will surely be blessed with fortune."

The bishop motioned to Senator Leontius. "The floor recognizes Bishop Ambrosius."

Ambrose stood up. "Thank you, Mr. Speaker. I'm sorry, Senator Symmachus, but I shall not permit you to place your altar in our cathedral—or in any church in our province. Your attempt to glorify these people, many of whom you call friends, is nothing short of evil. Your morbid attempt toward paganism shall not go rewarded. Perhaps you'll consider erecting your ship in one of our fine museums?"

Symmachus motioned to Leontius. "The floor recognizes Senator Symmachus."

"Thank you Mr. Speaker. Your Excellency, Christians pray all the time to those who've gone before them. Do you deny praying to angels, the Virgin, the Apostles, and an entire litany of saints? Do you deny asking them to intercede and pray to God on your behalf? I'll yield to the bishop."

"The floor recognizes Bishop Ambrosius."

"Thank you, Mr. Speaker. Senator Symmachus, I do not deny that we pray to those of whom you speak, for they are confirmed ambassadors of Christ. However, we do not know the spiritual disposition of those aboard the *Prize*. For all we know, these men and women posed as drunkards engaged in casual sex."

Murmurs arose among the assembly.

"ORDER . . . ORDER in the Chamber," yelled Speaker Leontius, striking his gavel down hard on the desk. "The floor recognizes Senator Symmachus."

"Thank you, Mr. Speaker. Bishop Ambrosius, you and I have been respected colleagues up to now. But, sir, how dare you speak of those men and women in that manner! These people gave their lives for this country! I'll yield to the bishop."

"The floor recognizes Bishop Ambrosius."

"I'm sorry, Senator Symmachus, but giving one's life for his country, though considered by many to be the ultimate sacrifice, is not the same thing as completing God's commission. The former requires great courage, the latter, grace from God. It's grace that makes the difference, Senator, and no one should pray to those who died without it. Senator, I shall not permit you, nor anyone else, to confuse matters of church and state."

Stronger murmers arose from the crowd.

"ORDER . . . ORDER in the Chamber," shouted Leontius, striking his gavel down hard again. "The floor recognizes Senator Symmachus."

"Thank you, Mr. Speaker. Bishop Ambrosius, this Chamber will no longer yield to your power. Ever since the royal family moved here, you lost having the last word on provincial government. Rest assured, Your Excellency, I'll go above your head and ask the President-Appoints for a proclamation on the issue."

Ambrose and Sister stood up to leave. "Do what you must, Senator," he said, "but your altar is headed for the fire."

Mr. Peters dutifully opened the limousine door upon the bishop's arrival. Sister scampered into the seat ahead of Ambrose, proudly smiling back at the irritated driver. After sitting comfortably in the limo's leather seat, the bishop, not wishing to engage in further conversation, turned on the television. They watched Director Leo weave his way through a crowd of picketers, making his way up marbled steps in front of the Federal Capitol.

"BRING BACK CONGRESS," one sign read.

"ONE PRESIDENT, NOT TWO OR THREE," read another.

A young reporter stuck a microphone in Director Leo's face. "Director, given the recent Goth attacks—and the Mexican buildup along our southwestern border—how do you plan to vote today?"

"Our by-laws are clear," he replied, "our nation can only support two presidents. Since President Valens occupies one office, the board must reject one of the Valentinian boys. Mr. Rutherford will speak to the matter today," he continued, pushing the microphone away from his face. "You'll know my vote after we thoroughly question him."

Sister Anne looked over at Amborse. "Which boy will they reject, Your Grace?"

"The lucky one," he replied. The bishop searched for the television remote. "This must be a recording," he muttered, "the directors are already in session." After finding the device stuck in the cushions, he flipped through channels before finding a live broadcast.

"That's correct, Director Stevens," said Larry Rutherford, President Valentinian's former adviser. "I've known both Valentinian boys since they were—"

"Mr. Rutherford," interrupted Director Cicero, "isn't it true that Ian is only five years old, so any policy decisions of his would likely be made by his mother?"

"Well . . . yes, that's probably true, but—"

"Mr. Rutherford," interrupted Director Cybele, "isn't it true Gratian lacks the will to kill, that he's nothing but a coward lacking in true leadership qualities?"

"Well, ma'am . . . he was raised by his kind-hearted mother, Marina, but it's unfair to label him a—"

"Mr. Rutherford," interrupted Director Leo, posing the panel's last question, "do you know how either boy would react if we encountered a Mexican invasion?"

Larry thought for a moment. "Yes, sir, I think either boy is capable of delivering a crushing blow." Rutherford smiled, remembering Caesar's exuberance over five activated Star Wars nuclear missiles.

"Milan General," said Peters, looking back through the rearview mirror. The bishop clicked off the television without waiting to hear the director's decision.

"Your Grace," said Sister, "don't you want to know the outcome?"

"We'll know soon enough." Ambrose and Sister entered the hospital, walking past a mound of cigarettes piled alongside its foundation. After avoiding a stretch of wet, pine-scented tile, they took the north elevator up to the seventh floor. There, they found Sheriff Crispus and Deputy Drusus guarding the door to the governor's room. Both officers rose from their folding chairs as the bishop approached. Drusus's chair collapsed with a clatter on the floor after his flashlight, latched to the back of his belt, caught against the ridge of the chair.

"It's good to see you again, Bishop Ambrosius," said the sheriff, "and you too, Sister."

Ambrose nodded at Crispus—and then quickly coiled his arm. Deputy Drusus unexpectedly grabbed his hand, attempting to kiss the Episcopal ring. "That's not necessary, Harvey," said Ambrose, "perhaps you should focus on righting your chair."

"We haven't had a Hun attack for days," the sheriff commented, wincing at the sight of his deputy's crack, exposed after he bent down to pick up the seat. "Maybe they've stopped trying."

"If only that were true, Sheriff," Ambrose replied. "But, we both know they'd wage war against the planet before backing down from a termination assignment. Sheriff, our only hope is for Mary to wake up from her coma." Ambrose smiled at the guards. "May I pass through now?"

After entering, Ambrose moved a cushioned chair closer to the bed and sat next to Mary while Sister Anne went off with Sheriff Crispus to get coffee. The distinctive inhale and exhale drone of a mechanical ventilator was the only sound in the room. "All right now," he said, placing a card on Mary's abdomen. The governor lay perfectly still on her back, eyes closed. "I'm finally getting the hang of this game," he continued, reaching into a brown paper bag. "B-22," he said aloud. "Hey, you've got that one." An exasperated look appeared on his face. "Come on, Mar, you'll never get a bingo if you don't pay attention—tell her girl." Lava lay snuggled atop Mary's left shoulder. She slowly lifted her head and opened her eyes after hearing his voice. The tabby rose to her feet, stretched her legs, walked over Mary, then plopped herself down on the other side. "You're no help," he muttered, hearing commotion outside the room.

"Drussy, you know perfectly well who I am; now let me through," said Hermie. The bishop listened to a half-minute of arguing before seeing his former legal secretary step into the room. She carried a large, overstuffed cardboard box in both hands.

Ambrose stood up and turned toward her as she entered. Besides the package, he noticed that she wore a colorful scarf wrapped tightly around her forehead. "Hey, Hermie," he said with a smile, "I can't imagine why you had a hard time getting past the guards."

Herminius set the container on the floor. "Drussy's such an idiot; he doesn't know a scarf from a headband." She tapped the box with her foot. "These are the things you never picked up, Ambrose; the box has been sitting at the firm for over a year. I figured you'd be here this afternoon, so I brought it along."

The bishop knelt before the box and began peeling back its flaps. "Gosh, I don't know what's in here anymore." He reached inside and pulled out a large black doll with hazel-brown, marble eyes wearing a lovely pink dress. "Made in Hong Kong," he muttered. "Hermie, I don't recall this doll being at the firm."

Herminius giggled. "Are you sure, Ambrose? She's got your eyes!" Then she continued in a more serious tone. "Actually, it arrived yesterday. Students from the university brought it to the firm in the late afternoon. They said it came postmarked from the UN in Kismaayo. Ambrose, doesn't Marcellina work there?"

At that moment, a nurse wearing blue scrubs and white sneakers walked silently into the room. "Don't mind me," she said, "I need to check the governor's intravenous drips and get her turned over."

Ambrose watched as she circled the bed. After raising her arms to examine a drip line, her sleeves pulled back, revealing colorful bands tightly wrapped around her wrists. She gave the bishop a malevolent glance a split second before extracting a box cutter from her pocket. "NO!" he shouted, rising up from the floor.

"DIE!" she yelled, lunging at the governor's throat.

Ambrose threw the doll at Mary's neck; it arrived just before the Hun plunged her murderous weapon. The point of the blade cut deep into stuffing but stopped short of piercing the other side. The disturbance awoke Lava, who hissed at the woman, then sprang at her eyes.

"AAHH," she shrieked, frantically prying the tabby from her face with one hand, shaking the doll loose from her knife with the other. "GET THIS THING OFF ME!"

Harvey ran into the room after hearing the ruckus, his flashlight no longer latched to his trousers. He tackled the nurse from behind as sounds of a folding chair collapsing reached them from the hallway. "You're not killing anyone today, honey," the deputy commented, stripping the knife from her hand.

Ambrose and Herminius watched the deputy handcuff the fuming Hun. After seeing them leave, Herminius reached out for the bishop's hands. "You're a hero, Ambrose," and then she added, "but that just makes things all the harder."

"What do you mean?"

Tears formed in the young woman's eyes. "Ambrose, Mary chose me as her healthcare agent." Tears flowed freely; her body visibly shook. "What should I do? Her brother Winston wants her life to continue, but her doctors want me to end it. How did I get stuck in the middle of this mess? I can't kill Mary; she's my friend!"

Ambrose put his arms around her. "Hermie, I know you've read her living will a hundred times over; you know she doesn't want to live like this. Still, I don't want to see her die any more than you do. But you won't be killing her; she's already dead. She has little brain waves—virtually no electrical activity whatsoever. Mechanical means alone support her life, and the doctors all tell us there is no hope of reversal. You will be releasing her, Hermie, not killing her. Mary's soul longs to see Christ—but it can't; it's trapped inside a broken body. Mary chose you because she knew you'd stay strong in this moment. Release her, Hermie; let her soul fly back to God."

Herminius's crying eased, but she kept her head resting on the bishop's shoulder. "If that's how you feel, Ambrose, why did you save her from that terrible Hun?"

"To save that terrible Hun; I didn't want her dying an early quick-sword death when she's still capable of doing God's bidding. That terrible woman may have a ways to go before her heart is cleansed, but everyone has a beginning."

Sister Anne and Sheriff Crispus returned with their coffee, rushing into the room. "We saw a Hun being taken away in handcuffs," Sister said. "Was anyone hurt?"

Ambrose walked past them in silence, thinking about something Governor Probus once told him: *Aurelius, this office needs someone who can move people, someone who can speak eloquently and motivate others to do things—things they may not want to do.* Tears formed in his eyes as he walked out the door.

Ambrose stared out a dark-tinted window as the limousine drove back to the cathedral. He had never considered Mary's death, not after she survived the initial explosion. *She's such a fighter, and medicine can do such miraculous things; I thought for sure she'd survive.* The limo drove past Lalia Channel; the river still flowed freely, but Ambrose saw himself falling on the ice. He could hear Mary's angelic voice: *Oh, Ambrose, are you all right?*

Sun shone low in the western horizon as the limousine pulled up to the church. Ambrose directed Peters to stop at the front of the basilica rather than drive to the rectory. "I need to pray," he said. He got out of the car and walked up the steps, carrying the cardboard container that Herminius had given him. Sister Anne politely opened the massive church doors so he could enter. As Ambrose made his way inside, he heard hammers and saws whacking and buzzing to his right. He set the box down on a pew and went straightaway to investigate the disturbance. "What's going on?"

"What do ya mean, ain't this your church, Fadder?" said a construction worker. "We're makin . . . oh, cripes, Hank, what the heck do you call this thing?"

"Altar of—"

"Yah, yah," interrupted the first worker, "Altar of Victory. It'll be real strong, you'll see. We're buildin' it out of solid oak."

"Under whose authority?" the bishop asked, feeling perturbed. Then he rephrased his question. "Did President Gratian approve this project?"

"Where the heck you been, Fadder? That kid ain't much of a president no more. Directors gave him two measly provinces to rule in the west; the rest belongs to his brother Ian." The construction worker lowered his voice to a whisper. "I hear Gratian got so upset he done got himself drunk before flying off to Colorado. And that ain't good," he continued, resuming a normal voice, "cause we'll need his help fighting Goths. President Valens declared war on 'em today. And it's about time, too, Fadder; they been gettin' away with murder. I hope we kick their butts all the way back to Africa."

The bishop grew impatient. "Who authorized the altar?"

"That little bugger—Ian. Fadder, I hear Senator . . . oh, cripes, Hank, what's the Senator's name?"

"Symma—"

"Yah, yah," interrupted the first worker, "Symmachus. I hear Senator Symmachus promised that little bugger he could throw the ball, you know, the football that is going inside here. Do you know what that boy said? He says, 'Great, I don't want to throw like a girl.' " The construction worker shook his head and chuckled. "Ain't that something, Fadder . . . children say the goofiest things."

The bishop stood still, pondering the situation. Sister Anne walked up to him; a stern look swept over her face. "Your Excellency, what are you going to do about this matter?"

Before Ambrose replied, Sisters Angela and Martin entered through a side door of the cathedral. Sister Martin ran down the side of the church while Angela furiously tapped her cane down the middle. "Reverend Mother, Reverend Mother," they both shouted, "something dreadful has happened to Catherine."

The apprentice arrived first. "Reverend Mother, Catherine is unresponsive; she may have suffered a stroke."

"Did you call 911?"

"Yes, Reverend Mother," replied Sister Angela, arriving a moment later, "Sister Henrietta called them on her phone. But Reverend Mother, she says the militia won't let the ambulance near us."

Ambrose's eyes grew wide. "Militia?"

"Yes, Your Grace," Sister Martin answered. "You can see for yourself through the windows."

The bishop hustled over to the north side of the cathedral. He looked out one of the large windows, which stood tall like a soldier. Peering out, Ambrose took note of the outdoor activities. He saw foot soldiers scattering across the grounds as well as Jeeps and other military vehicles setting up in position. Tanks swiveled around, pointing their gun barrels straight at them. Just then, the lights in the church went dark.

"Dang it, Fadder," said the construction worker. "My saw won't work unless you trip the breaker."

"Gentlemen, you're excused," said Ambrose, straining to see them in the dark. "You may come back tomorrow. Oh, and by the way, be sure to bring more of that oak." After he finished speaking, he felt his way along a pew until he met up with the sisters.

"What's going on, Your Grace?" Sister Anne inquired.

"I'll explain later; right now, I need everyone's help. Sister Angela, please return to the convent. You and Sister Henrietta prepare Catherine for a trip to the hospital. Oh, and Sister, I suggest taking the tunnel; it will be safer than traveling outdoors. Sister Martin, I need you to ring the bells—keep pulling on the rope until your arms can't take it!" Then he looked at Sister Anne with a melancholy expression. "I'm giving you the most difficult job of all. I need you to greet parishioners at the door."

"Your Grace, it's eight o'clock on a weeknight, who's going to come?"

"The cavalry, I hope. Look, Sister," he said, exploring her eyes, "if they come I need you to turn Arians away and allow only Nicenes to pass through. But Sister," he continued, sensing her pleasure, "give Arians a chance to convert before turning them aside. And one more thing, if any servers show up, tell them to light all the candles."

"What shall I say to the Corrigans, Your Grace? Ben and Louise are staunch Arians, they'll never convert."

"Let me know if they arrive, I'll handle them myself."

Sister Angela walked to the basement and traversed the tunnel at Bishop Ambrose's suggestion. She heard tanks moving overhead as she tapped her way toward the convent. Angela walked one hundred feet inside the burrow before hearing a horrific noise. She hastened her gait but soon came across a substantial object blocking her motion.

"Oh my gosh," she said aloud, "is this what I think it is?" Sister slid a hand across the grain and came across some writing. Engraved in a lower corner of the wooden box were the names *Gervasius & Protasius*. "Oh my gosh, my cousins make these coffins!"

Sister fought off the urge to converse with the decedent. "I'd love to stay, but Sister Catherine needs my assistance." Sister hopped on top of the coffin and swung a leg around to the other side. "If you're still here when I return, perhaps we can visit later." She lowered her feet to the ground and continued her progression. Sister had no more turned around than she crossed a second object. "Oh my gosh, another coffin caved into the tunnel!"

As she slid her body over the second casket, a ground-shaking rumble vibrated the burrow. The coffin's lid popped open. Sister couldn't resist the urge to stick her hand inside. "You're well preserved; you've got long, flowing hair, and your cheekbones are masculine and prominent. Sir, you must've been good looking."

Sister stroked down his torso until she came to his hands; they lay folded over a gladius. "You brandished a heavy sword, my valiant man; you must've been important." Sister palpated a hole where a gem used to be, then an engraving partway down the blade: *To Canthi, Love Mom.*

As she touched the decedent, Sister pondered all the feats he must have accomplished. *No doubt you pleased your master slaying fifty barbarians at once.* The sound of the cathedral bells high atop the steeple awakened her from her trance. "I must go, Canthi, there's important work to be done, but rest assured I'll be back to talk to you and your friend." Sister unstraddled the coffin and closed the lid, then resumed tapping her way through the tunnel. After walking a short distance, she felt unsteady, as if she might lose her balance. She also felt a burning sensation developing inside her head.

"Bishop Ambrosius, this is General Richard Collins With the third Army National Guard. Sir, We have you and your comrades surrounded. We've no desire to hurt anyone, but all of you must vacate the Basilica at once."

"Quickly, Sister," said Ambrose, "help me shut the windows!"

They heard bells clanging high atop the steeple as they hurriedly closed each pane. After the last one latched, a monstrous thud shook the glass. "My goodness, Your Excellency," Sister howled, falling back into a pew, "what on earth was that?"

"Tear gas, I suspect," he replied as more and more canisters struck windows. Bishop Ambrose took hold of Sister's hands and helped her to her feet.

"Your Grace, what do they want . . . what'd we do wrong?"

"Nothing, Sister; Lady Justina is seizing the church for her Arian beliefs." A faint smile came across his face. "I turned her away this morning—or as Sister Catherine would say, I pissed her off! Sister, I can't ask you to fight this battle; it's my head on a platter she wants. This situation is getting far too dangerous. I'm ordering you and Sister Martin to return to the convent at once."

An angry scowl swept over her face. "That venomous woman is hijacking my church for her own inscrutable beliefs?" With a savage look on her face, Sister stomped toward the back of the church. "If you need me, Your Grace, I'll be safeguarding the door!"

The bishop watched her storm off into the blackness. "Go get 'em, Reverend Mother," he said softly under his breath.

Sister Anne cracked open the massive doors. She witnessed guards stopping a handful of cars. *Oh no, they're not letting them pass.* Moments later, she watched several automobiles driving over the grass. Soon, a hearty glow from yellow headlights pierced the horizon. Tears welled in her eyes as she observed hundreds of vehicles breaching the hills of Orchard Park. "Our calvary is coming!"

Millie arrived first, still wearing her white bathrobe and slippers. "My fingers get a little stiff at this time of night," she said, "but I'll certainly do my best."

"Bless you, Millie. Oh, by the way, power in the church is out; the organ won't work. You'll need to use the piano."

Sister watched the elderly woman begin her ascent to the choir just as Mrs. Williams arrived at the door. "Naeem," Sister Anne asked, "are you Arian or Nicene?"

"What's dat!"

"Bless you, Naeem; please come in, how's Tavius?"

"I'm so proud of him, Sister. He plays a trumpet in da military band now. He don't fight Goths no more. You should see how handsome he looks in his uniform."

"That's wonderful, Naeem; I'm so glad he's out of harm's way." Sister turned around after watching the proud mother promenade into the church. Sister glanced out the door and saw Clarence Schmidt arduously making his way up the steps. "Mr. Schmidt, I didn't expect to see you tonight. Say, I need to know if you are Arian or Nicene?"

"I know where I'm goin'," he snapped, "why don't ya find somebody else that needs help?"

Sister let the elderly man pass without receiving an answer. *I guess they won't be putting me in charge of guarding the Gates in the hereafter.* Sister spotted the Mendoza family exiting their new silver Delont 383 half-ton pickup. She began counting family members when Tom Miller raced up the steps. "Hold it right there, young man, what are you doing out this late on a school night?"

Tom, doubled-over and gasping for breath, stopped to answer her question. "I came as fast as I could after hearing the bells, Reverend Mother," he panted. "Besides, I had to show Max I could still out-run him."

"Is your mother with you?" Sister asked her question while watching Tom's younger brother bound up the steps.

"No, ma'am, she . . . um . . . she kinda has another new boyfriend."

Sister shot him a disgusted look, placing a finger over his lips. "Say no more, Thomas; the bishop needs you and Max to light all the candles. Be sure to disperse them about once you have gotten them lit. Oh, and Thomas," she added, stroking his sandy-blond hair, "bless you and your brother for coming."

Sister smiled watching them run into the darkness. She turned around to greet the next parishioner when she spotted a yellow taxi. A ghastly expression came over her face; she closed and locked the doors. "Thomas," she yelled.

"Yes ma'am?"

"Please fetch the bishop before doing anything else."

Ambrose emerged from the shadows a few moments later. As he drew near, he heard pounding on the massive doors coming from outside the church. "Please open up," said the muffled voice of a stranger. "I need to see the bishop."

"What's going on, Sister; are troops storming the castle?"

"I don't think so, Your Grace, but who else pounds on wood with his fists?"

The bishop stared at her with inquisitive eyes, and then proceeded to unlock the doors. A cool breeze greeted him as he carefully unsealed the entrance. A middle-aged man dressed in black polyester prostrated himself on his knees. "Forgive me, Your Excellency . . ."

"Father Liguria, please get up," Ambrose interrupted, grabbing him by an arm. "Aren't you supposed to be in Central America?"

Liguria rose to his feet, tearfully glancing at Sister. She shot him a tight look in return. "I was, Your Excellency," he began, turning to face the bishop. "But I couldn't sleep; I couldn't eat. I constantly feared for my life. I tried emulating the archbishop, but I'm just not a missionary priest. When I heard about your brother's death and your need of a new churchwarden, I came back as fast as I could. Oh, I pray I'm not too late; I'll do anything, anything you ask."

"Ask him if he's Arian or Nicene." Sister interjected.

"Sister, please! You're hired, Father, but you may find things little changed from whence you came." Ambrose escorted the grateful man into the cathedral and pointed toward a corner. "We'll work on your inner shortcomings later, Father; right now, it's your outer strength I require. Over there, you will find an idolatrous altar masquerading as a wooden sailing vessel. I need you to rip it apart, piece by piece. Carry the wood to the middle of the church, under the cathedral's great dome. Once there, set it ablaze; it will keep us all warm later. It's made of solid oak, Father, so it should last us through the night. The workers promised they would bring more wood in the morning. But Father, don't make the fire inordinately large; I wouldn't want these trusty pews going up in smoke along with it."

Sister Anne took hold of Liguria's hands before he took off on assignment. "Welcome back old friend," she said with glistening eyes.

Then she peered over his shoulder and outside the door. "Your Grace, the Corrigans have arrived."

Ben bounded up the steps ahead of Louise. He had had his right knee replaced and felt rather like a new man. He had learned a lot about the procedure talking to Sister Anne's father before having it completed. He made his approach with an austere look on his face. "Bishop Ambrose, is it true this church is no longer Arian?"

The bishop nodded.

Ben stared angrily. "Well, Bishop, we're not too old to go elsewhere. Come, Louise, let's shake the dust from this place."

"Ben," began Ambrose, watching him turn around. "I won't try to change your mind, but could you and Louise find it in your hearts to deliver the gifts one more time?"

Mrs. Corrigan looked puzzled. "Are you saying Mass at this hour, Your Grace?"

"No, Louise, we're reading psalms and singing hymns. Oh, and we're giving away prizes to anyone putting the most positive spin on Job."

"Forget it, Louise," grumbled Mr. Corrigan, "they don't want us here anymore."

"Oh, Ben, we've been members of this church for years; the bishop needs our help," pleaded Mrs. Corrigan. After a long pause, he turned around and affirmed a nod at Ambrose.

"Bless you," said the bishop, "the gifts are waiting for us at the convent. I'll meet you there in a few minutes if you'll drive your Suburban around." Ambrose turned toward Sister after watching the Corrigans leave. "Sister Angela arrived safely at the convent," he began, "but she texted a cave-in at the tunnel. I'll need your veil if I'm going to get past the guards."

"Certainly, Your Grace," she replied, with concern in her eyes, "but they'll spot you walking alone. Take Sister Martin with you. Her arms may be shot, but I doubt you'll keep up with her legs!"

Ambrose smiled. "You know, Sister, ever since I was a boy at St. Frederick's, I've been dying to know what a nun's hair looks like."

Sister Anne, standing tall in the doorway, reached up and removed her cover. A golden halo surrounded greyish-brown hair as amber light from hundreds of vehicles showered past her. "Well?"

"Just what I pictured."

"Is everyone belted in?" Mr. Corrigan pressed gently on the gas and drove slowly away from the convent.

"Hit it, Ben, we've no time to lose," yelled Ambrose. He sat in the back applying last rites to Catherine. Sisters Henrietta, Angela, and Martin sat in the middle praying silently for their companion. Louise sat in the front, admiring her brave husband.

The Suburban weaved past several sword-carrying guards, but no one seemed to notice. Armored tanks, mounted with loaded gun barrels aimed directly at the cathedral, hovered large over the passenger vehicle. Mr. Corrigan floored it once his trusty car had gotten safely past the militia.

They zoomed down the expressway on their way to the hospital. Ben laid on the horn while swerving through lanes. The sisters clung to rosaries as Louise dug her nails into the upholstery. The nuns made the sign of the cross after the vehicle slowed for an exit. They turned right onto Harvey Devoe Boulevard, named in honor of the recently retired judge who was killed playing golf in the lightning. Mr. Corrigan drove the remaining three blocks to the hospital, taking a sharp left turn into the entrance after waiting patiently for a street-train. Then he pressed hard on the brakes, skidding the car to a stop.

"We'll do all we can," said one of the medics, wheeling Catherine into an examination room.

The group meandered into a waiting area. A nurse told them that a doctor would come along and explain everything in a minute. After waiting patiently for an hour, Sister Henrietta looked over at Ambrose. "Go check on her, Your Grace. You look miserable sitting here doing nothing. I'll text you when there's news of our sister's condition."

Ambrose politely smiled, and then left the room in search of an elevator. Unable to find one, he climbed 140 steps to the seventh floor. Upon entering the hallway, he saw Tiny seated in a metal folding chair outside the governor's room. "Hey, Tiny, are you here all alone?"

"Hey, Brozie . . . no, Scarzy's with me; he went for coffee. You know we caught two of 'em already. We got us an x-ray tech and a phlbo, phlibi—oh, you know, one them blood suckers. Did you know Huns is startin' to wear colorful wristbands?"

"You don't say?" After chatting a few minutes—mostly catching up on sports' scores—Ambrose asked to enter. The distinctive inhale and exhale drone of the mechanical ventilator was the only sound in the room. He slowly approached the bed. "Hey, Mar, it's Ambrose. Don't worry, I don't have any bingo cards with me; I'm told you don't want to play. I don't feel sorry for you, you know," he continued; his lips started quivering. "I know where you're going, and I can't blame you for wanting to go."

He got down on his knees and grabbed hold of her hands. "But I'm selfish, Mar; I don't want you to leave. I want to look into your emerald-green eyes, hear your soothing voice . . . damn it, Mar, I want to have coffee with you on the porch!" He closed his eyes and cried; his whole body shook with grief.

"BEEP, BEEP," sounded the ring from his phone.

Ambrose did his best to rein himself in. "I have to go, Mar," he said, rising to his feet. "I don't know if I'll be here tomorrow to witness your ascension; I need to hold down a fort. But know that I love you, and I always will." He headed for the door, then paused and turned around. "Do you want to come home, girl?"

"Meow!"

"All right, stay with her one more night."

Ambrose found the elevator and took it down to emergency. He knew instantly by their solemn faces that Sister Catherine had passed. He gathered the sisters together and they all bowed their heads, holding one another's hands as he prayed: "Lord, bringer of life; your love teaches and guides our hearts, and upon your authority, we return to the dust of Eden. Jesus, we commit the soul of Sister Catherine, and all the faithful departed, back to you. She lives in your presence; may she rejoice in your Kingdom now and forever, Amen."

After saying the prayer, Ambrose walked toward the Corrigans, who stood near the door. "Thank you Ben, and thank you, Louise, for all your hard work tonight and over the years. I don't know what we'll do without you. You'll be tough to replace at our Sunday service." He paused for a moment, and then added, "You don't have to stay any longer, the sisters and I will catch a cab back to the cathedral."

Mr. Corrigan spoke up. "I'm truly sorry for your loss, Bishop Ambrose; she was a fine woman. Catherine was the Reverend Mother when I went to school at St. George's; she truly was a gift." He paused for a moment, and then continued. "Bishop, Louise and I have been thinking. The whole reason we are Arian is that Archbishop Auxentius believed in it so strongly. However, I listened to your sermon last week, and, well, it made a lot of sense to me. I mean, the Father couldn't have created Jesus. He needed to use someone He loved, someone He could trust, to experience man's abandonment. He needed to use someone within the Godhead."

"What my husband is trying to say," interjected Louise, "is that we'd like to stay on with the church."

The bishop beamed a wide smile. "That's wonderful! Then I trust you'll be coming to our vigil. May we hitch a ride back with you to the cathedral?"

"Hitch away," said Mr. Corrigan.

Ambrose looked back at the nuns; he wasn't sure if they felt ready to leave. But, as he looked on, he noticed something odd. Sister Angela had broken away from the pack and was walking briskly toward him without using her cane.

"Now I know what people mean when they say you have Egyptian-blue eyes, Your Grace."

Ambrose looked astonished. "Sister, can you see?"

She nodded. "When I texted you about the cave-in, Your Grace, I left out the part about the corpses."

"Corpses?"

Sister stood in front of the bishop caressing his face. "Your hair isn't as long as his, but I doubt he has your olive-skinned complexion; still, you both have straight noses, and your prominent cheekbones are identical."

"Corpses, Sister?"

"Two coffins caved into the tunnel, very near where Marty's Landscaping removed the poisonous Agapanthus plants. That happened after the armored tanks shook the ground. I touched one of the bodies, Your Grace, after its casket lid popped open. That valiant guard, that brave protector, the one who's nearly as handsome as you—the one they call Acanthus—he repaired my vision."

The ride back to the cathedral held mixed emotions. Everyone grieved for Catherine, but Sisters Henrietta and Martin had a marvelous time pointing at street signs to help Sister Angela with her reading. Louise seemed content, too. She sat close to her husband, resting her head on his shoulder. Ambrose sat quietly in the back, mourning the loss of two people. However, his spirits rose after they snuck back in through a side door of the church. The Cathedral of Dionysius was alive with people singing and dancing, eating and conversing—and tall candles flickering and glowing. The church also had what appeared to be a small bonfire beneath its great dome.

"One more time, Millie," shouted Sister Anne. "Yes ma'am."

♫ Oh, when the saints go marching in
Oh, when the saints go marching in
Lord, how I want to be in that number
When the saints go marching in . . .

XV

NOBLE JUSTICE

Gratian chugged single-malt scotch and studied the balls on the billiard table. "Number three in the corner pocket," he said, setting down his glass. He rubbed blue-colored chalk over the tip of his pool cue, leaned over the green felt table, practiced a few strokes, and smartly struck the cue ball; solid red number three disappeared instantly down the hole.

His opponent stood by the table sipping champagne from a fluted glass. "Good shot, Gray. I can't believe what the directors did to you yesterday. Why would they give Ian more power than you?"

The emperor studied his next shot. "Well, at least I'm president somewhere—and I get to keep the Red House. Anyway, Max, don't say anything more; I'm through discussing it."

Maxima Constantia was a great granddaughter to Leonard Constantine I. She and Procopius had planned to marry until his untimely demise by heroin overdose following his speech in front of the Lincoln Memorial. Brigadier General Theodosius and presidential advisor Larry

Rutherford had convinced the Constantines that the real Procopius had died years earlier. "We told you this new guy was a fraud," they said, "and a junkie as well." Afterwards, the Constantines had encouraged Maxima to start dating Gratian.

She brushed her hand across his ass as he bent over to make his next shot. "Well, maybe I don't want to talk at all."

Caesar struck the cue ball, missing yellow number one by a country mile. "Now look what you've made me do." He glanced at two behemoth guards standing at the door, then lifted his glass and downed another gulp of scotch. "Did you have something else in mind?"

Maxima sauntered over and pressed her body to his; she lightly stroked his pool cue. "Maybe."

Caesar smiled. "I've reserved the presidential suite if you're ready," he said softly, setting the stick on the table.

Maxima nodded her approval.

The guards opened the doors allowing the nobles to exit the billiard room at the Chalet Aspenia. The place had become a casino mecca, rivaling the finest emporiums in Sin City, after President Valentinian had moved his family into the Red House. Under tight security, the couple walked arm in arm down a long corridor heading for the elevators. Before turning toward the lifts, Gratian spotted a lovely sign above a set of white doors: *Chapel of Love.* "What do you think, Max?"

Maxima, feeling the effects of the champagne, nodded her approval. "I always pictured myself wearing a beautiful dress, but blue jeans will do—at least I'm wearing something old and something blue," she giggled.

The couple married in less than ten minutes. "Sign here, Augustus," said the magistrate, handing him a pen. After signing the license, they continued toward the elevators. The emperor looked lovingly at his new wife. "You'll be wearing beautiful dresses the rest of your life, Max; we can still have a formal wedding if you'd like."

Upon arriving at their suite, Gratian carried her across the threshold, into the room, and set her on the bed. Maxima sprang to her feet, clasped his hands, and kissed the corner of his mouth. "I'll just be a few minutes."

Caesar watched her saunter into the bathroom. After she closed the door, he walked to the bar at the far end of the room and poured himself another scotch. He considered turning on the television to watch late-night news, but decided against it. *I'm on my honeymoon for Pete's sake.* After downing the drink, he got undressed and slipped beneath the covers.

Maxima emerged from the bath wearing a rose-colored bra and panties. "Oh, Gray," she began, eyeing him in bed, "you have to set the mood if you hope to get the food." She walked to the door, dimmed the lights, and turned on overhead music. Frank Sinatra's "The Way You Look Tonight" began playing. Maxima swayed to the music, sidling toward the bed. She cuddled up next to her man making sure to touch her breasts to his chest while draping her top leg over his. "I'm all yours, honey."

"Wait, Max, don't you want to get wet?"

Maxima put the fry stick to her lips and inhaled deeply. She held the smoke in her lungs for a good half minute. "Oh baby, that's good stuff, where'd you get it?"

"The magistrate gave it to me before we left the chapel." After she inhaled several more hits, he took the butt from her hand and set it on the bedside table. Then he rolled on top of her and began making love.

Maxima felt the drug go to work. "Oh yes . . . oh, yes," she cried out, "OH GOD, PROCOPIUS, DON'T STOP!"

The emperor's undulations came to a sudden halt. "What did you say?"

Maxima couldn't hear him over delusions playing out in her mind. "Oh, Procopius," she continued, her pupils still flaring, "HMMM, you're fantastic. Oh, please tell me you're not done?"

Gratian withdrew and jumped up off the bed. "My god, Max, you're still in love with *him*." He struggled into his jeans and ran out into the hallway. Several guards chased him down the stairwell and caught him entering the chapel. The president pushed aside two loving couples as he angrily advanced toward the judge. "I want an annulment," he demanded.

"But Mr. President, it's been less than an hour." Gratian's furious eyes sent him a stark reply. "All right, Caesar; I'll comply with your order. Just tell me you haven't consummated the marriage."

Gratian looked about the room, and then smiled a sheepish grin.

The magistrate closed his eyes and shook his head. "Then I'm sorry, Your Highness; I can only offer you dissolution. Let's see, now," he continued, thumbing through a ledger, "that will be seven thousand credits." After looking up from the book, he made a mental note of Gratian's scrawny image.

The president withdrew a Lottorola C200 from his pants pocket. After swiping the card, the judge waited patiently for approval. "A red light soon appeared. I'm sorry, Mr. President; you must have been unlucky at cards, you've only got five thousand."

Gratian pleaded his case: "But I'm backed by the United Provinces."

The magistrate shook his head. "I'm sorry, Caesar, but that holds little meaning."

Gratian appeared desperate. "Sir, there must be something you can do. Are you sure you can't tear it up, or scratch her loathsome name off the paper?"

The judge thought for a moment. He brought his face close to Gratian, catching the attention of the guards. "I'll tell you what, Augustus," he said softly, "since my father and yours were such good friends, I'll destroy the old license if you sign a new one with some other woman."

"What other woman?" After watching the magistrate shrug, Gratian dashed out into the hallway. He spotted a lovely woman walking with her mother toward the slots. He grabbed the woman's arm and turned her around, looking wondrously into her pearl-colored eyes. "What's your name?"

"Laeta," she replied, fixing her gaze on the wide-eyed, half-naked youth.

"Hello, Laeta," Caesar continued—he had a cockamamie smile on his face. "Laeta is such a pretty name . . . and oh, by the way, I'm Gratian, president of Pueblo and Tejas provinces. Perhaps you've heard of me; my friends call me Gray . . . you wouldn't perchance be single?"

After a few minutes of polite conversation, the couple entered the chapel and signed a marriage certificate to the elation of Laeta's mother. Then Gratian watched as the magistrate shred the old marriage license. "There, Mr. President," he began. "There's no trace of what happened before. I hope you enjoy your new wife."

"Thank you so much, Judge. Oh, by the way, I didn't catch your name?"

"Dwayne Shapiro, Your Highness. You may not know it, but our fathers go back many years. My dad served as an investigator with the special service division of the FBI. Our fathers worked closely together a year ago on this very day, right here where this chapel now stands."

"I remember now. Your dad gave my dad that Buick Roadmaster," he said excitedly. "I've got it with me, Mr. Shapiro; it's parked in the underground lot. Oh no," he continued, his enthusiasm diminishing, "but if I recall, a timberwolf jumped in through the window and tragically killed your father."

"Yes . . . something like that, Mr. President."

"I'm terribly sorry, Mr. Shapiro."

"It's all right, Augustus, I've moved on."

Gratian nodded, and then walked out of the chapel arm in arm with Laeta. Laeta's mother kept stride, sniffling into a kerchief not ten paces behind. After the chapel doors closed, a man emerged from the shadows and spoke sternly to the magistrate. "Why didn't you kill him? You twice had the chance!"

"Easy, brother," said Dwayne, "his guards would have run me through before I'd ever drawn my sword. Besides, I want to have some fun with him before he meets an untimely demise." The judge squinted, producing a sinister expression with his eyes, while bringing forth the first marriage license undamaged.

"How's that possible, brother, I saw you rip it up?"

"It pays to double as a blackjack dealer."

†

Bright sunshine nudged over the horizon; brilliant rays passed through St. Jerome's window high atop the cathedral's eastern partition. The bishop shielded his eyes from yellow luminescence upon awakening from uneasy slumber. He slowly sat up and began massaging his neck, thinking, *Gosh, these pews aren't getting any softer.*

Ambrose's Nicene vigil, in response to Lady Justina's Arian coup, started into its seventh day. Eleven hundred parishioners packed the church, reading Bible passages, singing hymns, and listening to Ambrose's sermons on Job. A bonfire beneath the great dome kept them all toasty warm during the evening. As everyone emerged from repose, Ambrose shoved Liguria's feet off his lap and rose to evaluate his surroundings. "They're all gone, Your Grace," shouted a parishioner, spying out a stained-glass window. "The militia is all gone!" Several yippies, woo-hoos, and other cries of elation erupted from the mostly yawning congregation.

Sister Anne cracked the main doors open; a brisk chill shot into the vestibule. "That's not quite true, Your Grace; I still see two tanks pointed directly at us."

"One's mine," echoed a man's voice somewhere inside the church. "I'm with him," sounded another.

"The other tank is mine," shouted General Collins. The soldiers, proud Nicene Catholics, had disobeyed President Ian's orders by joining the vigil midway through the week. Each of them, a phenomenal vocalist, could not pass up Millie's amazing piano music.

After surveying the scene, Sister Anne's misgivings soared after spotting something peculiar. "Young men," she shouted, "if you are responsible for those machines, then how come one of them is moving?" The soldiers looked at each other in disbelief—a second before the congregation awoke to an earsplitting noise. A projectile shot from the armored vehicle chiseled bricks off the steeple; everyone below felt its chilling vibration.

"Get beneath the pews," the bishop commanded. "Not you, Father," he said, grabbing hold of Liguria's arm. "I need your help to get everyone down."

Sister Anne peered out the massive doors, spotting the president's motorcade drive by the cathedral. The regal procession drove east along Lombardy Avenue heading for the vicarage. Sister eyed them shiftily while solemnly renewing her vows: *That venomous woman isn't hijacking my church. I don't care how much flack she throws at us.*

Just then, the soldiers pushed past her on their way out the door. "Excuse us, Sister," said one of the men, "we've got a date with an armored tank." The men ran across the lot and climbed aboard the moving vehicle. As they reached the top, another shot rang out, hurling them back to the ground. Fortunately, the projectile missed the church, setting a distant maple afire. "Get up," screamed General Collins, cupping his resonating ears. "We've got to stop this thing before it does any more harm."

The men regained their footing and struggled to the summit. Upon opening the lid, one of them remarked, "Looky here, General, we got ourselves two ladies." After five minutes of tempestuous battle, the men hoisted one of the infuriated pistillates out of the hole.

"Why, isn't that Della Bellanca?" Sister Anne inquired, speaking to the bishop, who had just walked up beside her. He remained quiet, gazing out the door over her shoulder at the commotion. "She owns the Pomona," Sister continued, "that fine Greek restaurant. Your Grace, does that make that tank a Trojan Horse?"

The bishop did not answer. He watched the soldiers pull another infuriated woman from the vehicle. Darlene Thompson came out kicking and screaming, sliding headfirst down the tank's plated backside, smearing her makeup along the way. "No, Sister," Ambrose finally replied, "I believe it's an armored tank in heat."

The widow of former prosecutor and gubernatorial candidate Leonard Thompson lay prone on the ground, weeping and trembling, attempting to block from her mind the notion that she had failed her husband. "I'm sorry I brought you into this, Della," she remarked, looking toward her companion. She rolled over and tearfully looked up at the men "Don't you understand; he must die . . . the bishop simply must die." Darlene looked past the soldiers at the cathedral. "Oh, how my Leonard longed to get even!"

The clerics bid farewell to parishioners as they watched the two misty-eyed women drive off in a squad. "Peace be with you," the bishop said, shaking hands, "and bless you for helping us in our time of need."

Soon after, Sister Angela walked briskly down the aisle. "Your Excellency, Lady Justina is in the rectory; she's demanding your presence at once."

Ambrose continued shaking hands with his followers, coiling his hand whenever they tried kissing his Episcopal ring. After a few moments passed, he looked at the nun. "Sister, I'll see her when I'm ready and not a moment sooner. Please direct her into the study; she can wait for me there."

Justina, seated in the cozy, ruby-colored chair, stood up in anger the moment he entered the room. "How dare you? Do you know I've waited for over two hours, Bishop . . ."

"Ambrose, my lady; Bishop Ambrose," he said, finishing her sentence. "And I've waited a week for your nails to dry so we can go over that Arian book you so cherish!" The bishop glanced around his library; the shelves lay as barren as they had been at the mansion—except for three soft-cover books stashed in a corner, their pages curled from usage.

The empress appeared offended. She would have stormed off in a huff if he had not mentioned the part about waiting a week. She sat back down and looked into his eyes. "Then you haven't heard the news, have you?"

"My lady, the church has no electrical power, and everyone's phones are dead." Just before delving more deeply into the matter, he heard footsteps approaching from the hallway.

"Your Grace," began Sister Martin, peering into the study. She froze upon seeing the empress.

"What is it, Sister?"

"Oh, I'm terribly sorry, Your Excellency, I didn't realize you had company. I came to tell you President Maximus began invading American provinces; we're at war with Mexico, Your Grace."

After she left, Ambrose resumed speaking to Justina. "So, that's why you pulled the militia—not because you changed your mind about Christ, but because you needed them for your protection. And let me guess; you're here because you're worried about Gratian?"

Tears welled in her eyes as she looked forlornly at the bishop. "I'm worried because he doesn't answer my calls, and his aides have no clue as to his whereabouts. Everyone believes he flew to Colorado, but no one seems to know where. Even Maxima doesn't respond to my messages. Oh, Bishop Ambrose, I'm afraid something awful has happened to him."

Ambrose pushed a box of tissues toward her. "Don't think the worst, my lady; Gratian may only command two provinces, but he's still a full-fledged president. He has our entire military at his disposal. Besides, didn't you tell me earlier that everyone has nothing but fond things to say about him?"

She burst into tears. "Oh, Bishop Ambrose, I must confess a lie; I've harbored it for years. Everyone thinks of me as an innocent girl from Kansas, but things are never as innocent as they seem. I am the daughter of Arturo Garcia Vega, commander of Los Zetas, the largest drug cartel in Mexico. My father falsified my identity and then arranged my marriage to President Adal Rodriguez. He did it, Bishop Ambrose, to merge his filthy business with the law. But Adal wouldn't play along; he all but divorced me after discovering the truth—so my father had him killed. Oh, Bishop Ambrose, Val didn't know anything about this;

he wanted to kill Maximus at the time. He went to his grave thinking that he had mistakingly sabotaged Adal's plane. Val always believed he'd received faulty intelligence—but it was my father who switched the planes!"

The bishop remained quiet.

"Val never thought I had the brains to understand these matters," she continued. "He thought I'd been born for only one purpose. But in truth, I knew about most things before he did. Anyway, before my father killed Adal, he forced me to start seeing Maximus. Oh, don't you see, my father was grooming him to be the next president. My father was starting things all over. However, this time, I wouldn't play along. So, after Adal's death, I sent Val and Marina a letter. To her, I asked if she would come to Mexico and make love to me; to him, that I had proof of her cheating. My plan worked beautifully, Bishop Ambrose. After Val discovered our affair, he divorced Marina and married me. He took me away from Mexico, far away from my kingpin father."

"Let me guess, your fears have resurfaced now that your husband is dead and Maximus is invading our provinces?"

Justina shook her head. "I don't know what he wants, if it's more power, or if he's acting on behalf of my father to kill me and my children. But right now, I fear for Gratian. How could I have so badly misjudged my stepson? I thought it absurd when you told me he would react badly if the directors reduced his power."

Ambrose walked around the desk and took hold of her hands. "What people say and what they hold in their hearts can be at odds, my lady; everyone has discord running through them. It's something we must all try to diminish before God will grace us with His presence. So, please, my lady, tell me how I can help."

She reached into her gold-studded purse and removed her phone. "I need you to speak to Maximus. You're a man, he'll listen to you."

"And if I do this, do you promise to be within the church and not lording your power over it?"

Justina nodded. Ambrose took the phone from her hand and pushed the call button. Soon, he heard the Mexican president's voice on the line. "Buenos díaz, Señora Justina, I knew you'd be calling."

"I'm sorry to disappoint you, President Maximus; this is Aurelius Ambrosius, Bishop of Dionysius."

"WHO ARE YOU? HOW DID YOU GET THIS NUMBER? IF JUSTINA IS THERE, PUT HER ON THE PHONE!"

"Mr. President, Empress Justina demands you break off your advance immediately. She needs you to return to Mexico at once."

Ambrose heard voices chuckling in the background just before Maximus reengaged in the conversation. "And if I refuse, Bishop, what then?

"If you have feelings for her, Maximus, you'll do as she asks."

"Feelings? My dear bishop, I've hundreds of women more beautiful than she!"

Justina overheard him; her face glowered as she lunged for the phone. Ambrose held her back while thinking up a reply of his own. "If you continue, Mr. President, you'll be met with heavy resistance."

Maximus chuckled again. "So far, I've encountered none."

"Well then, you're sure to encounter some." Ambrose grimaced, sheepishly looking at Justina. She rolled her eyes in disgust over his lame retort.

"You're wasting my time, Bishop. I'll take my leave unless you have something important to say."

"I'll make you an offer," Ambrose replied, sensing that time had reached a critical juncture. "If you'll stop advancing—and leave Gratian alone—I'll see to it the directors endorse your sovereignty over the provinces you've captured."

Momentary silence came over the phone. "Bishop," Maximus finally responded, "are you suggesting that I become an American president—

your nation's fourth reigning emperor? That's ridiculous; I plan to make these provinces Mexican."

"Mr. President," Ambrose replied, speaking flippantly, "that's the trouble with world domination today. Sovereigns like youself yearn to change the identity of the nations they conquer, housing everything under the name of their birthplace. Don't you think it wiser if you retained the captured land as a separate subsidiary? Wouldn't you rather be president of two countries than one?"

A brief silence ensued before Maximus spoke further into the phone. "I'd consider your offer, Bishop, but I've never heard of you; you've no authority to do as you say."

Ambrose stood tall and spoke unswervingly. "President Maximus, my name is Aurelius Ambrosius, avowed Doctor of the Catholic Tradition, adored Bishop of the See of Dionysius, renowned Exarch to this glorious and exalted nation. As superintendent archbishop, it is my solemn obligation to sanctify all federal law prescribed in this country. Mr. President, you'll indeed find me fit to endorse you."

Justina's eyes grew wide, her mouth dropped open.

"All right, Bishop, in that case I accept your offer; I'll stay put, and I promise not to harm Gratian should I run across him. But if I'm not sworn in by the end of the week, consider our deal a flop."

Ambrose clicked off the phone and handed it back to Justina. The empress stared at him in amazement, and then made a sarcastic remark, "Exarch? My god, Ambrose, you're not even in the running! And who do you think you are, making Maximus president of two countries?" Tears welled in her eyes when it finally dawned on her what he had accomplished. "Please forgive me, Your Grace; thank you for giving my stepson a chance." Justina knelt on the floor and kissed his Episcopal ring.

†

Buttercup sunshine gleamed through lucid windows at the east end of the oval office. President Valens sat in his leather chair, sipping java, reading an assortment of newspapers. "Shut the door, Theo, I don't want Al in here."

"Your wife needs an answer," replied the brigadier general, making his way toward the desk. "Have you reached a decision?"

"No, and I don't care to discuss it." The president kept his eyes glued to the paper as he spoke. "Have a seat, Theo . . . look here, this article says:

> Four women pleaded guilty to setting fire to the Akiba Synagogue, causing extensive damage to the sacred ediface. Apparently, three of these women participated in the first ever same-sex wedding in Dionysius hours after they attempted to burn down the church where the ceremony took place.

"Geez, Theo, what's the matter with people?" Theodosius shrugged his shoulders. "And look at this one," the president continued:

> "Seventy-three-year-old J. Celcius Nero, professor of religious studies at Dionysius University, pleaded guilty to three counts of sexual misconduct. Sentencing is set for one month from today.

"Geez, Theo, how old must a guy be before he learns to keep it in his pants?" Theodosius shrugged his shoulders again. After flipping the page, President Valens remarked, "Oh my God, Theo, take a look at this article:

> Incumbant Governor, Mary Peterson, still comatose after a blast that killed twelve and injured hundreds at the Dionysius Capitol, won the election today over Bang Yang, former partner in the esteemed law firm of Agrippa, Leontius, and Drusus. The governor unexpectedly survived after doctors terminated her ventilator. Many people believe

> her sweeping victory came because of unheralded support from popular radio host, Henry Llinos.

"Do you believe that, Theo? Dionysius elected a vegetable! What's this world coming to?" The general shrugged his shoulders once more. "And look here, Theo, you're mentioned in this one:

> Aurelius Ambrosius, Bishop of Dionysius, formally accused Brigadier General Adrian Theodosius of the brutal slaying of seven thousand protestors in Thessolonica, a small township west of Milan. The incident occurred while the town's penitentiary held the renowned gladiator, Victor Zetseva, on charges of killing Michael Mariano, the only inmate in over a decade to defeat a gladiator and win back his freedom. The bishop stated, 'The general will not enter Christ's church until he repents.' The general responded, 'I had nothing to do with their deaths; these people were cut down by insubordinate Goths masquerading as American soldiers.'

"I thought you ordered that raid, Theo?"

"No, Mr. President, I did not. I never cared much for my sister's late husband; I would never have ordered our troops to avenge his assassination. Moreover, my sister had many friends in that town; I wouldn't have wanted them killed." Theodosius quickly moved to an offensive position. "Caesar, Bishop Ambrosius is nothing more than a troublemaker, an unqualified local—a tyrant. He's at the heart of all this folly you're reading about."

Valens received a text on his phone. "Excuse me, Theo, but I'll just . . . what the hell?" The president looked up at his burly commander. "Theo, you might want to look at this. I'm receiving a report entitled: 'President Ian Welcomes Mexican President Maximus: America's Fourth Reigning President.' "

The general's eyes grew wide. "Sir, this is Ambrosius's doing. It's exactly what I'm talking about; there's no doubt he planted that ludicrous idea in Justina's pretty little mind."

The president scanned for more news. "Christ, Theo, look at this: 'President Ian nominates Bishop Aurelius Ambrosius as the nation's fourth Superintendent Archbishop.' " Valens shook his head. "Is Justina nuts? Why would she name him exarch when she spent all of last week using military might to oust him from his cathedral?"

The general leaned forward. "He's twisted her mind, Caesar; she doesn't know if she's coming or going." Theodosius shook his head. "Damn it, those directors should never have limited Gratian's power." The general flamboyantly lifted his arms. "How could those idiots reduce him to two tiny provinces? Didn't they realize Justina needed his help against the misguided antics of that asinine bishop?"

"Sounds like that bishop is getting under your stripes," Valens said, without looking up. "Speaking of Gratian, Theo, I left a message on his phone; I need his help fighting Goths. Have you heard from him?" Before Theodosius answered, someone knocked on the oval office door. "Quiet, Theo, it's Al."

"Jules," she shrieked, "you'd best be coming to my father's funeral today. He'd be mad if he knew you skipped out to attend that ridiculous parade."

"Tell her you're planning to do both, Mr. President," whispered the general.

Caesar gave a puzzled look at his commander, and then hollered, "Love chops; I plan to do both." They heard a forceful rap on the door just before all sounds in the hallway went silent. "She's gone, Theo; now what's this about doing both?"

"Sir, the funeral parlor isn't that far off the end of the parade route. My Treasure could . . ."

"My Treasure—I'll be riding my horse?" The president thought for a moment. "Genius, Theo . . . pure genius," he said, grasping the general's meaning. "I'll pull Petroneus's casket in the parade using my race horse.

Al will think that I am giving her father the ultimate respect he deserves. When we get to the end, I'll pull his fat ass into the parlor. Brilliant, Theo, how'd you think of it?"

"Give my sister Helen the credit. I talked to her the day after Petroneus's murder. She said that she had met a nice person in church whose father owns a stable here in D.C. She said to give him a call if we had any thoughts of giving that bastard a proper burial."

"I like the carriage idea, but there's still one problem."

"Sir?"

"My Treasure's a race horse, Theo. She won't pull his fat ass the entire distance."

"Then I'll have my people give that stable a call; we'll see if they've got any draft horses."

Ratta tattatta tat tat, boom boom . . . ratta tattatta tat tat, boom boom . . . tweet, tweet, tweet, tweet. The United Provinces Army Marching Band proudly walked behind Petronius's flag-draped coffin, playing trumpets, drums, and cymbals to another Sousa rendition. President Valens waved to the crowd from his place atop a white carriage drawn by a pair of cremello-colored breeding stallions—the draft horses had taken ill after a feed of bad oats. Tens of thousands of spectators lined Pennsylvania Avenue, exuberantly cheering as Augustus passed by them.

"We love you, Mr. President," yelled one parade-goer. "Kudos for ending the recession," yelled another.

Meanwhile, a dark-skinned, middle-aged man wearing military fatigues walked beside a filly a quarter mile down the road. "Excuse me," he said to the people nearby, "please let my horse and me pass through." He brought the equine to the edge of the street and waited until the emperor approached, releasing the reins when Caesar drew near. The horse trotted onto the road and danced in front of the stallions, which subsequently reared their front legs in protest. Then the males charged after the filly, instinctively protecting their herd.

"Whoa," yelled President Valens, with fear in his eyes. He clung tightly to the reins as the carriage jumped over the curb. Petronius's casket bounced wildly in the back; its lid popped open, revealing a corpse shot twice in the head—twice—by a Taurus revolver.

The bellicose stallions chased after the filly into the screaming crowd, knocking over seniors and toddlers too slow to sidestep their path. President Valens considered jumping the carriage, but disappeared along with it into an abandoned warehouse. Six guards and a young trumpeter named Tavius ran after him, endeavoring to save him from peril. People stood watching and praying, hoping they would shortly emerge from the depot. To their horror, however, came a sudden flash of light. The explosion disintegrated the edifice—along with the president, the guards, and the trumpeter—off the face of the earth. The sound from the blast soon followed.

General Fritigern stood with his back to the bedlam, talking on his phone. "It's over, Aashif; it's finally over. I've avenged my father's death—and the death of every Visigoth lying at the bottom of the Indian Ocean."

"I'm sorry you lost such good horses," replied Colonel Dirie.

The general closed his eyes and mouthed a short prayer to Allah, then made an inquiry. "How much C-4 did you pack into that warehouse?" Before Dirie answered, Fritigern continued. "Well, it doesn't matter. Aashif, don't contact me for a while; I'll be riding low in Toronto." Then a satisfied look came over his face as squads appeared in the distance. "Good work, Colonel; take the month off and have fun with your daughter. Oh, and if you see Muntisir, thank him for talking to Helen. But understand this: if that doll doesn't surface, I'll kill him myself."

††

Gratian sat behind the wheel of the Buick Roadmaster, driving south through the Roaring Fork Valley, heading toward the Red House. Laeta sat close to him reading text messages while her mother sat quietly in back. "Can you repeat that last one?" he asked.

"Uncle Jules wants your help against the Goths."

"Sorry, I mean the one before that."

"Worried sick, please kall when you can." Laeta studied the composition. "Did you know your stepmom spells *call* with a *k*?"

"That means she wants me on a secure line when I phone her. It means she has something important to tell me. My stepmom's a bit jumpy; she gets paranoid about things easily—must be her Midwestern upbringing."

They drove three miles through tall, lush pines before Gratian spotted something familiar. "There it is, baby, you can see the gorgeous red brick through the trees!"

Gratian pulled up to a wrought-iron fence guarding the property's perimeter. "Look, the 'For Sale' sign is still up." He left the car to unlock the gate—but to his surprise, the realty company hadn't secured it. "Our family abandoned this place several months ago, Laeta; I hope freaks haven't taken it over." After opening the gate, he returned to the car and drove to the Red House's entrance. A sickness came over him as he made his approach. "Damn it, the front doors are wide open."

"You can't go in, Gray," she cried, "at least let your guards go first."

Gratian signaled his men, whereupon they dashed from their vehicle, unsheathed their swords, and ran into the entrance. Gratian heard yelling and screaming, the clash of sword against gladius. After a few minutes, he got the "all clear" from someone inside. "Look, baby," he said, staring fondly at his bride, "I need you and your mom to stay here. If I'm not back in ten minutes, both of you leave here at once."

He kissed Laeta good-bye and saluted her mother, then exited the vehicle and stepped into the doorway. Caesar cautiously walked down a dark corridor heading for the parlor, passing several slain guards in the process. He turned a corner and stepped inside the room. Except for the russet-brown couch, the furniture lay covered in linen. He stared at the sofa, picturing himself talking with Justina after his father had suffered a stroke. He heard his stepmother say, "Your father loved you very much, Gratian; he was so . . . so proud of you, my son."

Gratian suddenly felt the tip of a sharp object poke into his backside; an unfamiliar voice soon followed. "Mr. President, be quiet and don't turn around. Throw down your knife and walk toward the pool, if you recall, it's in the back of the house." Caesar made his way rearward, passing his guards. Their lifeless bodies stood upright in a hallway, each run through by a sword that pinned him to the wall.

Colonel Dirie puffed on a Cuban cigar and basked in the peacock-blue pool with his daughter. His eyes glistened after spotting Gratian. "Well, well, well . . . Allah be praised," he murmured. "God has given me another opportunity to kill an American president. Gratian," he said louder, "welcome to my home."

Augustus spit on the floor. "My father built this house, Goth. It'll never belong to you."

Dirie smiled at Gratian before hoisting his daughter from the pool. "Get dry, Azziza," he said, setting her dripping body on the deck. "Daddy will be with you shortly, honey, but now I've got work to do." He signaled one of his guards. "Asad, give Caesar your sword."

Gratian looked over the thirty-inch gladius, taking hold of its imitation-wood pommel. He swished it back and forth, making note of its weight and balance. "If it meets your approval, Mr. President, please join me in the pool. Gratian didn't hesitate; he ran toward the water, raised the sword high, leaped into the air, and completed a cannonball. He hoped the splash would distract his opponent, but Colonel Dirie stood by unamused.

Metal clashed against metal as the men swung their swords. Dirie lightly jabbed at Gratian's hands, while Gratian slashed wildly at Dirie's head. The battle ensued for a quarter hour when one of them finally tired. Gratian, who had fought in full clothes and swung the heavier sword, stood staggering and gasping for breath. He stared at his opponent with defeat on his face, his arms exhausted, too heavy to lift. Colonel Dirie, meanwhile, resiliently smiled back. Dirie stabbed him in numerous places as the youth tried backing away. "You're bleeding, Mr. President, it's a shame you can't fight back."

Colonel Dirie had nearly exacted the final measure when Azziza suddenly appeared. "Daddy, you played with that man long enough," she said sweetly, "now help me dry my hair." The girl bent down to plug the appliance into an outlet partially hidden by a *Dendrobium orchid.*

Gratian, half conscious, took advantage of his only chance. With his last bit of strength, he heaved himself out of the water and flopped himself prone on the deck. Azziza, frightened by his action, became more incensed at the sight of his blood. Her scream was enough to scare the t-rex replica emerging from the flora. She dropped the hair dryer and ran off in frenzy. Gratian, meanwhile, reached out with his sword and batted the appliance into the water. He turned his head just in time to see Dirie's body electrocuted. Then he laid his head down on the tile and fell into a well-deserved slumber.

Gratian awoke a short while later, not knowing how long he had slept. After lifting his head, he saw Colonel Dirie, wide eyed, reclining at the bottom of the pool—the occasional bubble escaping his lips. The president painstakingly pulled himself into a seated position and reflected on what had happened. *Father, I killed my first man; I hope that makes you proud. Uncle Jules, he was a high-ranking Goth; I hope his death helps you out.* He rose to his feet and looked over his surroundings. Colonel Dirie's guards were gone, but he heard sobbing mixed in with a little girl's whimper. Caesar staggered toward Azziza, who sat curled in a poolside lounger. "I won't hurt you, little one," he said softly. "What's your name?"

"Zziza," she replied, tears forming in her eyes. "My daddy's mad at me; he doesn't want to play," she continued, pointing at the cadaver. "And he promised he'd buy me a new doll for my birthday."

Gratian looked at her with sad eyes. "Let's go upstairs and get you into dry clothes; we'll see what there is to play with." They walked together, sidestepping corpses, through two sets of hallways, up twenty steps to the bedrooms. Gratian limped badly, feeling his lacerations. He peeked into the master bedroom where he had last seen his father—dead, naked, and drooling from the mouth. They continued walking after a moment of silence, stopping in front of a guest room. "Is this where you're staying?"

The little girl nodded.

Gratian walked inside, hobbling toward a south-facing window. He widened a taffeta curtain done in a classic damask and opened its cream-colored shade. The Buick remained parked in front of the Red House. *Laeta and her mom must still be around,* he surmised. He turned back and walked toward a chest of drawers in the corner of the room. "Is this where you keep your clothes?"

"No," she replied, pointing to the closet.

The president pulled open the doors—his new wife and her mother tumbled out to greet them, each slain by a Mexican saber. Gratian leaped out of their way while Azziza pierced the air with her screaming. Augustus spun around—the last thing he ever did. A black-mustached soldier with a cross around his neck ran a gladius through him. Gratian's abdomen burned while the rest of him chilled. Choking on warm blood, his lean muscles quivered. He dropped to his knees as the sound of the girl's cry faded.

Maximus entered the room and knelt beside him. "Gratian, can you hear me?"

Caesar had not the strength to answer. He used his might to stay upright and direct his gaze at Heaven. *I killed a man, Lord, but for valuable cause, defending the home of my father. Forgive me, Jesus; please carve out this one exception.* Gasping for breath, he exclaimed, "If only Bishop Ambrose were here!" He fell forward, flat on his face expelling his last breath of air.

Maximus glared angrily at his men. "*Mierda*, I promised Justina I'd keep him alive!"

"Presidente, what shall we do with the girl?"

"Bring her," sounded his furious reply from the hallway, "a small token for Justina—for killing her sons and laying waste to Milan!"

††

The requiem Mass for Sister Catherine De Luca was nearly over. It had been delayed a week owing to Lady Justina's coup with the militia.

Although Sister had been old, there wasn't a dry eye in the establishment. She had been such an important member of the church over the years that Bishop Ambrose honored her before hundreds of her Benedictine colleagues. He faced her head toward the altar and draped her casket in a shroud of purple. He prayed the *Libera Me* standing at the front of her coffin while Father Liguria stoked frankincense walking down the aisle. Parishioners held onto burning candles as choristers voiced a melancholy anthem.

Sister Anne sat in a small room off to the side of the cathedral. She held Naeem Williams in her arms after two uniformed guards paid the simple parishioner a visit earlier that morning. They had said that her son was a hero, and how sorry they were that she had lost him in a warehouse explosion. Sister gently rocked the lachrymose woman back and forth, mouthing the choir's unhappy jingle.

After the hymn ended, Bishop Ambrose spoke to the congregation. "Grant timeless rest unto her, O Lord."

"And let everlasting light shine upon her," they replied.

"Sister Catherine's burial at St. Liberius is private," he continued, "it's reserved for her Benedictine colleagues, as well as her closest friends. However, anyone wishing to stay here for coffee and donuts in the basement is welcome." Ambrose finished speaking just as the cathedral doors burst open. A handsome, dark-skinned man wearing orange high-top sneakers walked up the aisle, waving a silver box overhead.

"Murderers," Muntisir shouted, turning around in full circle, scoping out the people. "America declares war on us—but know this; it was you who started the killing!" He continued waving the small box overhead. "Allah be praised; your elderly die naturally while I'm forced to avenge our massacred relatives!"

Naeem roused from sorrow after hearing the young Goth hollar. She had heard on the news that Thrivingi terrorists had caused the explosion. She shot up from the bench and raced out of the room in a tizzy. "You killed him," she screamed, "now I'm gonna kill you!" The half-crazed woman ran past mahogany pews near the altar, and then turned left into the main aisle, seeking revenge on the despot. She had just about reached him when Ambose released the brakes from Sister Catherine's carriage. The bishop pushed it along, preserving a small separation between the irrational woman and the reprehensible man. "Let me at 'em, Father," she cried.

Out of the corner of his eye, Ambrose saw Sister Angela leap out of her pew, tackling Mrs. Williams from behind in a manner befitting a Conqueror. "No, Naeem," she shouted, "Tavius doesn't want you to die."

Sister sat atop the shrieking woman, assaying a bruise on her elbow; Naeem, meanwhile, lay facedown, kicking and screaming. After the parishioner's insanity abated, Sister helped Mrs. Williams to her feet.

The bishop looked at Sister Angela inquisitively. "When did you take an interest in the living?"

"After I began seeing the pain on their faces," she replied. Sister grabbed hold of Naeem's arm and slowly walked the disheartened woman down the corridor. Ambrose looked over at Sister Anne, who had emerged from the small room in time to witness the spectacle. They both had surprised looks on their faces.

Muntisir laughed, putting away his dagger. He spat on the floor and then once again turned around in a circle to address the people. "Is that the best you can do," he shouted, "send a woman to oppose me?" He held the box in front of him and gestured as if to press a button. "All of you prepare yourselves for hell; that is where Allah will send you."

Ambrose pushed Catherine's casket back toward the altar. "I'm sorry to spoil your fun, Nadif, but your little toy is inoperable," his voice barely heard over the clatter rising up from a terrified congregation. Parishioners at the back began running toward the doors. "HE WHO WISHES TO SAVE HIS LIFE SHALL LOSE IT," the bishop bellowed. He watched with interest as they all sauntered back. "Now where was I? Oh, yes, your remote doesn't work, Muntisir."

The Goth looked up and smiled at Ambrose. "And how would you know that?"

The bishop smiled back. "Do you see my friend in the back, Muntisir?" Ambrose pointed to a lanky man standing in the back of the church. "He cut the power inside your router." Lierchetsky held up needlenose pliers in his right hand. After putting it back in his pocket, he felt the warm touch of a woman's hand wrap around his fingers. Tears filled his eyes as he turned his head to the side and saw Jennifer standing beside him.

"You're bluffing," Muntisir replied, zealously pushing buttons. But to his disappointment, nothing happened. He threw the device on the floor and sneered at the bishop.

Ambrose walked toward him. "I've known about you for some time, Muntisir, ever since you bombed the Capitol."

"You've no proof of that," he quickly replied, slowly backing up.

The lawyer in Ambrose began surfacing. "Isn't it true," he began, "that after you blew it up, you gained the respect and admiration of your superior, General Abdul Kareem Fritigern? In fact, he held you in such high regard that he commissioned you to retrieve sacred documents from his father's mausoleum."

"That's not true."

"You brought a doll with you to Thrivingi—I'm quite certain it wore a lovely pink dress. You intended to conceal the documents inside it. After you stuffed it and sewed the material together, General Athanaric's men discovered you at the compound. In your haste to get away, you threw the doll away."

"I didn't throw it away."

Ambrose smiled. "Pardon my error, Muntisir." He looked around at familiar faces in the congregation before continuing his interrogation. "After Athanaric left, you returned to the camp to retrieve it, but it was gone, wasn't it? Your precious doll went missing."

Muntisir remained quiet.

"Muntisir, unbeknownst to you, my sister invaded the camp just before you returned. She came to the camp as part of a peacekeeping mission to free the children held hostage. Marcellina found your precious doll, Muntisir. Unfortunately, Athanaric's men captured her and beat her to within an inch of her life. They threw her and the doll into a dumpster nearby."

"I'm familiar with Marcellina."

"But apparently not enough to care!" Ambrose raised his voice; his eyes shot a hole right through him. "You were in the area, Muntisir, but did nothing about it. You cared more for your precious documents than a human being—is that what Allah expects from you?"

Ambrose took a moment to compose himself. "Your brother traveled to Thrivingi after learning of my sister's disappearance. A merchant captain and his crew located her while your brother sanitized their ship. Fortunately, Aamir's efforts paid off: they found my sister and nursed her to health—at least well enough to send her to Germany. They gave the doll to a Wazigua boy, expecting him to give it to his sister. How am I doing so far, Nadif?"

Muntisir stayed quiet.

"Your sister, Aarifah, possessed the doll momentarily, questioning why it had been found in a warlord's compound. According to her, she would have given it to you to take to my sister if you hadn't been in such a hurry."

The bishop watched Muntisir shake his head, and then continued his closing argument. "She cleaned the doll and mailed it to the UN in Kismaayo, hoping it would reach Marcellina. Of course, being a bureaucracy, they knew little of my sister's disappearance. They thought she had gone home, so they mailed the doll to the only address they had on file—her student housing at the university. Naturally, none of the students living there had ever heard of my sister. Luckily, a legal card of mine lay taped to the side of the refrigerator. They brought the doll to my old law firm, whence my former secretary brought it to me."

Muntisir's eyes grew wide. "You have the doll?"

"The story isn't over, Nadif. I was playing a rousing game of bingo with the governor when my secretary brought me the doll. I must say, the toy proved useful; I used it to prevent the homicidal intentions of an atheist Hun. Because of that doll, Muntisir, that crazed woman's box cutter fell short of my beloved's cervical."

"Did you find the writings?"

"Not right away, Nadif." The bishop glanced over at Sister Anne, who stood tall in the doorway. "I gave the doll to our Reverend Mother; she's quite handy with a needle, learned sewing from her father. I wanted the doll repaired so I could give it to one of our young parishioners. Sister discovered the sacred writings when she stitched the fabric together."

Muntisir's expression turned somber. "Then she no doubt destroyed them."

"On the contrary," replied Ambrose, "Sister Anne has gained a remarkable tolerance for those passing leeward of our ship; you'll find the documents safe and sound at the Masjid Milan a mile down the road."

Muntisir closed his eyes and gave thanks to Allah.

"But know this, Muntisir," continued Ambrose, "mixed in with those scriptural texts was a paper scribbled in Mai Mai. Aamir translated the writing. You'll never guess what it said."

Nadif raised an eyebrow.

"It seems your General Fritigern also fled in a hurry. He left his terrorist plans behind in his father's mausoleum. You mixed them together when stuffing them into the doll. Fritigern's plots included not only attacking our capitol, but sabotaging our cathedral as well. I didn't learn about the former in time to stop you, but I've kept a close eye on you ever since. President Ian's militia encircled our church last week; they kept armored tanks pointed squarely at us. Fortunately, some of the soldiers proved friendly and sided with us. I asked them to video you placing bombs around our cathedral. You weren't too hard to spot, Muntisir; your orange tennis shoes didn't match your fatigues." The bishop looked over the congregation. "Have I proven my case ladies and gentleman?"

Muntisir looked side to side, wondering which way to run. Before darting off, however, he heard the innocent voice of a child behind him.

"If you want Aseta, mister, you can have her," said Elsa Mendoza, "but only if you say please."

Muntisir looked behind him—she held the doll in question. Sister Anne had given her the toy for her fifth birthday a few days ago. "I don't need your doll anymore, little girl; I'll take you instead." Muntisir scooped Elsa into his arms and unsheathed his dagger, holding it to her throat. "Stay back; everyone keep still, and no one will get hurt." Elsa started crying and dropped Aseta on the floor.

"Let her go," shouted Ambrose, walking toward the Goth.

Muntisir stepped backward, his back toward the third pew from the front. "Don't come any closer, Bishop; I swear I'll kill her."

Ambrose stopped. He looked over Muntisir's shoulder at an elderly man wearing worn-out sneakers, dirty tan trousers, a ball cap, a dusty brown leather jacket, and a dirty red ribbon pinned to his lapel. The elderly man looked steadfastly at the girl. Elsa, in turn, looked fearfully back at him.

"Help me, mister," she cried.

"I'll save you," Clarence muttered after hearing his daughter scream. He saw cobblestone sidewalks, old-fashioned streetcars, and Addie holding chocolate ice cream. He proudly waved to his beloved wife, Clarice, who stood tall, smiling near a street corner. He pulled out his six-inch stiletto Army knife and thrust it into the side of Muntisir's neck.

The Goth felt only a sting at first, but the modest sensation soon changed to burning, then gurgling, as blood accumulated in his throat. Muntisir clutched his neck, finding it hard to speak; blood trickled from his mouth. His legs began quivering; they soon gave out and dropped him to his knees. He began sensing the gravity of the moment, sensed Allah looming. He lowered Elsa to the floor surprisingly well for someone in shock who no longer possessed the strength to lift his arms. Muntisir remained upright, all the while gazing at Ambrose. Finally, he fell headlong onto the cathedral's myrtle-green marble floor, his orange high-tops spattered with blood.

Upon hearing sirens in the distance, the bishop looked out at the people. "The funeral Mass for Sister Catherine is over. Please go home to love and serve the Lord. Oh, by the way, anyone wishing to stay for coffee and donuts should head for the basement now." Most everyone dismissed his remark and made a beeline for the exits. Once again, however, before anyone could leave, the cathedral doors burst open. Lady Justina, her three daughters, Azziza, and President Ian and his guards, all stepped inside. The congregation—wishing they were elsewhere—bowed as the nobles made their way up the aisle. Everyone, that is, except Ambrose; he remained resiliently vertical.

"We're leaving, Archbishop Ambrose," said Justina, "but I hope to see you in Washington, D.C. once in a while now that you're our nation's new exarch. Then she looked down at Azziza. "Will you please find a home for this child?"

"Certainly, my lady, I know a wonderful man who wants nine more just like her," he replied, thinking of Aamir.

Sister Anne approached them and took the girl by the hand. "Come with me, little one; you'll simply adore your new daddy." As they began walking off, Elsa Mendoza stopped them.

"Would you like to play with Aseta?"

"Maali!" Azziza exclaimed, folding the doll into her arms. "My daddy promised she'd get her own room once we moved into a house in America." The two girls giggled as they walked off with Sister.

Ambrose redirected his gaze at Justina. "My lady, at what price do you leave?"

Tears welled in the noble's eyes. "Despite your winning performance, Archbishop Ambrose," she began, "Maximus killed my stepson, and he's begun invading more provinces; Mexican soldiers will reach Milan before evening. Since Jules—I mean President Valens—is dead, I asked Brigadier General Theodosius to assume Ian's presidency. I can't afford to lose another son."

"But my lady, can you afford to give your daughter in marriage to a man who won't repent of his sins?"

Justina's eyes grew wide; she didn't think anyone knew about that spousal arrangement. "I know you and the general don't see eye-to-eye, and that you blame him for the massacre at Thessalonica. However, you must not take your feud out on us. My daughter willingly accepts the hand of our president-appoint."

The archbishop directed himself at Galla, who stood close to her mother's side. He looked down and saw a sweet, innocent young woman not much older than fourteen. Galla wore a leather miniskirt, which appeared to ride high; black thigh-high boots, which could redden anyone's backside; copious makeup applied with a spoon, along with plentiful tattoos and piercings. People placed bets on the actual color of her skin. What's more, she had voluptuous cleavage large enough to resemble her hind side. "Is that true?" he asked.

Galla snapped gum in her mouth. "What's it to you? Teddy is a man, and I love him. God, Mr. Bishop, I just adore his big, round ass," she continued, sticking out her tongue, rolling her eyes toward Heaven.

Ambrose smiled. "Congratulations, Galla; I'm sorry I'll miss the wedding, but there's no doubt you're the unequivocal match for the Brigadier General. I'm positive you'll make a top-notch First Lady." Ambrose redirected himself to Justina. "My lady, what has . . . Teddy promised you in return?"

Just as Justina began speaking, a CL-20 smokeless propellant, found in the casing of nuclear missiles, switched on. The missile, stationed three miles above the earth's atmosphere, began positioning its nose at an exquisite red brick house situated deep in the trees of Aspen, Colorado.

Epilogue

Ambrose sat in the cathedra wearing his conical mitre. Time approached the end of Sunday's ten-thirty Mass. Three months had passed since the Stars Wars missile killed President Maximus and his troops advancing toward Milan. Residents everywhere, relieved that President Theodosius had thwarted the invasion, celebrated Christmas in gusto. Millie began playing the final hymn of the morning. Discovered in the Limburg Gesangbuch hymnal, its author is unknown.

♫ God Father, praise and glory
Thy children bring to thee.
Thy grace and peace to mankind
Shall now forever be . . .
O most holy Trinity, Undivided Unity;
Holy God, mighty God,
God immortal be adored . . .

Near its conclusion, the archbishop stood up. Taking hold of his crozier, he kissed the altar and descended its steps. Two priests—including Father Liguria—three deacons, and six altar servers came together in front of the tabernacle, genuflecting in flawless unison. Everyone turned and walked toward the sacristy—except Ambrose, who walked to the back of the church. Music continued as he passed 1,500 Nicene parishioners singing in perfect harmony.

Blissful parishioners began filing out through the massive doors at the back. Descending its concrete steps, they witnessed a group of energetic boys building a large snow fort across the way in Orchard Park. Some people nodded their heads as they passed by the archbishop; a few stopped by long enough to shake his hand. However, a good many of them waited in line to kneel at the archbishop's feet and kiss his Episcopal ring.

"Your Excellency, have you changed your views on marriage?" Walter Augustine, a new parishioner, asked his question while thumbing through the bulletin. The inquisitive lad was considering entering the priesthood.

"I'll say," interrupted Betty, directing herself at the gent. "The archbishop has gone from marryin' everybody to marryin' no one at all. And if that ain't enough, he's talked about nothin' but virginity the past seven sermons. I think he plans to write a book on the subject!" The flustered woman turned toward Ambrose. "You're scarin' my daughter; how am I ever going to become a grandmother? If you keep this up, there'll be no one left in Milan!"

Ambrose smiled. "How's Nancy doing, Mrs. Piedmont?"

"Goooood," she said, smiling back at him. "Mr. Llinos is paying her tuition just as he promised. Did I tell you she started at Casius College?"

"She's going to a fine school; you should be very proud. Say Betty," he continued, "if you want her to meet someone special, tell her to eat at the Dio. I'm confident she'll run into some wonderful people." He watched the happy parishioner walk off before turning himself back to Walter.

"Your Excellency," began the curious chap, "if you've got any time this afternoon, I'd love to know how you got your start."

After most everyone had left, Tom ran up to Ambrose. "Father," the youth began, "this really old-looking dude dressed in strange clothes came up to me outside. He came out of nowhere, Father, and handed me this letter. He said he didn't have time to talk, but that he wanted you to read this instead."

The archbishop took the missive from the boy, carefully reading it as he walked toward the altar. While under the cathedral's great dome, he turned round and asked, "Tom, do you know Mr. Lierchetsky?"

"Sure, Father, he drives that cool Mercedes."

"Stop him from leaving; tell him I need his assistance. Have him park in front of the doors, but keep the motor running."

Sister Anne saw his spirited expression. She walked over to inquire about the matter after stacking hymnals on a table. "What's happening, Your Grace?"

"I'm going to see Mary."

Her countenance fell; Sister had hoped for more exciting news. It had become his Sunday afternoon custom to visit the comatose governor at Burning Oak Manner Nursing Home. "Yes, of course, Your Grace, where does she get her will?"

"She's doing as I suggested; refusing to give up on the good people of Dionysius."

Sister Anne nodded. "Well, Your Grace, just keep watch of the time. President Theodosius is due at the airport in a few hours. My goodness, he sure has changed his tune. Is it true Galla talked him into repenting?"

The bishop shrugged. "She's not as dumb as she looks. Galla knows that repentance is the only way he'll be allowed back in church. So unless he apologizes before God, they'll never get married." Ambrose started walking toward the door. "Sister, would you please do me a favor and greet . . . Teddy, at the airport? And when I return, I'll need time to go over Father Palladius's ex-communication papers."

"Your Grace, you're not planning to keep our new president waiting?" Sister nodded her pleasure after seeing him smile. However, an uneasy expression came over her face a moment later. "Oh, I'm terribly sorry, but I can't fulfill your request. I'll be teaching catechism to a class of unruly boys."

"I can teach them, Reverend Mother," interrupted Sister Marcellina. "I finished checking up on my mother." She hobbled across the myrtle- green marble floor using axillary crutches. She wore lily-white vestments over her casts as she entered the cathedral's great hall. Marcellina was the newest member of their Benedictine Order. She had terminated her position with the United Nations in Kismaayo and became Sister Catherine's replacement. "Reverend Mother, if I can teach religion to mindless adults at the university, I think I can handle your busy little boys."

"Are you sure you're up to it, Sister? It's only your second week here."

Sister nodded as Father Liguria walked up to greet them. "Your Excellency, you're off to visit Governor Peterson a little earlier than usual; have the doctors noted a change in her condition?"

"No, not that I know of, Tarquitius," Ambrose replied, "but I have it on higher authority that she'll be coming around."

They heard the sound of a midnight-black Mercedes-Benz SL550 roadster revving its engine outside. The archbishop turned toward Sister Anne and handed her the letter. "Well, I'm off . . . you may read this message if you can." Without waiting for a reply, he sprinted for the doors.

Sister Anne spoke up just before he disappeared. "Your Grace, I thought you donated your car to charity?"

"I did, Sister. Mr. Lierchetsky kindly bought it back at auction." The archbishop gave them all a passionate look. "Oh, please; allow me this one indulgence!" With that, he smiled and scampered out the door.

The group anxiously turned their attention to the letter. "Read it, Sister," said Liguria, "I'm dying to know what it says."

Sister Anne held it close to her face. "It starts out, 'Most Reverend Aurelius Ambrosius, Archbishop. It is my honor' . . . oh, darn it all, these letters are too small for me to read. I can't go on without my glasses," she fretted, handing the document to Liguria. "Here, Father, you read the rest."

Liguria examined the letter. "Why, there's nothing here; I don't see anything on the page." He turned it over several times to double check for writing. "It's blank; there's nothing recorded," he continued in a troubled voice. He handed the document to Sister Marcellina. "This must be some kind of joke!"

Marcellina looked down at the letter. "I see the words perfectly, Father; they're as visible as the nose on my face." She cleared her throat and began reading aloud:

Most Reverend Aurelius Ambrosius, Archbishop,

It is my honor to write to you today; it seems you've settled nicely into your ecclesiastical position. Please know that I write this letter in strict confidence; only those whom God has confirmed can read it.

God is pleased with you, Aurelius. You have conducted yourself with a firm hand—yet with tolerance, dignity, and grace. First, you honored God by accepting his commission and relinquishing your secular existence. Then, you uprooted denominational Arianism, eradicated senatorial paganism, and precluded nobles from usurping the church. You even prevented the cathedral's physical destruction. We couldn't have asked for more. Archbishop Ambrosius, you are hereby confirmed! Heaven kindly awaits your arrival.

I've news from others that may interest you. First, your brother is here. Need I say he breezed past Judgment? He says to say hello, and that he was quite taken by your eulogy.

Archbishop Auxentius, the man you replaced, also made it past the gates and dwells with us in Paradise. Oh, I know what you're thinking, Aurelius, but the decision to end his life by slitting his throat with a knife wasn't his; it was mine. Since he wouldn't heed my letters, I planted that thought in his mind—see, I needed to make room for you, you understand. Of course, the archbishop had some explaining to do about that Arian nonsense he so firmly espoused, but all is squared away; it's all behind him now.

You'll be pleased to know that Sister Catherine joined us here as well. My, what a hoot; she has kept us in stitches ever since her debut. But in all seriousness, Aurelius, she was the tie breaker. Sister intervened on your behalf after listening to your prayers about Mary. She said you'd be pissed if you didn't have coffee with her on some porch. Well, since the Father wills that a man and woman should govern together, we opted to keep Mary there with you. You may go to her, my son; she'll be as good as new very soon.

I doubt I'll write to you again, Father. I'm confident you'll keep up the good fight. So with that, I bid you adieu.

Yours in Christ,
Cardinal Seneca

The organ started playing. Millie and the rest of the choir had remained after Mass to practice a hymn that Ambrose compiled. Sisters Anne and Marcellina, joined by Angela, Martin, and Henrietta, along with Father Liguria, stood quietly under the great dome of the cathedral—the cathedral that stood high on a hill looking down on Milan as a reminder to all that God was in charge.

Sister Henrietta, who was surfing the net with her phone, broke the silence. "It says here, Governor Peterson started moving her fingers after

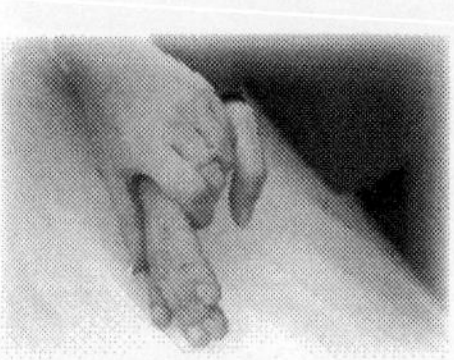

the archbishop's cat began sniffing at them. The article goes on to say that studies are underway to determine the healing power of felines. Father," she continued, "do you suppose that's how God did it in the beginning; breathed His life into man using one of the animals in Eden?" No one answered her; they all stared at the back of the church in awe of the man who had walked out its doors.

Appendix

† References

1. **Photographs.** The following list honors an amazing group of photographers who contributed to this book:

Pg. iii: *Blue Eyed Model in Suit*; © Curaphotography; depicting Ambrose.
Pg. v: *Fresco Renevation*, © Tupungato.
Pg. vii: *Basilica of Saint Ambrose, Milan*, © Arkanoide.
Pg. 1: *Bumble-bee on the Flowering Plant*, © Mykola Ivashchenko.
Pg. 3: *Bees on Spring Crocuse*s, © Marina Glebova.
Pg. 5: *Saint Paul Cathedral at Night*, © Joe Ferrer; depicting the Cathedral of Dionysius.
Pg. 11: *Smiling Older Man*, © Galina Barskaya; depicting Archbishop Auxentius.
Pg. 14: *Chess Figures with Book*, © Natalia Larina; depicting Father Palladius's chessboard.
Pg. 28: *Blue eyed Model in Suit*, © Curaphotography; depicting Ambrose.
Pg. 30: *Tough Vintage Guy*, © Curaphotography; depicting Mr. Mock.
Pg. 38: *Man Looking Over His Shoulder*, © Felix Mizioznikov; depicting Drew Lierchetsky.
Pg. 59: *Young Adult Woman*, © Sean Nel; depicting Marcellina.

Pg. 72: *Portrait of Handsome Black Man*, © Juliengrondin; depicting Aamir Nadif.

Pg. 76: *Two Girls Kissing*, © Konstantin Pigrov; depicting Jacqueline and Accalia.

Pg. 80: *Man in Black*, © Torsten Schon; depicting President Valentinian I.

Pg. 81: *Bad Face*, © Stryjek; depicting Acanthus.

Pg. 84: *Young Woman with Headband*, © Branislav Ostojic, depicting a Hun.

Pg. 99: *US Soldier*, © Susan Gottberg, depicting General Abdul K. Fritigern.

Pg. 101: *Silhouette of Soldier*, © Farek; depicting a Thrivingi soldier.

Pg. 105: *Face of Old Bearded Man*, © Fotandy; depicting Captain Caragan Riley.

Pg. 117: *Bees on Spring Crocuses*, © Marina Glebova.

Pg. 119: *Wild Woman Portrait*, © Mircea Bezergheanu; depicting Mary Peterson.

Pg. 120: P*raying Nun*, © Patrick; depicting Sister Anne.

Pg. 135: *Portrait of a Priest*, © Lisa F. Young; depicting Father Liguria.

Pg. 147: *Loving, Handsome Senior Couple*, © Maria Carme Balcells; depicting Senator Eugene Leontius and his wife, Agatha.

Pg. 151: *Lions*, © Kitchner Bain; depicting Osama.

Pg. 156: *Roman Legionary Soldier*, © Nejron; depicting Victor Zetseva.

Pg. 183: *Fire,* © Gemenacom; depicting the fire at Phi Beta Delta.

Pg. 188: *Philospher*, © Nikhil Gangavane; depicting Prof. J. Celcius Nero.

Pg. 196: *African Woman Drinking Coffee at Home*, © Hongqi Zhang; depicting Aarifah.

Pg. 210: *Woman Face Close Up*, © Nyul; depicting Lady Justina.

Pg. 216: *Shirtless Teenager*, © Albo; depicting Gratian.

Pg. 216: *Kid with Goggle*, © Tatyana Chernyak; depicting Ian.

Pg. 239: *Vampire Blood*, © Andrey Kiselev; depicting a victim at Thessalonica.

Pg. 240: *Cargo Ship*, © Parkinsonsniper; depicting the *Aigneis*.

Pg. 248: *Tall Ship Race Halifax 2009*, © Photo4emotion; depicting the *Prize II*.

Pg. 269: *Bees on Spring Crocuses*, © Marina Glebova.

Pg. 271: *Real Portrait*, © Vladakg; depicting Katie.

Pg. 272: *Sleeping Tabby Cat*, © Heysues23; depicting Ambrose's cat, Lava.

Pg. 295: *Sparkling Diamond Engagement Ring*, © Ryan Jorgensen.

Pg. 297: *Holy Bible*, © Janaka Dharmasena; depicting Origen's book.

Pg. 298: *Old Lady*, © Irina Drazowa-Fischer; depicting Millie.

Pg. 328: *Police Car on Side of Road*, © George Kroll; depicting a Milan Police car.

Pg. 333: *Sad Man Gets Drunk*, © Ruslan Huzau; depicting Dr. Murray Lynch.

Pg. 348: *Lighting the Menorah*, © Photowitch; depicting Rabbi Abiah.

Pg. 356: *Green Waste*, © Flynt; depicting a Thrivingi garbage bin.

Pg. 358: *Tank*, © Popa Bogdan; depicting a tank used by the Dionysius militia.

Pg. 363: *Calvary Dusk*, © Welburnstuart.

Pg. 377: *Crying Woman*, © Alena Ozerova; depicting Herminius.

Pg. 391: *Doll*, © Mila Atkovska; depicting Azziza's doll, Maali.

Pg. 401: *Smoking Male*, © Vanessa Van Rensburg; depicting Presidente Maximus

Pg. 412: *Sports Shoes*, © Klenova; depicting Muntisir's orange high-top shoes. (Note the photograph was cropped and rotated to hide text).

Pg. 417: *Senior Man*, © Laurin Rinder; depicting Clarence Schmidt.

Pg. 421: *Mystical Stairs to Heaven*, © Starblue; depicting Ambrose's walk into Heaven.

Pg. 423: *Veteran*, © Carolyn L. Marshall; depicting Brigadier General Theodosius.

Pg. 426: *Wedding Hands*, © Fotografescu; depicting Ambrose holding hands with Mary.

2. **Biblical Quotes:** All Biblical quotes expressed within are given numerical supra scripts. Text derives from Charles Caldwell Ryrie, PhD: *Ryrie Study Bible: New American Standard Translation,* Moody Bible Institute, 1978. My wife gave me the book on Christmas day in 1983, a year and a half before we married.

   [1] Mark 12: 28-30
   [2] Luke 1: 28-30
   [3] Mathew 6: 9-13
   [4] Mathew 27: 46
   [5] Luke 23: 46
   [6] John 19: 30
   [7] Mathew 27: 44
   [8] Luke 23: 39

3. **Mass Prayers and Responses.** Sentences ending with superscript "†" are taken from the Roman Missal, 3rd Edition, United States Conference of Catholic Bishops (USCCB).

4. **Hymns/Songs.** The text includes references to hymns and other songs because music played a big part in Bishop Ambrose's life.

5. **Speech Vocalized or Written by Bishop Ambrose.** These sentences end with a superscript letter:

   [a] Ambrose Letter XX, to Marcellina, par. 23, found at www. newadvent.org/fathers/340920.htm.
   [b] Discussed under the heading "Theology," found at http://religion.wikia.com/wiki/Ambrose. (Note that Ambrose did not say these exact words, but they have been attributed to him.)
   [c] On the Death of Satyrus (Book 1) par. 2, found at http://www. newadvent.org/fathers/34031.htm.

[d] Ibid., at par. 3.

[e] Ibid.

[f] Ibid., at par. 5.

[g] Ibid.

[h] Ibid.

[i] Ibid.

[j] Ibid.

[k] Ibid., at par. 27.

[l] Ibid.

[m] Ibid., at par. 41.

[n] Ibid., at par. 13.

[o] Ibid., at par. 6.

[p] Ibid.

[q] Ibid.

[r] Ibid., at par. 80.

[s] Discussed under the heading "Ambrose and Arians," found at http://religion.wikia.com/wiki/Ambrose.

†† *Glossary of Names & Places*

(Alphabetic Order)

Abbas................................ First mate to Capt. Riley aboard the *Aigneis*
Abiah, Rabbi...................... Head rabbi at the Akiba Synagogue
Acanthus............................ One of Pres. Valentinian I's best bodyguards
Accalia.............................. Jacqueline's lesbian lover; Beth's former lover
Adam, Adolphe.................. Penned the music "O Holy Night"
Addie................................. Clarence and Clarice Schmidt's daughter
Aegidius............................. One of Pres. Valentinian I's best bodyguards
Aegidius, Harold................ Professor Nero's attorney
Aeliana.............................. A large lake immediately north and west of Milan
Aemelia.............................. The name Ambrose would give his daughter

Agripa, Leontius & Drusus... Ambrose's law firm
Aigneis .... Merchant vessel named after Capt. Riley's mother
Akwasibah .... Michael Mariano's fiancée
Alatheus.............................. Captain serving under Gen. Fritigern
Alavivus.............................. Colonel serving under Gen. Fritigern
Agnomen............................. 4th largest city in Salamis County
Akiba Synagogue .... Jewish temple in Milan
Al-Mubarakpouri, R.......... Notable Islamic author
Alexander, Antoine .... UP's first superintendent bishop; its first exarch
Ali Nadwi, A.H................ Notable Islamic author
Ambrosius, Aurelius........... Governor; Archbishop of Dionysius; 4th exarch
Ambrosius, Marcellina........ Ambrose's sister
Ambrosius, Satyrus............ Ambrose's brother, Mayor of Trier
Amica, Stan........................ Salamis County prosecutor
Angela, Sister...................... Blind Benedictine Sister at the Cathedral
Antonia .... One of Jacqueline Meadows's lesbian friends
Apollo................................ Jewelry store in Milan
Aquilla .... Collegiate textbook author on world religions
Arius .... Deceased Christian preaching Jesus's creation
Asad................................... One of Colonel Dirie's guards
Aseta .... Elsa Mendoza's doll; also Azziza's doll, Maali
Aspenia, Chalet .... Temporary headquarters for Pres. Valentinian I
Athanaric............................ Military general and warlord in Thrivingi
Augustine, Walter............... Parishioner thinking of joining the priesthood
Aurelianis, Ambrosius........ Ambrose's father; former Mayer of Gaul
Aurelianis, Laura............... Ambrose's mother; witty and intellectual
Austin Hall........................ Law building at Harvard
Auxentius, Claudius........... Archbishop of Milan; UP's third exarch
Awanata............................ A river traversing through Milan
Ayuub................................ A Wazigua youth enslaved by Gen. Fritigern

†

Bakke, Mohamed Siad........ Goth leader before the commonwealth divided
Balba................................. Contributary to the Awanata River
Balba Stuarts...................... Rock band frequently playing at the Gallus
Bantu................................. A broad label for Africans speaking Swahili
Barnabus............................ School for the deaf, located in Milan
Bartelli, Santino................. Painted the Last Supper hanging in the cathedral
Basil.................................. Ambrose's boyhood friend; suffered Tourettes
Bassinis, Titus G................ Vatican cardinal; ordained Archbishop Auxentius
Beaverhead River................ River in the territory of Gaul
Bellanca, Della.................. Owns the Pomona; Darlene Thompson's friend
Bercu, Akiva...................... Authored a bill for rich states to buy poor ones
Binaisa, Dembe.................. Ugandan ambassador to the United Nations
Binaisa, Kukango............... Former president of Uganda
Bob.................................... Head of security for Pres. Valentinian I
Boots.................................. Darwin Cooper's dog; a golden Labrador
Bridges, Mathew................. Co-authored "Crown Him With Many Crowns"
Britannia............................ One of Jacqueline Meadows's lesbian friends
Brossan.............................. Collegiate textbook author on world religions
Bubalishious Bagel.............. Eatery attended by the O'Farland Garden Club
Burning Oak Manner........ Governor Mary Peterson's nursing home
Butler, Amy....................... Univ. of Dionysius student at Phi Beta Delta

†

Caecilius, Dr. Ornuf .... Pres. Valentinian I's personal physician
Caldwell, Taylor................. Notable Christian author
Camillus............................. Contributary to the Awanata River
Candria.............................. Last hub for train 15-B
Cappeau, Placid................. Wrote the words to "O Holy Night"
Cardea............................... One of Jacqueline Meadows's lesbian friends
Cassian.............................. One of Pres. Valentinian I's bodyguards
Cassius College.................. Private college in Dionysius
Chavez, Dr. Montoya......... Retiring UN ambassador in Kismaayo

Cicero.................................. Director voting on Gratian's and Ian's fates
Clampert, Johnny................. Possesses a car dealership in Thessalonica
Clarkston, Ms..................... Pres. Valentinian I's secretary
Clyde.................................. A regular at an illegal tavern in Kismaayo
Collins, Gen. Richard.......... Head of Lady Justina's militia
Conquerors.......................... Milan's professional football team
Constantia, Maxima........... Pres. L. Constantine I's great-granddaughter
Constantine, Leonard I........ Deceased president; changed the USA to UPA
Consular Tunnel................. A lengthy train tunnel in Gaul
Cooper, Darwin................... Prosecution witness to Mrs. Llinos's murder trial
Corrigan, Ben...................... Parishioner who often brought up the gifts
Corrigan, Louise................. Ben Corrigan's wife; a cathedral parishioner
Corvinus.............................. One of Pres. Valentinian I's bodyguards
Covington, Frank T............ Rear Admiral aboard the *UPS George P. Sanford*
Crispus, Maurice................. Sheriff of Salamis County
Cybele................................. Director voting on Gratian's and Ian's fates

†

D'Angelo........................... Capt. of the sailing schooner, *Prize II*
Danos, Mr.......................... Principal at Marcellina's grade school in Gaul
De Luca, Sr. Catherine....... Benedictine Sister at the Cathedral of Dionysius
Debbie................................ Marcellina's grade school friend in Gaul
Devoe, Harvey..................... District court judge of Salamis County
Dickies............................... Popular restaurant for Milan courthouse staff
Dio...................................... A casual restaurant at Cassius College
Dionysius........................... One of twelve American provinces
Dionysius University........... Where Marcellina received her doctorate degree
Dirie, Aashif...................... Visigoth soldier serving in Gen. Fritigern's Army
Dirie, Azziza...................... Aashif Dirie's daughter
Domitilla............................ East of Milan; third largest city in Salamis County
Dom Perignon..................... Fine champagne produced by Moët & Chandon
Domnica, Albia................... President Valens's wife

Domnica, Petronius............. Albia Domnica's father
Dorothy............................... Lady Justina's personal attendant
Douglas, Lloyd C................ Notable Christian author
Drusus, Harvey.................. Deputy sheriff of Salamis County

†

Eligius, Dick....................... Secretary of Dionysius Province
Elvey, George...................... Wrote music: "Crown Him With Many Crowns"
Equinas, Thomas................ Dominican priest of the Roman Catholic Church
Ezekiels............................. Local Milan bank hoping for national expansion

†

Fairbrook School................. Where Marcellina taught as a teacher's aide
Farthington, Michael........... Also known as Mr. Mock and William Keller
Fausta County..................... County adjacent to Salamis County
Flankston, Thomas C.......... Designed Prize II after the original *Prize* sank
Forks of Cypress................. A plantation home designed by William Nichols
Franz, Ignaz........................ Wrote hymn: "Holy God We Praise Thy Name"
Fredericksburg..................... A city in Virginia, northeast of Spotsylvania
Fritigern, Abdul K.............. Warlord general from Thrivingi, East Africa
Fritigern, Najid ... . Gen. Fritigern's father

†

Galla.................................. Pres. Valentinian I and Justina's eldest daughter
Gallia Belgica...................... Cemetery in Trier
Gallus................................. Old cabaret near the Univ. of Dionysius
Gaul................................... A UPA territory north and west of Dionysius
Gelasius, Aldfrith............... Archbishop who originally blessed the cathedral
Gervasius............................ Town near Ambrose's home in Gaul
Gervasius & Protasius........ Coffins made by Sr. Angela's cousins
Gladius Mercantile............. Online retailer of swords, knives, and machetes

Goose Head.......................... A world-class brewery in Milan
Gowon, Chijioke................. Security guard at the county courthouse; "Tiny"
Grata.................................. President Valentinian I and Justina's daughter
Gulf Cartel......................... A large Mexican drug cartel
Gwondoya, Androa............. Dembe Binaisa's eighteen-year-old nephew
Guamo................................ A street vendor along Lalia Channel

†

Hankonson, Dr................... History Professor at the Univ. of Dionysius
Harper, Steven.................... News reporter working in Dionysius
Hathaway, Marcia............. Police officer at the 5th Precinct, Milan
Hayes, Melva....................... Head receptionist at the Governor's Mansion
Heinz, William C............... Novice detective working for Salamis County
Henderson, Sen.................... Dionysius senator
Henderson Family................ Cathedral parishioners who drive a Cadillac
Henrietta, Sr....................... Benedictine Sister at the cathedral
Hensley, Warden................ Master warden at Stillwater Prison in Milan
Herminius........................... Ambrose's legal secretary
Hill, Grace L...................... Notable Christian author
Hortensi Place..................... Street where Ambrose's townhome was located
Huns.................................... Secret society that kills the weak and the dying

†

Ian....................................... Pres. Valentinian I and Justina's son
Insubres Colisseum............. Milan stadium where Conqueror's play football

†

Jackson, Jeremy.................... Wide receiver for the Milan Conquerors
Jackson, Lt.......................... Serving aboard the *UPS George P. Sanford*
Jackson, Teresa.................... Student in Marcellina's class at the university
Jacobson, Chris.................... Ambrose and Mary's political campaign manager

Jean-Luc.............................. Lady Justina's personal manicure attendant
Jenkins, Mr......................... Pres. Valentinian I and Lady Justina's butler
John, Father......................... Priest auditioning for the bishop of Dionysius
Johnson, Pete........................ Lineman for the Conquerors; a.k.a. "Big Pete"
Jorun.................................. Tanker that saved crew of the original *Prize*
Jovianus, Flavius................. Deceased president; preceded Pres. Valentinian I
Julianus, Claudius............... Deceased president; preceded Pres. Jovianus
Jupiter, John........................ Chief judge of the province of Dionysius
Juba River........................... River flowing through Thrivingi, East Africa
Jubaland.............................. Thrivingi; home of Aamir, Muntisir, & Aarifah
Justa.................................. Pres. Valentinian I and Justina's daughter
Justina, Valentinian............ Pres. Valentinian I's second wife
Jennifer............................... Drew Lierchetsky's girlfriend

†

Katie.................................. Deaf girl who called Ambrose's name in church
Keller, William.................... Michael William Farthington; a.k.a. "Mr. Mock"
Kiara.................................. Mary Peterson's co-worker at the sheriff 's office

†

Laeta.................................. Gratian's second wife
Lalia, Hanna........................ Lt. governor of Dionysius, served Gov. Probus
Lalia Channel...................... River channel cut from the Awanata River
Larson, Sr. Anne................ Mother Superior/Rev. Mother at the cathedral
Latrobe, Benjamin.............. Began Greek revival homes with Th. Jefferson
Lava................................... Ambrose's orange tabby cat
Lavinia Townhomes............ Ambrose's home as a defense attorney
Lazarus, Pirelli T............... Contractor who built the Cathedral of Dionysius
Lee's.................................. Dry-cleaning store across from Phi Beta Delta
Leo, William....................... One of Dionysius's Board of Directors
Leontius, Agatha................ Senator Eugene Leontius's stout German wife

Leontius, Eugene................ Senator of Salamis County; Majority Speaker
Lewis, C. S......................... Notable Christian author
Lezetti, Tommy.................. Linebacker for the Washington Liberties
Liberties.............................. Washington, D.C.'s professional football team
Lierchetsky, Drew................ Ambrose's friend and favorite investigator
Liguria, Tarquitius............. Cathedral Churchwarden; formerly Fr. Simplician
Lipton, Charlie.................. East Africa World Food program director
Llinos, Harold P................. Celebrity radio host on trial for killing his wife
Llinos, Carminea................ Deceased wife of Henry Llinos
Lolitta................................. Taught Justina's daughters how to apply makeup
Lombardy County.............. One of thirty-five counties in Dionysius
Los Zetas........................... Large Mexican drug cartel
Lucretius, Edgar................. Univ. of Dionysius's first president; Arts Center
Lynch, Dr. Murray............ Physician serving aboard the *Aigneis*
Lynchtown College.............. Where Prof. J. Celcius Nero received his PhD

†

Maali.................................. Azziza Dirie's doll; also E. Mendoza's doll, Aseta
MacDonold, George............ Notable Christian author
Magra................................. Japanese-owned automobile plant in Milan
Manchester Hotel................ Hotel across the street from the Courthouse
Marcus............................... Former chief justice of Salamis County
Manius............................... One of Valentinian I bodyguards at the marathon
Mariano, Michael............... One of Governor Probus's guards; friend of Tiny
Marshall, Catherine............ Notable Christian author
Martin, Sister..................... Benedictine apprentice at the Cathedral
Marty's Landscaping........... Company that contracts with the government
Mathews, Danny................. Milwaukee Hun aboard the *UPS G. P. Sanford*
Mathews, Mrs..................... Hun who tried killing Caesar at the marathon
Mauritius, Cindy................ Senator Mark Mauritius's wife
Mauritius, Mark................. Senator of Po County; Province of Dionysius
Max.................................... Altar server; Tom's younger brother

Maximus, Magnus A .... Mexican president; nephew of Pres. Rodriguez
Meadows, Jacqueline .... Marcellina's roommate at the Univ. of Dionysius
Mendoza, Francisco .... Husband of Lareyna, a.k.a. "Pancho"
Mendoza, Lareyna .... Wife of Francisco; parishioner at the cathedral
Mendoza, Antonio .... Oldest Mendoza boy
Mendoza, Elsa.................... Oldest Mendoza daughter
Mendoza, Mario................. Middle Mendoza boy
Mendoza, Miguel................ Middle Mendoza boy
Mendoza, Rafael................. Youngest Mendoza boy
Mendoza, Yesenia............... Youngest Mendoza daughter
Messalla.............................. South of Milan; 5th largest city in Salamis County
Milan.................................. Capitol of Dionysius, located in Salamis County
Millie.................................. Elderly organist at the cathedral
Mizrah, Beth....................... One of Jacqueline Meadows's lesbian friends
Mock, Mr........................... Michael William Farthington; a.k.a. "Wm. Keller"
Molly.................................. Scantily clad cheerleader for the Conquerors
Morpan, Mohammed........... Deceased general; ruled Thrivingi after it divided
My Treasure........................ President Valens's racehorse

†

Nadif, Aamir...................... Marcellina's friend; robotics professor
Nadif, Aarifah .... Aamir Nadif's sister; nurse living in Thrivingi
Nadif, Muntisir.................. Aamir Nadif's brother; student at the university
Nero, John Celcius............... Prof. of comparative religion at the university
Nichols, William................ Designed the Forks of Cypress plantation home

†

Octavius............................. Opposed Ambrose's father in a mayoral election
O'Farland Gardeners........... Landscaping club near the old clock tower
O'Leary Family................... Parishioners who drive a Magra Commando
Orchard Park...................... Playground adjacent to the Dionysius Cathedral

Origen .... Notable Christian scholar
Osama .... Five-hundred-pound sub-Saharan lion
Ostrogoths .... Muslims living along the coastline of Gruethungi

†

Padilla .... Premium cigars made by the Padilla Cigar Co.
Palisade Avenue .... Road leading to Marcellina's student apartment
Palladius, Wulfila .... Milan street-priest preaching Arian Christianity
Pete's Hardware .... Store in Virginia, near Valens's plantation
Peters, Mr .... Chauffeur for clerics at the cathedral
Peterson, Mary .... Ambrose's girlfriend; Governor of Dionysius
Peterson, Winston .... Mary Peterson's brother; attorney in California
Petroneus .... Pres. Valens's father-in-law
Phi Beta Delta .... Sorority at the Univ. of Dionysius
Phillip .... One of Sister Anne's alcoholic brothers
Philo .... Name Ambrose would give his son if he had one
Phoebus Law School .... Law school of Ambrose and Winston
Peterson Piedmont, Betty .... Henry Llinos's housekeeper; mother of Nancy
Piedmont, Nancy .... Betty Piedmont's daughter
Pomona .... Greek restaurant owned by Della Bellanca
Prize .... Capsized in eighty-knot winds north of San Juan
Prize II .... Goodwill ship sent by Pres. Valens to Thrivingi
Probus, Anicius .... Governor of Dionysius
Procopius .... Pres. Julianus's cousin; claims a presidential right
Protasius .... Town near Ambrose's home in Gaul
Pueblo Province .... One of twelve American provinces

†

Red House .... Home of Western UPA president in Colorado
Richardson, H. H .... Architect who designed Austin Hall at Harvard
Riley, Caragan .... Merchant Marine Captain of the *Aigneis*

Rodgers, Blake T.................. Warden at the Thessalonian Penitentiary
Rodgers, Helen...................... Blake T. Rogers's wife; Gen. Theodosius's sister
Rodriguez, Adalberto.......... Former Mexican President; Justina's first husband
Romanée-Conti..................... Estate in Burgundy, France; maker of fine wine
Roaring Fork Valley........... Affluent region in western Colorado
Rutherford, Larry............... One of President Valentinian I's top advisers

†

St. Clemens.......................... Hospital where Ambrose's mother received care
St. Fredericks....................... Ambrose's grade school in Gaul
St. George's.......................... Grade school owned by the cathedral
Salamis County.................. One of thirty-five counties in Dionysius
Sanford, George P.......... Aircraft carrier trasporting Visigoths to the UPA
Saphrax.............................. Colonel serving under General Fritigern
Savera, Marina................... Pres. Valentinian I's first wife; Gratian's mother
Scarsdale, Johnny................ Salamis County courthouse deputy
Schmidt, Clarence............... Widower; elderly parishioner at the cathedral
Scottsdale, Amy................... Television news reporter in Washington, D.C.
Sebastopoulos Family........... Cathedral parishioners who walk to church
Secret Carnival.................... Manufacturer of fine clothing
Secundianus, John L............ Deceased bishop; UPA's second exarch
Seneca, Giovanni................ Vatican cardinal
Shapiro, Dwayne................ FBI agent's son; magistrate at the Chapel of Love
Shapiro, Mr........................ FBI special services agent on crackpot theories
Sheldon, Charles.................. Notable Christian author
Sheraton Community........... Milan community where Senator Leontius lives
Sherpete, Abdirashid........... Goth leader before the Commonwealth divided
Simon & Garfunkel........... Amazing American singers and songwriters
Sinatra, Frank.................... World-renowned singer and entertainer
Spotsy................................. Spotsylvania County, Virginia, UPA
Stanton, John Martin.......... Milan mayoral candidate
Stillwater Prison................. A prison in Milan

Switzer Hotel .... Where Thompson began his run for governor
Symmachus, Judith .... Senator George Symmachus's wife
Symmachus, George .... Senator of Lombardy County, Dionysius

†

Tavius .... Son of Naeem Williams; serving in the army
Tatius, Father .... Vatican cleric who read Sister Anne's letters
Taylor, Demetrius .... Half back for the Conquerors, a.k.a. "Zip-Line"
Tejas Province .... One of twelve UPA provinces
Temani, Ali Abdullah .... Ousted Yemen president at the Battle of Mukalla
Tendenblat, Extavious .... Billionaire owner of the Milan Conquerors
Tendenblat, Julie .... Extavious Tendenblat's wife
Terentius, Joe .... Quarterback for the Milan Conquerors
Thessalonica .... Town in Dionysius, imprisoned Victor Zetseva
Theodosia, Natalia .... Priest who approved the cathedral's construction
Theodosius, Adrian .... UPA Brigadier General, a.k.a. "Theo" or "Teddy"
Theodosius, the Elder .... Deceased; Adrian Theodosius's father
Thomas Family .... Church parishioners; drive a Chevy station wagon
Thompson, Darlene .... Wife of prosecutor Leonard Thompson
Thompson, Leonard .... County prosecutor; gubernatorial candidate
Thring, Godfrey .... Co-author "Crown Him With Many Crowns"
Thrivingi .... Region in Southeast Africa
Tiberius, Aegyptus .... Milan mayoral candidate
Titus .... Second largest city in Salamis County
TNF .... Thrivingi National Front; ousted Gen. Morpan
Tom .... Altar server at the cathedral; Max's older brother
Townsen, Clara .... Chaperon for the Barnabus School for the Deaf
Trevororum .... A wealthy, remote suburb in Gaul, UPA
Troncais .... French National Forest
Troy, Ed .... Captain serving aboard the *UPS G. P. Sanford*
Trudeau .... Deceased captain of the mother ship *Prize*

†

Valens, Anastasia............... One of Pres. Valens's daughters
Valens, Jules......................... UPA president; brother of Pres. Valentinian I
Valens, Carosa.................... One of Pres. Valens's daughters
Valens, Galates................... Pres. Valens's son
Valentinian, Flavius, I........ UPA's western president; brother of Pres. Valens
Vergil, Mr........................... Student in Marcellina's class at the university
Vespids................................ Univ. of Dionysius's nickname
Visigoths............................. Sunni Muslims living in Thrivingi, East Africa

†

Wazigua.............................. Former refugees; the Nadifs are from this tribe
Wiley.................................. Dionysius Senator
Williams, Charlie................ Lineman for the Liberties, a.k.a. "Tractor Pull"
Williams, Charles............... Notable Christian author
Williams, Naeem................ Parishioner at the cathedral; Tavius's mother;
Winthrop, Sr. Mary............ Marcellina's fourth-grade Latin teacher in Gaul
Wright, Harold B................ Notable Christian author

†

Yang, Bang......................... Senior partner at Agrippa, Leontius, and Drusus

†

Zephyrinus, Ephraim.......... Head coach of the Milan Conquerors
Zetseva, Victor.................... Famous Gladiator; kills inmates at the Colisseum
Zion.................................... One of twelve UPA provinces

Priest is virtually the only one running his church, except one woman who gets the mail. P hears confessions - people whine + gossip more than confess their sins; some [illegible] of alcohol, others don't say anything. P's seminary friend comes to stay for awhile to help out (in reality, he is to stay permanently, for he is a pedophile) [illegible] proposes to let women be priests - or to at least start out by giving sermons, because other denominations do that and it's highly successful. So P asks his very dedicated receptionist if she wants to start giving sermons and consider going to the seminary

Proof

Goals

1. Sold to a million people
2. Made into a movie

- does book have awareness + events happening now?
- Rachel?
- Book: People, Plot, Prose
- Comparable sales
- Book must be available before sign event
- 5k on local level
- don't know how good a book is!

24724657R00267

- e-books

Made in the USA
Charleston, SC
03 December 2013